NEW YORK REVIEW BOOKS
CLASSICS

HARD RAIN FALLING

DON CARPENTER (1931–1995) was born in Berkeley, California, and grew up on the West Coast. He served in the air force during the Korean War, attended the University of Portland, and received a B.S. from Portland State College and an M.A. from San Francisco State College. Carpenter, his wife, Martha, and their two daughters settled in Mill Valley, near San Francisco, and he became good friends with the local writers Evan Connell and, especially, Richard Brautigan. His first book, *Hard Rain Falling*, was published in 1966 and was followed by nine other novels as well as several collections of short stories. Carpenter also wrote for the movies and television and spent a good deal of time in Hollywood, the subject of several of his novels. Plagued by poor health in his later years, he committed suicide at the age of sixty-four.

GEORGE PELECANOS is the author of sixteen novels and was a writer, story editor, and producer on the HBO series *The Wire*.

HARD RAIN FALLING

DON CARPENTER

Introduction by
GEORGE PELECANOS

NEW YORK REVIEW BOOKS

New York

THIS IS A NEW YORK REVIEW BOOK
PUBLISHED BY THE NEW YORK REVIEW OF BOOKS
207 East 32nd Street, New York, NY 10016
www.nyrb.com

Copyright © 1964, 1966 by Don Carpenter
Introduction copyright © 2009 by George Pelecanos
All rights reserved.

Library of Congress Cataloging-in-Publication Data
Carpenter, Don.
  Hard rain falling / by Don Carpenter ; introduction by George Pelecanos.
      p. cm. — (New York Review Books classics)
  ISBN 978-1-59017-324-4 (alk. paper)
  1. Problem youth—Fiction. 2. Swindlers and swindling—Fiction. 3.
Portland (Or.)—Fiction. I. Title.
  PS3553.A76H37 2009
  813'.54—dc22

                              2009012732

ISBN 978-1-59017-324-4
Available as an electronic book: ISBN 978-1-59017-390-9

Printed in the United States of America on acid-free paper.
1 0

INTRODUCTION

A couple of years ago the memoirist and fiction writer Chris Offutt urged me to read Don Carpenter's *Hard Rain Falling*, first published in 1966. As promised, it was the kind of infrequent reading experience that can only be described as a revelation. Inexplicably, the book has long been out of print, and its republication is cause for celebration.

Many debut novels boil and sometimes overboil with a voice edging toward manifesto; it's rare to see one hit the mark with the assuredness, maturity, and authority of *Hard Rain Falling*. It is not, as it has often been described, a crime novel, though it does concern itself peripherally with criminals and their milieu. I hesitate to classify the novel as either a literary or genre work because I'm not sure Don Carpenter would have cared about the distinction. By his own admission he aimed to write cleanly, with his intended audience the general public rather than the gatekeepers of academia. *Hard Rain Falling* is populist fiction at its best. It is not just a good novel. It might be the most unheralded important American novel of the 1960s.

The book begins with a prologue set in eastern Oregon in 1923. In the small town of Iona, a young cowboy named Harmon Wilder meets a sixteen-year-old runaway named Annemarie Levitt and impregnates her. She goes away to a home for unwed mothers and returns to Iona alone. Harmon Wilder becomes a hardworking employee of a ranch and a drunk with looks damaged by alcohol and the sun. Annemarie goes to live with the Indians. Harmon is killed at twenty-six when a horse kicks him in the head. Not long after, Annemarie ends her life with a ten-gauge shotgun. Carpenter finishes the prologue in typically terse style: "She was twenty-four at the time. The Indians buried her."

We first meet Jack Levitt, the abandoned son of Annemarie, in 1947. Having escaped from an orphanage, he now runs with a group of hard teenagers who hang on the corner of Broadway and Yamhill in Portland, Oregon. Jack is large, strong, and good with his hands. He can fight but has no other discernible talent. He's at the age when the brains of certain boys are disproportionately wired for impulsive behavior over conscience or reason. His needs are elemental:

> He knew what he wanted. He wanted some money. He wanted a piece of ass. He wanted a big dinner, with all the trimmings. He wanted a bottle of whiskey.

Jack's not a sociopath. He's a young man who's never been socialized or loved.

In Portland, Jack befriends Denny Mellon, a loose, larcenous boy, and Billy Lancing, a spectacularly talented, genial young pool player who has drifted into town on the hustle. "The color of his skin was a malarial yellow, and it was obvious from that and from his kinky reddish-brown hair that he was a Negro." The issue of Lancing's race will reappear throughout the novel, and Carpenter handles it with honesty. Also, Carpenter's descriptions of pool halls and the intricacies of various billiard games are top-shelf, as are his tours of the rooming houses, diners, and boxing arenas of the Pacific Northwest. Fans of Nelson Algren, Walter Tevis's *The Hustler,* and W. C. Heinz's *The Professional* will find much to admire in this book.

After an incident involving a break-in, Jack is sent to reform school in Woodburn. His stay includes months in solitary, detailed by Carpenter in a frightening, bravura piece of writing. Jack's next stop is a stint in the state mental institution in Salem. He is released; boxes semiprofessionally; does jail time in Peckham County, Idaho, for "rolling a drunk"; and gets work in eastern Oregon "bucking logs for a wildcat outfit." Drifting down to San Francisco, he meets up with Denny Mellon, now in his mid-twenties and a full-blown alcoholic, in a poolroom. They go to Denny's room in a flophouse overlooking Turk Street, and hook up with two brittle young women, Mona and Sue. Jack has his way with both of them. The sex is loveless, mechanical, and artfully described. Here Jack begins to feel the first touch of self-awareness and realize his true nature:

> You know enough to know how you feel is senseless, but you don't know enough to know why. Sitting in another lousy hotel room waiting for a couple of girls you've never seen before to do a bunch of things you've done so many times it makes your skin crawl just to think about it. Things. To do.

That you dreamed about when you couldn't have them. When there was only one thing, really, that made you feel good, and now you've done that so many times it's like masturbating. Except you never really made it, did you. Never really killed anybody. That's what you've always wanted to do, smash the brains out of somebody's head; break him apart until nothing is left but you. But you never made it.

Jack's realization is not enough to save him. He hits bottom with Denny Mellon, with Mona, with himself. He goes on a long drinking binge and considers taking his own life:

For a moment he felt a drifting nausea as his mind helplessly moved toward the idea of suicide. He steadied himself and faced it, as he had known all the time he must: I am going to die. Why not now? He felt cold and sick. Well, why not? What the fuck have I got to live for?

The whiskey bottle was in his hand, and he lifted it, holding it up before his eyes. Do I want some of this? Do I want another drink? Suddenly it was very important to know. If he did not want a drink, he did not want anything. If he did not want anything, he might as well die. Because he was already dead.

"Bullshit," he said aloud. "Bullshit. I'm just in a bad mood." He tilted the bottle to his mouth and drank, his eyes closed.

Jack stumbles once again, as he knew he would. Trusting the wrong people, not yet fully understanding the mechanics of a system that has kept him incarcerated his whole life, he's sentenced to adult time at San Quentin in Chino. There he meets up again with Billy Lancing, in for "bopping" a check. They become cell mates and confidantes. And, in what must have been a shocking plot development at the time of the book's release, they become lovers. Carpenter's handling of masculinity issues and homosexuality at San Quentin, where "the prison seemed alive with affairs," is matter-of-fact, nonexploitative, and frequently moving.

> One day while Jack was walking past the salad table with a stack of hot clipper racks, he happened to glance over in time to see one man slip a plastic ring on the finger of another man. Both were ordinary-looking men, one a burglar and the other a thief, but the expressions on their faces were ones Jack could never remember having seen on a man: one of them shy and coy, an outrageous burlesque of maiden modesty; the other simpering with equally feminine aggressiveness.

Billy confesses that he has fallen in love with Jack, and asks Jack for reciprocal words. Jack can't bring himself to say them or to give his friend one kiss. What happens next will chill the reader to the bone and has such a spritual impact on Jack that it puts him on a new road.

The next section of the novel takes place from 1956 to 1960 and details Jack's improbable but wholly believable transformation. Because Carpenter is a realist, he knows that the damage done to Jack at his very core can never truly be healed. So we leave Jack Levitt broken but not defeated, drinking a wealthy man's fine whiskey. It is an oddly optimistic ending, a gift from a writer who saw the beauty in the here and now. Jack has the day and a future. It is all any of us can hope for.

Hard Rain Falling tells a ripping good story, but it is above all else a novel of ideas. It falls squarely in the tradition of Ken Kesey's *One Flew Over the Cuckoo's Nest* and Norman Mailer's *An American Dream*, books that prefigured the counterculture movement in their challenge to conformity and the system. As in all good literature, it attempts to answer the question of why we're here and does so in a provocative way. It's the kind of novel that can and should be read many times over. It sent me back to my desk, jacked up on ambition.

Writers write for various reasons: money, fame, pleasure, posterity. Don Carpenter did not receive international acclaim or a great deal of wealth in his lifetime. Maybe he wanted it; it's not for me to say. I like to think that he was in the posterity camp. Certainly his work bears that out.

"I'm an atheist," said Carpenter, in a 1975 interview. "I don't see any moral superstructure to the universe at all. I consider my work optimistic in that the people, during the period I'm writing about them, are experiencing intense emotion. It is my belief that this is all there is to it. There is nothing beyond this."

And yet, he found a piece of immortality with this book.

—George Pelecanos

HARD RAIN FALLING

THIS BOOK IS DEDICATED TO MY WIFE
AND TO BOB MILLER

"They can kill you, but they can't eat you."

— FOLK BELIEF

Incidents in
Eastern Oregon

1929–1936

Three Indians were standing out in front of the post office that hot summer morning when the motorcycle blazed down Walnut Street and caused Mel Weatherwax to back his pickup truck over the cowboy who was loading sacks of lime. The man and woman on the motorcycle probably didn't even see the accident they had caused, they went by so fast. Both of them were wearing heavy-rimmed goggles, and all Mel saw was the red motorcycle, the goggles, and two heads of hair, black for him and blond for her. But everybody forgot about them; the cowboy was badly hurt, lying there in the reddish dust cursing, his face gone white from pain. The Indians stayed up on the board sidewalk and watched while Mel Weatherwax and one of his hands carried the hurt cowboy into the shade of the alley beside the store.

The doctor got there after a while and then he started cursing, too, as he sat on his knees and probed the cowboy's body with his fingers. Quite a few people were standing around, now, watching the doctor, and some women among them, but that didn't stop his cursing. It turned out there were some broken ribs, and moving the cowboy had probably rammed the broken ends through his lungs. He died less than an hour later, still lying in the alley, and by this time the sun had moved enough so he was out exposed to the heat again. One of the town women was standing over him with a parasol trying to shade him, but she was so busy talking to a friend that the parasol got waved around, and didn't do the cowboy much good. He had already died some time before the woman noticed it, and then she gave a little scream and jumped back and went off down the street looking mortified.

There was still a crowd around Mel Weatherwax after the body was hauled off and he was telling again what had happened when the young man from the motorcycle and his girl friend walked back into town. He had his goggles pushed up into his dusty hair, and she had hers down around her neck, and there was a purplish bruise on her cheek. They were both dusty and tired-looking, but the young man pushed his way into the crowd and said to Mel Weatherwax, "Hell, I busted my motor. Is there a garage in town?"

"Sonny boy," Mel said, "you just killed one of my cowboys. Nobody in this town is going to fix your damn motorcycle."

The year was 1929 and the Depression had already been on two years in that part of eastern Oregon, so Mel wasn't worried about getting another hand. But he was glad to have that boy there to blame the accident on, and once the idea caught fire with him he lost his temper and hit the young man in the face, knocking him back through the crowd, stumbling, until he came to rest right at an Indian's feet. The young man wiped the dust and sweat off his face with the back of his hand and looked up, grinning, at the Indian. A handsome young man, his teeth made brighter by the sunburn on his face. "I'm damned," he said, "a damn Indian." Then he got up and attacked Mel Weatherwax, and pretty soon some of the other men had to drag him off.

4

The girl stood back from it all, in the shade, and watched. She was slender, dirty, blue-eyed, and very young, and she looked tired, but she had a glitter in her eye as she watched the fight, as if she liked what she saw. After that, when anyone saw that look in her eye, he knew there was going to be some trouble.

With the fight over, things calmed down, and Mel, being defeated, offered to buy the young man a drink, and they all moved off toward the Wagon Wheel. With that job open none of the men out of work were going to let Mel out of their sight until he had made his pick. As it turned out, the young man got the job, and he and Mel and the other hand rode out of town in the pickup together, leaving the girl at the hotel by herself. On the way out to the ranch they picked up the motorcycle and put it in the back, and out at the ranch they tried to fix it, but some of the parts were broken, and the frame was bent. Harmon Wilder, the young man, told everybody he had stolen it in Oakland, California, and didn't care what happened to it.

There wasn't any funeral for the dead cowboy; he didn't have any family and, since it was early summer, all the men on the ranches were too busy. His body was put into a wooden coffin and hauled out to the ranch and buried there.

The next time the Indians saw the girl she was waiting on tables in the hotel restaurant. None of them went inside the hotel; they saw her through the big window that looks out over Walnut Street. In those days they didn't have jobs; they lived on checks they got at the post office from the Federal Government. The checks didn't stop until late in the 1930s when the lumber business got so busy the mills started hiring Indians. So in 1929 some of the Indians would come to town almost every day, and stand around in front of the post office, talking and watching the town goings-on. If the chance came up they would get some whiskey and take it off somewhere and drink it. They got to know Harmon Wilder pretty well, because unlike a lot of the other cowboys he didn't mind buying the Indians whiskey. He even went drinking with them once or twice. And once, when the two Federal agents from Portland came to town and closed the Wagon Wheel, Harmon and a couple of others drove up to Bend and bought a case of Canadian Club, and Harmon sold three quarts of it to the Indians. It seemed as if the whole town was drunk that night, although it was just millhands, cowboys, and five or six Indians. Those two Federal agents got into a fight trying to find out where the liquor came from, and one of them was hit over the head with an empty bottle and had to be driven forty miles to the hospital.

Not long after that the State police came and got the girl. Her name was Annemarie Levitt, and she had run away from her family in Portland, and she was only sixteen years old. She was gone all told for about six weeks, and then came to town again on the bus, took a room at the hotel, and got her job back in the restaurant. By this time everybody could see that she was pregnant. Before she went back to Portland, Harmon used to come in to town on Saturday nights and visit her for a while before he went over to the Wagon Wheel, but afterward he wouldn't even talk to her on the street.

By the time the first snow fell in late October, everybody in town knew her parents were not going to send the police after her again, and that she was not going to go back to Portland of her own free will. By this time of year the cowboys could come to town every night if they had any money; Harmon was lucky at cards, and so was in town quite a lot. He had not changed; he was still wild, still drank too much, but every once in a while he would stop by the hotel to see Annemarie, and at least once she hitched a ride out to the ranch to see him.

Annemarie Levitt didn't come to live with the Indians until late in the following spring, 1930, after she had gone up to Bend and had her baby at one of those homes for unwed mothers. She came back to Iona without the baby. No one knew which drove Harmon crazier, not knowing where or what his child was, or seeing the mother of his child living with the Indians. Maybe it wasn't either of those things; maybe it was what she did to his face.

She did not love Harmon any more; she proved that one afternoon not many weeks after she got back to town without the baby, and Harmon stopped her on the street. He was carrying a bottle of whiskey and was half drunk already, even though it was only the middle of a gray winter day; stopped her, said something to her nobody else could hear, and then laughed and tried to give her the whiskey bottle to have a drink, and she took it and swung it in a wide arc, upward, hard, and smashed it against the side of his face and sent him flying. The snow that had been plowed off the street and scraped off the boardwalk was lying in hard dirty heaps, and Harmon tumbled over the snow and left a bright smear of blood on the crust and ended up face down on the hard ice of the street; and Annemarie stood there with the neck of the bottle in her hand, laughing at him, and then threw the neck down on top of him and walked off, leaving him there in the street with his jaw broken, his cheek cut open, the blood pouring out hot and then freezing to the street. There were a few people who saw the whole thing from across the street, but nobody stopped to help Harmon; his reputation in town was already too bad for him to expect any help, and finally he got up himself and staggered down the street to the Wagon Wheel. Some hands finally took him to the doctor and then drove him to the hospital. No, she did not love him any more. Maybe she hated him. Maybe that was strong enough to bring her back. Then, when she hit him with that whiskey bottle and laughed to see him helpless and his blood freezing to the street, she stopped hating him and started hating herself.

Portland had driven her crazy. Even at sixteen she hated it; she was the despair of her family, the only child; wild, already in trouble with the police once or twice before she met Harmon and on impulse ran off with him; she would sit in her room upstairs after her parents had sent her to bed and wait for them to go to sleep and then get dressed again and go out the window and catch a streetcar downtown; but when she came back she would come right in the front door, and if they were waiting up for her she would lose her temper and tell them to mind their own business, and if her father tried to slap her or spank her she would hit him and scream at him until he just stopped trying, and then she would go back upstairs and into her room and lock the door. She must have met Harmon on one of these expeditions downtown because one night she just didn't come home.

Harmon's face was ruined; he lost all the teeth on the left side, and there was a scar running from just under his left eye through his lip and down his chin; his face now had a caved-in look to it, and his blue eyes lost all their brightness, and he was just plain mean from then forward until he died; living the life of a good hardworking cowboy, maybe not the kind of life he might have dreamed about in Oakland, California, but, for him, good anyway: eighteen hours a day when the cattle were on the range, half the anger cooked out of him by the sun, the dust, the hot acid smell of his horse under him; the work, even in winter, the thousand irritating must-be-done tasks attendant to cattle, drawing his surplus energy out through his arms and legs until there was barely enough for one yelling Saturday night a month left in him, one night to drink and smash windows and batter any face that presented itself.

He used to write letters, and come to the post office every chance he got to see if there were any answers. It was not long before everyone knew what he wanted. He wrote the letters to orphanages and State homes all over Oregon, trying to find out if there were any children in them named Wilder or Levitt; but he would come out of the post office and sit down on the bench and open his mail and crumple the letters up after he read them, his face black with rage, and so everybody knew he hadn't found the child yet. Maybe the urge to find the child got cooked or burned out of him too; after a while he gave up, and people stopped thinking about him because he did not come to town any more at all, but stayed out on the ranch. Cowboys move around a lot, changing jobs, but not Harmon. He stayed with Mel Weatherwax until he died. Mel said he was a good cowboy and did not talk much, and if you left him alone he caused no trouble. Whatever made him run away from Oakland to the

Wild West seemed to have been taken care of, one way or another. Maybe what he wanted was freedom. Maybe he looked around and saw that everybody was imprisoned by Oakland, by their own small neighborhoods; everybody was breathing the same air, inheriting the same seats in school, taking the same stale jobs as their fathers and living in the same shabby stucco homes. Maybe it all looked to him like a prison or a trap, the way everybody expected him to do certain things because they had always been done a certain way, and they expected him to be good at doing these strange, meaningless, lonely things, and maybe he was afraid—of the buildings, the smoke, the stink of the bay, the gray look everybody had. Maybe he was afraid that he too would become one of these grown people whose faces were blank and lonely, and he too would have to satisfy himself with a house in the neighborhood and one of the girls from high school and a job at one or another factory and just sit there and die of it. So he ran for the only frontier he ever heard about and became a cowboy. But of course he brought it all with him when he ran, and it kept at him, jabbing, destroying, murdering, until he himself was all gone and nothing was left but a man's body doing work. And finally that died too. It was an accident. A horse kicked him and he died the next day of a brain hemorrhage; he had been trying to knock loose the balled ice under the horse's hooves, and he slipped and wrenched the horse's leg and the horse kicked out and got him right on the temple, and that was the end of him. The accident happened in 1936, and he was twenty-six years old, almost twenty-seven. He never did get to see his son.

Neither did Annemarie. She had been living with the Indians for a long time now, and seemed all right, but when she heard about Harmon's death, something went out of her—something the massed hatred of the white people of the town had failed to diminish in all that time—and a few weeks later she killed herself with a 10-gauge shotgun. She was twenty-four at the time. The Indians buried her.

PART ONE

The Juveniles

1947

There were worse things than being broke, but for the moment Jack Levitt could not think of any of them. He stood on Fourth Avenue in downtown Portland looking into the window of a novelty store, his hands in his pockets, his heavy shoulders sloped forward. Two items caught his eye, the first a not-very-convincing puddle of plastic vomit, colored a bilish yellow, with bits of food sticking up from the surface; the second a realistic heap of dogshit, probably made out of plaster of Paris and then colored brown. Somebody made these things to sell. Somewhere there was a factory in which workers stood at assembly lines and turned these items out, and the workers got paid for it. Jack wished he could think of something like that to make money with. But he knew he had neither the imagination nor the energy for inventive work. He smiled to himself. When you're broke, all kinds of crazy ways of making money come into

1 3

your head. Rolling drunks. Walking into a store (like this one, for example, empty except for an old man in the back reading a newspaper) and grabbing the guy by the shirtfront, giving him a couple of pops on the mouth, and emptying the cash register. . . . Or he could go down to the labor employment place on Third, a few doors up from the burlesque theater, and try to get a job. Except that all along the Burnside skid row there were men standing out on the sidewalk or leaning against buildings, and there would be a whole cluster of them at the employment office, trying to get work. When Jack had first run to Portland a few months before, he had thought all these men were bums, but they weren't. They were just workers out of work. Fishermen, dock workers, lumberjacks, fry cooks, men who had been to barber college, and only a few winos. Gypsies, too, whole families of them sitting out in front of their storefront homes, and Jack knew the gypsy girls, the pretty ones in their costumes, would smile and wink at you, and beckon you into their place, offering what no gypsy woman ever delivered, and then, once inside, asking for some money "to bless," and gypsy men would begin to glide out of the curtained shadows. . . . The men were mostly used-car dealers, and would race around town in dusty old cars, stopping people and asking if they wanted immediate cash for their car, or offering to repair dented fenders. They would say that they would remove "that ugly dent" for three dollars, and if you went for it, five or six of them would pile out of the car with hammers and start banging away on your fender, and they would turn your one big dent into dozens of small dents, and then demand three dollars *apiece,* surrounding you and arguing furiously about the sacredness of a contract and they had witnesses; and if you absolutely balked and refused to pay anything at all, they would offer to buy the car. If you didn't want to sell, they would eventually go away, but not without argument. Another great way to make money. Only, Jack was not a gypsy.

He was, in fact, a young man who had a hard time getting work. Not that he wanted to work, but he did want money, and right now, in daylight, that seemed the only way. He was seventeen, and very hard-looking. He had penetrating, flat, almost snakelike blue eyes which ordinary citizens found difficult to look into, and his head seemed too large for his body, accentuated by the mop of wild blond curls he seldom combed. He looked mean without looking angry, and his huge fists seemed capable of smashing skulls, almost as if they had been made just for that. Jack was not the picture of the model employee, and even when he smiled there was too much ferocity in his expression to relax anyone.

Yet he was only a boy, and most of the hardness was a mask, developed over the last dozen years of his life because he had discovered that nobody was going to protect him but himself. On a smaller, thinner, less powerful-looking boy, his expression might have been mistaken for self-reliance, and commended.

He turned away from the window, taking his hands out of his pockets, and began to walk up the street. People who saw him coming got out of his way. It was a gray Portland day, and this helped him to feel sorry for himself. He was down to his last few dollars and locked out of his hotel room. He had quit his job and did not know where he could get some more money. He was legally a fugitive from the orphanage, and in that sense "wanted." He did not feel "wanted"—he felt very unwanted. He had desires, and nobody was going to drop out of the sky to satisfy them. He tried to milk a little self-pity out of this thought, but it did not work: he had to recognize that he preferred his singularity, his freedom. All right. He knew what he wanted. He wanted some money. He wanted a piece of ass. He wanted a big dinner, with all the trimmings. He wanted a bottle of whiskey. He wanted a car, in which he could drive a hundred miles an hour (he had only recently learned how to drive, and he loved the feelings of speed and control, the sharpness of the danger). He wanted some new clothes and thirty-dollar shoes. He wanted a .45 automatic. He wanted a record player in the big hotel room he wanted, so he could lie in bed with the whiskey and the piece of ass and listen to

1 5

"How High the Moon" and "Artistry Jumps." That was what he wanted. So it was up to him to get these things. Already he felt better, just making a list of his desires. That put limits on them. And he knew that every single one of his desires could be satisfied with money. So what he really wanted was lots of money. Say, ten thousand dollars.

He was really in a good humor when he got to the poolhall which was one of his three hangouts (the other two were a street corner and another poolhall), and he ran down the stairs cheerfully, and when he saw his friend Denny Mellon he called out, "Hey, daddy, have you got ten thousand dollars you can loan me?"

Denny frowned and said, "What do you need it for?"

"Houses and lots," Jack chanted.

"Well, okay. I thought you was going to waste it on war bonds or somethin."

A few minutes later Jack was involved in a game of ten-cent nine-ball, and he had forgotten all about his troubles.

Jack was not friendless. Shortly after coming to Portland he found the location of the local hard kids and joined them, and in the gang he had a certain status as one of those who would stop at nothing, one of the really tough boys, like Clancy Phipps and his brother Dale, a leader because (so it seemed to the rest of the boys and girls) there was no proposition too dangerous for him. In Portland the hard kids were called "the Broadway gang" and they hung out at the corner of Broadway and Yamhill. The gang started during World War II, and still goes on. These were the kids who were not liked or wanted enough at their high schools, or who despised school themselves, and who wanted the excitement Downtown promises; the ones who were in trouble with the schools, the police, their parents— nearly everybody—and so gathered together into one loosely knit gang. There were perhaps fifty of them, boys and girls both, and the makeup of the gang was in a constant state of flux; members would vanish into the Army or jobs, or get married, or make friends at their own schools, or go to the reformatory in Woodburn, or leave the state and go to New York or San Francisco; and new members kept coming along, many like Jack, to be recognized and admitted to the group on the criteria of toughness, a lack of conventional morals, a dislike of adults, and a hatred of the police.

Most of them were like Jack Levitt in that they wanted a lot of money and wanted to do anything they pleased, at least for a while; but most of them saw it differently: they wanted to enjoy themselves *now*, because they knew in their hearts that soon they would get jobs and get married and start having families (like their own), and the fun would be over. If they seemed too noisy, too wild, too defiant, perhaps it was a little out of desperation, because lying before them were endless years of dull existence, shabby jobs, unattractive mates, and brats with no more future than themselves. Jack did not see things this way, and there was no reason why he should have. He did not know who his parents were, and he did not expect the future to be a repetition of the past because that was unthinkable—he at least had a vision of the future which included a wildness in itself, a succession of graduated pleasures and loves and joys, and if it was going to be a struggle, that was all right, too; he knew how to fight for what he wanted. In fact, that was almost all he did know. There were buried terrors, too; but he hoped that part of his life was finished. In this sense, he was that odd combination, a cynical optimist. His hopes were vague and even childish, but they were at least hopes, and their vagueness was a blessing; for many of the others, the future was all too clear.

At about the same time Jack Levitt ran down the steps to the poolhall, another boy whose future was vague, yet to him full of promise, got off the bus from Seattle. His name was Billy Lancing and he was the last one off; a slender, bony-shouldered boy of sixteen, hawk-faced, with sharp, too-old, calculating eyes. The color of his skin was a malarial yellow, and it was obvious from that and from his kinky reddish-brown hair that he was a Negro. He wore a white windbreaker and carried a small blue canvas overnight bag, which he put into a ten-cent locker there in the Greyhound depot; then he walked downstairs to the men's rest room, slipped a nickel into one of the pay-toilet slots, and entered. When he came out the locker key was inside his stocking, under his right instep. This was important: inside the bag, along with all his clothes, were fifteen ten-dollar bills, rolled tight and kept together by a doubled rubber band—his caseroll, money he had won and scrimped and saved to make his break from home.

The key safe, he went to one of the sinks and ran cold water over his hands, and then splashed it over his face. The men's room was full of sailors, and their talk and laughter bounced strangely off the tiled walls, an insane barrage of fragmentary noises. Except for the echoing quality it sounded to Billy just like his home in Seattle, the continual clatter and chatter of the people who lived in their housing-project apartment: his father and mother, his brothers and sisters, his old aunt from the South, his three grandparents; a home in which someone was always up, meals were always being prepared, somebody was always getting ready for work and someone else just home and having a drink of whiskey; the radio going, a child crying, another screaming with laughter; his aunt's constant low bubbling voice from the corner beside the stove, talking about the times in the South and the cold and the rain; or his father and grandfather arguing Boeing this and Boeing that. When Billy thought of home he thought of noise, and now in the men's room of the Greyhound depot in Portland, almost two hundred miles from the housing project, the old fear of suffocation, of being strangled by the noise, came over him again, and he felt his gut tighten and his palms go moist. I'm just scared of Portland, he thought. That's all there is to it. Like any other kid. He went back up the stairs and out into the street.

Heavy gray bellies of clouds hung low over the buildings of downtown Portland, but it was not raining yet, and the sidewalk was dry. Billy looked at the blue-and-white street sign:

Fifth and Taylor. He knew from what they told him at the Two-Eleven in Seattle that there were three poolhalls in downtown Portland: the Rialto, on Park, between Morrison and Alder; Ben Fenne's, on Sixth, between Washington and Stark; and a place everybody called "The Rathole," on Washington between Fourth and Fifth. The top action was supposed to be at the Rialto, but Billy decided that he would like to try out the other places first. He walked over to a driver leaning against a Yellow Cab and asked him directions, and then began walking down the hill, toward Washington Street.

"The Rathole" was easy to find: a red neon sign, over an entryway between a hole-in-the-wall lunch counter and a real-estate office, saying "Pool–Snooker–Billiards" and a stairway down. As Billy started down, two businessmen were on the way up, laughing about something. One of them gave him an odd look and then turned sideways to let him pass. The stairs were incredibly dirty, and the concrete landing at the bottom was stained and covered with litter, smelling of stale vomit and urine. There was a small green wine bottle lying on its side in one corner, and next to it a paper bag from which the neck of a second bottle stuck out. Billy turned right and pushed open the swinging doors and walked down three more steps into the poolhall.

To his right, a glass cigar counter with a few stale-looking wrapped sandwiches on top, a horse-pinball with the usual player bent over it, a telephone booth, a man in a white shirt, probably the proprietor, leaning against the counter and giving advice to the pinball player; to his left, six tables in a row, all pool tables. Three of them had games going, and there was a row of theater seats against the wall, with clusters of idle watchers opposite the active tables. Beyond the cigar counter Billy saw an entryway leading to a back room, and through it he could see the corner of a snooker table, and past that, more theater seats. There was a lot of noise coming from the back room, and with his hands in the windbreaker pockets, Billy walked over and leaned against the entryway. There were three

1 9

snooker tables, and all three had games going; businessmen with their coats off, probably playing four bits a corner while they ate their lunch, laughing, all friends, all playing together every day at noon. One of them, Billy saw, was a policeman, plump, loose-faced, chewing on a sandwich. Billy was just about to turn around and leave when he felt something on his shoulder.

He turned and looked directly into the proprietor's face. The mouth was tense, the words were harsh, but behind gold-rimmed glasses the gray eyes looked troubled, as if the eyes were trying to tell Billy not to mind the words, not to blame the proprietor. But then again, Billy thought as he went back up the stairs, maybe the old fart was just excusing himself. Billy paid no attention to the actual words; whether they were "Beat it, nigger," or, "Take off, nigger," or just, "Blah blah, nigger," did not matter to him and he did not remember; it was not important; "The Rathole" was not the kind of place he was looking for. It was a dirty, two-bit joint full of pastime players and horsebettors in out of the weather; there was nothing for Billy there anyway.

Ben Fenne's was different; he could see that right away. It was another basement, but the staircase coming down was wider and had been swept off; at the bottom there was a barbershop to the left and the poolhall to the right, and it was a bigger room, with a higher ceiling, more tables, more action; and instead of a cigar counter there was a long bar, of dark wood, behind which two white-shirted men worked, drawing beer or cooking on the griddle. A quick glance around the room showed Billy that there were no other Negroes in the room, but he expected that; there were no Negroes at the Two-Eleven in Seattle, either, or hadn't been until Billy persisted, and finally was permitted to hang around. For that matter, he had even developed a reputation of sorts in Seattle as the "Kid Nigger," who always played his best and showed real talent as a straight pool or one-pocket player.

The first table to the right was billiard, and there was a three-handed game of 31 going on. Feeling the hard-action tension in his gut, in all his muscles, Billy walked over to the counter behind the billiard table and perched himself up on the stool in the corner, leaning against the wall as he turned to watch the game. He felt the thrill of action in him, almost as if he were going to get into a game for a hundred dollars right then. It was a good feeling, and his hands were dry now and he could swallow easily. He almost laughed, he felt so good.

Pretty soon the counterman came over to him, wiping his hands on his stained white apron: a short man, monkey-faced, tired-looking, with thick, hairy forearms.

"What'll it be?" he asked Billy.

Billy felt the laughter trying to bubble up out of his throat, because he knew what was going to happen, knew what had already happened. The counterman had chickened out; he had come over to tell Billy to leave, and then had chickened out.

"I'll have a hot dog and coffee with cream," Billy said to him.

The counterman's hands were on the bar, and he drummed his fingers once and sighed. "Okay," he said.

When he brought back the sandwich, a thick, rubber-skinned hot dog cut in half and placed between thin slices of white bread, he had to tap Billy on the back to get his attention.

"Here's your sangwich, kid. Thirty cents with the coffee. Eat it and go, okay?"

"Did you think I wanted to *sleep* here?" Billy said innocently. Then he smiled his big show-off smile at the counterman, and pointed a long bony finger at the mustard pot down the bar. Automatically the counterman reached for the mustard and slid it to Billy. "You know what I mean, kid," he said.

Billy ate his sandwich and sipped at his coffee, pretending to watch the billiard game; but actually he was casing the place, looking over all the tables to see where the gamblers were and what the action was. To his right was another billiard table, only with a keno rig on it—a wooden rack with a brass edge at one end of the table, with numbered holes in it for the balls. Keno was a purely gambling game, and a sign above the light rack of the table said, "Open Game, Ten Cents Per Cue," which meant that anybody (well, practically anybody, Billy thought) could get in. He debated whether to make his stand here, and then decided against it. Because at one of the pool tables in the middle of the room there was a nine-ball game going on, between players not too much older than Billy, and there were plenty of watchers, sitting or leaning against other tables, whispering and making side bets. That would be the place.

After he finished eating he wiped his mouth daintily with a paper napkin, crossed the room to the toilet, and washed. When he came out, he went to the middle of the room, near the nine-ball game. He eased himself into a high-backed wooden chair, hooked his feet into the rungs, crossed his hands over his belly, wanting to laugh, wanting to let out a yip of joy, and said in a boyish, niggery voice that could be heard all over the poolroom, "Befo you-all *tho* me out, who wants to take my money? Who wants a black boy's hard-earned money?"

The place went dead for a moment as everyone stopped what he was doing and turned to look at him. Then slowly, some embarrassed, some uninterested, they went back to their games and talk, and the noises of the poolhall resumed. But Billy expected this; he knew that among them, probably around the nine-ball or keno table, some people were wondering what his game was and how good he was at it; wondering if they couldn't take his money before the houseman threw him out. Billy also knew the houseman, wherever he was, would be over soon to do just that unless one of the regulars begged him not to, at least not until he had trimmed Billy.

As it turned out, the houseman himself made the offer. He was a medium-sized, well-built man of about thirty, with a leather apron on. He came up behind Billy and said, "What's your game, boy?"

Billy turned and looked up at him. "I'll play anything."

The houseman said, "Why don't you stay over on Williams Avenue, where you belong."

"I'm from Seattle," Billy said. "I never heard of Williams Avenue."

"Colored neighborhood," the houseman said. He stood patiently, his hands in his hip pockets.

"Sure," Billy said. "Warped cues, ripped-up tables, dented balls, and ten cents on the nine. What do I want with a place like that? I got a *future* in pool."

"Nobody's got a future in pool," the houseman said. "But I'll play you, just to see what you got. Straight pool all right with you?"

"That would be just fine," Billy said.

"Two dollars a game? Fifty points?"

"Just fine."

"How about letting me see your money?"

Billy laughed softly and took out a fold of bills, with a ten on the outside. "Now how about I see yours?"

"Smart little fucker, aint you," the houseman said.

"You want me to beg to get to play here?" Billy asked.

The houseman thought about that, and had to grin. "Well, I guess not," he said.

I'm entertaining, aren't I, Billy thought, and for a moment he felt a twinge of disgust with himself; he knew what he was doing was just a form of uncletomming. But the hell with that; it got him what he wanted. Maybe they started out by tolerating him, but they ended up respecting him, because the only thing that counts in a poolhall is how well you shoot.

"Let's see your money," Billy said. At once he wished he hadn't; it just slipped out of him. But the houseman didn't get mad; he laughed and pulled out his roll.

"New *hustler* in town," he announced to the crowd that was beginning to gather.

"Little boy *black*," Billy chanted as he came back from the bin with a cue, "will take your *jack!*"

That got a few laughs, and Billy could feel the tension in the room lessening. He hoped the houseman was one of the best, and he hoped, of course, that he could beat him. It would help.

At sixteen, Billy Lancing was already a brilliant pool player. He had the smooth stroking action only the young and the great ever get, and a young sharp eye, and above all, and what made him great, the inner necessity to win the money; because money meant everything in the world to Billy. He had learned how to play pool at the YMCA, and after the first rudimentary difficulties with bridge and stroke and eye, saw that for some reason or other, nobody else at the Y could beat him. He discovered that he had a talent. And he knew that down at the colored poolhall three blocks from home men played pool for money. At the age of fourteen he made his debut at the colored poolhall, and after the grown men got over laughing at the picture of him leaning over the table, outsized cue in his hand, they saw that he was winning all the games and taking all the money, and cute or not, he was a menace. The owner of the place took care of that, and barred Billy for being underage. So he went downtown to the Two-Eleven, shivering with fright. Of course they threw him out; and that made him angry. He came back, and they threw him out again, and then he bet one of the men who took him down the elevator that he could beat him in bank pool, and the two of them rode back up again, both angry, both silent, and played on the number one table with everybody watching, and Billy got so far ahead in the first game (playing ten miles over his head in cold anger) that he made his last three banks contemptuously one-handed; and from then on he was the official mascot of the Two-Eleven poolshooters, and eventually, the best of them. A regular child prodigy, one of them called him.

The houseman won the toss and Billy broke the balls safe, but it was not a good break and the houseman started to run, six, ten, fourteen balls, and Billy reracked and the houseman fired in the loose ball and broke into the pack, spreading the balls all over the lower end of the table, and the houseman ran another ten balls before he missed. A total of twenty-five on the wire; half the game. But Billy was not worried; he was in action, and action was what he liked best. If the houseman had run fifty and won the game it would not have bothered Billy, as long as he had money in his pocket to back his play, and as long as he had his right arm. He leaned against a table and watched the houseman shooting, seeing the bright Kelly green of the new felt, the way the overhead light glowed off the balls, and beyond the table the seeming darkness of the rest of the poolhall, sensing the perfect security of knowing where he was and knowing he belonged there. Finally the houseman missed and wired his score. Billy advanced on the table, chalking his cue and sizing up the layout at the same time.

One of the watchers said, "Hell, John, you aint run so many balls in your life."

The houseman grinned and said, "Keep the fuck outen the game, bigmouth."

"You shootin over your head," the watcher said.

Another, younger voice said, "I'll give anybody two to one John beats the nigger."

Billy turned quickly and squinted into the gloom. "Who said that?"

"I did." The speaker was a grinning young man with dark red hair and freckles, and a dimple in the middle of his chin. He pulled a fold of money out of his shirt pocket and waggled it at Billy. "Want a piece of this?"

"I'll take five for ten," Billy said.

"The kid *is* a hustler! Okay, you're on."

Billy ran thirty-eight balls before he missed, feeling the charge mounting in him as ball followed ball into the pockets and rattled hollowly down the return troughs beneath, until the pressure was finally too great and he missed what should have been an easy cut into the side, and left the cue ball in the open. John the houseman, his face tightened into concentration, bent over the table and began to run, but missed his breakshot on the next rack and left Billy wide open. John sighed, put his cue down on top of an unused table and went to the back of the place and collected the time from some snooker players who had quit playing, and by the time he got back to his own game it was over: Billy had run out.

"Who said you could shoot while I wasn't lookin?" he said angrily.

"You didn't say nothin," Billy said. "I didn't even see you leave."

"Christ Almighty, John, he win fair and square," one of the watchers said. The red-headed kid handed Billy a five and five ones with an expression of disgust, and John paid Billy his two dollars.

"Another game?" Billy asked him.

"You're too good for me, kid," John said. Somebody yelled "Rack!" and John moved off to answer the call. Billy threw some balls out on the table and began shooting them, waiting for somebody to challenge him. But it was quiet now, around his table, and he began to wonder if maybe he wasn't going to get thrown out anyway. The action-feeling was deserting him, and he began missing easy shots. After a while he quit in disgust, racked the balls, put his cue away and found John.

"How much do I owe?"

John rubbed his face. "Nothin. It's free if you win."

"I mean for the practice," Billy insisted.

"Shit. Two minutes? Be two cents."

"I wouldn't want to owe nobody anything," Billy said. I'm pushing it too far, he thought. What the hell's the matter with me? But he dug into his pants pocket and came up with a nickel. He handed it to John, who stared down at the coin with puzzlement, almost disgust.

"Hell," he said. "I'll just take it and buy me a Coky-Cola. Thanks, kid." He went off toward the bar, and Billy waited a moment and then sat down and watched the nine-ball game. There was nothing else for him to do. For eight hours on the bus he had been preparing himself for this entry into Portland, this triumph, and it had come and gone so quickly that it did not seem to have happened at all. It should have been more dramatic; somebody should have yelled about a nigger in the joint, people should have taken sides, and he should have silenced it all by his brilliant play. But it didn't happen that

2 6

way at all, and now he sat there, twelve dollars richer, ignored, another idle watcher. Almost as if he already belonged.

The red-headed kid flopped down in the chair next to his, crossed his legs, and began picking his teeth, watching the game before them.

"You could beat all these guys," he said to Billy. "You just get in from Seattle?"

"Just got off the bus," Billy said. The red-headed kid had lazy green eyes and an easy smile; Billy liked him right away. He got out his cigarettes and offered one to the redhead.

"Thanks. You ever play at the Two-Eleven up there?"

"Yeah. All the time. You know Seattle?"

"I been up there a couple times with my old man. You ever play on them big snooker tables? You play good snooker?"

"Well enough," Billy said. "I play all games."

"You want to make some money playin snooker?"

"Do I have to lay off to do it? I never lay off."

The redhead chuckled. "You don't have to do nothin but play. They got snooker players up at the Rialto; you don't have to lay off or fake it or anything. All you got to do is go up there and get in the game. You don't have to hustle; they'll hustle *you*." As an afterthought he said, "My name's Denny." He reached out his hand and they shook.

Billy thought for a moment. "How about that Rialto? I heard a lot about it in Seattle. Is there anybody up there can beat me?"

Denny laughed. "Oh, man, you're good, but you're not that good. There's plenty of guys up there can beat you. What's your high run?"

"Fifty-five," Billy said.

"Fifty-five. You ever hear of Joe Cannon? He *owns* the Rialto. You think you can beat him with your fifty-five? And not only him. How about Reuben Menashe? Bobby Case? Bobby's only about fourteen but he can wipe your ass. He went down to Frisco about a month ago and made eighteen hundred playin nine-ball at Corcoran's, and they were *spottin* him the seven eight cause he's so young-lookin. Can you beat these guys? You better stick to snooker. They got a bunch of snooker fiends up there that think they run the world; it'd take em a month to decide you were too good for em, and by then you'd have all the money."

"I don't want to play no snooker," Billy said. He did not know why; there was something in his mind about being the best, but he did not want to face that. Because, he thought, it's not the truth. I don't want to be the best. I aint the best. I'll never be the best. But he did not want to play snooker, take the sucker's money, while all the time the really good players were laughing at him. As a matter of fact, he had forgotten all about Joe Cannon; he could not understand why. Everybody knew about him. He was a really good player, and one of the few who had made money at the game, enough to buy his own pool-hall and cardroom. The very thought of playing him frightened Billy; he knew his hands would feel heavy, the cue foreign to his grip, the balls distant. And Joe Cannon wasn't even the best. He was just the best in the Pacific Northwest, and already people were saying he was getting too old, spending too much time playing poker, and his stroke was way off lately. Yet Billy was afraid to play him. I'm only *sixteen,* he told himself angrily. *What's all the fuss?*

"How do I find this Rialto?" he asked Denny.

"Let's go," Denny said. "I'll take you up there. I wanna hamburger anyhow. They aint got hamburgers in this joint." He called out, "Hey, Levitt, I'm goin up to the other joint."

Jack hardly looked up. He was beginning to feel desperate; he had played and played, and all he did was lose his money. This morning he had left his hotel for breakfast, and returned to find a padlock on his door. He knew that he would not be able to get his stuff out of the room until he had paid the fifty-odd dollars he owed, but instead of sitting down and planning what to do, he had gotten into a game of pool. He wondered now why he was so stupid. He missed an easy shot, and swore angrily, throwing his cue down on the floor. John the houseman came up to him and said, "Don't bust the equipment, sonny."

"Aw hell, I quit," Jack said. "How about puttin my time on the wire?"

John looked at him carefully, and said, "Okay. One time."

Jack grinned. "How do you know I'll pay?"

"Shee. You'll pay. You got to, or you don't get to hang out in here."

Still grinning, Jack shrugged his shoulders and said, "Well, I guess you got me by the balls."

"I guess so."

Jack went back outside. It was drizzling slightly, and the cold moisture felt good on his face. He walked up toward the Corner, up Sixth Avenue, and stopped once in a record store to listen to some new Stan Kenton. It was one of the things you could do if you didn't have any money. But it got boring, finally, and he went on. Everything seemed out of kilter. It hadn't been like this at the orphanage; there you had something you were supposed to be doing all the time. He hadn't expected to miss that. But he did. He had to admit it. He went past the Orpheum Theater on Broadway. A war picture was showing, and he wondered if he wanted to see it. He knew a way to get in without paying; you went up to the guy taking tickets and said, "I'm supposed to pick up my kid sister," and just walked past him. If he had any guts he'd throw you out, but most of them didn't. A couple of weeks before, Jack and about seven others who had been hanging around the Corner bored and broke had busted into the United Artists by running single-file past the ticket-taker without saying a word, running up the stairs to the balcony and then splitting up and taking seats. None of them had been caught, and later, in the middle of the picture, Denny, sitting down in the front of the balcony, yelled, "Count *off!*" and Jack yelled, "One!" and somebody else, "Two!" while the usherettes ran around looking for them. It had been fun, but stupid. He did not want to see the war movie. It would be full of shit. He walked on up to the drugstore on the Corner and drank a Coke and waited for something interesting to happen.

His friend, the red-haired Denny Mellon, came into the drugstore about an hour later, and by this time Jack was almost going crazy from boredom. He was not the only member of the Broadway gang in the place, but he sat by himself anyway, to nourish his boredom; he did not like the bunch at the other end of the counter, grouped around Clancy Phipps. Clancy had just done six months in the county jail for stealing a portable radio out of a car, and everyone was listening to him be ironic and hard about life in jail. Denny sat down next to Jack and said, "Shit."

"What's up?"

"Oh, balls. I took this nigger kid up to the Rialto, meanin to hustle him out of all his gold. I had a great scheme goin. I was gonna get him to play snooker with Hatch and them old farts on the middle table, get his confidence all built up, you know, an then when you showed up, get him in a nine-ball game between you and somebody like Bobby Case, an cut him up. You know, you play safe, and Case shoot out. The best part is, he'd beat Hatch and them guys easy, see, and then we'd get all his gold an all their gold, too. Only, you didn't show up an didn't show up, and in comes Case with that crazy bastard Kol Mano, an *they* got him."

"How much did they get off him?"

"Christ, about fifty bucks. Shee-fucking-*it!*"

Jack laughed. "It wasn't your money."

"It should of been."

"So you're broke, too."

Denny showed his teeth in an Irish grin. "Nope. I got about ten bucks."

"Loan me five."

"Nope. In about ten minutes I'm gonna walk down to the Model Hotel and buy myself a nice juicy piece of ass. I been thinkin about it all day. I ain't had a piece of ass in a week."

"You're a real buddy," Jack said. Suddenly he wanted a girl, very badly. He had been to the Model and the Rex, and a couple of the other whorehouses, with Denny and alone, and right now that seemed like the most delightful thing they could do. It was so nice and businesslike, and the girls smelled so good, and seemed so attractive. . . .

"Listen," he said to Denny. "You got ten, we take five each and that gets us both in. You just can't leave me sittin here."

"Why not?" Denny grinned. "Tell you what: while I'm sittin there on the bed watchin the girl strip, I'll *think* about you, just once. Okay?"

"You prick," Jack said, but he knew that Denny would take him along. It was one of the things he liked about Denny. Jack could not understand why Denny was so friendly, so open and so easy with his money, when he had any, but that didn't make any difference. It didn't bother Jack that he would be bumming Denny's last five dollars, either. He reasoned that if Denny didn't want to share it, he wouldn't. He wasn't *forcing* him.

"Let's go," Jack said.

"Naw, it's too early. Let's try to hold off. But man, I do really feel horny, don't you?" Abruptly, he changed the subject. "That nigger kid just run away from home. Man, he shoots good pool, but he's a fish. Anybody with larceny in his heart would of smelled a dead rat, the way them guys was cuttin him up. But he just looked more and more pissed off, and kep shootin better an better; but no use. The best fuckin stick in the world can't beat that kind of action."

"If somebody pulled that shit on me, I'd break their fuckin heads in," Jack said.

"Sure you would, but what's a little guy to do?"

"Fuck the little guys. Hey, let's *go!*"

Denny laughed. "*Smell* that sweet pussy!" He wheeled around on the stool and stood up. "Let's race down Broadway!" He ran out of the drugstore, and Jack followed.

They raced down the full length of Portland's main street, dodging in among the evening crowds, bumping into not a few irate citizens. The light was red when they got to Burnside, but they ran across the street anyway, causing cars to brake sharply and drivers to blow their horns in anger and frustration. Jack, dancing through the traffic behind Denny, raised both hands in the standard gesture of contempt, his middle fingers extended. When they got to the other side and were among the skid row crowds, they slowed down to a walk, panting heavily and catching their breath. Above them, under the red clouds, two gigantic neon signs threw colored light on the wet streets: one saying JESUS THE LIGHT OF THE WORLD with a traveling scriptural message beneath it in blinking lights; the other a gigantic glass being filled with beer from a gigantic tap, all in blinking lights: BLITZ-WEINHARD BEER.

The Model Hotel was on the corner of Sixth and Couch Streets, above a grocery store, and had two entrances. The boys ran up the stairs leading from the unlighted side entrance, and even before they got to the top they could smell the strange, exciting woman-perfume smell of the whorehouse.

"Oh, boy!" Denny said. He grinned at Jack eagerly, and Jack's manly pose, just assumed, collapsed in giggles.

The maid came around the corner of the corridor and smiled at them and said, "Evenin, boys. Is you of age?"

"I'm thirty-six," Denny said.

"I'm forty-two," Jack said.

The maid laughed and led them down the corridor to the waiting room.

Less than an hour later, they were standing on the corner of Sixth and Burnside, wondering what to do with themselves. They had spent all their money, compared girls, and exhausted the subject of sex entirely. Now Jack was feeling restless and irritated with himself for no reason, and wondering what he was going to do for scuffle money. Without any particular destination in mind, they began walking up Burnside, toward the stadium area. Denny was silent as they walked, but Jack could not keep his thoughts to himself.

"God damn it, I need *gold*. We got to figure out some way of gettin some gold. It's not even eight o'*clock*, for Christ's sake."

"What'er you so pissed about? I'm broke, too."

"Yeah, but you can always go home and get eats and a bed. I'm out in the stony, man."

Denny put his hand on Jack's shoulder. "Lissen, you can sack out at my place for a couple days. I told you that before."

"*Fuck it!* I want money!"

They stopped walking. They were in a section of automobile showrooms and deserted used-car lots. Jack was wishing desperately that some fool citizen would come along so Jack could smash him, drag him in back of the used cars, and take his money. But there were no citizens around. There weren't even very many cars going by.

He looked at the used-car lot. In the back there was a small white shack with a night light showing through the window in the door.

"Let's bust in there and see if they left any gold around," he said to Denny.

Denny looked surprised. "Okay," he said. He followed Jack across the gravel of the lot and watched as Jack picked up a rag, wrapped it around his fist and punched the glass in the door. Jack reached through and opened the door from the inside, and they both stepped in, Denny throwing one glance back at the street.

There were two desks with barely room to get between them, papers all over the tops; a few calendars on the walls, and a large rack with keys on nails. Jack started going through the drawers of one desk, and after a moment's hesitation, Denny started in on the other. All they found were blank forms, messy

33

files of completed loan applications and title changes, and half an apple, which Denny threw in the wastebasket.

"Shit," he said. "We left fingerprints all over the goddam place."

"So what? Nobody's got my prints. They got yours?"

"Hell no. Fuck it. No money. Let's get out of here."

"You scared?"

"Course I'm scared, you nut. Let's go."

Jack was looking at the board of keys. "Let's take one of their goddam cars and race hell out of it."

They took the keys to a 1946 Cadillac, found the car, and drove it off the lot, smashing through the thin guard chain across the driveway, hearing the posts holding the chain splinter and crunch. They drove up Burnside, Jack behind the wheel. It never entered his mind that he had just committed grand theft, among other major and minor crimes. All he knew was that at last he was behind the wheel of a fine automobile, there was plenty of gas in the tank, and the evening was ahead of them. He did not think about money again for almost an hour.

After taking the Cadillac out on the highway and opening it up a few times, Jack and Denny came back to Portland, and for a while drove through the expensive curved streets of Council Crest. Driving the big, powerful car at top speeds had been terribly exciting, and now they were calming down, not talking, just looking out the windows at the rich people's houses. The plan was to abandon the car up here and walk back down to the downtown section.

"Hey, I been in that house," Denny said, pointing. Jack pulled the car over, and peered through the gloom. The house Denny meant was back behind a hedge and trees, and the second story, which they could see from where they were, was dark and deserted-looking.

"You remember that kid Weinfeld?" Denny asked. "This is his joint. I come up here and had *lunch*. He owed me eight bucks from snooker an we come up here to collect. God, what a mansion! You never seen anything like it. They got a room for every fuckin thing you can think of; the old man's got his own bar, all that crap. They must be damn near millionaires."

Jack looked up at the blank dark windows of the building, set in its framework of damp firs, beneath a roof that seemed to have a dozen chimneys. "God," he said.

"They're really rich bastards," Denny said. "In fact, they're takin a vacation in Mexico. Weinfeld come around last week askin if anybody wanted any dirty pictures or anythin."

"The place is empty?"

Denny looked at Jack. He began to grin. "Empty as hell, man. What'er we waitin for? Let's ditch the car an *bust in!*"

"Sure to be money laying around someplace," Jack said. "What a fuckin *break!*"

The Weinfelds were not rich and the house was not a "mansion," but the boys had no experience at all with the really rich, and so could not tell the difference. Weinfeld owned a small shoe store specializing in work shoes and odd sizes. He made a comfortable living, and his home was a comfortable one; in 1947 it would have been worth about $20,000. It was surrounded by hedge, lawn, and trees, and there was heavy, ornate-looking furniture in all the rooms; deep, wall-to-wall carpeting in most of the downstairs, and one very large, extremely beautiful blue Persian carpet in the living room, its border ornate designs in white, maroon, gold, and blue. The boys stood in the middle of this carpet, looking around themselves at the most splendid home they had ever seen outside the movies. Jack noticed that most of the windows in the house had the thick double-draperies that could be used in blackouts, and so he pulled them and turned the lights on. There was a large fireplace, and over it a mantel adorned with small delicate glass figurines of animals; and above that there was a picture—an oil painting—of an attractive, pleasant-looking woman in a white dress with a blue sash. The picture had its own little light above it, which went on with the wall lights when Jack flicked the switch. (The switch bothered him; it made no sound, no *click*, but the lights went on anyway.)

"My God," Jack said.

"What'd I tell you?" Denny said proudly. "Aint it a mansion? We ate lunch up in his room. He's got a room all to himself up there, with his own desk, and all kinds of crap all over the walls. He must be a lonely fucker, er why would he come down to the poolhall?"

For a while they forgot all about their purpose in breaking into the house, and explored.

"Holy cats," Jack said. "Did you see this *shower?* One sprayer up on top, *four* on the sides. Man, they must stand in there and just plain go out of their minds. An the control aint two handles, it's one that goes from cold to hot."

The master bedroom was on the main floor and in the center was a large double bed, with gilt posts and a white headboard. All the furniture in the bedroom matched and there were sets of pictures on the wall. On the bed was a coverlet of gold satin, and Jack could not resist throwing himself onto the bed. "Man!" was all he could say. He lay on his back and looked up at the crystal light fixture in the ceiling.

Denny began at last to go through the drawers in the high bureau. "This guy must have fifty pairs of socks," he commented. In one top drawer he found cuff links, an old worn gold ring (which Denny pocketed), and assorted trinkets, but no cash. Jack got up and helped him, going through the woman's vanity table. Then both of them examined the suits in the man's closet, finding only ticket stubs and a few pennies.

"Where's that bar?" Jack wanted to know. "Maybe there's some booze. I could use a drink."

"It's in the basement. Let's go."

The party room had a red tile floor, a fireplace (*another* one! Jack thought with amazement), brightly colored cushions on metal furniture, and a polished wood bar at one end, with three leatherette-capped stools. Jack sat at the bar and Denny went around behind. There were several bottles of liquor visible on the backbar, and Denny discovered a small refrigerator, which proved to be about half-full of bottled beer. Denny held up one of the glistening bottles and said, "Lookie. West Coast brand. What fuggin cheapskates. What'll it be?"

"A boilermaker, my good man."

"Lessee," said Denny, examining the bottles on the backbar; "do you want Scotch, bourbon, rye, or maybe gin?"

Jack giggled. "Make it Scotch and rye. I ain't never had either."

Denny took two pilsner glasses, put them on the bar, half filled them with a mixture of whiskies, and then added beer from one of the bottles, which he then tipped up and drained. He and Jack tapped their glasses together and drank.

"Whew. Jesus H. Christ!" Denny said after a moment.

Jack grinned at him expectantly. "Let's have some more."

"You know, this has been a hell of a night, man. We get laid, race all around hell in a Caddie, an here we are drinkin expensive booze. Do you reckon this is how the rich folks live?"

"If we only had some money," Jack said. "I wonder where they keep the spare cash."

"Have a nother drink, baby."

"I wonder when they're comin home?"

"Aw hell, I seen the kid Wednesday or Tuesday. They won't be back for a week. Hey, we can stay all fuckin night."

"That's what I was thinking. Have another couple of drinks, find the money, sleep, an cut out just before dawn."

"What if we find a couple thousand bucks! Hey, we could go to Mexico, too!"

"Lemme try some of that gin now," Jack said. "I never drank any of that, either."

THREE

Billy lay in his bed in the Couch Street hotel and half-listened to a dim, fragmented conversation between a man and a woman in the next room. He was familiar with the subject of the conversation; he had heard it a thousand times at home: The war was over, the easy West Coast money was being pulled out of Negro reach, prices were going crazy, finance companies were getting stonyhearted again . . . Billy grinned bitterly. It's like they wanted the war back, so they could make more money.

The man in the next room was trying to convince the woman that they should move to Detroit, where he was certain he could get work; she, on the other hand, did not want to leave her mother's family. The argument went back and forth dully, and Billy stopped hearing it. He had his own troubles.

He got out of bed and took off his jockey shorts and went to the sink in the corner, turning on the hot-water tap. A thin stream of water fizzed out, barely lukewarm, and Billy took his washcloth out of his bag and gave himself a sponge bath, standing on the hotel towel and drying off with his own thick, fluffy towel. It always made him feel good to get clean, made him feel sharp and aware, and he smiled at himself in the mirror, and then, for fun, showed his teeth in a chimpanzee grin. Still naked, he brushed his teeth. They were small, well-formed, beautifully white, and he was very proud of them, as proud as he was of the small corded muscles of his arms and legs. He was skinny, bony-shouldered, yes, but it was deceptive. He watched the muscles of his forearms as he scrubbed his socks against each other and then rinsed them out; muscles he had built by doing pull-ups and the rope-climb at school; and for a moment he regretted having left school. But the feeling did not last; if he lacked the easy comfort of going to school, he had something far better—his freedom of action. That was more important than reading all those books about the white world that were such lies even *he* could see through them. This was much better.

Except for the thing that had wakened him from his sleep, the eye-opening, sudden awareness that he had been hustled the evening before. It had come to him with the impact of a kick in the chest: that pair of guys at the Rialto had cut him up, and done it easily. But what had made him sit up, fully awake and completely angry, was that he had let it happen. He was no mark. How had it happened? What had he been thinking about?

"Stupid!" he hissed at himself as he got dressed. Pure case of buck fever, so excited by the idea of playing there, playing the best in Portland, that he forgot all about hustling, just automatically pretended that everybody in the world was just like him and wanted to play their best, for themselves. He could just see those two guys, in the men's toilet or someplace, splitting his money. Laughing at him. Well, they had a right to laugh; he had been a fool.

The voice of the man in the next room rose in sudden, wall-shaking anger: *"But what we goin do when Cholly Chill gets heah?"*

Billy made a face. Southern accent, very heavy; Billy could imitate that kind of accent easily. The guy probably came West for the easy war money, and now he was worried about what to do when winter came. Too bad for him; go back home and pick cotton and eat hog jowls, or whatever the hell they did in the South.

Do you know how lonely you are?

Billy was startled; it was not quite a voice, more than a thought. *What*, he thought, *lonely? I been lonely all my life. You mean homesick.* He laughed aloud, but it was a sick laugh, fake and unconvincing.

He had been in Ben Fenne's an hour, practicing straight pool, when Denny and Jack Levitt came in. Looking at Denny's bland Irish face, Billy wondered if he had been in on the hustle the day before. He *did* look tore-up and unshaved, as if he had spent a wild night on somebody's money, and that was enough to make Billy suspicious of him, even though he came right over to Billy and laughed and said good morning, and introduced his friend Jack Levitt. This one was *something else,* too, the meanest-looking kid Billy had ever seen, with cold dead blue eyes, a head too large for his already large muscular body, blond curly hair, ruddy skin—just plain mean-looking, that was all. Billy shook his hand and felt his stubby fingers take a good hold on his own, and yet not squeeze too hard like a man trying to impress people. Billy decided he was afraid of Jack Levitt, and would do his best to have nothing to do with him.

"What's on the fire this morning?" Denny asked him. "You want to run up to Rialto and make some gold?"

"I'll play you, here and now," Billy said.

"I'm broke," Denny said. "Anyway, you're too good for me."

"I don't go up to no Rialto for a while," Billy said definitely. "You know what happened to me up there. Don't you?"

"Sure," Denny grinned, "you got your ass waxed. So what? There's plenty of guys up there you can beat."

"What's in it for you?" Billy asked. "Why you bein so *kind* to me?"

"We make side bets on you, man. You win, we win."

Billy had to laugh. "On your *guts?* Against your own *friends?*"

"Money's money, baby. We need all the loot we can get."

"Well, I found a home, you know? And I'm gonna hang around here for a while; see if I can't get up an *honest* game."

"You're chickenshit," Levitt said shortly.

Billy went back to his practice, turning his back on the other two. It made the skin on the back of his neck crawl to do it, but he had no choice. He shot carefully, and had to concentrate to keep his fingers from shaking. He heard them talking behind him, and then finally they went away.

It was Saturday, and toward noon the poolhall began filling up. Many of the customers were in their teens, and these congregated around the two small snooker tables in the back, playing pink-wild snooker or sitting in the theater seats and making side bets, or just sitting watching. The keno game had four players, all men in middle age, and the rest of the tables and the bar were crowded. There were two horse-pinball machines behind the telephone booths at the inner end of the bar, and both had players and circles of watchers around them. The radio was on to a baseball game, adding to the babble of voices, clicking balls, the electric clunking of the pinballs, and the noise of the ventilating fan. The long dark room was blue with smoke and moist with humidity. Billy saw that men coming in from outside were wet, although it hadn't been raining an hour before. Rain, that was one thing he hadn't gotten away from; it rained in Portland almost as much as in Seattle. Of course to Billy rain was interesting for only one thing: it slowed down the cloth, and he had to shoot a little harder than usual to get the balls to perform properly.

After a while, John the houseman came up to Billy and said, "You got to get off the table now."

A pang of fear ran through him, and a split-second afterward embarrassment and anger; he knew he wasn't being kicked off the table because of race, but because there were players waiting, and it was policy to kick off practicers when there were two- or three-handed games waiting. But he could not help feeling that first reaction, and when he turned to John and shrugged, he saw in his eyes an expression of understanding, almost wariness. John said quickly, "Players waitin."

"Yeah," Billy said. He paid his time and put his cue away, and then, idle, went over and stood watching the keno game.

Keno is played on a standard billiard table; at one end is a wooden platform raised almost an inch above the level of the felt, and along its front edge is a brass ramp. There are four rows of holes in the ramp, spaced alternately, and each hole is numbered. In the exact center of the platform is a starred hole. Any player whose ball lands in the starred hole gets a keno and the point value of the ball. If the ball or balls land in any other hole, the player gets the value of the hole, and if the number on the ball matches the number of the hole, he also gets a keno. The game is played with a regular set of fifteen pool balls, racked at the other end of the table. In the game Billy was watching, each keno was worth fifty cents from each player, and the player with high score when all the balls were on the rack got a dollar from each of the other players, less any kenos. Each game ended with a flurry of calculating and arguing over the score, but Billy saw at once that there was plenty of money changing hands. It looked like a game worth getting into.

Keno looks like a luck game, which is its chief attraction to poor players, but as Billy stood and watched, now drinking a bottle of Coke, the players with the best stroke always seemed to come out ahead. There was more to the game than met the eye; it was not enough to ram your cue ball into another ball so that it banked around the table and ended up on the platform, although that is just exactly what most of the players did. Players came and went; at one point, as Billy watched, there were six of them, and a man with the placid face of an idiot stood by the blackboard keeping score and talking about the game like a sports announcer. But the good players, without seeming to, always managed to play their cue ball back to a bad position for the next man, and instead of just getting a ball up onto the platform, played it so that it knocked into other balls, rearranging them on the platform and making higher scores. Also, the good players seemed to know the precise strength a ball needed to roll up to its keno hole and stay in it, without bobbling out or flying off the end of the table. Still, it looked easy to Billy, and he itched to get in.

He fidgeted through three or four games, and then finally got in without half-trying. A tall red-faced man who had been losing steadily as Billy watched, cursing his bad shots and bad lays as bad luck, finally got out in disgust when he had to pay off eight kenos and game. "Shit, this sure as hell aint my day," he announced. He walked up to the wall rack to put his cue in it, and instead, thrust it into Billy's hands. "Here," he said. "*You* try it."

Billy moved up to the table, picked up a piece of chalk, and stood there chalking the cue, and no one seemed to object. One of the players said to him, "You follow me," and he was in. Apparently, his money was as good as anybody else's. The action-feeling started to come over him, and he felt good; he could feel it thickening in his throat, and deep in his belly was a sense of anticipation almost sexual. When it was his turn to shoot he bent over the table slowly, savoring the feeling. He banked the six-ball off the side rail with the speed and direction he assumed would make it go up onto the ramp, hit the twelve-ball, which was in the center keno hole, displace the twelve, displace the ten-ball behind it, and give him a score of at least twenty-eight plus keno, maybe double keno if the ten kept rolling and landed in its own hole in the back row. Instead, the six sped up the ramp, glanced off the twelve without moving it, skipped over the top of the ten and off the back of the table, coming up against the bar with a crack.

The idiot at the scoreboard chanted, ". . . and the new money *jumps* the rail and draws a *blank!* Next shooter, Mister Frank Bartholomew, *if you please!*"

There were five players in the game, and it was a long time before Billy shot again. But he was not conscious of the wait; he was too busy watching the shooters. When it was his turn, high man had a score of 32, and there were two kenos on the board. He sized up the lay of the balls carefully. Somebody yelled, "Shoot the fuckin shot," but he paid no attention. This time he had a clear shot, no bank necessary. It was the five-ball, whose holes were in the back row; he could try for a keno and five points, but now he distrusted his stroke for this game, and suspected that if he shot a direct shot he would go off the back again. There was a cluster of balls in the middle of the platform, two of them not in holes but just leaning against other balls. The shot would be to play the five into the pack; but if he did so, his cue ball would also go up onto the ramp, and wipe out his score. Billy's stroke was good enough for him to be able to hit the five with lower left draw so that the cue ball would end up going back and forth across the table, but to do so he would have to hit the five too hard. There were other balls to shoot at, but none of them in good position. There was only one other alternative; to massé the cue ball so that it curved up behind the five and drove it straight into the pack instead of at an angle; then the cue would spin backward. But this was a circus shot, extremely difficult, and making the shooter look like a show-off and a fool whether he missed or made it.

But it was the only shot by which he could catch up. So, estimating carefully, stretching his fingers into his high, massé bridge, Billy fired. The cue ball took off in one direction, then curved sharply up behind the five, struck it, and zipped back to the end rail, where it hit two other balls and came to rest. The five rode up the brass, powered by spin the reverse of the cue ball's, hit the pack, imparted its spin to the other balls and knocked them free; they wobbled, and then settled in other holes. The five itself landed in the two hole, but Billy got the score from four other balls as well: a total of 44 points.

"Jesus H. Christ," somebody muttered.

"What, no kenos?" cried the idiot, "forty-four points for the gennleman, stepped out into the *lead* . . ."

Billy felt better.

An hour or two later, when he looked up toward the door, he saw Denny and Jack Levitt coming in again. But he did not care; he was not even interested. He could make plenty of money right where he was; he was already twenty-odd dollars ahead, and there was nobody in the game who could really beat him. He knew he was having beginner's luck, too, but he was glad for that; he would take any luck he could get.

Denny came up to him after a while and said, "Hey, how about loaning me a buck?"

Automatically, Billy reached into his shirt pocket and pulled out a crumpled dollar and handed it to him. "Don't spend it all in one place," he said.

"Thanks, baby. I'll pay you back tonight." He went up to the bar and yelled, "Twenny nickels!" Later, Billy saw him at the pinball machines, standing stiffly and slamming the machine with his palms, cursing and begging. Billy laughed to himself. What a mark! Playin a *machine!* To Billy that was like throwing the money out a window. But he didn't care; he was getting rich right here.

Jack Levitt sat on a high stool between the number one billiard table and the keno table, watching Billy. It made a game more interesting if there was somebody in it you were rooting for or against, and Jack wanted to see Billy win. He knew already that Billy was a phenomenon, a natural like Bobby Case. It was a pleasure just to watch him shoot, even in a game like keno, full of slop and bad luck and yelling. Jack wished there was something he could be great at, some skill or talent he could find in himself that would give him something to do. He was a good fighter—no one anywhere near his own size had ever beaten him, in or out of the orphanage—but that was different, because every man ought to be able to defend himself, with his fists or a knife or a gun or whatever came to hand. That was basic. No, he wished he had some *talent,* like Billy's for pool, that would make him as busy with himself as Billy seemed to be. And anyway, a talent like Billy's was worth money; that was the end result of talent—you made money against the less talented. So there he was again, back to the old need: money.

Last night had been a failure. Fun, yes; but they had searched the house from top to bottom and found no ready cash at all. Of course, there were a lot of things they could have stolen and tried to sell: clothes, radios, phonographs, several cases of liquor (none bearing the Oregon State Liquor Tax stamps, Denny had noted with admiration), and more canned and dried foods than Jack had ever seen outside the orphanage, as if the Weinfelds expected another war and wanted to be prepared. But

Jack and Denny had ditched the Cadillac and had no intention of going near it. They had even wiped their fingerprints off it, feeling both sheepish and hip. They couldn't walk through residential streets carrying goods, even before dawn. So they had gotten drunker, played the radio, fooled around, cooked some food in the kitchen, and then slept. They had played rock-scissors-paper for the right to sleep in the big bed on the main floor and Denny won, but unfortunately fell asleep with one of Weinfeld's big Cuban cigars in his hand and burned the gold satin coverlet pretty badly before the smell woke him up. There were three bedrooms upstairs, two obviously girls' rooms, and Jack had slept in the boy's room, so drunk he didn't even bother to take his shoes off.

But no money! A day and a night had passed, another day was passing, and nothing had changed. He did not even have enough to buy some lunch. Of course he would not starve in the pool-hall; he could always bum twenty cents for a hot dog; but that wasn't any good. All his stuff locked up in his hotel room, the clothes he was wearing getting rancid (it had been a delight showering in the Weinfeld's amazing five-spray, tiled shower, but when he put his clothes back on he could smell them, and they seemed damp against his skin, disgusting) . . . in fact, his whole life, since he had quit his second job two weeks before, had been rapidly going down the drain.

He had been working as a delivery boy for a blueprint company, and quit after an argument with the manager. The manager, a gray man with yellowish eyeballs, had accused Jack of taking money out of petty cash. Jack had taken the money, all right—all the delivery boys did, as a matter of course—but he knew it could not be proved and he denied it. When the manager still looked suspicious, Jack told him he could take his job and stick it up his ass. Then he demanded the wages due him and walked out. He had hated the job anyway; running all over downtown Portland with huge unwieldy rolls of blueprints, always running, never enough time to walk, then sweeping the place out and having to put up with the bossiness of the printmakers, who for lack of any real authority tried to push the boys around. And besides, the place smelled of heat and chemicals, and nauseated him. He could not understand how people could work there and even claim they liked it.

Since then he had been living on his wits, and not doing a very good job of it. Now he was really up against it, for the first time in his life; really at the point where he had to decide if he was going to let *them* run his life for him (as *they* always had in the past) or whether *he* was going to run it. So far, since his romantic dash for "freedom," he had run it right straight into the ground. How easy it would be to just give up and let *them* take over again. Go back to the orphanage where he had a bed and meals and clothes issued to him, where he worked because they told him to work, went to school because they told him to go to school. . . . But it would only last another year or so, until he was eighteen. Then even the orphanage would kick him out. But he could do what a lot of the others did, join the Army. They said the Army would take care of you; three squares and a flop, and all you had to do was obey orders; there wasn't a war on, so no danger of getting your ass shot off; just a nice, easy life, uniforms, barracks, *chow*, and marching around with a rifle.

The very thought of it made Jack sick to his stomach. He knew it was not for him. He had run away from the orphanage in the first place because he was the toughest boy in the place and there was no more challenge for him and he was going crazy from boredom. Or something. The Army would be the same; he would feel that dull surge of hatred when somebody tried to tell him what to do, and sooner or later he would pop somebody and they would throw him in the stockade.

Well, he *could* get a job. Do what he was told. Bother no one. Dry up and blow away. Ffft. What was the difference?

He watched the green bills disappearing into Billy Lancing's pocket at the end of almost every game. There was getting to be quite a wad in there. Jack felt hunger for that money. He wanted to walk up to Billy and just take it away from him. Why not?

Why not wait till he leaves, follow, catch him in a lonely place, brace him, take all the money and the hell with it? Jack felt a tickling of emotion he could not identify, something to do with the Negro's *talent*, and it might be unfair (odd word!) to steal his money . . . but the thought passed, and he decided if he had a chance, he would do it. He hoped the kid wouldn't hate him for it. What difference did that make? He and the kid weren't friends; every time the kid glanced at Jack his eyes veiled over with what Jack knew was fear; hell, the kid probably hated Jack, and every other big mean-looking white.

Denny came back and sat down next to Jack, grunting with disgust. "Shit! That goddam machine is *fixed*, you know that?" He felt through his pockets. "You got a cigarette?"

Levitt brought out his pack, took out the last two, and handed one to Denny. "You got any gold left at all? I'm gettin hungry."

"I wonder how come that rich bastard didn't have any cartons of smokes layin around," Denny said. "Cigars, but no cigarettes. What a prick!" He lit up and puffed. "Ahh. Money? No, I aint got no money. Maybe I can borrow another hog off that nigger." His eyes widened with surprise. "Hey. I got an idea!"

"Are you kiddin?"

"No, really. Listen, that kid's folks won't be home for probably another week. Let's go back up there tonight, get some chicks, man, and throw us a little *party!* We can't just *leave* all that booze up there! We'll have a little party, and then take all the rest of the booze with us in somebody's car an stash it someplace. Man, we could stay drunk a *year!*"

"Or we could sell some of it off," Jack said.

"Yeah, but first, we could have ourselves a nice quiet little party, some cunt, some guys, real quiet, you know, but really live it up."

"I could use a party," Jack admitted.

"I got to try to borrow another buck from the nigger. I think I'll ask him to the party," Denny said, and he jumped up and went over to where Billy was standing. Jack watched their faces, saw Billy look puzzled, then almost angry, and then saw him laugh, just before he approached the table to make his shot. Denny came back and sat down.

"Did you ask him to the party?" Jack said. "What the hell do you want *him* along for?"

"Sure I asked him, why not? Maybe we can get up a poker game and get that fuckin money out of him." Denny scratched the dimple on his chin. "You know, he's a smart little fucker; I says to him, 'How about comin to a party with us tonight?' an he says, 'What kind of hustle is this?' an I says, 'No hustle,' an he says, 'What the hell you want with me at your party?' an then he says, 'Oh, I get it, you want my nice green *money* for your party!' an I says, 'Hell yes, man, that's part of it, but what the hell do you care? You aint got no friends in Portland, an you must want white friends or you wouldn't come hangin around the white parts of town, so what do you care? You wanna come?' . . . an he thinks about that for a minute—I could tell he didn't like it out in the open like that, but what the fuck—an then he says, 'Hell, okay, what do I care.' He's comin."

"I still don't see why you asked him," Jack said. "He's a nigger. Tell you the truth, I was thinkin of followin him out of here and coldcocking him for his money."

Denny frowned. "Hell, that's nothin to do. I mean, he comes in here. . . . No, I mean, so he's a nigger, so what?"

Jack thought about that. All right, so what? He had always been told that niggers were bad people, but no one had ever said *why. They* told him. That was enough to make it a lie.

"Yeah," he said vaguely. "I guess you're right."

"Oops! I forgot to bum another buck!" Denny exclaimed. He jumped up and went back to Billy. Billy laughed and said loud enough for everyone to hear, "Since when did I take you to raise?" but the hand went into the pocket and came out with a dollar, just the same. Denny crooked a finger at Jack and they sat at the counter and had hot dogs and coffee, and Denny bought a package of cigarettes for each of them.

"You know," he said, "this nigger's a good guy."

"He's a sucker," Jack said.

"No he aint," Denny insisted. "He's *honest*. There's a difference. Anyway, I didn't hustle him, I *ast* him."

"I don't see the difference."

"Well, I'm gonna pay him back."

Jack thought, and then said, "You mean, you're gonna pay him back the two dollars, or the money we whipsaw him out of tonight?"

"The two dollars, naturally."

Jack laughed. "I get it."

"Why should I pay him back money I *win?*"

"Hello, tough guy," a hoarse voice said. Jack turned around and saw Kol Mano, and behind him, Bobby Case, both wearing leather air corps flight jackets over cashmere sweaters, slacks, and highly polished cordovan shoes.

Mano and Jack shook hands, formally. Mano was one of those people who shook hands, almost as if it were a sort of game. Jack liked him; he, too, had a talent. Not a specific talent like pool, but a generalized talent for making money and living his own life. Kol Mano was in his early twenties, and when he spoke he held a finger over a hole in his throat. He had been in World War II and had been wounded and sent from France to a hospital in England. Even before he got out of the hospital he was deeply enmeshed in black-market rackets, selling watches and other PX material, and even some hospital supplies. He was given the Silver Star, released from the hospital, arrested by the MPs, and given a general court all in the same ten-day period. He held a dishonorable discharge for a while, and then it was changed to a medical, and he was now on 100 percent disability. He had the dreamy eyes of a lush and the delicate fingers of a cardshark, and he was both. Everyone considered him a little crazy.

But he was not crazy; he was the coolest head Jack had ever met. When he was not gambling in the cardroom of the Rialto, or out in front hustling a little pool, he could usually be found in his hotel room across the street, in bed, awake. Sometimes he would spend weeks in the Veteran's Hospital across the river in Vancouver, having his throat worked on. With his finger over the hole in his throat he spoke in a hoarse whisper, but without it a faint whistling sound obscured everything he said. When he was playing poker he would often keep a lit cigarette in his mouth and blow the smoke out through the hole. "Keeps the enemy off balance," he said.

"What's the action, Levitt?" he asked Jack. He treated most of the people around the poolhalls with a silent contempt, but he was friendly to Jack, acting as if they had known each other all their lives, almost as if they shared a past, a secret, something only they could understand. Jack didn't know what it was all about, but he didn't care. He liked Kol Mano, and liked the feeling of being in his confidence.

"There's your pigeon," Denny said, pointing, "but he knows you guys cut him up yesterday."

Bobby Case said, "I don't have to cut him up. I can beat him." Bobby was fourteen and looked twelve because of his smooth girlish skin and his slenderness; but there was already a hardness around his mouth and suspicion in his eyes. He looked sullen and passionate, and he hated people making any reference to his age, as if it was something to be ashamed of. He slouched over to Billy, his straight blond hair hanging down almost over his eyes, and said, "You want to play some pool?"

Billy looked at him narrowly. "Heads up?"

"What else? What do you want to play?"

"Wait a sec," Billy said. He made his shot, and then ignored Bobby Case until the game was over; paid his losses and then moved away with Case.

One of the keno players complained, "He's takin all the money out of the game!"

"What you want him to do," Mano said hoarsely, "give it the fuck back?" He winked at Jack, and Jack grinned.

Denny, Jack, and Kol Mano followed the other two over to

a pool table, and John the houseman joined them. Already Jack could sense an electricity in the place: this was to be a game to watch—the competition between local genius and newcomer. The fact that both "geniuses" were so very young made no difference to the atmosphere. Jack wished desperately that he had *something* in him that could make a place go electric.

John the houseman waited, his hands on the balls in the rack, for them to decide what kind of game they would play.

"What's your best game?" Case asked Billy.

"I'll play anything," Billy said.

"You play one-pocket?"

"Is that your game?"

Case looked almost angry. "Yeah, that's my game. You want to play?"

Billy said slyly, "What'll you spot me?"

Case walked away in disgust, and then walked back. "Even up," he snapped.

"Okay," Billy said. "But if you is too good, I'se gwine to de *rack*."

Denny whispered to Jack and Mano, "Shit, Bobby ought to give him eight to five, no? This is no game!"

But he stopped whispering when Billy said, "What you want to play for, twenty dollars?"

"One-pocket," John said disgustedly, and he racked the balls, filled out a time card, and stuck it in the glass light shade.

Case, now really angry, stared at Billy. "Twenty is fine."

"Goddam," Denny said. "What's everybody so pissed off about?"

"Why fuck around?" Case said, tossing his hair back out of his eyes. His girlish mouth was white around the edges.

Denny threw himself into a chair. "There goes the fuggin poker game," he said disgustedly.

"Is there a poker game?" Kol Mano asked politely.

"There was. Gimme a cigarette, will you? No, wait a sec, I got a pack. Hey, you guys wanna come? We're gonna have a party. You got a car?"

"Sure I have a car," Mano said. "What did you think I was, a bum like yourself?"

Denny winked at Jack, and said to the other, "You been in the black market. Maybe you're the guy to handle this deal."

"What deal?"

Denny explained his idea, and Mano listened thoughtfully. "Sounds okay to me," Mano said.

Jack was a little surprised. Actually, Denny's plans had sounded just a degree or two crazy to him. "Hey, you think it's really okay?"

"Why not?" Mano said. "We have a little party, then steal some shit. What's wrong with that?"

"What about the cops?" Jack said lamely, and wished he hadn't. He did not want to lose Mano's good opinion.

"Cops. Balls. If I worried about cops, I'd have to lock myself in my room and do nothin. Fuck the cops."

Watching the slow, chesslike moves of the one-pocket game, Jack decided that Billy was going to win the money, and he liked him for that. Although Bobby Case was the better player, Bobby was letting something bother him; he was playing angrily, contemptuously, as if to show that he could beat this nigger without half trying. His movements were more rapid than cautious, and he shot before taking enough time to size up the lay of the balls; his face was rigid, attempting to mask the anger in his eyes. Every time he tried a shot that would have been stupendous if he had made it but only made him look silly when he didn't, Billy Lancing would step up, take his time, walk all around the table—idly, nervelessly, calmly—make his decision and then shoot either a tight, frustrating safety or plunk a ball into his pocket. Even when he shot to make a ball, he left the cue ball tight, not caring whether he had another good play or not; and although Bobby Case—due to a lucky run early in the game—had five balls to Billy's two, Jack felt with intuitive certainty that Billy would win. He pointed a finger at Kol Mano and said, "Ten dollars on Billy."

Billy was on the other side of the table, chalking his cue, and he looked up with unveiled surprise into Jack's eyes. "You bettin on me?"

"Sure. You gonna win, aint you?"

They continued to look at each other, and Jack felt something unidentifiable passing between them, an unexpected warmth, a communication—and he felt himself forced to break his eyes away from the contact. He looked over at Mano. "How about it?"

"You're on," Mano said. He took his finger off his throat and made a farting sound.

Of course Jack did not have ten dollars. He was betting on his guts. But that didn't make any difference; if there was a fuss, Mano just wouldn't pay off. No harm done. Jack was suddenly sure Billy would win.

He did. He never made two balls in a row, but he never scratched, either, and while Bobby Case made runs, he also scratched and left Billy wide open. The game ended 8-7, and Case racked rapidly and angrily for the next contest. Billy stood and waited, the new twenty tucked down into his pocket.

Mano handed Jack two fives. "Again?"

"Shore."

Denny went, "Ahem!" and Jack gave him a secret look which implied, wait, and you'll share all the profits. Denny replied with an expression of utter disbelief.

"Bobby was foolin around," Mano said. "This time he wins the money." Mano had been circulating in the crowd, getting down bets, and now that Billy had won the first game, he found takers for all his money.

But Billy won again. He broke safe, and Bobby saw a chance to make a circus shot, took it, and missed, and Billy slowly but surely, carefully, ran eight balls and won the game in less than five minutes.

"Some hustle," he said. "Are you ready to take the wraps off, raise the price, an lock me up?"

Bobby wiped his mouth, tossed his hair back, and nodded without looking at his opponent. "Fifty," he said in a low voice.

"Less see your fifty," Billy said. Jack wanted to laugh out loud. What pefect timing! What a deadly insult!

Case looked over at Kol Mano, who shook his head.

"Make it for ten," Case said. He pulled out a handful of bills, all ones, and spread them on the table.

"You mean *eight*, don't you?" Billy asked innocently, moving the bills around with the tip of his finger.

"Awright, goddammit, eight. You want to play or don't you? You going to quit on me, like a chickenshit?"

Billy looked disappointed, but Jack could see that underneath he was tense and excited, perhaps even frightened. "Aw," Billy said, "you callin me names. An I thought this was a friendly game." Then he pretended to get mad. "For *eight* dollars? Are you kidding?"

Denny chanted, "The *game* . . . is . . . *over!*"

John the houseman appeared out of the crowd of watchers, took down the time card and scribbled on it, glancing over at the clock by the entrance. "Be a dollar even."

"You lost, *pool shark*," Billy said to Bobby Case. "You pay the time." He left the table, put his cue in the wall rack, and went into the men's room. Bobby paid John his dollar and came over to Mano. He grinned boyishly, like a ten-year-old caught stealing at the Five-and-Dime.

"You blew it," Mano said.

"Billy was shootin the eyes outen them balls," Denny said. "You didn't have a chance."

Jack felt let down. He had won twenty dollars, of which he honorably owed half to Denny. The bills were in his pocket, but he knew they wouldn't buy him much, even if he didn't split. It was enough to have fun on, but not enough to get him out of his bind. "Rat shit," he said distinctly.

"What'er you bitchin about?" Mano said, his finger to his throat. "You win twenty, an I'll bet you the whole twenty that's all you got."

Jack stood up over Mano, his hands in his hip pockets. "I won't bet you. You're broke, probably." Even Mano laughed.

"Did somebody say somethin about a party?" Case asked. "Let's go do something."

"That's tonight," Denny said. He pointed to the clock. It was five to three. "What'll we do for the afternoon?"

"Is that all?" Case said. "Jesus, I thought it was about eight. I been up all day."

"You should have stayed in bed," Mano said dryly. "You cost me eighty hogs."

"I'm sorry; I just lost my stick," Case said. He looked young and shy, all his former anger gone.

"'You lost your head, you mean," Mano said.

Billy returned from the toilet. "Am I still invited to that party?"

"Hell yes, man," Denny said. "But that's tonight. What'll we do *now?* I can't stand this fuggin poolhall."

"I got to see a man," Billy said. "Whyn't I meet you here about seven or eight?"

"No, hell, let's go to a movie or somethin," Denny said lamely.

Jack and Kol Mano exchanged a knowing look: they knew that Billy wanted to get away and stash some of the money, and Denny knew it and didn't want him to get away.

"What about that poker game?" Mano said, not to anybody in particular.

"Hey, yeah," Denny said. "Do you play?" he asked Billy.

"Never played in my life," Billy said. Everyone knew from the way he spoke that it was a damned lie. "I'll see you guys tonight, huh?" And he walked out, small and jaunty, his white windbreaker a flag of victory.

"You got to admire the little cocksucker," Mano said. "He's not only got talent, he's got brains enough to keep hold of his money. I'll bet nobody whipsaws him the way we did yesterday. He was just nervous and wanted to prove himself; it won't happen again." To Case he said, with some severity, "You take a lesson, *punk:* don't lose your temper. Your money goes with it."

"Fuck you," Case said dully. He was not holding a cue; he looked lost.

"I know what," Denny said brightly, holding up one finger, "Levitt's got twenty; let's go to the Model Hotel an get fucked."

"On *my* twenty?" Jack said.

"On *my* twenty," Mano amended. "Good plan. Share the wealth."

"You guys go ahead," Bobby Case said.

"What's the matter, won't they let you in?" Denny asked.

"I just don't feel like it."

"Good boy," Mano said. "Let's go." As they walked up the stairs he said to Jack and Denny, "I know a place where you guys can get served; let's take the extra five and have a few beers."

Jack did not feel any regret. After all, what else could you do with twenty dollars?

FOUR

Billy got the full force of his lonesomeness that night, back again at Ben Fenne's, half-waiting for Denny and the others to come and get him for the party. There were only a few games going, nothing for Billy—at the keno table some college boys were playing for ten cents a game—and so he sat at the counter back of the keno table and near the pinball machines, nursing a cup of coffee, waiting, trying to pretend that he was not waiting; trying to pretend that he did not want the other boys for friends, only opponents. He felt like a fool.

It was odd how he had dreamed about it, when he had gone back to his room to stash most of his money and then lie down for a rest. He remembered parts of the dream vividly: he had given Denny twenty dollars to guarantee that he wait for him; how he had said to someone—it wasn't really Denny, in fact,

Billy thought it might have been a Negro kid—exactly the same words he told Denny, "Now you don't have to sweat me out." Only in the dream everything had been so mixed up. He had been playing pool, all right, but out in a wide green field, with white clouds above. The grass was like a golf green, and he had been lying down, shooting the pool balls. The sun had been hot on his back, and there were other kids around. They seemed to be all about ten years old, and he thought that maybe in the dream he had been a kid, too. He was the only one playing pool; the rest of them were on the edge of the field, picking flowers. Then it got confusing. One of the kids came up to Billy, holding a bunch of flowers up to his face—Billy could see him again, grinning through the flowers—and for some reason, Billy handed the kid some money and said, "Now you don't have to sweat me out."

He sipped at his coffee, and then glanced at the clock. It was twenty after seven. He shrugged to himself. Something was bothering him, and he was certain that it wasn't just Denny. Something about the dream. Was it money he had handed the kid? He tried to focus the picture in his mind. There was something. . . . Then he got it. But it was even crazier. It wasn't money, it was his right arm the kid took. Billy could now remember thinking with mild amazement that it hadn't hurt to take off his right arm. Right is might, he thought; no, that's bassackwards. And what had he said? "Now you don't have to let me out." His aunt at home had a couple of dream books which she used to consult regularly; maybe she could explain it to him. He tried to laugh, but the memory of the images still bothered him. The wide field, a place he had been before, as a kid. Probably a football field. Clouds, sure, you could always expect some clouds in Seattle; the funny part was the warmth on his back, which he could still almost feel. "Now you don't have to let *me* out," it seemed in his recollection, because all the other kids finished picking flowers and then ran down the street; but they weren't going home. He was the one that had to go home, up over all those hills; they were all going downtown to sell the flowers or something.

"Your name's Billy, isn't it?"

Billy looked up into the white face, startled, and said, "That's right."

The man was obviously a plainclothes cop; big, beefy, hard mouth. But he seemed friendly enough. "Could we talk back here?" he asked Billy.

"Sure." Now thoroughly frightened, Billy followed the cop to the back of the poolhall, where they sat down next to each other. Billy sat forward, letting his hands fall between his legs. He wanted to press his hands together, to keep them from trembling, but he didn't. "What's up?" he said. He smiled at the cop weakly.

"Got a guilty conscience?" the cop said.

"Don't everybody?"

The cop didn't like that. Billy noticed something strange about his field of vision; he could see the cop's face clearly, but around it was a sort of rainbow aura, and everything else was misty and indistinct. The face, the big, white face, looked a little sour at Billy's last remark, and it said, "No. Not everybody. You're new around here, aren't you?"

"Yes, sir," Billy said. "I just come down from Seattle to visit my aunt."

"You won a lot of money this afternoon, Billy. But you had a lot when you came in, too. Where'd you get the money?"

"That fifteen dollars was my trip money, sir."

"When are you going back to Seattle?"

"Sunday night, sir. On the train."

"That's good," the cop said. He stood up. "Just a friendly talk, boy. No harm. You're a pretty good pool gambler, boy."

"Yes, sir. Thank you, sir."

You motherfucker!

Billy stood, trembling with rage and relief, and watched the cop amble back to the bar, where he picked up a half-empty glass of beer and drank from it. *God damn you,* Billy thought, *you rotten cop motherfucking bastard!* Billy knew he had been braced just because the cop saw him and wanted to pass the time; had probably hoped that Billy would have fallen apart under the questioning and confessed to a couple of rapes and assorted chicken theft and mopery; braced him as a matter of routine, known that Billy had lied to him and didn't care; just passing the time; probably off duty and having a beer before going home or on duty. Billy's whole body trembled, and he walked into the men's room and threw cold water on his face, and then wiped it off with a paper towel. He stood up at the big smelly urinal and tried to urinate, but it would not come. He stood there, trembling, waiting, occasionally shaking himself angrily. "Come *on,* dammit, pee!" he said through his teeth. But he knew all his rage was not directed at the cop; there was something under and behind it; the thought that they had not, after all, sent the police after him.

Why didn't you? Why haven't you tried to find me?

He wanted to burst into tears. It loomed over him: he was alone, unwanted, unsearched for, hounded by the police, useless, black. But even that didn't matter; not the blackness. He wasn't even black, just yellow. That didn't matter; he could pat flour all over his face—he had done that once as a little kid—and they would still ignore him or laugh at him; it was *him,* not the blackness; him they didn't want and let run away and did not care if he ended up in a strange jail and left to rot. With the dreadful clarity of self-pity he saw himself as he really was, a frightened little baby who hadn't the guts to stand up to the accident of his birth, who hadn't the character to make the world like him or eat it. Just another yellowbelly, just another fool who gave money away and hoped people would take pity on him.

"What the hell, I thought you fell in," Denny said to him, grinning. He stood up to the other urinal, flipped out his penis, and began to piss noisily. "Man, you're gray in the face; did that fuggin cop scare you?"

Billy pretended he was finished, and went to the sink. "Hell yes, man."

"He's an asshole," Denny said. "Do you colored guys ever sunburn?"

Billy looked up at him. There was no mockery in Denny's face. "Sure," Billy said. "Just like anybody else."

"I mean, you got sort of red hair, like me. Red-haired guys burn like hell, no?"

"That's why I like to stay down in a nice cool poolhall," Billy grinned.

"Yah, but your balls get moldy. Less go party-time."

Well, well, Billy thought. Well, well.

He promptly forgot all about being the hero of a coward's nightmare, and by the time they got to the top of the stairs and piled into the car, he was bubbling with humor, and when he got up on Jack Levitt's lap—the only place he could sit—he said, "Now, every time we go over a bump, you owe me a dollar."

"Have a beer," Levitt replied.

"Make him pay for it," Bobby Case said from the front seat. "He's got all the fuggin money."

"He don't pay for *shit*," Denny said. "This party's on *me*." Everybody in the car laughed, except Kol Mano, who was intent on cruising Broadway one more time, in the hope that they could pick up some girls. When they went past the Corner, there were a few guys leaning against a car in front of the drugstore at whom Denny blew a loud razzberry.

Bobby Case said to Billy seriously, "You know, you and me ought to go to Frisco. There's a hell of a lot of money down there, and they'll spot you like crazy; we could cut those old fuckers up for a fortune. I did it once before, and they all thought I was just lucky."

"That's an idea," Billy said. "That's an idea."

"Goddam," Denny said, "you two'd be murder together."

There were three boys in the car Billy had never seen before, and one of them said, "I don't actually think you fooled anybody in San Francisco, Case. I think those men just couldn't *stand* the idea of your beating them."

"That's true," Billy said to him. The boy who spoke looked about eighteen, and had a high forehead and a long, inquisitive nose and almost no chin. "I've seen that in Seattle; guys who just couldn't take the idea of bein beat by some colored kid." He laughed. "They were my *meat!*"

"I've got your meat," Denny laughed.

"Now, that's *two* dollars," Billy laughed. Mano turned away from his driving for a moment with an impatient look, and Billy wondered if, after all, he didn't like Negroes. Well, if he didn't, fuck him. The others didn't seem to mind. He guzzled beer from the bottle Levitt had passed him from the opened case on the floor, feeling the cold needles go down his throat. Tonight, he thought, I'm gonna party like the world was comin to an end.

FIVE

The party got out of hand almost immediately. The original idea had been a poker game to trim Billy Lancing, with a party to drink up as much of the free liquor as possible and haul the rest away—all very quiet behind the blackout drapes of the expensive home—but the poker game fizzled out, and then, to get some girls, they had had to invite too many people. It rapidly developed into a brawl.

The first odd thing Jack noticed was that Kol Mano disappeared only a few minutes after they had arrived. He had parked his car almost two blocks away, under some trees, and when they got to the house, sneaked around to the back and gone in, Mano had said, "This is uncool." Shortly after Denny had shown Mano all the stacks of cased whiskey, Mano vanished, and Jack decided that a couple of the cases of whiskey were gone, too. Mano probably hadn't planned to stay at all, and vaguely Jack felt as if he had been taken. Mano *was* strange; people had hinted that he was a drug addict, a queer, lots of things, but Jack didn't know anything about it; he only saw Mano as a very cool man who never seemed to be too far from the money. Now he was gone. Jack had been meaning to sit down and have a talk with him. He shrugged. Some other time. There was the party going on.

Somebody had gotten on the telephone, and now there were about fifteen people running around the house, nearly two boys for every girl from the look of it; and Jack meant to get himself one of the girls. Just because he had been to the Model Hotel the day before and again that very afternoon meant nothing. He wanted a girl very badly. Some were even pretty, and he decided he wanted the prettiest one for himself.

He wandered through the three floors of the house, a bottle of Scotch in his hand, looking over the action. There were kids everywhere. None of them had ever been in a house like this before. Most of them, like Denny, lived in crowded homes in places like St. Johns or Sellwood, or Northwest Portland, and the sight of all this wealth subdued them. They just walked around at first, almost intimidated by the near-presence of the rich and powerful owners of the property, looking in the closets at the racks of expensive clothing, in the bureau drawers packed full of silken things. But after a while the whiskey and familiarity dulled their sense of being in a museum, and they began to get noisy, and to act as if they were in an ordinary home, having an ordinary party. Only Jack, Denny, and Billy Lancing knew for certain that they were committing a crime by just being in the house. They had told the others that they had permission from young Weinfeld. Bobby Case knew, too, but after wandering around for half an hour, he stole some of the kid's clothes (which fitted him very well) and left the party.

On impulse, Jack went out into the hedge-rimmed garden

in back of the house. There was a lawn, and the large black shadows of trees darkened the area to the rear of the garden. The sky above was clouded and tinted red from the lights of downtown. Faint noises came from the house; not loud enough, Jack felt, to be heard in the houses of the neighborhood, but light shone through amber window shades, and that could be seen—it was only in the front of the house and on the main floor that there were blackout drapes. Jack began to wonder if the neighbors would know the people were supposed to be on vacation. He did not know anything about how neighbors were supposed to be; he did not know that in upper middle-class neighborhoods such as this one, neighbors frequently did not know each other personally, did not even nod in greeting if they saw one another; he did not happen to know that the Weinfelds were Jews, and that there were no other Jews in this particular section of the neighborhood. So he began to be worried about what would happen if anyone saw the lights in the windows or heard a fragment of noise, a laugh, or a yell and decided to call the police.

He took a drink of whiskey and coughed. If the cops came, they would probably walk up to the front door and ring the bell. There were three or four cars parked out in front. The cops would notice these cars, and the boys they belonged to would be out of luck. But not Jack. When the cops came in, he would go out the back door. He looked at the hedge in the back. He could get over it easily; it was only about six feet high. He would have no trouble getting away. He relaxed.

But then, if he did get away (assuming the cops showed up at all), he would still be right back where he started: broke, locked out, etc. He felt a stirring of anger, not at society for failing to have provided him with money; not at himself for his refusal to work; but at the situation itself, for existing. Damn it! he thought. He took another drink of whiskey. There was nothing he could do about it now; so he might just as well get as drunk as he could, have fun, find a girl, and worry about later later.

"Hey," said a voice out of the black. "Takin the air?"

"Who is it?"

"Billy."

They approached each other. Billy, too, had a bottle, and they stood together for a few moments, drinking silently. Finally, Jack said, "What you doin out here? Takin the air yourself?"

"Yeah. This's not much of a party, is it?"

"Well, you know."

Later, when Jack had plenty of time to think about it, he wondered why he had not taken this golden opportunity to coldcock Billy Lancing and get his money. He had plenty of time to think about it, and he went over every possible motive in his mind. It wasn't because he and Billy were friends, and even if they had been, Jack saw no reason not to do it; Billy had money, lots of it, and Jack needed money. And it was not because Billy was smaller and defenseless, even in a way trusted Jack not to take advantage of this accidentally private meeting; no such motive had ever stirred Jack in his life. And it certainly wasn't because Jack didn't think of it, or because he was afraid to, or because it seemed unethical to invite a person to a party and then rob him (that had been the original idea of inviting Billy). In fact, in all the time Jack had to think about it he was not able to come up with a logical, reasonable answer. They stood there in the garden and talked, and then they went back in the house. That was all that happened. It was inexplicable.

A great deal was going on inside the house. In the basement party room, three couples were dancing, and one lone boy was behind the bar trying out different exotic combinations of liquor. When Jack came in for another bottle, this boy was holding up something greenish in a milk-shake glass and grinning like a mad scientist. Jack took the glass from him and sipped at the drink; it tasted like sour candy. He gave the glass back and picked up a bottle half-full of Cutty Sark. He looked at the dancers. They all seemed to be elsewhere, moving slowly to the radio playing "Dream."

65

It seemed so cozy. He went upstairs. The living room was empty. Several of the glass animals from the mantelpiece had fallen or been dropped on the hearth, and were broken. The nice lady in the white dress with the blue sash looked out into the empty room with a nice, pleasant, warm smile, not noticing what had happened to her ornaments. Her beautiful Persian rug, too, had been damaged by cigarette burns and some spilled liquor, but she did not see it; she was looking off into the distance. Jack saluted her with his bottle and went into the kitchen. Denny, Billy Lancing, and three other boys were sitting around the kitchen table, talking. The room was full of smoke. Somebody had been cooking something on the stove, and it had boiled over and burned. There were long yellowish-black streaks down the side of the stove, and the gas was still on under a blackened pot. Jack went over and looked in, but he could not tell what had been cooking. The boys at the table seemed to be talking about another party, not this one, one that had happened in the past. Jack could not quite make out what they were saying. Either they were drunk, or he was. Perhaps they were all drunk. Jack's ears buzzed, and his legs felt long and rubbery. One of the boys at the table finished his bottle and tossed it across the kitchen. It tinkled. Jack grinned. That was a funny thing to do. He looked at his bottle. Too full.

"I want a cigar," he said. No one answered him. He wandered out of the kitchen. Where were the cigars? Oh, yes, in the "Library." Jack knew this room he was looking for was called the "Library" because he had seen movies in which people had such rooms. It was a room full of books, a small room, but still, full of books. And there was a desk. He and Denny had searched through the desk the night before, looking for money. The son of a bitch that owned the desk did not keep money in it. The fool. Jack wandered around until he found the room. The light was off, and he flicked the mercury switch (which did not click) and caught a boy and a girl on the leather couch. Jack saw a flash of white thigh as the girl turned quickly toward him, smoothing down her skirt. Her face was smeared and puffed, her lips parted over two prominent rabbit's teeth. The boy sat up, his long Hollywood haircut all messed and down over his forehead. He had pimples and the beginnings of a tiny mustache.

"Beat it," Jack told them.

"Well I really," the girl said.

"What the hell," the boy said.

But they left, and Jack started looking for the cigars. There was a cupboard under a glassed-in section of books. They were in here, he thought, squatting down. He got out a cigar, licked it down, bit an inch off the end, and lit it. The cigar tasted raw and burned his throat as he inhaled. The rich life; rich folks smoke these fuckin ropes; I'm gonna smoke em if it kills me. He looked around the room. Books. Money hidden behind the books. Of course. Where else? Got to be money in this house, must be behind the books. He began sweeping books off the shelves, and looking behind them. After a moment he sneezed; it was very dusty behind the books, and the dust had a particularly acrid smell. He swept the books off the open shelves carelessly, and they tumbled to the rug, spines cracking, dust flying. Jack did not find any money. The glassed-in shelf of books was locked. That would be where the money was. Jack picked up a copy of *Wake of the Red Witch* and used it to smash the glass on both sides. He dropped the book and reached in. Have to be careful, now, and not get cut. And open every book; maybe twenty dollar bills will be between the pages of the books. He pulled out a thick little book called *The Perfumed Garden* and riffled the pages. No money in it. He threw it across the room. He pulled out more books, most of them dealing with the Civil War, riffled them, and dropped them on the pile on the floor. He finally found some money. A Confederate twenty-dollar bill, used as a bookmark. It took him a long time to decide what it was. Then, holding the worthless money in his hand, he really lost his temper, kicking the stack of books and cursing in a deep, enraged voice. He looked around for something vicious to do, but the room was already a shambles, and so, stepping over the books or kicking them out of his way, he left, still holding the Confederate money.

As he passed through the dining room, he saw a boy lying under the table, his mouth open, snoring. Jack stared at him, and then got down and stuffed the twenty into the boy's mouth. The boy gagged, his eyes opening, bulging, and he turned on his side and began vomiting on the rug. Jack said, "I'm sorry, dint mean it that way," and went back into the kitchen. He wanted an egg salad sandwich. And there was only one way for him to get an egg salad sandwich. And that was to boil some eggs, chop them up, add mayonnaise, find some bread, and *make* the sandwich. He jerked open the refrigerator, and looked through it. There was plenty of food in it, but no eggs. "What the fuck is this?" he said. He swept some of the bottles and packages out of the refrigerator, and heard the cracking of glass.

"Hey, we gonna go get some air," Denny said into his ear. "Come on, you look drunk."

"I *am* drunk," Jack said. He wanted to tell Denny all about the books, but he could not find the words. He followed Denny and Billy out into the back garden. Maybe now we'll pop the little fucker an take his money, he thought.

The three of them sat on the damp grass and lit cigarettes. Jack still had his cigar in his hand, but he did not smoke it; he just let it burn.

"God damn," Denny said through the gloom. "What a rotten goddam life. You know what?"

"What?" Billy said dully. He did not sound drunk to Jack. "Aint you drunk?" Jack asked him.

"Feelin no pain," Billy said.

"Shit. I bet you don't drink."

"Sure I drink."

"Chickenshit nigger mother."

"Aw," Denny said. "You know what? I'm gonna join the Marines. No shit. Get out of this rotten life. School. I hate school."

"Me, too," Billy said. "But I just took off; I aint going to join no Marine Corps."

Jack drew the clear cold air into himself, held it a moment, and let it out. The air almost cleared his head.

"Marines?" he asked. "What the hell for, Denny? Are you gone crazy?"

"Aw, shit. I aint gettin nowhere. I cut school all the time, get caught, get suspended, my old lady eats my ass out, then I got to go to school again. I don't do nothin there, just sit around. It's the shits. I don't do nothin down at the poolhall neither. I just wastin my life. You know what? You know what Clancy Phipps tol me? He says, 'You join the service now, while you can, cause after you get a record you can't get in.' Aint that an awful thing? Here all his fuggin life he wants to go in the fuggin Marines, an so he cops a radio an gets six months an now the Marines won't take him. Me'n his kid brother Dale, we're gonna join together. Dale Phipps, nex his brother, he's the toughest fucker I ever met in my life. Him'n me, we're gonna join."

"He aint so tough," Jack said. He felt envious, but not enough to join the Marines. "You know what? The Marines is worsen prison. You really got to snap shit."

"No," Denny said seriously. "In the Marines, sure, you got to toe the line, but man, they're *tough*; you got to be good to make it. That's worth doin."

Billy said, "Man oh man. But they're on your ass day an night. Me, I'm goin on the *road*. I figger I'm good enough, fair country poolshooter, an I can make my own livin."

"Gee," Denny said. "That's great. You really got the talent, too. You got a skill, see; I aint got one. So all I can do is join the service. An the Marines are the cream of the crop. See?"

"Yeah," Billy admitted. "But Jesus, what a way to go."

"Fuck you guys," Jack said dully. "You got your ambitions. I don't." He was feeling very sorry for himself.

"No," Billy said. "I know it's gonna be tough, me bein colored an all that; but I figure I can take it, cause I got the skill, see? An that makes all the difference. My old man, shit, he's got no skills or nothin, so when they layin off all the colored people he goes out of his head, runs around the house drunk an cryin over himself. An there's a lot of us to feed, man, so I just cut out, you know? I mean to make it."

6 9

"You will," Denny said with admiration. "You got the guts, an Kol Mano says you got the brains. Hey, tell me one thing; how much money you got on you? No kiddin, we won't take it; I just want to know how much you won today an how much you stashed. Come on."

Billy laughed lightly. "I brought twenty; I win almost a hundred today."

"God!" Denny said.

"Balls!" Jack said. He got up, his joints already rusty, and moved back toward the house. He could still hear them talking about their future plans as he went into the house. It was not a significant moment for any of them, but later on, when Jack had plenty of time to think, the moment took on significance: it was the last time he was to see either of them for years. He thought about them, both of them, often, as he sat in darkness and dreamed away his past; thought of Denny's friendliness, his openhearted kindness; blew it up all out of proportion, made Denny into a kind of saint in his memory; effectively destroyed the real Denny—thought about Billy and about his talent, his courage, exaggerated him as he did with Denny, so that both boys became almost symbolic of what he lacked, or what he dreamed, in darkness, that he lacked. Then he forgot about them as he forgot about almost everything. But that was later.

Right now, all he wanted was sleep. He was utterly drunk, and sleep seemed as desirable as a woman. He made his way upstairs, and looked into the boy's bedroom. There was a couple on the bed. He said, "Excuse me," and went to one of the girls' rooms. It was empty. He got onto the bed, his body almost dead-weight, felt the coolness of the coverlet under him, and passed out.

SIX

They really did not know what to do with him. He refused to tell them who he was, or how old he was, or anything at all. They took him down and booked him as John Doe and threw him in City Prison to await magistrate's court.

It was not easy to do. When he awakened, turned over, and saw the two big plainclothesmen standing over the bed, he only blinked his eyes once, and then started fighting. He did not really try to get away; it did not occur to him that it would be possible; he just started fighting. One of the officers had to hit him along the side of the head with his lead-and-leather sap, and then Jack's legs went out from under him and with one last wild, swinging left, he collapsed to the rug. They handcuffed him while he was still groggy, and then one of the officers stood straddled over him and hit him in the face, to let him know how things were. It did not occur to him to resent it.

They marched him down the stairs, and he got one last quick look at the house. The living room was a shambles; drapes torn, vomit and cigarette burns on the carpet, a lamp overturned, its shade askew. He did not realize how much the house reeked of smoke and vomit and urine until they opened the front door and he smelled fresh air. "Whew," he said. It was the first remark he addressed to the officers, and it also turned out to be the last.

For once it was sunny in Portland, and Jack saw on the front lawn the bright diamondlike glitter of broken glass. They climbed into the black police car, one officer in front and one in back with Jack, and drove down the curved streets toward the heart of the city. The motion of the car made Jack sick to his stomach, and his head hurt. He leaned over and vomited onto the officer's lap, felt something jarring, heard a loud sharp noise, and passed out again.

It did no good to search him; he had no identification at all. He probably would have been arraigned, tried, and sent to prison if one of the policemen hadn't recognized him from Ben Fenne's. The policeman spent his lunch hour at the poolhall playing keno almost every day, and he knew Jack's name. As a matter of routine, they checked the records and learned that he was a Missing Person, and to their dismay, a juvenile. So instead of being sent to prison, in Salem, he was sent to reform school, in Woodburn.

A Death on the Big Yard

1954–1956

SEVEN

Denny had gotten his growth since Jack had seen him last; he was now at least three inches taller than Jack, heavier, his face filled out and his red hair receding slightly from his temples. But there was no mistaking his greenish eyes or his smile—still boyish, even though Denny was twenty-four or twenty-five. They were sitting in a Market Street poolhall and Denny was telling Jack a funny story:

"What a mess. We was goin to take this gambling joint down in South City, an the guy who cased it said all you have to do is grin at the guy at the door and he lets you in, an then pull the guns and yell for everybody to hit the floor; the money's right there in a big wooden cabinet between the tables, an the cat with the green apron has the key, dig? Well, it sounded easy; the caser said no problem. He always said that, no problem, cause he never went along so everything was always real easy, all you got to do is scare hell out of everybody an pick up the money. What a joke.

"So anyway, I'm standing there at the door telling the guy to lemme in, wearin this big topcoat with my hands on the guns in my pockets, and he swings the door open and I blaze in there with the guns out, yellin like hell, and everybody's jumping for the floor an tippin tables over an turning green and all that shit, and there I am standing there lookin at myself in one of these great big mirrors, you know, set into the far wall. Man, I like to shit right on the spot. I knew goddam well there was a couple of nasty wops or something back of that fuggin mirror with a couple of big tommy guns or shotguns or something, you know, laughin their asses off at me an just itchin to shoot. So there I am, starin at myself, and everybody in the room is cuttin out or yellin or eatin sawdust on the floor; and I decide to fire a couple shots into the mirror, you know, to scare them off or something, and then I thought, oh, fuck it, and went for the guy with the green apron and he opened the money box and gave me the cash like he did it every day or didn't give a shit, and I stuffed the money in my pockets and yelled for everybody to stay down an split. Man, I could practically *feel* them bullets going up my ass, but I got all the way out to the car an nothin happened, and I jumps in and tells Tommy, '*Make it!*' and we zoom off, an nothin happened at all. Can you figure it?"

He laughed and looked at Jack puckishly. "You know, them poker clubs are legalized, and the next day's paper said we got away with eighty thousand dollars. So I knew why the guys back of the mirror didn't just cut loose and turn the corpse over to the cops; the boss himself was probably back of the mirror and says, 'Hey, let the asshole rob the joint; we'll clean up off the insurance company.' "

"How much did you really get?" Jack asked.

Denny snorted. "Eighteen hundred, total. What crooks!"

Jack smiled. He was glad he had run into Denny after so many years. "So you're a big thief now," he said.

"Well, I ain't done anything for a while. We really got

fucked up. Let's get out of here." They got up and left the pool-hall where they had accidentally met, walked up Turk Street a few doors, and went into a bar. It was the middle of the afternoon, and there were only a few people in the half-darkened place. They took a table in the back, and Denny said, "We was gonna knock over Playland, out at the beach, you know? We really had a big one planned, this caser guy I was tellin you about, he worked on it for weeks, goin out there, wanderin around, lookin for the money and getaway routes and stuff, and then we got together a bunch of guns, too; man, we must of had ten or twelve guns, rifles, automatics, revolvers, tear-gas guns, everything; and so one night we go out there, Tommy, the guy that drove for us, had just bought himself a brand-new personal car, and we had all the guns in the car, like, and we went out there, and Tommy parks the short and we get out and look around, ride some of the goddam rides, play the machines, really have a pretty good time, and then we go back to get the car, and man you wouldn't believe it—Tommy'd parked the fucker in a *tow-away zone!* It was gone. The cops had took it to one of their garages. Guns and all. So we were out of business, like. Tommy took off for Mexico. It was his car, registered in his name and everything. You ever go to Mexico?"

"Once or twice," Jack said. "Down through Laredo and that's about all."

"What have you been doin with yourself all this time?"

"Well, you know."

Denny waited a few moments, but Jack did not say anything more, so he laughed. "Well, yeah."

"I been boxing," Jack admitted. "Southwest circuit, Los Angeles. I just quit."

"Hey, no kidding? A fighter?"

Jack nodded and drank some of his beer. He did not add that he had also bucked logs, worked in a cannery and a furniture factory, robbed gas stations, rolled drunks, and lived in half a hundred arid furnished rooms, pretended the vacuum was freedom, wakened almost daily to the fear that time was a dry wind brushing away his youth and his strength, and slept through as many nightmares as there were nights to dream. He just sat and smiled at Denny and saw what time had done to him and wondered, now comfortably, why he was so bothered by time. It happens to everybody this way, he thought, we sit here and get older and die and nothing happens.

"Listen," Denny said. "This is great. I got a couple of chicks on my back; picked up one of them and the other come along, and we're all stuck together. You can take the other chick, okay? What'd be greater?"

"Too much," Jack admitted. He felt something coming loose inside him, and he decided that he was glad it was going away. This would be much easier. There would be time to think.

Denny's hotel room had one double bed and a very small single bed over in the corner. Sitting on this Jack could look down at the crowds of people on Turk Street, eddying around the entrances to theaters, clubs, hot-dog palaces, magazine stands, barbershops. He had a barrel-shaped thick hotel glass half full of whiskey in his hands, and Denny was spread-eagled on the double bed, thumbing through a comic book. There were comic books all over the room, and girls' clothes piled on both chairs, dripping off onto the thin carpet. Packages, empty sacks, wadded string, yellow-orange cheeseburger wrappers were on the floor and under the beds, and in the corner beyond the small bed Jack was on were the torn halves of the room's stock Bible among the dust motes.

How do you wake up? It was one thing to know that you had been asleep all your life, but something else to wake up from it, to find out you were really alive and it wasn't anybody's fault but your own. Of course that was the problem.

All right. Everything is a dream. Nothing hangs together. You move from one dream to another and there is no reason for the change. Your eyes see things and your ears hear, but nothing has any reason behind it. It would be easier to believe in God. Then you could wake up and yawn and stretch and grin at a world that was put together on a plan of mercy and death, punishment for evil, joy for good, and if the game was crazy at least it had rules. But that didn't make sense. It had never made any sense. The trouble was, now that he was not asleep and not awake, what he saw and heard didn't make sense either.

Mishmash, he thought. You know enough to know how you feel is senseless, but you don't know enough to know why. Sitting in another lousy hotel room waiting for a couple of girls you've never seen before to do a bunch of things you've done so many times it makes your skin crawl just to think about it. Things. To do. That you dreamed about when you couldn't have them. When there was only one thing, really, that made you feel good, and now you've done that so many times it's like masturbating. Except you never really made it, did you. Never really killed anybody. That's what you've always wanted to do, smash the brains out of somebody's head; break him apart until nothing is left but you. But you never made it.

Even before the reform school had shown Jack its worst he had tried to kill a guard, so the urge had been in him already; he knew that he, or the urge to kill in him, was not the result of a process of brutalization in the reformatory, he was not a victim of their stupidity and cruelty. Actually, the reform school was a model of life without artifice, without the gilding of purpose and reason to brighten the truth: that men were units to be taken care of and kept quiet—nothing else mattered except you weren't supposed to kill them. Jack did not understand this last rule, and the only way he could comprehend it was to think that if the guards killed all the prisoners then they would be out of work. Either that, or they didn't have the guts. He had a long time to think about it.

The guard—night watchman, really, but a man who thought of himself as a guard—had called them out of their cottage late at night just to brace them against the wall and accuse them of unnatural sex practices and walk up and down in front of them, daring them to make a move, while he sent his yellowish eyes up and down their bodies looking for signs of perversion; a stupid, illiterate central Oregon hick who couldn't get any other kind of job, lantern-jawed and snaggle-toothed, ordering the boys around because they were the only humans on earth who had to stand still for it, his awful eyes gleaming with desires he didn't have the guts to satisfy—and when the kid next to Jack giggled sleepily and muttered something, the guard shot his hand out and grasped the kid by the neck and jerked him out of the line, down onto his knees, and backhanded him across the face. The kid yelped in surprised anger, and Jack, out of control, feeling the pure blast of pleasure, moved toward this perfect target for his ambitions, spun the guard, hit him twice and knocked him against the wall of the cottage and fell on him, driving his fists coldly and carefully into the guard's face and throat, Jack's knee coming up into the guard's groin sharply; picking him up and slamming him against the wall, one hand on his throat and the other smashing into his face—murdering him with his hands. And he would have killed him, too, if the other watchmen hadn't heard the noise and come and pulled Jack away from his victim, clubbed him and dragged him down to the punishment cells—the hole—and left him there naked, the murder urge still burning unsatisfied in his heart; left him there for four months and three days—126 days without light—to remember, to think, to dream about his discovery.

The punishment cell was about seven feet long, four feet wide, and six feet high. The floor and walls were concrete, and there were no windows. In the iron door near the bottom was a slot through which he passed his slop can, and through which his food and water were delivered to him. They did not feed him every day, and because of that he had no way of knowing how much time had passed. After a while time ceased to exist. Time stopped in a strange way. First, he was aware that there was no present, no such thing as a moment; there was only the movement of his thoughts from past to future, from what had happened to what would happen. Then what had happened ceased to be real, as if his mind had invented a past his body could not remember; his senses were betraying him into dreams and the dreams eventually lost all contact with the senses. At first, he could not see because there was no light in his cell; then that became a delusion, and he could not see because he could not see, and then even that lost its reality, and he could not see because there was nothing to see, and never had been—his mind had tricked him into believing that there were colors and shapes, and he knew that there were no such things. At times, all his senses deserted him, and he could not feel the coldness of the concrete or smell his excrement, and the small sounds he made and the sounds that filtered in through the door gradually dimmed, and he was left alone inside his mind, without a past to envision, since his inner vision was gone, too, and without a future to dream, because there was nothing but this emptiness and himself. It was not uncomfortable, not comfortable. These things did not exist. It was colorless, senseless, mindless, and he sometimes just disappeared into it.

But then there would be a clank and a rattle at the door, followed by the smell of the food, and everything would rush back into him as the smell of the food hit him and aroused him and he would begin to tremble and slather and giggle, quickly locating his bucket and passing it out in exchange for the food and the cup of water; and for a few seconds every sense in him would rush into full operation and his mind would unfold in a glorious picture of what the food would be, and he would stick his fingers into it, whatever it was, and he would begin to gobble the food wolfishly, stuffing it into his mouth and swallowing, greed and terror knotting his stomach so badly that after only a few seconds he would feel engorged, and as likely as not begin to vomit up the food. Afterward he would lie back, panting from the exertion, and wait for the excitement to pass; then he would slowly and carefully eat what was left, and then drink his water. Then he would sit cross-legged in the middle of the cell, waiting for the reaction. Because sometimes they put soap powder into the food, he did not know why, and he would have to put up with the humiliations of diarrhea for hours. Jack never knew whether his food was going to be dosed or not; he could not, after the first few times, taste the soap, or feel the grittiness on his teeth, and so he would just have to sit and wait for the first cramping pang to hit him. There was no question of not eating; when they put the food into his cell he gorged himself without thought. It did not matter if they fed him twice in an hour, the same thing would happen. After a while he did not even hate them for it.

When he was first thrown into the hole what bothered him most was not the lack of a blanket, the cramped space, or the early terrors of the dark; it was the fact that he was naked, that he had been stripped of his dignity. It did not matter that there was no one to see him; what mattered in increasing dimensions of hatred was the humiliation of his nakedness, which seemed to deprive him of any kind of pride, took away his self-esteem, his humanity, his right to think of himself as a man. Squatting over his bucket, waiting for the next hapless squirting from his agonized bowels, he would dream of a future in which they would eventually let him out and there would be somebody there for his rage to murder; dreaming of the glory of that murder. It was a thought he clung to as long as possible, and it was always the last thing to desert him as he slipped again into nothingness: they had taken away his dignity, and he would kill them for that.

He went through self-pity very quickly. It occurred to him after he had been in endless darkness beyond all question of time that he would die in there, simply die of the immense loneliness, and that when he died no one would know about it for days, and when they finally did find out, they would unlock the door and remove his body and put it into a wooden coffin and bury it somewhere, without a marker, and that they would put into the files that his case was terminated, and that Jack Levitt was no longer an administrative problem. He would be dead, and gone, and nobody would mourn his death. They would be relieved, because they could terminate his file. They would get a sense of satisfaction from having the whole file completed, and maybe they would send to the orphanage and get all the papers on him there, and send to Portland and get the police report on him, and write to the places he worked and get his work cards, his pay records, every piece of paper on earth with his name on it, and make a big bundle (no, not so big, a small folder, maybe a Manila envelope) of it all, and take that out of the ACTIVE file and put it into the INACTIVE file, and then in a few years when they needed the space in the big green filing cabinet, they would take his folder out of the file and burn it, and he would be gone from the earth, and not one single human being on the face of the earth would know or remember who he had been, or care that he was gone. Not one single human being on the face of the earth would mourn his death.

Thinking about this made Jack cry to himself. But then, another thought came to save him from it; his mind told him that he would not care if any of them died, either. People were out there dying, and he did not care. If they all died, he would not care. It did not matter to him. So why should *they* care for *him? He* did not care for *them.* Fuck them. Each and every one of them. He laughed to himself, a rusty, creaking sound. He felt almost hopeful.

There were six punishment cells, and communication of a sort could be made by yelling, but most of the time it required too much effort, or Jack's senses were gone and he could not hear. But sometimes he did. He could hear other boys being brought in, yelling, cursing, some of them crying, and he himself suppressed all feelings of pity for the others; they did not pity him. They probably thought he was some kind of hero. Well, fuck them, too. Maybe in the cells they would learn the truth as he had, and know that nothing existed but a single spark of energy, and that spark could die for no reason, and existed for no reason. Then they would understand that it does no good to cry out, because a spark of energy has no ears; the ears are a lie, a joke, a dream, to keep the spark going, and there is no reason to keep the spark going. Any more than there is a reason for letting it go out. Maybe they would learn not to hate the guards, either, because the guards and everybody else on earth were prisoners in dark cells like themselves and just did not know it, and in fact they were in a worse prison than Jack was, because they were imprisoned by their own limits, and he was only imprisoned by them. He had found their limits—they would not, could not, just take him out and shoot him, and they could not let him run around loose, because he would not take any of their shit, and so they had to lock him up and feed him and dump his piss and shit for him, all because they had these limits that he did not have. If he had an enemy, he would kill that enemy. He would stop at nothing. He would kill that enemy quickly, get him out of the way, and then he would not have that enemy any more. But they couldn't do that. They were goddam lucky he did not have an enemy. Because if he did he would get out of there and find his enemy and kill him. As it was, there was nobody he hated, no single human life he needed to kill, and so, instead, he would just sit here and wait for them to let him out, and then he would kill the first living human he saw. That would teach them.

But even this thought, which could build itself to manic proportions, would fizzle away, and he would be left with nothing, not even madness.

Only once more, after the episode of self-pity, did he approach breakdown. He had just eaten, and for a change there was nothing in his food, and for a few moments he was experiencing a kind of contentment, hearing the sounds out in the passageway, thinking about nothing in particular. He heard the guards bring in a boy, and the boy was sobbing. Jack could tell from the sound of the sobbing that the boy was probably very young, maybe only twelve. Jack heard the cell door being opened, and then closed, and the sobbing muffled. He heard the guards go past and out. Then the new kid started screaming. It was a shock to Jack. He had never heard a sound like it. It was a sharp scream, as if the boy were in agony. Then Jack heard him calling for his mother, and then the boy screamed again, even louder than before, and Jack got frightened. He could feel a scream of his own rising in his throat, a terror in his own heart; he yelled for the boy to shut up, and heard the other boys in the cells yelling at him; but the new kid would not stop, and Jack and the others started yelling for the guard to come in and get him out of there. Jack was feeling panic; he was afraid that if the other boy did not stop screaming he would go crazy, but the boy would not stop; the screaming went on for hours, and then finally a single guard came in. Jack knew it must be nighttime, because it was only one guard that came in. During the daytime, or any time they brought a boy in or let a boy out, the guards came in pairs. So it was night, and the one guard went past Jack's cell and called in to the new kid, "Shut up in there, God damn it." The kid cried out that his stomach was hurting, and the guard was silent for a moment, and then said, "He's only fakin," and left. Jack and the other boys started yelling and screaming in rage at the guard's cowardice, because they knew the guard had been afraid to open the cell without a partner along, and Jack again thought he was going to go crazy; he yelled and swore and sobbed in rage, until there was nothing left in him and he lay on the floor of his cell face down, trembling with his hatred of the guard and his rediscovered terror of the dark. The only sounds that could be heard now were the low moans of agony from the new kid, and eventually they, too, stopped, and the punishment cells were silent. This silence was even more terrifying, and Jack bit his lips bloody to keep from screaming himself.

In the morning, when the doctor and three guards came, the boy was already dead. He had died of a burst appendix, and Jack could hear the furious anger of the doctor and the mumbled embarrassment and self-defense of the guards. But the boy was dead, a boy Jack had never seen, and he felt despair for himself again.

There was an investigation, and the night guard was fired. When the State Senator who was in charge of the investigation got to Jack's cell, he asked through the door how long Jack had been in there, and Jack did not answer. The State Senator sent one of the guards for the punishment records, and Jack for the first time learned how long he had been in there, the State Senator saying in an amazed, almost hushed voice, that according to these records, this boy has been in this cell for 87 days, and with shock making his voice tremble, the State Senator demanded that the cell be opened and the boy brought out, and Jack did not know whether the State Senator was planning to free him or just wanted to see what kind of animal could live in total darkness for 87 days without dying, because when the door opened and the faint light blazed against Jack's eyes, something dark and joyful exploded inside him and he hit the State Senator, grabbed at him, and tried to murder him, out of control, feeble, fumbling, helpless, nevertheless with his hands on the State Senator's throat and his fingers squeezing, odd noises in his ears, almost drowned out by a roaring sound from within; and then the guards pulled him off the Senator and threw him back in his cell, and the State Senator went back to Salem and the investigation went into file thirteen, and that was the end of that.

When they came to let him out, the day before his eighteenth birthday, they opened the door and jumped back, four guards crowding the passageway, one of them holding a white canvas restraining jacket. But Jack stood up and walked out into the passageway calmly, his eyes shut. The first thing he said to the guards was, "My eyes hurt like hell." He was blindfolded, to protect his eyes, and taken, inside the restraining jacket, to a place where there were two psychiatrists to examine him. The plan had been to transfer Jack from the reformatory to the State mental hospital, because the authorities did not feel in all conscience that they could let him go and the law said they had to give up his custody when he turned eighteen. The two psychiatrists asked Jack a lot of questions, and he answered them calmly, blindfolded, and in the restraining jacket and the pants that two guards had slipped onto him, sat in his chair and lied to the two doctors and told them he felt ashamed of himself, and that when the Senator had opened the door Jack had been having a nightmare and he was sorry; but to be on the safe side he was transferred to the State mental institution in Salem, locked in a room in a long brown corridor, and given thirty days' observation by the staff. He actually saw a doctor only four times, for fifteen minutes each time, and after the first visit he was given mopping to do and was permitted the use of the observation ward day-room. At the end of the thirty days he was let out, still wearing dark glasses, his skin pale and raw. He knew he was just lucky. He knew that it was an accident that they had come for him at a moment when he was perfectly rational. If he had been deep in his dream of murder, as he had been when the State Senator visited, then he might have spent the rest of his life in the insane asylum. He was just lucky they had come for him in one of the few moments of sanity. He had happened to be urinating at the moment he heard the guards in the passageway. So he had not been off-balance. He had managed in all the time of transition afterward to keep a tight control on himself, and his eyes helped. His eyes hurt so fiercely that he concentrated on the pain as a way of keeping from thinking of murder; and by the time they let him out of the insane asylum, he had himself under control. He worked in eastern Oregon, bucking logs for a wildcat outfit in the mountains between Oregon and Idaho, for half a year, letting the sun and the hard work burn strength and calm into him, and when at last he got fired for fighting, it was all right, because he was not trying to kill the man; the man had gotten drunk and started bothering Jack, and so they fought, but as men fight, not animals, and after they both got fired they went to Boise together and got good and drunk together, and Jack knew that he was going to be all right. He was afraid that he would dream about the hole, but he never did. Or if he did, he never remembered it in the morning, and that was what counted. Jack wanted to have a good time for himself, and night-mares would have spoiled the delicious pleasure of sleeping in a bed.

When the girls finally burst into Denny's room Jack felt a little depressed, but at the same time there was the usual ex-citement new things, especially girls, brought. They were two of a kind: long-haired, thin, with sharp, wolfish faces and children's mouths gone hard. Their thin hard bodies were dressed in new, almost identical, black cocktail dresses, shiny blue pumps, and black hose. Too much eye makeup, cheeks too pale, eyes too small, brows too sharply drawn, voices brittle and toneless with self-imposed coolness. Beneath it all Jack could see that the girls were both plain. But the attempt to be hip, to dress like four-bit New York whores, was in itself stimulating.

Denny jumped up from the bed and introduced the girls as Mona and Sue, and they nodded, neither of them meeting Jack's eyes, poured themselves glasses of whiskey, and plopped down on the bed, each with a comic book, and began with apparently deep concentration to read.

Denny grinned at Jack. "They're shy," he said. "How was the movie?"

"What a drag," one of them said.

Jack sighed, and sat back down. He had been through so many scenes like this one. Everybody knew what was what, but nobody wanted to be straight about it. They would go on like this—bored, indifferent, edgy, too hip to live—until they got drunk, and then somebody would turn on the radio and they would dance in the tiny space between the beds, and somebody would push somebody down onto the bed, and in the darkness the four of them would be sorted out into fornicating couples almost at random, with the light coming in through the window shade, and later somebody would throw up, and some time after that somebody would suggest that they switch partners, and after an hour of dull bitching they might or might not, and everybody would fall asleep from alcohol and boredom, and the radio would keep playing through their fuzzy dreams, and eventually they would all have to wake up. So much waste, he thought. He shook his head, trying to rid himself of this overwhelming sense of waste. He had come to San Francisco to think, and he was not going to do it. He was always doing the easy thing, the thing that first came to hand.

One of the girls on the bed, Mona, looked over at him and smiled cutely. "Got a bug in your ear?"

"Let's turn on the radio and dance or something," Jack said to her. "Let's do something." He wanted to get it over with, like a job of work or a fight.

"It's not even dark out," Mona said. Primly, he thought. As if dancing in the daytime was square.

"Let's go get some Chinese food and go to a nightclub," Mona said. She threw her comic book fluttering across the room. "I already read the goddam thing."

"I'm sick of Chinese food," Denny said. He was standing in front of the mirror over the sink, inspecting his teeth.

"You hardly ever eat Chinese food," Sue said. She was the brighter of the two, Jack thought; something about her eyes, a glint, something. He decided she had some sense. To Jack she said, "Every time we go to a Chinese restaurant he eats a hamburger or something. Honest to Christ."

Denny said calmly, "Listen, I've puked more Chinese food than you ever ate."

Mona laughed sharply. "I bet you have. You're a real puker. Mister Puke, that's you."

"Stick your nose up my ass, and I'll blow your brains out," Denny said without turning his head.

Mona grinned at Jack. "He's so *salty*. Do you have a suit?"

Jack admitted that he did. His clothes were in a quarter locker at the bus depot.

"Let's get dressed up and go someplace really expensive," Mona said. "All we ever do is go to crappy joints."

"That sounds good," Jack said. "I'll get a room here in the hotel and take a shower and change." He got up and swallowed off his whiskey. It was not hitting, but he did not expect it to, yet.

Sue leaned forward and whispered into Mona's ear. Mona's calm and serious eyes were on Jack as she listened to the secret message. She whispered back to Sue and said, "I'll go with you."

"We'll see you guys in about an hour," Denny said. He and Jack looked at each other. "Hey, baby; good to see you." It was almost embarrassing. Denny really appeared happy about the whole thing. As if they had been old and dear friends, instead of poolhall buddies who happened to run into each other in another poolhall.

Jack and Mona left the hotel and went up Market toward the bus depot. The street was heavily crowded with people just getting off work, and with soldiers, sailors, Market Street bums, and shoppers. Mona walked beside Jack with her hand on his arm. He faintly disliked this gesture of too-sudden intimacy; he did not like people touching him. He was used to it; people always seemed to want to touch a boxer as he was entering or leaving the arena, especially leaving, if he had won, and it was a little disgusting, like the old woman who had gotten into his dressing room once in Phoenix and wanted to pay him five dollars to watch him take his shower.

"Look at all the goddam squares," Mona said to him. In the twilight her face was harsh and pretty, her mouth slightly twisted in disgust. They were all alike. They were hip and anybody who worked for a living was square. Especially anybody over thirty. But then he felt a little that way himself, only not as hip and square; something else, something they didn't have words for. He really did not understand people who worked for a living. But he did not really dislike them, only the ones who tried to push him around. And there weren't very many of those.

When they got inside the bus depot, Mona said, "I wish to God I was going someplace. I hate bus depots. They always make me think I'm not going anyplace. I want to go to New York or LA or something. Don't you?"

"I just came from LA," Jack said.

"By bus?" Mona looked imperious, as if there was no question of going anywhere by bus. Jack left her standing by the entrance while he went for his suitcase and overnight bag. When he got back she was talking to two sailors.

"Let's go," he said to her.

"Don't interrupt," Mona said without looking at him. "I'm talking." One of the sailors eyed Jack nervously. They were both young and smooth-cheeked, with the slack mouths of punks. One of them was trying to grow a mustache, and he had his hand resting on Mona's arm. He looked at Jack, and let his arm drop to his side. Jack turned away and went out the door and walked back to the hotel alone.

He got a room only a few doors from Denny's, unpacked his clothes, squared the room away, undressed, and went in to take a shower. He let the hot water run hard on the back of his neck; lately the muscles there had been cording up tight, and he had discovered that hot water loosened them as well as or better than whiskey. Before every fight he had spent almost an hour in the shower, letting the water run over him, and nipping at a pint. He had always been about half-loaded when he went into the ring. The whiskey calmed him down, and he could be more mechanical. Castelli had told him he had two great problems as a fighter: his skin broke too easily—bled too much, and he had a tendency to slip from boxing to street fighting if he seemed to think he was losing. He could control the last with whiskey, but the first had spoiled what might have been a solid career as a boxer. It got around that he cut easily, and so his opponents would go for his face and make him bleed, and he lost his last seven fights through TKOs, boxing the final rounds with a film of blood over his eyes and the salty taste of it in his mouth. This is what made him get wild, and he was an easy mark for any half-bright fighter. Prado Vasquez, a kid he liked and drank with, almost killed him the fight before his last one, when there was so much blood in his eyes that he stopped moving for a second and tried to wipe his eyes and Prado (Jack could see the tight little Oriental face) got him setting solid, a short blow to the point of the jaw, and for the first time in his career Jack went out, and came to in the dressing room. For a couple of days after that he felt as if his heart had come loose, and after one more loser Castelli cut him loose.

But that was all right. He was getting tired of it. Everyone was being entertained but him.

While he was drying himself there was a tapping on the door. "Who is it?" he said.

"Who did you expect?"

He opened the door and let her in. His nakedness caught her

by surprise, and for a few moments she was disconcerted into silence, walking rapidly across the room and looking out the window into the light shaft. He continued to rub himself off.

"Well, really," she said at last. "Aren't you proud of yourself."

"You can leave if you want," Jack said. "But I don't think you want to."

"You know everything, don't you."

He laughed at her. "Are you going to take a shower?"

She actually looked embarrassed. "I guess so," she said.

But Jack didn't want to be mean. "Listen, you girls can use my room to clean up in and change, and I'll wait with Denny. Are they through in there?"

She closed an eye and squinted at him, as he put on his underwear. "How come you walked off on me? I was just talking to a boy I used to know. You have a good build, do you know that?" She made a face. "Sure you know it."

"You go get your things while I finish dressing," he said.

As she was passing him she stopped and then came close to him, reaching to touch the muscles of his upper arm. Jack noticed that she had orange lacquer on her fingernails, and that one of the nails was cracked. He could smell her perfume and it made him suddenly dizzy with expectation; there was a shout in him to throw her to the floor, but he stilled it; he knew that they would certainly make love and there was no reason to be brutal; it would be better—more delicious—to move into it slowly. He waited, his eyes on the small curve of her breasts.

"What a body," she said, almost to herself. She held her mouth up to be kissed, and Jack kissed her softly and cupped her buttocks in his hands and pulled her toward him.

"Turn off the lights," she said. "Pull down the shades, too. It's not dark enough in here. Don't look. Unhook this for me, will you? Wait a minute. Okay." She got on the bed with him, her thin, innocent body visible in the half-light, and they made love, Jack hungrily, Mona nervously, and when it was all over she pushed him away and turned facedown on the bed, her arms rigid at her sides. Jack got up and went into the bathroom, and then came out to get dressed. She was still in the same position.

"What's the matter?" he asked her. He was used to variations of this reaction, and it irritated him. She was trying to make him pay for his fun by being distant, guilty, and then, inevitably, bitchy.

"Nothing," she said. "Go away. I want to get dressed."

"Why don't I send that other girl over with your stuff from Denny's room?"

"You do that little thing." Her voice was muffled by the pillow, but it still crackled with dry bitterness.

"Are you pissed off? What's the matter, didn't you make it?"

"Shut up."

"I'll send what's-her-name, Sue, down here with your stuff," he said.

She sat up and looked at him. "Pay me ten dollars."

Jack laughed. "What for?"

"You know."

"Are you trying to turn yourself out? Are you kidding?"

"Pay me ten dollars," she said stubbornly.

"The first rule is, get the money first." He went out and down to Denny's room. If the girl wanted to be a hustler, he thought, she was shit out of luck. A hustler has the larceny; she always thinks of the money first. He knocked on the door impatiently; he wanted a drink of whiskey.

EIGHT

The girls did not know what Denny did for a living, but it did not matter, as long as he had plenty of money and didn't mind spending it. By little things he said, by his attitude of pretended boredom and suavity in front of the girls, Jack knew that Denny was having a high old time, that this life of girls, clubs, comic books, and whiskey was all Denny wanted out of life, and that the mystery of where and how he got his money enhanced his own sense of importance. This was not like the Denny Jack remembered from Portland; the old Denny had not done any faking at all. This was one of the things that time had done to him. This, and the thickening, and the wariness around his eyes. And there were hints that sometimes Denny got too drunk, blacked out, and went wild.

But nothing happened that night; actually, they had a pretty good time. They went to an Italian restaurant on the edges of the Tenderloin where the headwaiter wore a shiny tuxedo and called the girls "Madam" and showed them to a formica-topped table and pulled the table out so they could get into the leatherette booth, and their waiter wore a white jacket and music was piped in and a bottle of wine placed on their table. Mona put an ashtray into her purse before they left. After dinner they went to a night-club on Jones Street that featured strippers and a pair of comedians and the girls drank whiskey sours and Denny and Jack straight whiskey, and during one of the strippers' acts, the drum-beats sharp and explosive, the light on the stage brilliant purple, Mona leaned over close to Jack and pressed her fingers into his thigh and said, "Do you think I could make it as a dancer? I mean, as an exotic dancer?"

"You have a great little body," Jack said to her, and he meant it, still feeling her body in remembrance, looking forward to the time when they would be back in his room alone; watching the stripper with erotic detachment, and glancing over at Mona to see her watching, too, a look of wolfish hunger in her eyes, made fantastic by the purple reflection.

But when they got outside in the sharp air the first thing Mona said was, "What a crummy hole. Jesus."

"I wonder how those old hags keep their jobs," Sue said.

"Call them old?" Denny laughed. "I seen a couple strippers in Seattle a while back that make these chicks look like high-school kids. Man, one of them old bags must of been fifty, her old boobies flopping around; I swear, I wondered why her false teeth didn't pop right out of her mouth, the way she was jumping around up there."

"That's why they use those colored lights," Sue said. She and Denny were arm in arm in front of Jack and Mona. "That way you can't see the wrinkles."

"No, that's not right," Denny said. "The colored lights are part of the act. They're sexy, that's why they use them."

"I don't see anything sexy about colored lights. I bet a strip act would be twice as sexy in bright lights."

"Naw, you just don't understand," Denny said. "It's more mysterious with the colored lights." He turned and walked backward, and asked Jack, "You been to Mexico; you ever see one of them shows down there?"

"A couple," Jack said.

"Strip shows?" Mona asked.

Denny and Jack both laughed. "A lot like that," Jack said. "Only, kind of vulgar."

"What's the big mystery?" Sue wanted to know.

"No mystery," Jack said. "No mystery at all."

"Stag shows," Denny explained. "Chicks stickin bottles in themselves and screwin donkeys, and that kind of crap."

"Good God," Sue said. "Those Mexicans, they'll do anything. How *filthy!*"

"Well, the time I was in Tijuana the chick who took on the donkey was an American. Redhead. About forty. Some guy told me she used to be in the movies."

"Guess what kind of movies," Jack said.

"No, really. She was supposed to have been in Hollywood movies. A starlet or something. She was about forty when I saw her. Me and Tommy had a good thing going down there and we was out of our minds all day every day. That's a funny town. Did you ever see a bullfight?"

Jack said he had not.

"They stink," Denny said.

They went to Denny's room. He got out his whiskey bottle and the glasses, and they each had a drink. Sue was already drunk, and she gagged a little on hers, frowned, and then drank some more.

Denny winked at Jack. "This one really puts it away."

"Lissen," Sue said. She winced. "I could do a goddam better striptease right here and now than them goddam old bitches any day. You want to see?"

She began wriggling and snapping her fingers.

"Turn on the radio," Denny said.

"Oh, really, Sue," Mona sniffed with disgust. She went over and snapped on the radio, and in a few seconds, while everyone stood still and waited, rock and roll music began to play. Sue got into the beat, and jumped up on the bed, her face a counterfeit of abandon, and began rocking back and forth on the springs. Trying to keep the rhythm she reached behind to unsnap her dress.

"Christ," she said, "I can't do it." She sat down, cross-legged. "Goddam it." A commercial played on the radio, and Jack went over and switched to another station. But Sue did not get up and try again.

"They got trick dresses," Denny said.

"Do you want to dance?" Mona asked Jack. "It's dark now, if I turn out the lights."

As they danced, Jack wondered what twists of personality would make a person ashamed to make love in the light, and yet not mind having another couple in the room, as long as it was dark. It seemed so dishonest. But as they danced he kept drinking from his glass and rubbing against her body, and after a while nothing much mattered; he was blurring into a good peaceful sexual drunk.

The rest of the night got more confusing as he got drunker, and he liked that, he wanted to hold on to it; as the liquor pulled him away from himself Mona's body touching his pulled him back in, and he was in a state of increasing amniotic suspension. There were vague things that happened; someone predictably threw up in the bathroom; somebody fell over the corner of the bed; later on, one or both of the girls started crying about something, and eventually Jack mumbled that it was time to go back to his room and took the small moist hand in his and muttered good night to the radio and opened the door into the overbright, eerie, empty hallway and staggered down to his room, fumbled for his key, got the door open and the DO NOT DISTURB sign in place on the outside knob, and pulled her into the room without turning on the light and started kissing and pulling her clothes off and then his, and getting her on the bed, his wet mouth all over her body; dizzy, befuddled, really too tired to make love, but, having intended all evening to make love, bullishly going through with it, deep in his mind the blurry conviction that he would swallow her, licking her body, sinking his teeth into the mound of hair, focusing on nothing but the pure gratification of his urge to investigate her with his tongue and fingers while she thrashed beneath him; finally exhausted by sleepiness lying back and feeling distantly, rosily, the way she mounted him at last and brought him with a snapping vigor back to one long second of daylight before he passed out.

He did not realize until the real light, gray, of morning, that he had slept with Sue instead of Mona, but did not care even then. He was hung over and feeling burnt inside; still erotic, only this time awake, and in the light. He began kissing Sue's breasts and belly until she moaned and put her arms around him and spread her legs for him, her eyes shut, his cracked open, looking down, watching himself enter her, seeing her hips move sleepily, feeling her tighten just at the moment he was ready to come himself, letting go, feeling her body pull it into herself in bucking spasms; and then, with his mind empty, falling asleep still in her for another long doze of contentment.

When he woke up the second time, Sue was awake, sitting up, and staring at him.

"What's the matter?" he asked her.

"God, you're mean-looking," she said. "My head hurts." She pulled the sheet up over her small breasts, and Jack saw bruises on her shoulders, tiny purple marks almost like tattoos. "Mona's going to kill me," she said.

"Why?"

"Don't you know? She's really got the hots for you."

The information pleased Jack. "How about you?" he asked. "Do you have the hots for me, too?"

"Denny's my boy friend," she said. "Oh, God, he'll kill me."

"Listen, what do you think they're doing?"

She made a face. "You dragged me in here."

He got out cigarettes and matches, and they smoked for a few minutes without speaking. Jack wanted some coffee and a drink of whiskey.

"You know," she said. "It's a good thing you showed up. It was getting kind of shitty in there with the three of us. I used to worry about Mona laying there listening to us." She giggled. "I was afraid she'd say something, you know?"

"Why didn't you have her crawl right in with you?"

Sue looked startled. "Are you kidding?"

"Hell no. What's wrong with that?"

"*Three* people?"

"Bad scene?" Jack asked. He was smiling at her obvious discomfort. "Aint you never kissed a chick?"

But Sue did not want to talk about that. "But we couldn't split up; we're best girl friends. So it's a good thing you guys happened to run into each other."

"Didn't Denny try to get rid of her, though?"

"He's so sweet. I bet he's not even fooling around with Mona. I bet they both passed out, too."

"Did you pass out?"

She looked at him oddly. "Sure. Didn't you? We didn't *do* anything, did we?"

"You don't remember?"

"Of course not." She did a bad imitation of a girl trying to remember. "Gee, I don't know. I was so drunk. Did I throw up or anything? My head sure hurts."

Under the covers, Jack put a hand on her hip, but she pushed it away.

"Daylight bother you?"

"Close your eyes. I have to get up and go to the toilet."

When she got back she climbed into the bed after only a moment's hesitation, and snuggled up close. "Don't do anything to me," she said, "I just want to get warm and sleep."

"All right," he said. "I'm fucked out anyway." He giggled, and a sharp pain passed through his forehead.

"You bastard," she said. And a few moments later, "Did you really give Mona ten dollars?"

Jack was surprised. "Did she say that?"

"Yeah, but I think she was lying. Did you?"

"Why, do you want ten dollars, too? Hell, I ought to charge *you*."

Sue was quiet for a long time, and Jack thought she had gone to sleep, but finally she spoke. "I think she's afraid she's going to turn into a prostitute. She gets real scared sometimes."

"What about you?" he asked.

"Give me another cigarette. I'm sorry for her; she's really scared. But I'm not. I don't give a shit what happens to me." She looked at him over her cigarette, now sitting up again, her breasts exposed. "Last night," she said. Her eyes glittered oddly. "That was the first time I ever . . . well, you know? What you did to me. I remember. I never felt like that before. Is it you?"

"No," he said. "Maybe you just got drunk enough to forget about worrying."

"Oh, God," she said. Her face twisted itself into a babyish frown. "You didn't just *screw* me, did you? Didn't you use a rubber or anything?"

"No. You remember, you know I didn't."

"But I'll have a baby. Oh, Jesus Christ."

"Are you going to worry about it?"

"No. The hell with it. Screw me again. What do I care?" She puffed angrily at her cigarette, stubbed it out, and put her arms around him, her mouth on his chest.

"I can't," he said. "I'm gettin old."

"I don't care. Piss on it. I'm just a whore anyway." She began to cry on his chest. He was amazed. She had gone through about ten emotions in ten seconds and now she was bawling. But that was just like a whore, wasn't it? All of the whores Jack had known very well, no matter how cool and businesslike, turned hysterical in the end, went on shit or fell in love with other whores or sat around talking about suicide or pretending they were catching tuberculosis; and suddenly Jack knew that Sue and Mona were going to be just exactly what they were afraid of, and that so far no smart pimps had gotten hold of them and taken them over the bumps, or they'd have been turned out long before. It was just a matter of time, and Mona would learn about getting the money first, and Sue would forget about liking it; the life would soften them, and tears would come easier and love harder. It was depressing. A life of prostitution seemed so drab. But then he had to admit that the girls weren't really cut out for any thing else, except maybe working behind a counter somewhere, going out with small-time sports and fading out into drab mar riages and the bitterness of obscurity. Either way. What difference did it make? He felt a little sorry for them, for Sue, now silent and pretending sleep, and then he corrected himself angrily. To feel sorry for them was to pretend that he was any better, and worse, to pretend that he cared about them. Which was nonsense, both ways. He had whored a little himself, hadn't he? What else could you call boxing? Of course, he had enjoyed boxing for a while, but then the girls would probably enjoy hustling, if only for the outlaw feeling it would give them, and the money and the sense of daring. But of course that never lasted.

There was a knock at the door. Jack got out of bed and went to the door and asked who it was, and Denny answered. Jack opened the door.

"What the hell's goin on?" Denny said angrily; "you took my girl!"

"He didn't lay a hand on me, Denny, honest to God!" Sue said from the bed.

"That's right," Jack said. "I was so goddam drunk I dragged

off the wrong girl. No shit, I was so drunk I just hit the sack. We just woke up."

"Bullshit!" Denny looked betrayed and furious. His face was puffed with sleep, and his eyes red.

"Honest to God, honey."

"Shut up!" Denny turned to Jack. Their faces were only a few inches apart. "Smart bastard! I thought you was my friend!"

Jack made himself relax. "What's the matter, wouldn't Mona come across?"

Denny swung at him and Jack blocked the punch easily.

"Don't start anything you can't finish."

Denny stared at him stupidly. "You're a boxer."

"That's right. It wouldn't be fair."

They stood that way for a few moments. Jack felt the tangle descending on him, and had an urge to tear it away, but he kept control of himself and said, "Listen, don't get upset. We really didn't do anything. Honest, Denny."

Finally the old Denny asserted itself, and he grinned. Jack noticed that his teeth were dirty. "Okay," Denny said. "I'm sorry."

He kept apologizing all day, and it bothered Jack, because he had decided that he preferred Sue to Mona, and he didn't know what to do about it. He did not want to hurt Denny, perhaps because it seemed so easy to do. Denny had changed a lot, he decided.

After two weeks of it Jack was ready to quit. He could feel the tone deserting his body each morning when he got out of bed—a dull ache here, a thickness there—and he was tired, awfully tired, of the way their lives were going: a constant round of movies, dinners, long afternoons in the poolhall or across the bay at the track; bouts of lovemaking that by their very sameness destroyed any desire in him to make them different, coupled—practically glued—to Mona, whose only contribution to the act was to hook her legs around his and give her hips an occasional jerky thrust; who, during the few times he tried to investigate her body with his mouth, cried out in frozen anxiety and pushed his head away, leaving him with the choice of either quitting entirely or going ahead with what now seemed so unattractive; thinking, magnifying, Sue's response to their one night together, until at last his mind was making a distinction between what he was doing with Mona and what he wanted to do with Sue, as the difference between satisfying an itch and making a discovery. He had never thought about sex in quite that way, and it gave focus to an otherwise endlessly empty round of days, and kept him involved with Denny and the girls when otherwise he might have checked out of the hotel and left them, gone off and done the serious thinking he had come to San Francisco to do in the first place—or so he sometimes thought.

To live intimately with any person, however, is to pursue understanding, and after two weeks Jack felt that he knew more about Mona than there was to her, and since he was not going to release any of the hidden parts of himself to her, there were not even the satisfactions of being understood. Mona was a crafty girl but she was not intelligent in any real way; she had a line of patter to cover almost any situation she could expect, but when the unusual happened, she hid quickly behind a barrier of sarcasm, or a comically old-fashioned morality.

She might come home from an afternoon of movies and shopping on Jack's money, to find him on the bed naked, a can of beer in his hand, reading *Ring Magazine*. Nudity offended her.

"My God," she would say, standing there with an armload of packages, "were you born in a barn or something?"

Jack would not bother to reply, and she would tap her foot angrily for a moment, and then begin undoing her packages.

"Look what I got on sale at the City of Paris," holding up a forty-dollar cashmere sweater or a cocktail dress.

"Try it on," Jack would suggest.

"Don't you even care what it cost me?"

"I gave you a hundred, you spent it all."

Triumphantly, she would waggle a handful of bills in front

of his eyes. "I did not! I've still got eighteen-fifty left for
tomorrow!"

"Try it on."

"Close your eyes, now."

"Oh, Christ."

She would flounce into the bathroom to try on her new
clothes, shoes, gloves, or whatever, and then make an entrance.
Jack would stare at her. "That's very nice on you," he would say
without conviction.

"You don't like it. Screw you."

She was right; he didn't like it, or her. He did not think she
looked good in anything. On the other hand, he thought—Sue
looked better and better every day. He wanted her. He did not
know why he did nothing about it. He wondered why Sue herself
did nothing about it. Although they were friendly, Sue made a
point of never being alone with him, or giving him secret looks,
or even addressing remarks at him.

One morning he woke up to see Mona sitting in the chair by
the window, crying into her handkerchief.

"What's the matter?"

"Oh, never mind." She was wearing only a slip, and her
long hair was hanging down in front. Without makeup, her face
looked plain and childlike, but her mouth was twisted in bitterness. "You'll kick me out," she said.

"Come on, what is it?"

She admitted tearfully that her period had begun. "You won't
let me stay with you now. I'll smell bad for a week and you
won't be able to make me." She tossed her hair back angrily,
and Jack saw the shine of tears on her cheeks. "Goddam being
a woman! It's *shitty!*"

Jack had never thought of it that way. Of course it was
shitty, having to go through the bleeding and cramps, and have
the babies or worry about having them; but that was the nature
of things, and he could not, even with this small insight, really
feel sorry for her. But he said, "No, now listen, don't worry."

But she did have a right to worry, because all that was holding them together was their need to use each other. Her period was the same as if he ran out of money. So she had a right to some reassurance, because he did not really want to be rid of her. This surprised him a little. He was very nice to her all day, but as if to test him, she was moody, spiteful, and sullen. That night she had a sick headache and bad cramps, and the others went out without her. They went to a movie, and afterward, Sue went back to her room alone. Jack and Denny stopped in a small bar.

"Listen, I'm running out of bread," Denny told him. "I got about twenty-five left. I don't know where it goes."

"I'm getting a little short myself," Jack said.

Denny drank a shot of whiskey and followed it with half a glass of beer. He wiped his mouth. "Why don't we dump the chicks and go over to the East Bay? I know a liquor store we can score off of, down in the spade part of town. The cat has about fifteen hundred in a floor safe in the back, where there's a little desk in a hallway between the front of the store and the place he keeps his cases. The clerks all know the combination. All we got to do is go in there late when the clerk's sittin at the desk eatin, scare hell out of him, and get him to open the safe."

"I haven't done anything like that in a long time," Jack said.

"We got to get money someplace," Denny said. "Lissen, Tommy cased this one himself before he went to Mexico; we were gonna knock the place over just the two of us, because you know there wasn't enough for everybody, and it'd only take a couple guys to pull off. Tommy went into the joint to pick up a pint or something, and there wasn't anybody in the store, and like he was gonna just go around the counter and tap out the till, when he sees this curtain at the back, so he goes back there and pulls the curtain back, and there's this sandwich and thermos jug on a table, and this guy comin up from way in the back, and Tommy hears a toilet back there flushin, and the guy comes runnin up with a magazine in his hand, but not quick enough, cause Tommy sees under the table the open door to the safe, one of those round countersunk jobs. So he gets his pint and cuts out. But we never did get around to it. He had to take off for Mexico. But we could do it. It's a lockup."

Jack was on the verge of saying, "All right, let's do it," but something stopped him; not fear, certainly not the illegality—he had done much worse things—but perhaps the very cheapness of it. Robbing a liquor store, was that what he was cut out for? He had come to the city to think, and now he was being offered a proposition that again would make thinking unnecessary—but it all seemed so endlessly dull; an infinite series of holdups, parties, girls, bad dinners, and worse hotel rooms—he could not see any difference between this and working for a living, and with working there was not that nagging anxiety about being braced by the police. Jack had known a lot of people who stole for a living because they were bitter, and many who stole almost sexually, getting a secret charge out of the act. And Denny. He did not know why Denny was a thief, unless it was just habit.

"Why don't you get a job?" he asked.

Denny looked at him strangely. "Fuck that shit," he said. "Is that what you're worryin about?"

"Not really," Jack said.

"Lissen, man, I seen enough fuggin shit to last me the rest of my fuggin life. I seen guys get killed for nothin, I mean *nothin*, man. Fuck that shit."

"Were you in the Korean war?"

"I was in the Third Marines, man, me and Dale. Remember Dale Phipps? He's still in. He's a staff sergeant now, I think. Man, what a bunch of shit that was. You know what that cocksucker did? We was on patrol him and me and we bust into this little hut. It really stunk in there, an the only light was from this greasy dish or somethin, and there was an old man sittin in the corner and this gook officer on top of this woman in the corner, on some straw or somethin, an they all look up scared when we bust in, the officer's got his pants down, you know, and Dale sees all this and lets out a laugh and shoots the officer right in the forehead, man, the back of his head spatters all over the woman's face and she lets out a yell and Dale plugs her, too, in the chest, and then he turns and shoots the old man. Goddam, I never seen nothin like it; just about one second and all three dead, laying there, and Dale turns to me and laughs and says, 'How come you didn't shoot anybody?' and I says, 'Jesus Christ, Phipps, what the fuck are you doin?' and he gets a mean look on his face and yells at me, 'I'll kill you too, you motherfucker, if you tell on me!' an we got the hell out of there, an I asked him later what the fuck he shot all those people for, hell, the gook was on our side, you know, and he grins and says, 'What the fuck difference does it make?'"

Denny squirmed uncomfortably, and scratched his cheek. "He shot them because he got the chance to, you know? Man, I used to dream about it. That crazy bastard. He would of killed me, too, and we was partners."

But the pustule had burst now, and Denny laughed. "But that aint why I turned thief. It scared the shit out of me, but so did the whole goddam war. It's funny, at the time it didn't seem *wrong*, or anything, just, well, like he went crazy, and I was scared of bein hooked up with a crazy man. Lots of guys went crazy. I know one guy, there was another guy with the same name as he had who got killed, and this guy didn't find out about it, see, but the Corps sent his mother a telegram sayin he got killed in action, and he finds out about *that*, see, about a month later, and so he knows this *other* guy with the same name was killed, and his mother was tryin to collect on his insurance, and man, he just plain flipped out. He run out and tried to get himself killed, but his sergeant coldcocked him and sent him to the hospital. I guess he got a discharge. I met Tommy when I was gettin out, and we hooked up together. He had some great plans."

Denny looked sad, now. "That's what I ought to do. Run down to Mexico and find him. He run out on me, the bastard." His eyes were intense, almost glassy. "We got to get some money, man. We just got to."

"Why don't you hold up the joint alone? I don't want to go. Fuck it."

"What's the matter? Listen, I know a cat in Oakland'll sell us a couple guns, and we can steal a car. Take this one quick and we both head for Mexico. Ditch these goddam broads. I'm burnt out on Sue, anyway. She's the worst lay I ever had in my life."

"No," Jack said. "I'm sick of fooling around. I'm not going on any holdup."

Denny was puzzled. "Why not? You got to."

"No, I'm not."

"Yes you are."

"You don't own a piece of me, buddy. You ran out of money, that's your tough shit. I can't help you."

It soaked in. "You're just like that son of a bitch Tommy," Denny said. "He run out on me. Now you're runnin out on me."

Jack was half-tempted to say okay and go on the robbery, just to please Denny, who looked so offended and angry. But that was no way to run his life. It was disgusting; Denny was acting as if they had sworn themselves to blood-brotherhood.

"I'm not runnin out," Jack said. "I just don't want to go. I want to think. Something's wrong." He got up. "I'm going back to the hotel."

He was half-undressed when Denny showed up. He opened the door a crack and Denny pushed his way into the room.

"Shh," Jack said. "Mona's sacked out."

Denny was in the middle of the room, in a near-crouch. Jack looked at him curiously.

"What's eatin you?" Then he saw the knife in Denny's hand, saw it just in time to ready himself as Denny's thrust came. Everything fell away. Jack's left hand snaked out, not shying from the open blade, and he caught Denny by the wrist and with his right hit Denny sharply on the ear and then jerked him down, letting go as Denny was falling to chop him on the exposed neck, missing the neck but hitting the jawbone below the ear, hearing and feeling the snapping bone under his hand. Denny gave a grunt and a sudden sharp bark of anguish; and as quickly as the murder had filled Jack it drained away, leaving him standing there over the helpless man at his feet, his body beginning to quiver in reaction. Even now he could not help thinking: I'm like a machine, push the button and I act. I could have taken the knife away from him without all this. I don't even know what's the matter with him. But he pushed the wrong button and here we are, and I might have killed him. He could not have hurt me, and I could have killed him.

"What's going on?" Mona said. She was sitting up in bed. "What happened to him?"

"Never mind," Jack said. He kneeled down beside Denny. Blood was pouring out of his mouth and nose, and he looked up at Jack with stiff pain in his eyes. He tried to speak. Nothing came out of his mouth but a bubbling noise. The knife, a six-inch bone-handled Case, lay on the carpet, its well-honed blade face up. The last time Jack had seen the knife had been a few days before, when Denny had been cleaning his fingernails with the smaller blade. He picked it up and folded the blade into the handle and put it into his pocket.

"Are you all right?" he asked Denny. He knew he had betrayed Denny and Denny had come to knife him for it. He understood this, although he could not understand why, or why he felt bad about it. Denny's eyes were clear. They looked at each other. Jack had never seen such a look of pure intelligence in Denny's eyes before. It was as if he knew something now that Jack would never understand. But the look faded into pained puzzlement and Denny moaned, the blood thick and black in his mouth.

"All right," Jack said. He got Denny to his feet and took him over and sat him in the chair by the window, on top of a pile of Mona's clothes. Denny sat there in a stupor, blood spattered all over him and still flowing from his nose and the corners of his mouth. His jaw hung slightly open. Jack started to get dressed again, and Mona jumped out of bed, naked except for underpants, and went into the bathroom. She came back out with a wet washcloth, and bent down over Denny.

"Hold your head back," she said to him. She began dabbing at his nose and mouth. The cold touch of the washcloth must have revived him slightly, because he growled deep in his throat, pushed Mona aside, and came at Jack in a crouch. Without thinking, Jack clipped him on the point of the chin, and he went down heavily, his head bumping against Jack's knees and then down onto the floor.

"Get dressed," Jack said to Mona. He got down and went through Denny's pockets, removing his wallet and money. When Mona finished dressing, they carried Denny back to his own room. Sue was asleep, and they woke her up, got her out of the bed, and put Denny on it. He was still unconscious. Sue started cursing Jack, her eyes burning with hatred. Mona took her out of the room. Jack got on the telephone and called the clerk at the desk and told him that Denny had been mugged on the street and made it to his room and passed out, and to call a doctor. The clerk said he had seen Denny come in and he had looked all right, and Jack told him to wait a minute, and then went down to the lobby and gave the clerk a twenty-dollar bill.

"You don't have a mark on you," the clerk said with a grin. He was a tall, thin man with one drooping eyelid, and when he smiled, his teeth showed long and yellow. He reached for the jack on the switchboard.

"I tell you, he got rolled. You tell it that way, too. You saw him come in, and then you called the doctor. Right?"

"Anything you say, hotshot."

The next morning Jack told Sue to clear out. She had gone back and slept in her own room after the doctor had Denny taken away, and Jack went there to tell her.

"He hasn't got any more money, and he'll be in the hospital for quite a while," he told her. "So you better go back where you came from."

"You bastard," she said. "I really hate you. You didn't have to do that. You're a boxer."

"Well, you can stick around if you want," he said. "But on your own money."

He went back to Mona. She had done a strange thing the night before, after everything was all over and they were in bed. She had kissed him and said, "You're really a killer, aren't you."

He said nothing. He felt odd. It had been so quick, so thoughtless, and so stupid. He was not paying much attention to Mona, or what she was doing.

"You're a real man," she murmured; "You're what I want, I always knew it, I love you. I truly love you." She pulled the covers back and said, "This is what you want me to do, isn't it?" But it was no use. Even for this, Jack could not rouse himself, and Mona seemed, if anything, pleased. She stopped trying after a while, and lit a cigarette.

"I'm glad we're rid of Sue," she said. "That's good. They been holding us back. Now we can do stuff. I always thought Denny was a dumb guy anyway, and I'm sick of that Sue. She's so dumb. She had eyes for you. She told me what you did that night she came in here with you. I was so mad. I could have killed you for it. But I guess that's when I found out I loved you. She was so mad when you lied to Denny. She hates him. I bet she's glad you beat him up. He's so silly sometimes. All he wants to do is drink and lay around. He's got no ambitions at all. Let's go to Hollywood or Las Vegas or something. I really want to get out of this dumb town. I always used to think San Francisco was such a groovy place. We came down here once when we were supposed to be in a cabin at Rio Nido and spent two days running around and I never saw anything like it, so when we took off we came here. But it's so dumb after a while, don't you think? I want to go to Hollywood. We could get an apartment. Not another crummy hotel room. A nice apartment in one of those big motels where they have a swimming pool and bars and everything, and I can go out and take sunbaths. San Francisco is so cold all the time. We could even buy a car and go racing around and go down to the beach and everything. Maybe we could go to Mexico. Do you want to go to Mexico?"

She poked him. "Do you?"

"Huh?"

"Want to go to Mexico. We could see a bullfight and everything."

"Where do we get all this money?"

She wrinkled her nose. "Money. You can get money. You can go out and box some more, can't you?"

She snuggled down next to him. "Oh, we can have such a great time."

The next morning, after he had told Sue to leave, he settled down in the room with a bottle of whiskey and started drinking. He wanted to think. Mona was fussing around in the room, the radio on to a rock-and-roll station, and she began to bother him. He couldn't get any thinking done. Finally he asked her to go out and leave him alone.

"Are you going to give me any money?"

He handed her a twenty.

She looked at it distastefully. "That's not enough to do anything with."

"Go to a movie."

"I'm sick of movies. You're drinking too much. When are we going to leave?"

"Go on, get the fuck out of here."

"Don't you swear at me."

"Get out of here before I knock you on your ass."

She stared at him murderously. "Don't you talk to me like that!"

He took another drink, and continued to stare out the window.

"I hate you!" She stamped out and slammed the door. After a moment, Jack got up and turned off the radio, and then went back to staring out the window.

He drank all morning and all afternoon. The whiskey was not leading him anywhere. He kept drinking it just to keep from going backward. Everything seemed quite clear except the first step. He did not know what to do first. He was buried inside his skin, bones, and nerves, and he would have to get out of there if he was to understand his pain. If it was pain. He knew people suffered agony, and he wondered if what he felt was agony. It did not seem like the descriptions of agony. He wondered if it wasn't just self-pity again. At the orphanage they had gone to religious services every Sunday morning in the dining room and listened to different preachers tell them that God loved them especially because they were orphans and that they had a hard lot in life, but the hardness of their lot gave them a precious opportunity to be particularly saintly in their conduct, to be obedient, to be moral, without having placed in front of them the temptations toward sin that come to children who have sinful parents around them, tempting them away from the path of goodness by their bad example; how they, the children of the orphanage, were the results of the sins of their fathers, and yet at the same time had this great opportunity to lead blameless uncontaminated lives of purity and virtue; to obey the rules and be the especially beloved of Jesus Christ, who Himself disowned His own Mother and made Himself into an orphan, so to speak; and how they, the children of the orphanage, were actually better off and luckier than the children on the outside, because in the absence of the love of parents and the misguided behavior of parents, they could come directly to the love of Jesus Christ and therefore the love of God Himself under the direction of the orphanage administration. But it did not take much thinking on their part to see that if Jesus Christ and God approved of the administration of the orphanage, in fact preferred it to home and parents, then they were the enemies of the orphanage children because if that hollow cavity in their souls was the love of God then God was the ultimate murderer of love.

Because the children of the orphanage were taught, all week long every week of their lives, that the difference between good and evil, right and wrong, was purely a question of feeling: if it felt good, it was bad, if it felt bad, it was good. The food at the orphanage did not taste very good, and the children were taught, told, that this food, this unappetizing oatmeal or dish of prunes or boiled-to-death vegetable, was nourishing and good for them and would make them strong and capable of much hard work; and that the candy they got from the ladies who visited was at once a treasure and a sin, because while the candy tasted beautiful, it did them no good and after they ate their candy and thanked the ladies, they had to go in and brush their teeth and get rid of the last traces of flavor, because candy, that delicious rarity, rotted everything it touched. And they were told that presents were not good, because presents were possessions, and possessions were fought over and caused bad feeling, not that the authorities would take their presents away from them, only that the authorities had a way of making the children feel guilty about possessing them. And of course the pleasures of the body—running, jumping, laughing, masturbating—were sins, particularly the last, but all the others were too because they disrupted the routine, were contagious and threw things off schedule, and were not to be permitted except under certain well-defined circumstances. And Jack could remember particularly the feeling of near-rage at being told that for the next hour they could go out into the yard and have fun and jump and run and play, and remembered his desire to stand stock still and refuse to enjoy himself. And then, unable to control himself, running, skylarking a little desperately, a knot of anything but joy in the center of him, under the approving eyes of the authorities. And work, they were taught that work was good, especially hard work, and the harder the work the better it was, their bodies screaming to them that this was a *lie*, it was all a terrible, God-originated, filthy lie, a monstrous attempt to keep them from screaming out their rage and anguish and murdering the authorities. But they did not, because they knew that nobody, not the ministers, not the ladies who visited, and least of all the authorities themselves, believed it, any of it, because they did not act as if they believed it. They acted as if they believed only one thing: that force and force alone governed. And this the children believed too, in their hearts, and most of them dreamed of the time when the power of force would be in their hands.

The trouble was, it was intangible. It was not in the hands of anyone. While Jack had been there, most of the boys had blamed the man who was in charge of the orphanage as the center of power; they had believed that all that happened to them and all that did not happen to them originated with this one tall, heavy white-haired man. But then one day, during the middle of Jack's wing's play period, they saw the man walking across the yard, his hands behind his back, his head tilted forward—the way he always walked when he was angry and determined—saw him suddenly stop and look straight up in the sky and give a grunt and fall backward, saw him fall with a thump onto the frozen ground and saw him carted away, and learned the next day that what they had seen was the death of this man, taken by a heart attack and dead before they got him indoors and got his clothes off. And that night all the boys in Jack's wing nourished a secret joy at the man's death and many of them thought in their hearts that they would be set free now that the center of power was gone, or at the very least that their lives would change in some magnificent way and they would be free at last of the man's mechanical tyranny; some of them even thought that candy would be passed out to them. But they learned. Very quickly there was another administrative head to the orphanage and he was different in appearance only. So it was an intangible; not a man, a set of rules. It would not even do any good to steal the rules away from the office and burn them, because there wasn't even a book in which the rules were kept. It was just that the authorities knew the rules. You could kill them all and the rules would remain. This was the great virtue of rules, they were told in somewhat different context.

But, and this is what puzzled Jack now, once you grow out of this, once you learn that it is all nonsense, that what you thought as a child was nothing more than the excuses of self-pity, what did you replace it with? You had a life, and you were not content with it; where did you aim it?

The whole idea of a good life was silly. Because there was no such thing as good and bad, or good and evil. Not the orphanage way, with good equaling the dull and painful and stupid, and evil the bright and delicious and explosive; and certainly not the simple reverse of this—it would be all very well to live purely to have fun, but what did you do after you had had all the fun you wanted? It would be like aiming your whole life at getting a sandwich, and then getting it, eating it, and having nothing left. It was just as stupid to spend your whole life avoiding pain, because you could see right away that this would logically mean locking yourself up in a room and letting the authorities take over, bring your food, take away your excrement; even if the authorities provided entertainment for the senses, you would still be a prisoner. . . .

It seemed so bleak. He swallowed a sip of the warmish whiskey and continued to stare out the window. The quality of the light had been changing and now everyone on the street seemed identical. He could see them out there, obsessed not with their destinies but by some simple problem of today: to do a piece of business, to finish shopping, to catch a bus, to bum a cigarette. Nothing important, except to themselves. The only difference is that I am in here, and they are out there. What do we want?

He searched his mind very carefully, and could find nothing he wanted. It seemed as if he had never wanted anything in his whole life. But that was not true. As a kid he had wanted lots of things. In the orphanage it had been simple. When he had wanted something, he took it. If he got caught, he accepted his punishment. He had always known that what he had wanted most was freedom, escape from the orphanage, and when he was ready, he escaped. That was all. Then he no longer wanted his freedom, because he had it.

In Portland, before they threw him into reform school, he had wanted things, too. Very simple things, that you could buy with money. Such as whiskey. Or women. A fast car. Well, he had all those things now, except the fast car, and he did not want any of them. No, that was not true. He had them, and he didn't want to be without them, but they didn't work. They didn't make him feel better. They just helped him stay alive.

For a moment he felt a drifting nausea as his mind helplessly moved toward the idea of suicide. He steadied himself and faced it, as he had known all the time he must: I am going to die. Why not now? He felt cold and sick. Well, why not? What the fuck have I got to live for?

The whiskey bottle was in his hand, and he lifted it, holding it up before his eyes. Do I want some of this? Do I want another drink? Suddenly it was very important to know. If he did not want a drink, he did not want anything. If he did not want anything, he might as well die. Because he was already dead.

"Bullshit," he said aloud. "Bullshit. I'm just in a bad mood." He tilted the bottle to his mouth and drank, his eyes closed.

He ran out of whiskey about six in the evening, and started to get up to go after some more. But he could not move. He was on the bed and he could not find the right nerves to activate to swing himself off the bed. He decided to take a nap instead. He kept his grip on the neck of the empty fifth as an anchor, and began to drift off into dizzy dreams, among them a dream in which the girls came into the room and hovered over him, their faces white and cruel, and then vanished before he could sit up. Later on, when he awakened, he remembered that dream and checked his pockets and knew it had been real. He was still groggy and drunk, and it all seemed very funny to him. The girls had gotten away with more than a hundred dollars. But he had more stashed in the closet, the last of the money Castelli had saved for him, and he got it all out and put it in his pocket and went down and bought three fifths of Canadian Club and carried them back to the room. He was not hungry, but he got it into his head somehow that he would like a piece of ass, and he decided to sit there on the edge of the bed and wait for Mona to come back. Very slowly he undid the first bottle and took a drink. He remembered how bad he had felt earlier in the day, and how he had secretly known, all the time he had been thinking those bad silly angry thoughts, that sooner or later he would feel better. He giggled to himself. Every time it happened he got drunk and felt better. Even the hangovers were good, because they made him think clearly but without agony. He wanted Mona. That was a good thing.

He knew she would be back; the room was still littered with her things. When she came back he was going to fuck hell out of her and throw her out. He felt cruel and mean. He would not let her take her stuff. He was going to tell her it was his stuff, since he had paid for most of it, and he was going to keep it for the next two-bit whore he shacked up with. That was a laugh. Mona was so prudish. To call her a whore was so accurate; the burr would hit the nerve and she would screech and hit him. He wouldn't mind. He would laugh at her and rip off her clothes and screw her once again, and then throw her out in the hall naked. That would be a good lesson for her. And maybe she would finally be a good lay if he could just get her mad enough to thrash around.

But it palled; everything finally got old if you dreamed about it too much; everything but drinking, and with drinking you could always throw up and start over. Eventually, he passed out.

He awakened in the middle of the morning. Mona was not there, but her junk was still littered all over the place. He took a drink of whiskey and just made it into the bathroom in time to throw up. He felt light and empty, but there was only one thing to do; get another shot of whiskey into himself and keep it down. He finally made it, sitting very still to keep the nausea from bulging up into his throat, and in a few minutes he knew he would be all right. He stayed on the bed all day, drinking. His mind was utterly empty. Mona unlocked the door once and stuck her head in, and when she saw him on the bed the head disappeared. Jack did not even bother to wave.

A long time later, Jack told Billy Lancing all about what finally happened:

"I had been drinking for so long and not eating that everything was hollow and weird; I felt like some kind of crazy mystic who keeps seeing visions that his eyes can't remember; I wasn't really drunk any more after the third day, I was just living on alcohol and pissing pure sugar, and the whole world was sharp and blurred at the same time. I remember one of Mona's comic books was on the floor by the bed and I sat there looking down at the cover. It had a picture of Batman and Robin on it, grappling with some dirty thugs on a city street at night, the most weirdly beautiful city I'd ever seen in my life. Batman was saying, 'This looks like The Joker's handiwork!' and one of the thugs was saying, 'What the!' and Robin was saying, 'Somebody wants us out of the way!' and I was sitting there trying to figure out why all these beautiful people were arguing, even though everything they said made perfect sense to me. The comic book was upside down and so I was looking at the picture backwards, but that made it even more real, and I'd heard somewhere that we really see things upside down and then our mind turns them right side up, and I think I was trying to right everything in my mind when they knocked at the door. It was a terrible effort, and burned up a lot of my whiskey.

"I got up and stood in the middle of the room, trying to swing the door around so it would be upside down and she would come in walking on the ceiling with her skirt around her ears, and said something like, 'Come on the fuck in,' and waited a second and then the door exploded, just blew up in front of my eyes, and two guys came running in waving guns. I thought for one second that Mona had hired a couple of redhots to come and take the rest of my money and get her stuff, so I grinned at the guys and said, 'Hi, fellas.' They saw me standing there naked and put their guns back. When I saw the belt holsters I knew they were cops and so I headed out the door, but one of them got me by the ankle and I went down, out in the hall. A man and woman were coming down the corridor, and I looked up at them and they looked down at me, and I said as clearly as I could, 'Excuse me,' but it must have come out wrong and the woman screamed and the man did a funny thing; he was a mousy-lookin little guy with a mustache, I figure he must have brought the woman there to the hotel for a little side action, anyway, he wrinkled his little mouse nose at me, and stuck out his foot and kicked me on the shoulder. Then they both turned and went fast down the hall, and the cops dragged me back to my room, made me get dressed, handcuffed me, and took me down to the Hall of Justice. Just as we were coming out of my room, the bigger of the cops put his hand on my shoulder and asked me if I wanted another drink, and I said yes, and he went back and got one of my bottles and I took a long one, and then he took one, put the bottle back, and said to me, 'Boy, we're going to kill you.'

"I felt glad. I really liked that cop. He told me the truth, that cop did, and I really liked him for it. I wanted to reach out and kiss him, or at least shake his hand. He was a good cop."

NINE

They took Jack down to the old Hall of Justice on Kearny Street and put him into one of the cells in the city prison. When they booked him down at the desk several hours later he was still sleepy and half-drunk, and beginning to feel the early tremors of a long illness. But even so, he heard the list of charges and began to understand that something had actually happened and he was not having a dream. He was not sure what the specific charges were but he knew there were a lot of them, all bearing different numbers from the penal code. What made it real for him was the way everyone was so distant and polite. He felt a gush of warmth for the detectives, the desk man, the deputies. When they took him back to his cell he fell asleep thinking about how nice everyone was.

The next morning in Municipal Court he found out what the

charges were. By this time he was really sick; hung over, his arms and legs hollow, his belly a hard knot, his face burning with fever. The assistant district attorney, a large man in a brown suit, with reddish hair and a peaked, sunburned face, read out the charges in a droning yet somehow angry voice, standing at his table, holding the sheet of lined onionskin paper up before his eyes, telling Jack and the rest of the court that Jack was charged with statutory rape, resisting arrest, drunk and disorderly, and theft. In the same bored angry monotone he said, "We have a foreign warrant on him, too, your Honor."

"Well, let's hear it, let's hear it."

"This just came in this morning, your Honor; it's a warrant for kidnap, Balboa County. If it hadn't come in on time I was going to ask you to hold him on the local charges or bind him over to Superior Court."

Jack and the judge looked at each other for a moment, and then the judge shook his head slowly. "Hold for Balboa County," he said, writing on his disposition sheet. Jack had never been in Balboa County in his life; but he did not think it was unusual. The way he felt, nothing was mysterious. Everything seemed rational. If they had taken him out and hanged him in public he would not have been surprised, and if they had just let him go, he still would not have been surprised. They took him back to his cell and he went back to sleep. He woke up several times during the day with attacks of diarrhea, and although he was nauseated he could not manage to vomit. He felt lucky to be able to sleep.

Late that afternoon two detectives came and got him and drove him up to Balboa County. The two detectives sat in the front of the big black-and-white station wagon and Jack sat in the back. They had welded steel eyelets to the floor in back, and Jack wore leg chains that were fastened to the eyelets. Back of his head there was a grill of steel mesh, and each of his hands was outstretched and handcuffed to this grill. The two detectives were very nice to Jack, spoke to him, and let him smoke. The one who was not driving had to hold Jack's cigarette for him, turned halfway around in the seat, but he said he didn't mind. Both detectives said they were sorry about having to truss him up like that but it was regulations. "Some of your felonies," the one who was not driving said, "we just use the cuffs; but on your capital crimes we got to use the leg chains, too."

"You know, though," the driver said, "it cuts both ways. I mean, you're pretty safe all locked up like that. A couple of our guys were haulin a prisoner just like you are, I think the guy cut up his wife and killed her or somethin, and the guy drivin was goin like a bat out of hell and this dumb fuckin farmer comes puttin out of a side road, blind, and whacks right into the side of the vehicle and knocked it ass-endways, it goes off the highway, turns over a couple of times and ends up on its top. The guy drivin held on to the steerin wheel and he was okay but the guy sittin next to him got throwed out and spilled his brains all over the street; caved in his head like a punkin; but the prisoner, why, he was just sittin there as pretty as you please, upside down, all chained in, protected, not a scratch on him, yellin his head off to get him out of there before the fuggin thing blew up. You never saw anything like it."

The other one grinned back at Jack. "So we got these safety belts now"—he held up the end of a seat belt and waggled it at Jack—"but piss on em."

"I got mine on," the driver said. "You never know."

The other one said, "How the hell can I administer to the prisoner's needs if I'm strapped in? I'd have to strap in and then unstrap every ten minutes."

"It's your ass," the driver said. "You're the one in the ninety-percent seat."

"Seventy-percent seat," the other corrected.

At the county jail, someone noticed Jack's fever and called a doctor, and Jack was taken to the county hospital. They had no prison ward at the hospital, so he was placed in a private room with wire mesh over the windows. The door was locked and a policeman was stationed outside the room. Jack was sick for almost two weeks, in a near-delirium, but he did not speak once during that entire time, not even to the doctors. His case was diagnosed as a bad attack of influenza.

When he had been drunk, everything had seemed rational; now nothing did. He did not know why he had been arrested. He could not understand why he had been charged with kidnaping and brought to this place. He could not understand why he was sick. At one point he was certain he was going to die. His body temperature kept dropping, and got as low as 97, and he felt cold inside, as if the life was deserting his cells and soon there would be nothing left of him but meat. In his delirium he thought that if he died they would prop his corpse up at the table in the courtroom and still go through the motions of the trial, calling witnesses Jack had never seen in his life to testify to things he had never done, and in the end the jury would bring in a verdict of guilty and his corpse would be taken to the gas chamber and gassed, and then it would be taken out and buried; and through all this he would be floating above it, watching, listening, trying to understand what was happening to his meat and bones, to the body he used to inhabit; and the corpse would just sit there, dead, in its chair, rotting, beginning to stink, everyone else in the courtroom pretending that the corpse did not stink, and he even saw his eyes shrivel, and finally drop out of their dead sockets and roll down onto the floor, and saw an attendant come over and pick them up and put them into his pocket, and the eyeless corpse just sat there, getting smaller and yellower as the trial droned on, and finally, when they carted it off to the gas chamber, it was so small and so light that one man carried it under his arm like a doll, and how tiny it looked in that big chair, eyeless, toothless, the nose half eaten away with decay, as the tiny octagonal room filled with the mists of cyanide gas and the corpse got soggy with it and began to fall to pieces so that several men had to pull it away from the chair in fragments and dump the fragments into a bag, and it all kept coming apart in their fingers, but they did not mind, they were even telling jokes to each other and laughing as the bits of soggy flesh and rotting bone stuck to their fingers and they had to wipe their hands off continually, stuffing the bag full and joking about the odor; while he, Jack, his spirit, hovered over them and watched and refused to speak. It was obscene, he knew this, but it did not move him.

He even dreamed that Denny accused him and he was being tried for his betrayal of Denny, and Denny was saying to him, yes, you betrayed me, you are my friend and you refused it, but Jack said, no, you don't have any right to move into my body and take part of me as yours, but Denny said, yes, of course, I have every right to do that, you are my friend, I have a right to your body and your mind, to all of you, because I love you and need you, and everyone has this right, to take love away from each other and inhabit one another's souls, but Jack said, no, no, I am my own body and soul and you are not part of me, you have no right, but Denny said, you don't understand, we all have this right to each other, and no man is entitled to privacy because your privacy is my murder, don't you see that yet, don't you understand that just by being alive you are open to me, and I to you? Don't you understand now? And Jack said no, he kept saying no, not to Denny because Denny was gone by this time, taken off to the hospital himself, and Jack was alone, not suffering, free of Denny; convicted but free. He knew that he could not afford to hate Denny, because that would be the same, that would be giving himself up to him. But he was gone, and with an incredible sense of sadness, Jack realized he would never see Denny again, and he felt something shred away and dissipate, something important; not Denny, something important, some part of himself, vanishing.

But eventually he got better, and they took him back to the county jail, and the day after that he was brought in for a conference with the District Attorney.

His name was Forbes and he was a very fat man, large, big-boned, without any of the weaknesses of self-indulgent fat, but with the strength of pure bigness, a powerful barrel of a man, whose heavy florid face was pleasant rather than jolly, his mouth sensual but not cruel, and his eyes hard and alive and humorous.

1 2 3

When Jack sat down across the desk from Forbes he knew right away that there was going to be no phony stuff; in other circumstances, Jack probably would have liked him.

Forbes had a Manila folder in front of him, and he flipped it open and read silently for a moment. "I don't believe a word of this," he said to Jack. "But don't think I won't try you on it. If I have to, I will. Are you going to cooperate?"

"No," Jack said. He wanted a look at the papers in the folder, but he refused the idea of asking.

"I didn't think you would. You look like a tough boy. I don't have to tell you not to get tough around here. We have your record from Oregon, so we know you know how things go. You're no cherry. Will you make a statement?"

"No," Jack said, but the big man had already heaved himself up out of his chair and gone over to the door behind Jack, opened it, and called out, "Myra, would you come in here, please?" When he got back to his desk and settled, he said to Jack, "Talk loud, she's kind of deef." The woman, about fifty, with brightly dyed red hair and a petrified face, came into the room and sat in a chair by the window. She had a notebook and a pencil ready, and she twitched a smile at Jack and said loudly, "All right, dearie."

District Attorney Forbes began asking questions, and the woman began writing; after each question, both of them would pause and wait for Jack to answer, and when he did not, the District Attorney would say, "Refuses to answer," and go on to the next question. They were ridiculous; they had nothing to do with Jack. From the import of the questions, Jack understood that he was supposed to have been in Balboa County about six weeks before, in a car, to have picked up Mona and Sue in front of the Ritz Theater at gunpoint—forced them into the car with a threat of bodily harm if they did not comply—driven the pair of them to San Francisco, and installed them in the hotel. He was supposed to have threatened them by saying he would have them arrested as prostitutes if they did not stay, and he was supposed to have forced them to perform acts of a sexual nature, and to have lived with Mona in a state of unlawful carnal co-habitation. Further, a wallet was found in his possession, belonging to someone named Dennis Mellon; and Jack was asked to explain this, and to explain the fact that Mr. Mellon was at present in the University of California hospital in San Francisco, suffering from multiple fractures of the jaw. Jack was also asked to explain why he assaulted two police officers who had come to his room to question him. He answered no questions, and explained nothing. He also refused to sign a statement denying everything. The woman went out of the room, and District Attorney Forbes sighed.

"I talked to San Francisco a couple of times," he said. "What probably happened is these two girls got braced by the vice squad, and the boys had nothing better to do, so they made up a story for the girls to cop out to. They probably told the girls they'd have to waste away in the juvenile home for the next four or five years if they didn't lay the blame on somebody else. Hell, there was a missing persons report on both the girls laying around the SF police station for about a month. Trick is, to find out how much of Mona's statement is bullshit, how much true. Did you pick em up at the theater?"

Jack said nothing. He wanted to ask several questions, but he did not.

Forbes went on: "I'll give it to you straight. This girl's father swings some weight around here; he's been in this office four times already, fartin fire and telling me he's going to have my ass if you aren't sent to the gas chamber on the Little Lindbergh Law. I know the girl. She stinks. Just another two-bit chick, stupid enough to go tough. I know both the girls. Sue Franconi is all right, but don't think she won't get up on the witness stand with Mona and lie you right into San Quentin or worse. She'd do it to save her ass, and to tell the truth, I don't blame either of them. You shouldn't, either. You've been in juvenile, you know what it's like.

"Now, these other charges are still open in San Francisco. I told them I wanted to try the kidnap charge here, and if you get convicted of anything at all, they'll probably drop. I'm going to ask the grand jury to indict you for kidnaping, and that'll get Mona's old man off my neck; and by the time trial rolls around, he'll be up to his ears in some other wild-ass scrape of hers, and we can accept a lesser plea of contributing or something from you, hear it before a judge, and you'll be doing your little bit in county jail before he knows what happened. Anyway, by that time I'll be renominated and he can't touch me for another four years."

He looked at Jack intently. "I'll lay the whole thing out for you. If you don't cop the plea, if you want to fight it out, you'll probably win your case. I can get you a damned good lawyer, and he'll beat it. You can probably find somebody who saw the girls leave town, maybe the bus driver. You can get the clerks from that fleabag hotel down in the city, and they'll probably testify in your behalf. You'd have no trouble beating it, and you know it. It's as phony a charge as I ever saw. It's got vice squad bull written all over it. I'm just telling you so there'll be no mistake. I ain't trying to trap you. You can beat it, and I'll have a big defeat on my record in an election year, and Mona's daddy will raise all sorts of hell, and I'll look stupid. But I'll tell you what I'll do if you try that: I'll drop the case and take my medicine, and you'll go back to San Francisco and face the statutory rape charge. That one you can't beat, and you know it. I won't lift a finger to get that charge dropped if I have to drop mine. It's out of my hands anyway. You'll do time on that one, plenty of time. Do you see what I'm getting at? I'm telling you I can fix the rape charge and the rest of it, if you'll cooperate with me. If you won't, tough tiddy."

Jack saw. If he pled guilty to the charge he was innocent on, he would not be tried on the charge he was guilty on. It was even kind of funny. As to the rape charge, he realized now that he had always known the girls were underage, but had never given it a second thought. If he hadn't known, or suspected, it would not make any difference anyway. It was still a felony. It was a joke. Nobody ever went to jail for screwing. Except that they did, all the time. But none of that made any difference. You didn't go to jail for what you did; you went because they caught hold of you and didn't know what else to do, and so they put you in jail. They. Yes, they. The filing cabinets in the orphanage. The city hall. The parking meter. The hotel-room door. Batman. Never anybody real sending you to jail. The cops didn't do it. The District Attorney didn't do it. His *chair* is doing it. Sending my meat and bones to jail, and I got to go along. That's all. Nothing personal.

"Fuck you," Jack said to the District Attorney's chair. He felt enraged, seduced, raped. He felt hate, but he couldn't do anything about it. He wanted to scream. He began saying, "Fuck you," over and over again, sitting erect in the chair, his hands at his sides, his face empurpling with frustrated rage, tears coming out of his eyes.

"This won't do," the District Attorney said. Jack stopped, and stared at him through the film on his eyes. "Think about it. No hurry. I'll send your lawyer down right after the son of a bitch gets back from his goddam fishing trip."

Jack lived in the Balboa County jail for 66 days, awaiting trial. It was not his first county jail. The jail was on the top floor of the courthouse building and took up the whole left side of the floor. There was a long corridor with a concrete wall on one side and bars on the other, and in the corridor was a desk, manned by a county deputy during the day and unmanned at night. At the left end of the corridor was a concrete-reinforced steel door, and to one side of it was a steel judas window six inches square. Outside this door was another short corridor which ended in a barred gate, and beyond that the elevator foyer and the doors leading to the visitor's room, the lawyer's consulting rooms and the women's and juvenile divisions of the county jail. When the prisoners were being taken to the visitor's room or to see their lawyer, they were led past the elevators, but that was all right, because the elevator doors were enclosed in a tiny barred cell of their own; persons emerging

127

from the elevators found themselves in a small cell that could be opened only by the man sitting at a desk just out of long hand-reach from the cell. There was a deputy at this desk day and night.

The felony tank itself was behind the bars that made up one side of the long corridor. It was an open room, surrounded on three sides by cells that were never locked except for special prisoners. The men slept in the cells and spent their days in the big bullpen, where there were some tables and chairs and a couple of long benches. No matter where the prisoners were, in the cells or out in the bullpen, the deputy sitting at the desk in the corridor could see them, and if there was any trouble, a riot or anything of the sort, the deputy could quell it by using the fire hose curled against the wall beside the desk. There was no place in the tank the deputy could not reach with his fire hose. The lights in the tank were controlled from the desk, but there was one, in the ceiling of the bullpen, that never went out. At nine o'clock a deputy came in from the elevator foyer and flipped the switch, extinguishing the lights in the corridor and two of the lights in the tank, but the one in the middle always stayed on. All the light bulbs in the tank were covered with heavy wire cages, but the one in the middle had been worked loose, and after the deputy left the men often climbed up on a table and unscrewed the bulb so they could sleep in the dark. The place smelled of damp concrete, creosote, and sweat.

When a prisoner or suspect first arrived he was wearing the clothes he was arrested in, minus any belts, suspenders, neckties, or shoelaces with which he could hang himself in a fit of depression. If the prisoner or suspect was indicted by the grand jury, held over, or convicted by the municipal or superior courts, his personal clothing was taken from him and he was issued a light blue work shirt and darker blue dungarees. Every Friday these were exchanged for clean ones, and the dirty ones sent to a Laundromat owned by one of the deputies. This cleaning cost was deducted from the prisoner's pay or from his fund of money down in the property room, and was one dollar per cleaning.

The prisoners were divided into three groups. The first group consisted of trusties, who did not live in the felony tank but at a farm outside the city limits, where they slept in barracks and grew some of the food consumed by the other prisoners and by persons in the county hospital. In order to be a trusty you had to have been convicted of a misdemeanor and doing more than thirty days' time, and to exhibit a spirit of willingness to reform. The trusties were mostly farmworkers who had been caught drunk driving or gambling; some of them were just ordinary citizens who had been found guilty of one thing or another and could not get probation. Several were in for failure to provide child support.

The second class of prisoners included those who were not admitted to trusty status but who had money downstairs in the property room. They lived in the felony tank and spent their time playing cards, talking, reading, or just sitting around in the bullpen. No one was allowed on a bunk during daylight hours.

The third class of prisoners had neither trusty status nor money. They had to do all the work in the tank and were paid a dollar a day for their efforts. This money was placed in their accounts each Friday, minus one dollar for cleaning. These men made the beds, cleaned out the cells, mopped down, washed the walls, disinfected, carried out the graniteware pails that were used for toilets, and acted as intermediaries between the tank and the outside.

The prisoners in the tank were fed three times a day and exercised twice a day. In the morning, after lights-on at six-thirty, the working prisoners cleaned up, took out the slop pails, and then brought in a big aluminum kettle full of black coffee and two trays of mugs; and, following this, brought in two trays of bowls and spoons and a kettle of oatmeal mush. Some of this breakfast was actually eaten by prisoners who had no money, always with expressions of rage and disgust, because the unsweetened coffee always tasted like chlorine, and the oatmeal, without sweetening and only thinly mixed with powdered milk, tasted like nothing at all.

The prisoners who had money, working through an established route of intermediaries, ate whatever they wanted, having it sent up from the restaurant in the basement. The cost of these meals was twenty-five cents above the listed price, and the extra money went to the deputy who carried up the food. Other articles could be had from the deputies: books, magazines, newspapers, etc., for which the carrying charge was also twenty-five cents above purchase price, except for cigarettes, which were a set thirty-five cents a pack. The prisoners were not allowed to have cartons of cigarettes.

The noon meal for the prisoners without money was the big meal of the day, and was usually a bowl of vegetable stew with meat flavoring, or macaroni and cheese, tea, and two slices of bread. For dessert, there were prunes. The evening meal was bread and jam and tea. Everybody, even the prisoners with money, ate the bread and jam, because the jam was made and sold to the county by the wife of one of the deputies, and was considered excellent. Even the deputies on duty would have some.

For exercise, at ten in the morning and three in the afternoon, all the prisoners lined up two or three deep in the middle of the bullpen, the tables and chairs all pushed aside to make room, and did calisthenics under the personal direction of the sheriff of the county, who stood in the corridor and did all the exercises himself, bellowing out the count in his deep manly voice. He was a very popular sheriff, and was justly famous for his belief that county prisoners were more than a mere administrative and economic problem, that they were *men,* too, and needed to keep their strength up if they were to lead useful lives on the outside. When, due to the pressures of outside business, the sheriff could not make it for the exercise periods, a deputy would read the exercises from a mimeographed sheet in a bored voice, sitting at the desk in the corridor. Each exercise period lasted fifteen minutes, and no one was excused except violent prisoners, who were locked in their cells. Even the prisoners with money had to exercise.

Jack Levitt was brought in on a Thursday, late, and all the other prisoners seemed to know he was being held on a capital crime, and they let him alone. The deputy led Jack to an empty cell and Jack got onto the bunk and fell asleep in only a few minutes. The next day he was taken right out to wait for his interview with District Attorney Forbes, and that night, after he was brought back, he was taken with the others down the corridor to the shower room; but he was not yet given a set of dungarees. After his shower he was conscious of the musty odor of his clothes, and it bothered him a little. Nobody talked to him except to tell him where to go and what to do. None of the prisoners spoke to him at all, although one very young Mexican grinned at him once.

On Saturday he had a visitor, and was taken with the others who had visitors down the corridor, past the elevator cage, and into the long visitor's room. The prisoners went locked together by wrist chains, led and followed by deputies carrying billy clubs, and as they passed the elevator cage, one of the prisoners moaned. The elevator cage was full of civilians, mostly women, with a sprinkling of children and men. The man probably saw his relatives, saw a look of embarrassment on their faces, and moaned out of humiliation.

The visitor's room wasn't really a room, but a series of cubicles. Each prisoner selected a cubicle and stood in it. There was a thick glass, and a telephone. On the other side of the glass was exactly the same thing, and the visitor walked along, looking for the familiar face. They talked over the telephones. It was always very noisy and confusing. Long-time prisoners who were already convicted of a misdemeanor went to a different place, where they could actually sit with their families or friends, under the eyes of two deputies. This room had easy chairs and couches, and a nice view of the distant vineyards and the mountains beyond, through the meshed windows.

Jack wondered who his visitor could possibly be, knowing it was not his lawyer, because they had small private rooms for

131

legal conferences. He was surprised, then, to see Mona on the other side of the glass, making a girlish face at the arrangement. When she saw Jack she smiled and picked up her telephone.

"Are you mad at me?" she asked him. She cupped the phone against her cheek and shoulder and held her hands out in a gesture of helplessness, as if to suggest that destiny was being unkind to both of them. She was wearing a man's Pendleton shirt and Levis cut off above the knees. Her hair was combed out straight and there was a bright yellow bandeau holding it back rather primly. She looked about thirteen, Jack thought, without all her makeup. It made him feel better, not worse, to see her looking so young and almost innocent. Not really innocent; there was still that expression of rapacious stupidity around her eyes, makeup or not. Jack felt an uncontrollable desire to act as if he didn't mind being in jail, and he grinned and stuck out his tongue at her. "I aint mad," he said. "Just horny."

"I had to," she said. "They would have put me in reform school for just years." She told him her version of what had happened, and he listened quietly. He wondered why she had bothered to come and tell him. She said, "I can't understand why that man made me say you had a gun. Mister Forbes says the gun part could get you into terrible trouble. He wanted me to change my story, but Daddy says if I don't stick to it he'll make me go to boarding school." She made a face. "Wouldn't that be awful?" She put a hand over her eyes in dismay. "I mean, not as bad as this place. But still, who wants to go to boarding school with a bunch of little lesbians?" She shifted her weight from one foot to the other. "Is it shitty in there?"

"I've been in worse places," Jack admitted.

"This town's a real drag. After the trial's over, I'm going to take off for LA or Las Vegas or someplace. San Francisco's a real drag, too. Nothing to do at all."

"Why don't you take off right now, if you're gonna take off?" Jack wanted to know. "Then there won't be any trial."

"Daddy says if I take off again he'll find me and then they'll put me in reform school. I just can't." Her face looked sincerely upset for a moment. "Don't think I don't want to. Me and Sue both. Sue hates me. But she signed one, too. She copied hers from mine. Goddam it, I didn't want to!"

"Forget it," Jack said, not because he didn't wish she would run away, but because he knew she would not, and he sensed that the guiltier she felt, the worse it would be for him; she would reach out for something outside herself to blame, and there he would be, an easy and helpless target. He wanted her to feel nice toward him, not guilty. "Listen," he said. "It's not your fault at all. You couldn't help it. Don't blame yourself." He smiled stiffly, hoping she would see that he didn't mind being in jail at all.

"I have to go," she said. "My boy friend, this boy, anyway, is out in the parking lot waiting for me. We have to go to this dance and picnic thing."

So that had been it. She had wanted to show off to her new boy friend. Or maybe old boy friend. Look at me, I got friends in jail. God *damn* women!

On the following Monday he met his lawyer in one of the little conference rooms.

The lawyer's name was Costigan and he was a short trim man with snapping eyes and a sharp, very intelligent face. He got right down to business. "I understand you have well over two hundred dollars down in the property room. Is that correct?"

"Yes," Jack said.

"That's not enough to pay my fee," Costigan said.

"Then you're shit out of luck, aren't you," Jack said.

"I'm entitled to something for my services, don't you agree?"

"Sure. But I thought the District Attorney assigned you to me."

"District attorneys don't assign. They're just lawyers. Stanley merely asked me as a favor to take your case. Judges do the assigning when assigning is done. The point is this: when you go down to muni this afternoon you're going to be bound over for the grand jury and the judge is going to assign you an attorney. He'll pick me. We worked it out. But the point is, I think I'm entitled to some money for my work. You have two hundred; do you know where you can get more money?"

"No."

"Then, don't you think you at least ought to give me a hundred? I know how it is in that tank, but I ought to get something."

"No. You don't get any of it. I'm gonna need it all."

"Then," the lawyer insisted, "I'm not to be paid anything?"

"I guess not."

Costigan shrugged quickly and said, "All right. I just thought I'd ask. How do you want me to handle the case? Do you want me to plead you guilty or not guilty?"

"To what charge?"

"Why, kidnaping."

"Hell no. I thought——"

"Never mind what you thought. If you plead guilty at muni the judge will hold you for superior court, and then you can change your plea to not guilty and skip over the grand jury. I'll ask for a continuance to work up my case until the heat blows over and the nominations are all made, and you can change your plea to guilty of contributing, and we can hear it before a judge and pass up the jury trial. It's all very simple. All you have to do is cooperate. We handle San Francisco from here, tell em you pleaded guilty to kidnaping, they might as well bury their charges, and then when nobody's looking, switch to contributing."

"Why is he doing this for me?" Jack asked.

The lawyer looked surprised. "Forbes? Stanley Forbes? Hell, why do you think?"

"It beats me," Jack said.

"You're innocent, aren't you?" Costigan raised his eyebrows. "Isn't that reason enough?"

"I guess so."

"Then you'll cooperate?"

"Shit, why not?"

Costigan smiled quickly. "That's thinking. Anything I can do for you? You'll probably draw a year upstairs. You might even get out to the farm, but you'll be out of circulation for a year, anyway. Anybody you want me to call?"

"No."

"Okay." The lawyer smiled. "I know it's rough in there. Just bear up. I was in jail myself once; got caught down in Carmel with a bunch of beer in the car. Had to stay in jail all goddam night. I know how it is."

They shook hands formally, and later in the day, at the afternoon session of municipal court, met again; Jack pleaded guilty to the charge and was held for superior court, just as Costigan had said. The judge did not even have to appoint Costigan as his attorney, because when Jack's name was called, Costigan stepped forward and said he was acting as the accused's counsel. It simplified matters. Everyone, Jack thought, was doing his utmost to simplify matters, to make the administration of justice run smoothly. Even he was. He could have balked, he could have been stubborn and ethical, but it wouldn't have done anything except run him right into the gas chamber. And if he had really been guilty, it would have been different. He would have been right in there, trying to make any deal he could get.

As a final gesture, Costigan asked for bail for Jack, but the judge refused because it was a capital case and Jack was not local. When they took him back upstairs he was permitted to change his smelly civilian clothes for a set of dungarees, and they offered him a pair of workshoes, but he asked if he could keep his loafers. The deputy thought it over, bit his thumb, and finally said okay.

Jack was not really concerned about his guilt or innocence; or even about the giant abstractions of Guilt and Innocence. In his life he had already committed enough crimes to be jailed for a thousand years. Armed robbery, battery, statutory rape, and for that matter even kidnaping as it was defined in the State of California. He and two others had robbed a store and then forced the owner to come in the car with them at gunpoint and then drove him out into the country so he couldn't call the heat down on them until they were far away. That was kidnaping.

Shortly after he had quit working in eastern Oregon, he had gone all over with a partner pulling a short-change racket that involved the changing of a twenty-dollar bill for a package of cigarettes; he imagined he had done this enough times to *deserve* at least a hundred years in prison if he got a year on each count, so he was not feeling particularly *innocent*, at least in the eyes of the law. As for the true crimes of his life, the crime of being born without parents, the crime of being physically strong and quick, the crime of not having a puritan conscience, the crime of existing in a society in which he and everybody else permitted crime without rising up in outrage: well, he was purely and perfectly guilty here, too, as was everybody else. So that didn't matter, either. The trick was to keep from being "punished" for his "crimes." He decided that to fight the authorities, to balk, would in a sense be admitting that they were right and he was wrong. But of course there wasn't any right or wrong. So it was better to cooperate, to do *anything* that would lessen his punishment.

Except that in his heart he felt deep personal rage at himself for cooperating. It made him grind his teeth together to keep from shouting out his self-hatred, from beating himself against the concrete wall of his cell; the thought kept ballooning up in his mind that they had no right to treat him like an animal, no matter what he had done or not done. All night long, in his cell, he burned with hatred. It did not matter what he thought, it was how he felt; and alone in the darkness of his cell, with the muttering noises of the tank around him, he felt like murdering the universe.

TEN

In a way, the Balboa County jail was run on democratic principles, which was not true of a jail in Peckham County, Idaho, where Jack had spent nearly three months a few years before. He had been given three months in Peckham County for rolling a drunk, and as soon as he got put in he knew that this was going to be a hard three months. The Peckham County jail was run very tightly by the deputies, with no inmate control at all. There had been no corruption and no graft. Jack had been told that a few years before the jail had been one of the worst in the nation and that a reform administration had cleaned it up. The prisoner who told him this, a tall lean man in for failure to provide child support, first greeted Jack by grinning and saying, "Welcome, Comrade, to the Union of Soviet Socialist Republics. Don't spit on the sidewalk."

It wasn't long before Jack saw what he meant. The reform administration saw to it that there was no outside food or anything else for the prisoners with money. The tank was very well lit all the time, and the inmates were under constant supervision, to see that there would be no gambling, arguing, fighting, or unnatural sex practices. Each man had to do his share of the work, and long-term prisoners spent most of each day in a gravel quarry out in back of the jail. During the day the prisoners who were not in the gravel quarry sat around the tank and did nothing. At night they were locked in their cells. The county authorities were proud of the fact that there was no sanitary court in their felony tank, and that all prisoners got equal treatment.

"And it works, too," said the tall prisoner. "This is a very humane place. We all get equal treatment, and we are all simply desperate to get out of here and never come back. There is no coddling, and money is not king, and a prisoner who does not cooperate is placed in isolation to brood over his antisocial behavior. And the rest of us, according to the depth of our imagination, just sit here and go out of our minds. But quietly, of course. When I came in here, I was a mild socialist. I suppose I dreamed of a world in which all men received equal treatment before the law, and the function of the law was to see that everyone received equal treatment. Perhaps I even dreamed that in a mildly socialist world, we might even stop murdering each other's children, since there would be nothing to gain from it. I have been in here two weeks now, and when I get out I'm going to make a very formal ceremony of going down and registering as a Republican. I have been in here two weeks, and like all the rest of us I have been stripped, absolutely stripped, of every single emotional and intellectual value, every basic urge, every desire; everything that distinguishes me as a human being from other human beings, or even from other animals. My privacy is gone, my pride is gone, I have no status, nor is there any way to get any status in here. My sexual urges, as weak as they are, have no possibility of satisfaction. My other appetites have been reduced to the point where I eat, drink, sleep, crap, piss, scratch, and yawn all for the same thing—the mere satisfaction or rather, reduction, of a primal itch I'd be better off without. Which has all made me realize that I do not want *your* supper, because it is just like *my* supper. And I had always thought that this would be a good thing! 'Remove,' I said to myself, 'the impetus to private ownership, and you have made the first giant step toward removing the causes of injustice in the world. There would be no greed if there were no possessions, no jealousy, no envy, perhaps even no hatred.' "

The tall prisoner laughed. "What a dream! I've been in here two weeks, and already I know that I would give my right arm for something to be jealous about, for something I desired enough to steal, or even kill for. I feel dead; even though I know I'll be out of here soon, I can't really believe it, and even the quality of my daydreams has changed to the point where I now realize that everything I dream of and desire could cause that same desire in another man, and that I might have to fight another man to get it. Even my wife. Do you see? Suppose I loved my wife: Couldn't somebody else love her, too? And then wouldn't we have to fight over her? And if we fought, wouldn't one of us have to lose? And if one of us lost, wouldn't *he* be the victim of injustice? Because by what right does he lose the object of his desires?

"You see, I've always dreamed of a world in which this wouldn't happen. And here it is, right here in the tank. A perfect socialist utopia, in which those desires which cause conflict are satisfied by being lopped off. Just think what it would be like if some evening one of us, just one of us, got something *extra* for supper? Wouldn't we all be excited! We'd all scheme and dream about how we could get it away from him. Say, a banana cream pie. We would lust after it passionately, because it would be the only thing in the tank to lust after; and we would dream of getting one of our own somehow. We would look up to the fellow who had it, admiring and hating him at the same instant, kissing his ass and wanting to murder him, just so we could be the one with the banana cream pie. And if I were the one with the extra something, wouldn't I be in a terror for fear somebody would take it from me, or simply murder me just because I had it! But at least we'd be *involved*.

"Jesus Christ!" he exclaimed, his face contorting with sudden pain. "What I wouldn't give to be involved!"

Then he smiled again, bitterly. "But I'm the one who dragged my imagination in here with me. What a gift!"

Later on the tall prisoner repudiated everything he had said. "I told you, I'm going out of my mind. When I get out of here I'm going to toe the old line and pay that support money to my stinking wife and never come back here as long as I live." He got out two weeks later, and then, about six weeks after that, he came back in. This time he did not even acknowledge Jack's hello, but went to a corner, sat down, and would not speak to anybody. A few nights later he threw his plate of stew across the tank, and was led out and taken to solitary. Jack never saw him again.

Balboa County jail was different; not much better, but certainly different. Here, the inmates of the tank ran the tank. There was a sanitary court and it was run by a man named Mac McHenry, who was judge of the court because he was strong and smart and ruthless, a natural leader. Jack came up before McHenry on Tuesday night.

It was after lights-out and the deputy was gone from the desk. Jack was lying with his hands back of his head when he saw some of the men gathering out in the bullpen, under the one light. One of them seated himself at a table, and another, a tall Negro, stood on the table, his arms folded. Four other men stood behind the seated man and the rest gathered on the sidelines. Jack was the only man still in a cell, and he pretty well knew what was going to happen. The tank was absolutely quiet. Jack lay there, wondering whether it was worth it to resist. Since he had decided to cooperate with the District Attorney, the idea of resisting seemed to have lost some of its savor. He had been resisting all his life, struggling against any encroachment on his personal self, and it had gotten him exactly nowhere, or what was even worse, it had gotten him exactly where he was; if anything, worse than nowhere. It would be so much easier to drift with events and simply let things happen. But just as he had about made up his mind to do this, two men came and tried to drag him out to the court, and he reacted automatically, his body resisting, while he thought to himself how silly it was to fight.

From his prone position he gave one of the men a short jab in the face, using his follow-through to spring up off the bunk and land the toe of his right shoe a glancing blow on the other man's chest. On his feet, he grabbed one of the dazed men by the shirt and hit him as hard as he could on the Adam's apple, letting him go and whirling on the other man, who was leaning against the bars, his mouth open, panting and rubbing his sore chest. Jack uppercut him on the point of the chin and the man lifted slightly and then slid to his knees before falling forward on his face. The first man had gotten through the doorway on his hands and knees and was lying doubled up on the floor of the tank, holding his throat, making hawking, wheezing noises. Blood and a thin trickle of vomit were dripping from his open mouth, and his face had turned black. Jack picked up the other man and threw him unconscious out of the cell. He stood by the doorway, waiting. All of the other men were looking at him.

The man sitting at the table was grinning. "Well, well," he said in a soft Southern voice. "Walter, turn off the light." The Negro who was standing on the table reached up and undid the wire mesh and quickly unscrewed the bulb. The tank went black. Jack heard rustling noises as he positioned himself directly in front of the cell door. He felt, rather than saw, the first man coming in for him, and he kicked out where he thought, hoped, the man's groin would be, and was rewarded by a surprised scream out of the darkness as his foot sank into flesh. But that was his only moment of triumph; in a couple of seconds he felt himself pinioned, smothered by men. Nobody tried to hit him, but they kept his arms behind him and he could do nothing. They carried him out of the cell, and in a few moments the light went on again. Behind him Jack could hear a man sobbing.

McHenry had not moved from his place, and the big Negro was still standing on the table. Men held Jack right up to the table, and McHenry said, "We got to hurry this. Those guys will have to go down to the dispensary." He looked up at Jack and said, "I'm the judge of the sanitary court. You like to killed a couple of my deppities. I'm going to fine you for that. You got to learn the rules of this tank, and I'm going to fine you for not coming along. Do you have any money?"

Within, Jack was amused and distant, but all he could think of to say was, "Fuck you."

McHenry laughed, his gray eyes almost disappearing behind wrinkles of merriment. "I'm going to fine you for that, too. Matter of fact, I happen to know exactly how much money you got downstairs. Tomorrow, you just tell the deppity to transfer fifteen dollars from your account to mine. It ain't legal, but he'll do it. My name's McHenry. You'll get the rest of your fine tomorrow night. We got to hurry. Rest of the fine is fifty whacks. You want to know what a whack is? You want to know the rest of the rules, so's you don't go around busting the rules?"

"Fuck your mother," Jack said.

McHenry shrugged, as if it was out of his hands now. "Beat shit out of him and put him back in his cell. Tomorrow night court con-venes again. Get the deppities in here for them guys been fightin."

The Negro jumped down from the table, and while the men still held Jack, began hitting him in the chest and belly, hard short chops, his breath coming in grunts at each blow, until Jack went blind from the pain and heard himself distantly whimpering. After that he could remember nothing. He was told later that after he was put on his bunk unconscious all the other prisoners started yelling, and after a while the deputy out in the foyer came in, and then brought others up from downstairs, and they carried out the men Jack had wrecked. The one Jack had knocked out came back the next day, but the other two went to the county hospital and Jack never saw them again. If he had he would not have known them.

The next morning he was sitting by himself on one of the benches while the "outs"—men without money who had to do the work—cleaned up. He felt all right, he was still in pretty good condition, and if he ached all over it was not a new sensation. He noticed McHenry sitting at one of the tables with two other men, a big man, heavy, thick, as hard as teakwood. McHenry turned toward Jack and nodded to him, smiling, and then said something to the others and got up and came over. He sat down on the bench beside Jack and said, "A few aches and pains, Levitt?"

"A few," Jack said.

"We got to have rules," McHenry said.

"I know it. All you had to do was ask me."

"Send you a subpoena, hey? Okay, I did it wrong." He held out his hand. "Shake?"

It was impossible to refuse the hand.

"Breakfast on me this morning," McHenry said. "While we eat I'll tell you the rules of the tank. That is, if you want to learn them."

They sat alone at one of the tables and had buckwheat cakes, bacon, scrambled eggs, and coffee, while McHenry told Jack the rules. They were really very simple and logical, and their function was to make the tank livable. Everyone in the tank is automatically a member of the sanitary court and is fined three whacks or three dollars; everyone must wash himself thoroughly in the weekly shower and keep as clean as possible the rest of the time, or is fined three whacks or three dollars; no one is allowed to make unnecessary noise after lights-out or is fined as the judge sees fit; no one is allowed to resist the judge or is fined as the judge sees fit; no fighting is allowed; no one is permitted to steal from his fellow inmates; no one is allowed to speak out against his fellow inmates, or is brought before the court and fined at least fifty whacks; no one is allowed to make a fuss in the open visitor's room; anyone caught cheating at cards is banned from the game and fined all the money in his pocket automatically, etc. etc. They were, Jack realized, reasonable rules, and it was either have a sanitary court to administer them, however badly, or be at the mercy of the deputies. Jack already knew what that was like. This way, everybody had a sense of being at least partly responsible for his own welfare, and of course it made life a lot easier and more profitable for the deputies. It also made life easier for the inmates who had money, and it wasn't even too bad for those who had to do all the work. Because by the end of every week they had six dollars clear and could get into a poker or crap game and run it up into a fortune and not have to work any more. This almost never happened, but then it *could* happen; at least there was hope.

After the delicious three-dollar outside breakfast, Jack was more than willing to listen to reason and to cooperate. He knew that if he didn't his life would be made miserable. He would have to eat inmate food. The hell with that, he thought. There was also the matter of his being beaten half to death every night or so if he didn't cooperate. He remembered what his rebellion had cost him at the reformatory in Oregon, the long endless time in the hole, and he thought, the excellent breakfast warming his belly, what a fool he had been.

As they smoked their after-breakfast cigarettes, McHenry asked, "Well, how about it? You coming along?"

"What about tonight?" Jack bargained. "I guess you want to give me those fifty whacks."

"I never did tell you what a whack is, did I? Well, it's one whack across the bare ass with this-here belt." McHenry was wearing a thick leather belt, and, Jack saw later, was the only man in the tank who had a belt at all. More cooperation from the deputies, he thought. Oh, how everybody cooperates. But this was tangible, just plain old naked force. You don't cooperate with naked force, you just sit there and take it. Which made Jack wonder why McHenry was asking for his cooperation, instead of just *enforcing*, since he obviously had the power to do so.

"I'll tell you about them fifty whacks," McHenry said. "I'll drop that if you're willin to go along, and if you just transfer about twenty-five dollars into my account downstairs. Above the fifteen. Hell, you got lots of money."

"Okay," Jack said. "That's fine." He understood now. McHenry was afraid of him, afraid that Jack might just want his job as judge, and might be strong enough and determined enough to take it away from him. "I'd be happy to cooperate," Jack said, and they shook hands again. There appeared to be an expression of guarded relief in McHenry's eyes. Jack remembered what the tall prisoner in Idaho had said, and he hoped the man had been wrong; but he could see, now, that even in here and with these rules of self-government there would be no such thing as fairness; that the big and the strong and the rich would naturally be better off. That was why he was being offered a way out.

"I wouldn't touch your racket," he said to McHenry. "You know what you are? You're just another *screw*. You're in here, but you're just like the deputies. Don't worry; I wouldn't want to be you and have to worry about guys like me."

"Now, you got a point there, Levitt," McHenry said, not bothered at all. "I *was* worried about you. But man, if I don't run the tank, somebody's got to. These guys don't know what's good for them, they'd live just any ole way if there wasn't any rules. And the deppities can't control from out there; you know that. If there wasn't a sanitary court guys'd be rattin on each other inside ten minutes, just to get special treatment. Now, that's shitty and you know it."

"Sure," said Jack, "so you run things for everybody's benefit. And I'll help you, too, because I dig that special treatment myself."

"Doesn't everbody?" McHenry grinned.

They understood each other perfectly now, and for a few weeks Jack was permitted, with a nod and a thank you to his strength and his ability to use it, to remain on the edges of the simplified social structure of the tank. For a while this suited him, because, as he reflected ironically, he had been wanting some time to think. Except for the more or less constant noise, the county jail was a fine place to think. Of course there were distractions. New prisoners were brought in and old ones released, and it was always interesting to find out who the new people were, and how they reacted to the tank. Most of them had been in jail before and would be again, and considered jail only a transitory phase; some were citizens, upset, angry, baffled, frustrated, frightened, terrified that they would stay in jail the rest of their lives. But most of the citizen trade went to the drunk tank downstairs. One night an old man was brought in for assault with a deadly weapon. They got the story from the deputies: The old man lived with his son's family, and his granddaughter had been gotten pregnant by a boy, and there had been a conference of the two families in an attempt to fix the responsibility and decide what to do. At first it was decided that it was the boy's fault for making the girl go all the way; then they blamed the girl for allowing the boy to take these liberties with her (they were only juniors in high school), and then both sets of parents decided to blame themselves for not raising their children properly, and finally, after much self-recrimination, it was decided that modern society itself made it impossible to raise children properly, what with the movies and television and violence, too much sex in the magazines, and the way girls dressed these days; and the old man, who had been sitting in the background listening in disgust, finally went upstairs to his room and came back down with his double-barreled 12-gauge shotgun and terrified everybody by pointing the deadly weapon at the boy and telling him by God he would do the right thing by the girl or the grandfather would come looking for him and would find him no matter how far he ran and when he found him he would blow a hole through him, by God. The boy let out a scream and jumped through the picture window, and cut himself pretty badly, and the boy's parents called the police right after they called the ambulance. It did not occur to them to blame the grandfather's actions on society.

The consensus in the tank was that the old man had done right, and what young people needed was to be shown who was boss. It was remarked by Mac McHenry that the most difficult and noisy prisoners were invariably young. The old man, his eyes bright and interested, told the others, "Boys, that old bird gun of mine has come handy more than once. When that little girl, the same girl, mind you, was about four years old, we lived in Santa Rosa—that was just after I retired, I was a plumbing contractor for thirty-two years, boys—the people next door had this Doberman pinscher, meanest-looking dog I ever saw in my life; I told the owners of the dog, I said, 'If that dog gets loose and comes around here you'd better look around for some place to bury him,' that's what I told em, but that man was just so proud of his big dog, and the dog stayed out there in their backyard on a long rope, and roamed around crapping on the lawn and digging up the flowers and looking mean. Hell, that was no dog to have in town. If I had my way all those big dogs, especially the Dobermans, would be taken out and done away with. Well, anyhow, boys, little Darcy (aint that a hell of a name for a child, boys?), she went on over into their yard one afternoon to have a close look at that dog, and naturally, the dog, being a brute with no more brains than a nitwit anyway, just bit that child right on the arm, and Darcy came running home to me crying and bleeding like hell, and I fixed up her arm and called the hospital and went upstairs and got my bird gun and went over and blew that there dog right into dog heaven. Then I got in my car and drove Darcy to the hospital and left her there and went on down to where this man worked—he was in the life-insurance business—and went in and told him, 'Sir, I shot and killed your dog. Here's seventy-five dollars; that's what you paid for the beast, take it.' He stared at me, his lips working, and wanted to know what happened, and I told him, and he looked at that money in my hand—I always carry plenty of cash, you never know—and started cursing me under his breath, but by God he took the money and he even counted it, and I went home. His wife never spoke to me again."

"You killed a *dog?*" said one of the prisoners. "That was tied up and couldn't get away?"

"I did just that, sonny. Damn brute."

"You had no right to do that."

"Horse-frocky, sonny," said the old man. "Now, if you boys will excuse me, I got to get some sleep."

The old man got out on bail the next day, and Jack heard later that he had been convicted and given a one-to-five sentence, suspended, and two years on probation. Jack thought the old man had done right in both cases, but most of the men in the tank were upset and angry about shooting the dog.

Citizens like the old man usually got out on bail, or if convicted of a misdemeanor were sent right out to the trusty farm, but there were a couple of exceptions.

The first of these was a man in his middle twenties who lived in Sausalito, in the adjoining Marin County. He had, according to the wry tale he told, been driving home from a party in Redding, horribly drunk from the last few hasty nightcaps, and not long after he crossed the Balboa County line he decided he was just too drunk to go on, too sleepy, and so he pulled his car over and went to sleep. He was awakened by a flashlight in his face. The police made him get out of his car, turn around, lean against the side of the car and be searched. Then they made him walk a line, and they smelled his breath. They searched the car, too. He was taken in and thrown into the drunk tank, and in the morning, with the rest of the night's crop of drunks, he came before the municipal court. He was charged with being drunk on a public highway. He explained to the judge that he was not driving, but sleeping. The judge asked him if he had gotten to where he was arrested by driving in a drunken condition, and he said yes, but that he had stopped driving because he realized he was drunk. The judge said that didn't matter. He fined the man $250 and the man lost his temper and yelled at the judge, and was given ten days in the county jail for contempt of court.

"So I'm in here for not drunk driving," he explained. "Ain't that enough to frost your balls?"

Jack corrected him. "No, you got sent here for yelling at the judge. You got *fined* for not drunk driving."

This particular citizen was very popular while he was in the tank. He played shrewd poker and won a lot of money, marveling that the men got to play cards all day and saying he wouldn't mind coming here every so often just to get in the game. He appeared before the sanitary court, took his few token whacks and fines with good humor, obeyed the rules of the tank, was friendly to everybody and did not act superior, and at the end of his ten days went downstairs to the cafeteria and left money and orders for packs of cigarettes to be delivered in his name to "the boys on the top floor." He was a chemist by profession and everybody admired him for his education, breeding, and good manners.

Jack envied him; he had his work, which he loved, and he had a good life and a good attitude toward life. He and Jack were the same age, too.

The other citizen was different. This man was in his fifties, an executive for a hardware company, and his case made all the newspapers. He, too, had been driving home drunk, but instead of pulling over to go to sleep he fell asleep behind the wheel while going sixty or seventy, and his car plowed into a parked car full of necking teenagers. Three of them were killed at once, both girls and one of the boys, and the other boy was in the hospital with a bad concussion and a broken collarbone. The executive got out of his car, saw what had happened, and ran off. Two policemen found him hiding in a backyard, and he offered the policemen fifty dollars each if they would let him go. It was stupid; his car was back there, wrecked, but the executive seemed a little out of his mind. When the police refused the money, he hit one of them and tried to get away. So he was booked for manslaughter, attempted bribery, and assault on a police officer. When they brought him into the felony tank early in the morning the first thing the prisoners heard him say was, "You can't do this to me!" So everybody knew he was a citizen. They all said that.

After his indictment for manslaughter (the other two charges were dropped) the man was returned to the tank and had to dress in dungarees. His bail had been set at fifty thousand dollars and no one had put it up for him. He was a pompous, florid man with silvery hair, and he looked absurd in dungarees, like a millionaire going to a costume party. There was a subdued excitement among the prisoners; to most of them this man represented their chief enemy, respectability, and cruelly they wanted to see him come up before the sanitary court and have his pants pulled down and his ass whacked, to watch him silently while he discovered that his dignity could be taken away from him so easily, and that for once he was at the mercy of the underdogs. Nobody spoke to him all day, and he sat in his cell, alternately holding his head in his hands and groaning, or jumping up to pace back and forth in his cell. All the prisoners knew this was a violation of tank rules, but they said nothing.

The executive, however, was not brought before the sanitary

court at all. The next day, McHenry went into his cell and stood in front of him, and they talked for almost an hour, and McHenry came out and called the deputy at the desk over to the bars and whispered to him, and then the deputy went out and came back later with a tray of food for the executive.

When the executive was not visiting his lawyer, he stayed in his cell. He refused to speak to any of the inmates except Mac McHenry, and Mac let it be known that he, Mac, wanted the man left strictly alone. He winked at Jack. "This boy has power on the outside. We fiddle with him and the whole thing goes."

The executive got out just before Jack, his lawyer finally arranging bail.

Somewhere along the line Jack began to be angry, in a deep, personal way that had nothing to do with the tank or the inmates. They could not be blamed for the way they acted, and if Jack began to hate the sanitary court and McHenry, it was not because he did not understand the need for the inmates to run things, or at least pretend they ran things. He understood that; but he hated it anyway. He did not even get to hate McHenry in person, because he was only the toughest and shrewdest of the lot, not the worst; and if he was gone the number two tough nut would take over the court, and that could have been Jack himself. He could feel it in himself, and he often thought of the sense of pleasure that could come from the power; and he hated himself for it. And he could not hate the deputies, because they hadn't put him in jail, they were only there to see to it that he *stayed* in jail. They were just doing their job. Certainly, a few of them were getting rich off the inmates, but Jack could not think of any reason why they should not. If they didn't, somebody else would. Everybody was just doing his job, making the machinery run smoothly. And so Jack could not hate anybody, or blame anybody, but himself. And in the end he could not even hate himself, because he had not willed himself into jail; he just tried to live his life his own way and that ran against the grain and he ended up, almost accidentally, in jail. And he could not hate *accident*. That was crazy. He had to admit that he had been proud of himself, and that he nourished the memory of his long stay in the hole years before; that he had assumed he would be able to do his time standing on his head because the hole had been so much worse; but now he was in doubt. He was getting older. The boredom of it all, the sameness, the constant noise and smell of the tank, were driving him crazy. The fact that he was in was driving him crazy. He lost all his contempt for the executive; the executive was right, they can't do this to me. They have no right to do this to me, or to anybody else. He hated them all. But it was crazy to hate them. So he decided he was going crazy.

It was a relief for him to go berserk at last; it was an act of pure rationality that had nothing to do with McHenry or the poor fool Mac was taking over the bumps. It was an expression of sanity, a howl of rage at a world that put men in county jails. Everything finally got to be too much and he let go of his passion.

The man was a farmworker, probably a *bracero*, and he could just barely understand English. He had picked fruit for a couple of weeks, on his knees under the straight lines of prune trees, and one night he got drunk in a poolhall and pulled a knife on a man. He got a year for pulling the knife, and he was not sent to the trusty farm because he had a record of disobedience from his last stay in jail. On the night of his sanitary court trial he stood in front of McHenry stupidly, not comprehending what Mac was telling him. As usual, Jack stood well back, his arms folded, watching the whole procedure. Mac was in an odd mood; he kept asking the *bracero* if he was willing to pay his fines, and when the man did not speak he gave him more fines to pay or more whacks to suffer.

It disgusted Jack to see Mac, in his pleasant drawl, making fun of the man simply because the man was weak and stupid and Mac had the power. The *bracero* probably thought Mac was a legal official, and he hesitated and stammered, and finally made everybody laugh by saying, "Wock? Wass a Wock?"

Mac was tickled. "I'll show you what a wock is. Take his pants down."

It tore away in Jack, and he came up. He was really out of control, but he seemed calm and possessed. Inside he felt passionate.

"McHenry," he said, his voice trembling only a little, "you're about the most chickenshit Southern cracker I ever saw in my life. I bet you got a hard-on right this minute. I bet this is how you get your kicks, you fuckin hillbilly. Aint you ever heard of women?"

McHenry understood instantly and fell back in his chair, wildly signaling, but he was too late. Jack dived at him across the table, and they rolled on the cement floor, punching and grunting, before anybody could stop it.

The fight only lasted a few minutes, and was broken up when they saw Jack beating McHenry's head against the concrete, his fingers dug into McHenry's shoulders. Mac's eyes were bugging out, and blood was coming from his mouth and spattering on the floor, and when they pulled Jack loose Mac slumped down unconscious, his eyes still open. He came back the next morning with a bandage on his head. There was no concussion or anything more serious than a few stitches. Mac must have talked to the deputies before he came back, because they came in before morning and locked Jack into his cell. He stayed locked in until he left Balboa County.

Even the smoothest-running county political machines have their flaws. In this case, the particular judge who was supposed to hear Jack's case upset the smooth operation of the machine. Costigan, the lawyer, told Jack all about it, his voice dry and bitter. The judge said he would not accept such a drastic reduction of the charge, from kidnaping to a misdemeanor charge of contributing to the delinquency of a minor. It was none of the judge's business, but he made it his business. All in private, of course, the judge told District Attorney Forbes and Costigan that he thought Levitt ought to do some time, and not county jail time. He hinted that if the District Attorney brought the man Levitt up on a contributing charge, the judge would give him the year in the county jail, and then make it a point to get in touch with San Francisco and have them prosecute on the rape charge. So that the man Levitt would get out of his year and go right back in. Costigan was very bitter about it, but Forbes said he knew a way out of the dilemma. Jack could plead guilty to having had intercourse with the girl right in the car, still inside Balboa County, and they would drop the part about the gun and the force to make it statutory. He asked the judge about it and the judge said he would go along with that and give Jack a very light penalty, perhaps one-to-five.

"That's the best we can do," Costigan said. "I'm awfully goddam sorry."

"I don't give a shit," Jack said. He was empty. He had been empty since the assault against McHenry. For once, everything ran smoothly. He was tried before the judge, waived the waiting period, and was sentenced at the same time. The next day he left by station wagon for Chino, chained up in the back, leaving Balboa County the same way he had entered it, only with two uniformed deputies instead of two detectives. Both of the deputies were taking courses in criminology at San Jose State, and had requested the assignment because they wanted to see the center at Chino. They were going to write a paper about it.

ELEVEN

The heavy leather belt tight around his waist buckled in the back. The chain of his handcuffs passed through two steel-reinforced holes in the front of the belt, and he could not move either hand more than a few inches. When he wanted to smoke a cigarette he had to bend his head down to his hands to take a puff, and of course one of the guards had to give him the cigarette and light it. Passed through the handcuff chains was another chain leading down to his leg-irons, which were clamped onto his ankles in such a way that he could move his feet only enough to shuffle; and the connecting chain was too short to allow him to stand erect. He and the other two hard cases had to be helped onto the bus, along with the others who were making the trip from the center at Chino to their final destination at San Quentin.

The three hard cases sat right in front, under the eyes of two riot guns. The window next to the driver was open, and the hot wind blew into Jack's face; but it was better than no air at all. He sucked it into his lungs as if it was to be the last air he would breathe; he had never forgotten the feeling of suffocation that would overcome him sometimes in the hole, and he could see nothing in the future but an endless repetition of the hole. He had the answer to all his questions now. He knew what he loved. He loved freedom, and this long bus ride was going to be his last chance to sense it, to use his eyes and ears and lungs on the world, the real world, before he was locked again in endless darkness. He did not feel sorry for himself. He was too busy trying to draw the world into himself, trying to *be there.*

The hard case sitting next to Jack muttered and cursed throughout the hot valley morning, his chin on his chest, his eyes shut. He was completely crazy. He was about forty years old and had been a Certified Public Accountant and a Notary Public. One night about three months before, he had come home from his office and gone into the kitchen and gotten a butcher knife, gone in to where his invalid wife was sleeping, and stabbed her more than three hundred times. Then he dragged the body out the side door and stuffed it into the trunk of the car and drove off. Several neighbors saw him and had called the police even before he left the neighborhood. He drove around with the body for hours before they finally got him. He had appeared rational at the trial, and did not break down until later. Everyone at the Chino center was afraid of him, even though he behaved rationally in front of the authorities until time to leave for San Quentin, and then he broke down again. The other hard case sat behind Jack in a seat by himself. He was a Negro, like most of the other passengers. He had the tab on his file because he had resisted arrest and tried to break out of the county jail. He was going up for ten years for armed robbery. These three were the ones the guards watched.

When the bus stopped at a small roadside diner, the sun blistering overhead, the prisoners were taken in shifts to eat and go to the toilet, and while this was going on the three hard cases were made to get out of the bus and lie face down in the ditch beside the highway, with the guards taking turns standing over them holding a riot gun. Jack lay face down in the ditch for over an hour, the sun burning his skull, the gravel hard against his cheek, thoughtless again, his mind and senses cleared of all obstructions; the nerves alive and waiting for the guards, the State, the authorities, to make one tiny mistake, open one tiny crack through which he could burst; not escape, that was impossible and unimportant; no, *burst*, destroy, kill, show them he had no limits and they would have either to break him or kill him, and the only way they could break him would be to kill him and he knew they, it, did not have the courage to do that, and he did. Waiting, then, for a tiny slipup, perhaps a softness in one of the guards, a momentary weakness or a careless mistake, the riot gun slipped a little too close while the guard lights a cigarette. They were all one to Jack. He knew the rules now. They wouldn't kill him unless he killed them. Then they would kill him. And he would not have to go back in the hole.

Jack was very much afraid now of going to prison. He re-membered the long endless moments of the approach of insanity in the hole; not the coming of relief in the form of delusion, but of cold wet terrifying madness, when nothing made sense and all illusions made him tremble with fear: all sounds made his body jerk, all dreams were awakened from in cold sweat and deadening dread of the unknown—madness, an eternity of fear. He could smell the gravel and feel it cutting into his cheek.

The back of his head felt as if it was going to explode from the heat. He knew he had to move his head, turn over the other way. The smell of the gravel made him want to throw up, but he was frightened; if he threw up perhaps his intestines would come loose and hang out of his mouth. He was afraid that if he turned his head the guard would misunderstand and blow his head off; yet if he did not turn his head, raise it up, let the gravel sticking into him fall loose, he would go mad. Sweat trickled down and burned into his eyes. He was afraid to blink; they would see that and the butt of the riot gun would come down on the back of his head and spill his hot brains out over his hair and down into his eyes and he would surely go mad in that instant before death and die screaming; and remain screaming for eternity.

They had to help him back into the bus anyway, but even if he had been unchained he could not have made it alone. One of the guards gave the hard cases sandwiches and coffee after the bus got started again, and Jack felt the old wolfish hunger swelling up inside him, and made himself sit still, the sandwich in his lap, the paper cup of hot coffee in his hand, until the feeling subsided. Then he began to eat. It was a tuna salad sandwich, full of bits of celery, and it tasted very good, but the back of his neck hurt from having to bend down to eat. And the coffee was even harder. He had to suck it up from the paper container because he could not get the proper angle on it to tilt the coffee into his mouth. He got only a few hot sips before he gave up and asked the guard for a cigarette.

"Here you go, buddy," the guard said. Jack left the cigarette in the corner of his mouth, blowing the smoke out his nose. He looked at the guard. A puffy, tired face. Even in his summer uniform the guard looked hot and tired. There were patches of sweat under his arms. Jack saw that his fingers on the riot gun were pressed white; so the man was tense. He had probably been tense all morning. In fact, Jack thought, the man was probably tense all the time he was at work. Probably every time he came to work a piece of whatever held him together disintegrated, vanished, and he would go home that much less than he had been. He would go home from work at night, the tension still stiff in his muscles, and have a drink of beer. Chino was hot; maybe the guard had a little patio out back of his house, where he had a canvas chair. He would take his can of beer out there, let himself down in the chair, and begin to drink, waiting. Maybe his wife would be out under the late sun, gardening. He would speak to her. She would straighten up, turn, smile. The glare would make it hard for him to see her smile, but he would know, and a little of it would slip away. It would take part of him with it, but it was worth it. Then he would remember that on the next day he had the run to San Quentin again. For a few seconds he would think about trading off. Or telephoning in sick. He would take another sip of beer, and then another. He would pull his hand away from the arm of the chair and light a cigarette. He would sigh, as if to clear his chest, but it wouldn't work. His wife would sense that something was wrong, and she would suggest that they go to the drive-in movie that night with some friends. He would nod and notice that his teeth were pressed together, and he would put his hands on the muscles below his ears, rubbing them gently, trying to soften them. He would know that he ground his teeth in his sleep. His wife would have told him, and often when he took naps he would wake up with the sweet deathly taste of blood in his mouth. His face was puffy because he ate too much. Eating made him feel good. It was practically the only thing that did.

Jack daydreamed all this; the guard merely sat, his fingers on the riot gun, and sweated. Every once in a while he looked out the window at the hazy valley, as if to catch a glimpse of the view. The guard probably loathed his job, Jack thought, but didn't have the guts or the ambition to do anything about it. But then, maybe he had no choice. He didn't look like the kind of man who would find work easily.

"How long you been a guard?" Jack said.

The guard's eyes wavered on Jack for a moment. "No talking," he said.

Jack's sympathy closed up. "But I have to take a piss," he said.

"Me too, man," the hard case behind Jack said. "How about we taken a piss?"

"Let's all PISS!" Jack shouted. The words were hardly out of his mouth when he saw the gaping eye of the riot gun almost touching his nose. He giggled. "Shoot, fuckface."

The guard across the aisle swung his gun onto Jack. "Don't pay him no mind," he told the first guard. "If he smarts off, crack him one."

"Your mother sucks off niggers," Jack informed the second guard.

"Hey, man," came a faint protest from behind.

"Present company excepted," Jack added.

"Well, I don't know if I like *that*," the Negro said.

"You guys shut up," said the first guard.

"Never mind," said the second guard. "I pity these poor guys."

But the first guard still looked hurt. "You guys know the rules. No talking."

"*And,*" added the man behind Jack, "no pissin."

Jack got tired of the game. He lapsed into silence, and after a while the riot gun moved away from his face. He saw a smirk appear on the face of the second guard. He almost spoke. But it would have been useless; the second guard would think he had shut up out of fear, and nothing Jack said or did would change his mind, and anyway he was probably right. Jack decided the second guard was probably very happy in his work. That's my revenge, he thought, to make him out a bastard. What about the driver? Bet he's a bastard, too. The good guys are all chained up, and the bad guys have all the guns and salary. Hee hee.

"What'er you grinnin about?" the second guard asked him.

"Nothing. I was just plotting my escape."

"Take us with you," the man behind him said, and there was an odd urgency in his voice. Then he giggled. "Oh, please, man, take us with you."

The second guard smiled. "Okay," he said with a paternal gentleness.

Throughout the whole day, the man next to Jack had been muttering and cursing.

"Will you shut the fuck up?" Jack said to him finally. The man turned his eyes to Jack, and for a moment Jack was frightened by what he saw, an empty coldness in the eyes that seemed to go nowhere. Not dead eyes, but terribly alive and so out of place in that meek clerkly face. Jack turned away and watched the valley darken in the twilight. They were on the freeway now, among the afternoon traffic. He watched the cars surge around the old bus, almost all of them with only the driver and no passengers; hot, tired-looking men. Thousands of cars, thousands of men, free to drive home on the freeway in empty cars, and Jack envied them terribly.

TWELVE

The Negro who had been sitting behind Jack on the bus wanted to go to prison even less than Jack. His name was Claymore. He was not a very hard case, even though he had held up a grocery store with a gun. But he kept trying to escape. When the police of Watts, California, came for him, he jumped out the back window of his apartment and they caught him in the alley with a twisted ankle. Then he tried to get out of the police car when it stopped at a red light. He did not offer the police any violent resistance, he just tried to get away. At the police station, handcuffed to one of the officers, he tried to sidle away from the desk, and when they jerked him back he said he wanted to go to the toilet. Claymore did not try to escape again until municipal court. He tried to walk out of the courtroom after being bound over for trial, and at the actual trial, three weeks later, he tried running. But that didn't work, either. He tried to get out of the county jail three times, and once got as far as the elevator, but when the doors opened at the main floor they were waiting for him. There was nothing they could do but chain him up like an animal. They did so reluctantly, because he did not look at all dangerous.

They had showers after their chains were removed, and sat in a corner of the gigantic dining hall in San Quentin, eating supper. "I just continually want out," Claymore said to Jack. "Hell, I got ten years to do."

Jack was still in isolation when Claymore tried his first escape attempt from Quentin. He was missing for three days. He had been assigned to one of the factories and on his first day at work he vanished. Everyone was mystified. They found him near the end of the third day, stuffed up into a ventilating shaft. They put him in isolation for a while, and a couple of the counselors tried talking to him. They convinced him that it would just hurt his chances of early release if he kept trying to escape. He agreed with them and they sent him back to work. He worked for three weeks in the varnishing room of the furniture factory and then disappeared again and was not caught for well over a month. They got him in Colorado, in a stolen car. The authorities of two states and the Federal Government talked it over and the Federal Government said they could handle him, so they tried and convicted him of crossing a state line in a stolen car, and sentenced him to five years in Federal prison; after which he would be returned to California to serve the full ten years of his previous conviction. Because of his record, Claymore was sent finally to Alcatraz, and when the news of his capture and trial filtered back to San Quentin Claymore was already serving time only a few miles across the bay. Nobody ever escaped from The Rock.

"That Claymore boy has a lot of heart," Jack's cellmate said. "But I do wish I knew how the hell he got out of here. Don't you?"

This cellmate was a Negro who refused to be classified as a Negro; his name was Billy Lancing, and he and Jack had known each other briefly several years before. When Jack got his job in the kitchen, Billy pulled some strings and they became cell partners. Billy looked different: his hair was paler red, his face sallower, and at one point in his career as a crossroader and pool hustler he had lost all his front teeth, which had been replaced with brilliantly white, obviously artificial teeth. To set them off, Billy had capped both his eyeteeth in gold, and all this gave his frequent grin a multicolored look. Otherwise he was much the same as Jack remembered him, small, narrow, giving the appearance of being in the last stages of tuberculosis.

Jack did not know how to take him. Billy talked a lot, and Jack wanted to be let alone. There was something wrong with San Quentin, and he wanted time to think about it.

"Can you figure it, man," Billy continued. "He gets out of here and then gets caught in a stolen car. *Surrounded* by *evidence!* Man, if I ever get shut of this place I won't spit on the *street!*" Billy laughed. His voice was high and soft, but his accenting was comical, almost a parody of how a Negro was supposed to talk. Of course, when he had been shucking the authorities about his racial background, he had been entirely white in his accenting and posture. The only things negroid about him, really, were his lips and nose, and he argued vehemently that this was surely not enough to make him eat and sleep with, as he phrased it, "a bunch of boogies." When the authorities finally gave in, Billy collected twenty-eight packs of cigarettes from other inmates who had bet him at two-to-one odds he wouldn't make it. He had no cell partner until Jack came.

Jack's placement in the kitchen instead of one of the factories came about in this way: When he first came in he was placed in isolation, "on the shelf," until he was brought before a counselor. The counselor had not been wary with him, and did not pretend that he knew more about Jack than Jack did, which was an unusual experience right there, and made Jack begin to feel uneasy. And yet, the counselor was not a con-lover. Jack knew these: men and women—an enormous number of women—who were simply fascinated by institutional types. They were always showing up at the orphanage or the reform school, ostensibly to observe or even to help out, but actually, as far as Jack was concerned, to satisfy their urges, to look through the bars at the wild animals. They had a certain glassy look to their eyes which Jack recognized, and the trick was to spot these people and make them give you money or candy, or, at the reform school, get the men among them aside somehow and ask them if they had a bottle in the car and would they sneak it in. On visitor's day at the reform school some of the boys would be given the job of handling the parking lot, and these would rifle the glove compartments, and when the sucker sneaked out to his car to get the bottle, it would probably already be stolen. Jack imagined these con-lovers liked the idea of being stolen from.

But the counselor wasn't one of these. He was a short round man with a pink face and delicate fingers, who looked as if he had a hangover. He looked through Jack's institutional records, blinking wearily, and then smiled at Jack.

"Well, how about it? What do you want to do here?"

The question stunned Jack. Nobody had ever asked him before. He sat there and didn't say anything. He felt very uneasy. The counselor talked on, about other matters of adjustment, and then came back. "Well, you're here, and you'll be here a while. Why waste the time? What do you want to accomplish?"

Again, the question frightened Jack and he did not answer. They took him back to the shelf, which was merely a section of single cells away from the main population. He knew now that San Quentin no longer had a hole. This frightened him, too. He was prepared for the hole; he was not prepared for anything else. He was afraid if he opened his mouth he would begin yelling for help. It was absurd, but that was the way he felt.

When they brought him back a couple of weeks later, the

counselor smiled affably. He did not seem to have the hangover this morning, and he was quite brisk. "Well. Back again. Sorry about the long wait; the case load around here's terrible. Now, let's get this done, shall we? I'm going to assign you to the furniture factory for the time being. I don't have to tell you it helps to be sort of busy around here; and there's plenty to do. None of it's make-work. I hope. And I've noticed on these records that you're just a few semesters short of high school graduation. Would you like to finish up here? We have some pretty good instructors. You can get a certificate from the GED and the Great State of California making you a bona fide high school graduate, if you want. Then you can go to college and become a brain surgeon. Work in the plant mornings, and go to school in the afternoons. Study in the evening. Want to try it?"

There was only one way for Jack to react: he had to push.

"I won't do it," Jack said. "Fuck your factory."

"Don't you like that kind of work?"

"Drives me batty. I've done it before."

A look of sympathy passed over the counselor's face. "I know what you mean." He did not seem bothered by the virtual "fuck you" Jack had flung at him. "Well, what *would* you like to do? I can't find out unless you tell me."

The softest job in the prison was kitchen work. "How about the kitchen?" Jack said. "I'll work there."

"You will, hey?"

"Sure. And, go to school, too. I mean, if you can work it."

The counselor fussed with his papers. "We'll see," he said. Jack went back to isolation, expecting to feel justified and triumphant, but all he really felt was disgusted with himself. He was acting like a child. He was in isolation for another week, and then transferred to Billy Lancing's cell and told that his schedule would be work in the kitchen from 4:30 A.M. to noon, with yard break, and then school in the afternoon. He could not understand it. Billy's schedule was the same, except that he spent his afternoons teaching elementary arithmetic. "Ah'm a fuckin mathmatical *genius*, baby," he told Jack with a delighted grin.

THIRTEEN

Jack spent his mornings mopping the dining hall, feeding one of the gigantic steam clippers, scouring pots and pans, all the KP duties of a newcomer to any kitchen, and in the morning break on the yard stood by himself in the sun. He ate early chow with the kitchen workers and then went on pass to the classroom and spent the afternoon in the oddly nostalgic atmosphere of learning. It was, in fact, the slowest part of the day. Their teacher was a convict, sent up for the usual white-collar crime of bad checks, a thin, egocentric man whose instruction moved painfully slowly, as slowly as if not more slowly than the dim comprehension of the dullest student, most of whom were much older than Jack. The young ones were nearly all fuckoffs from the factories and not even vaguely interested in grammar or English literature or California history. Jack was always glad when the day ended and he could go back to his cell. He brought his books with him and it was much easier just reading the books than studying them. And Billy was there, too, with another installment of his autobiography. Not that Billy wasn't interested in Jack's past or that he wanted to monopolize the conversation; just that Jack was not really talking yet. He was still trying to absorb the sights and sounds of the prison; it was his new home, and he expected it to be, almost wanted it to be, his home for the rest of his life. Because to think any other way was to hope, and he hoped he had given up hope.

Evenings were the best part of the day. After the bustle, the noise, the omnipresent danger and the constant sense of enforcement, being at home in a two-man cell was almost restful, even though there was always a threshold of noise that never lessened throughout the night, and even though there was another man sharing the semi-privacy. It was Jack's luck that the other man was someone he could like and someone he could listen to with interest.

It was clear, of course, that Billy wasn't talking just to hear himself, or to tell Jack about his adventures. By recapitulating the past Billy was in a sense getting out of the present, getting back into the world outside, as if by the magic of speech and memory he could for a few hours free himself from the cell, and as far as Jack was concerned, it worked. It not only drew Billy out, it took Jack with him, by the very simple fact that Jack could not think about Billy and think about himself at the same time. So, for a few hours each evening, the two of them wandered around the northern parts of the United States, living, reliving, the life of a small-time gambler. Those things Jack thought he would miss most, the colors and tastes of life on the outside, came back to him as he tried to picture the things Billy talked about, and often afterward he would lie on his bunk and wonder with some inner excitement if he wasn't developing a hidden resource in his imagination; if there weren't, after all, ways of beating the joint without actually leaving.

But he knew better. When the excitement went away, he was left with the sour knowledge that Billy was trying not so much to escape via his memory, as to find out, in fact, why the harmless, lonely life he lived had led him straight to prison. Not the specific crime; he knew what that was, but the things that changed him into a man who would commit such a crime. He had written a phony check and been caught for it; that was his crime. But what he wanted to know was, how did it happen that a wise fellow like himself had done such a stupid thing. He never did find out, but he told some good stories.

"Man, I tell you the queerest thing ever happened to me was up in Idaho. I'll *never* figure that cat out if I live a thousand years. I was in this all-night joint; I come about a hundred miles to get in this crap game in this guy's garage, you know, and man, I spent a *good* half-hour losin every penny I had, an so I cut out an went for this all-night poolhall an was just sittin there out of the weather watchin some old white cats playin billiards an wonderin where in *hell* I was gonna get some *food*. Man, you can say what you want about this joint, but you get three squares and a flop, and when you *aint* got em, they're *somethin!* I thought of everythin. Hock my stick? What stick! My magical Willie Hoppe Special? What a joke! I bought that son of a bitch about a month after I left Seattle, you know I just *had* to have one, an then some cocksucker in Walnut Creek, man, took and busted it over his knee when I wiped him out in snooker. I got another one later; left it at Whitehead's when I got busted at last. Sell my ass? Sho, I read about cats doin that, you know, they get busted an sit around the bus depot cussin like hell, an then some cute guy comes along an gives em half a million to cop their joint; well, shit, I thought about it, but I didn't want to, and man, I didn't even know *how!* I thought about bustin into a house an stealin the family fur coats, but shit, I'm too chicken-shit for that kind of action, and anyway, what the hell do you do with a fur coat? I didn't know any fences. You hear a lot of shit about that. Man, every big-city poolhall's got about fifteen guys always hangin around tryin to sell you a watch or a radio or somethin, but you never see these guys with any bread, do you? Hell, no!

"Anyhow, I'm sittin there in this poolhall and in comes the guy; it must of been two in the mornin, dressed in this business suit, nice-lookin guy, maybe fifty, looked like an *executive,* you know? He sits down and watches this billiard game, too. There wasn't nothin else happenin in the joint; one old guy in back cleanin off the tables, the houseman asleep back of the candy counter, you know; and then this executive comes up to me an wants to know if I want to play rotation for two dollars or somethin. *Rotation!* Well, shit. Maybe he's a queer, I think, and now's my big chance to sell my ass; but then, you know, maybe not. I says to myself, Billy, you been an honest man all your goddam life, and now you're *broke!* Play on your guts, Billy, and take that man's two dollars, and if you lose, let him try to find two dollars worth of your hide. I don't know who that cat was or what he thought an never did find out, but he sure wanted to play. So I did it, I got up an played him rotation, half scared he'd find out I was broke, half scared he'd beat me; but hell, he handled a cue like it was a deadly snake, and man, he couldn't hit his ass with a six-by-eight.

"We played, and I kind of kept it down an beat him by about ten points, man that game took twenty minutes, and he pulls out this wallet and opens it up, and you can see me kind of leanin over to look inside while I'm rackin the balls, and he pulls up two singles, bran new lookin, an throws em on the green and wants to play for *four!* Well, I says to myself, you got money for breakfast. You could throw it in right now, because your dream came true; or you can play on your guts *again* an get hustled into jail. Maybe the cat's a cop or somethin. But screw it, I played him an beat him out of the four, still wonderin if the cat ain't a hustler I just never met, waitin for him to throw me the okey-doke, but he doubles the bet another time or two and still can't hit a lick, and finally I think to myself, Billy, this john don't know the way home, and I cut loose myself and wrapped him up. Man, we started playin for fifty dollars a game, and I'd break and run every ball off that table sometimes, and he'd just be polite and say 'Nice shootin, you got talent,' or somethin, an give me the money and I'd rack the balls again an let him break and he'd go *zong!* and miscue or bounce the cue ball halfway across the room, and I'd shoot my sixty-one points, and out would come that wallet! I thought it would never end. I thought I was still sittin there having a dream. Finally the cat says, 'Thank you for the games, I seem to be broke, could you pay my share of the time?'—lookin anxious like he was violatin the *rules;* pay his share? *I had two thousand fuckin dollars!*"

Billy's laugh was easy, but his eyes glinted with remembrance of his riches. "Two grand." He looked at Jack. "Did I run back to that crap game, even before I ate breakfast? Is a bullfrog green?"

"Oh, don't tell me," Jack said. "You didn't lose it?" He felt almost sick at the thought. He could almost feel the thick wads of money slipping out of his own pocket.

"Lose it? Lose it? Are you out of your mind? Don't you know anything about luck? I come into that crap game like a madwoman flingin shit, an won another nine hundred before everybody fled. Man, I just got out of there and *trod* on Idaho lookin for somebody I couldn't beat." He laughed again. "Lose it? *Hell* no! You think this story's hard to believe; listen to this: Man, I took that money an thought an thought what to do with it, and I ended up goin to *college!*" His eyes were bright, almost feverish. "Ain't that a *bitch?*"

"Man, do you have any idea how many niggers there is in night school? They're *scared,* baby, they quit high school just like I did an go out an face that tough Cholly world and stand around on street corners an *sneer,* an when they get home they got no money an they wasted all that good sneerin; and up jumps the *Army,* an they hear their old man yellin around about *automation,* and it just scares the shit out of em. Night school! That's the scene! Man, they're so fuckin dumb, the most of them, they get all worked up and come to these classes, an then act just like they was back in high school, layin around payin no attention an thinkin the teacher's got it out for em cause they're black. Most of em. I made it through night school in a year, man, flyin low, spendin my days in Hollywood shootin pool, and I was gonna register at UCLA but this old dream of mine caught hold of me somewhere, and I went home to Seattle. I wanted to go to the University of Washington, right there in Seattle, and live near my folks, all that shit, you know; and man, I got there an my family was *gone,* every last one. I don't know where the hell they went. I should have wrote. Anyway, I went to the University, got a *conditional* acceptance, signed up for a bunch of wild-ass courses like French, biology, history, English composition, you know. Moved into a dorm, bought me some *sweaters,* dig; went to football games, all that shit, studied like hell, but man, how *cold!* What did I care?

"I didn't want to go to college; that was a bunch of shit. It was okay for some of them guys; hell, they was gonna end up runnin the country, you know? College is okay for them an for the cats who want to find some nice safe hole and crawl in it, but that wasn't *me.* I know, because I wasn't there three months before I had me a poker game goin in my room, an I was pushin benny at final time; taught them college athletes how to play nine-ball at the rec hall an was just *rollin* in money. Sure I studied. All the goddam time I'd be up all night hittin the books, but it didn't make any difference; the only courses I got anywhere with were biology and algebra; the rest were Cs and Ds, an you know *me,* daddy, I got to be up in the top or I don't play. So, shit. After a while, I felt like an asshole. You know, the worse thing in the whole fuckin world is to wake up in the middle of the night, when you're helpless, man, an think to yourself, Billy, you're a phony. You went to college because your heart ached, an now your heart aches *still!* What's the matter, you sick? You lonely?

"I wasn't the only one. There was cats all over that college wakin up scared. Some of em did it for *fun,* you know, sittin around drinkin coffee an talkin about *life;* with this now there aint no God so what the hell we gonna *do* time; some of these cats would come an bang on my door and come in an want to talk about niggers, what a hard lot they got, an want to score for some benny or make me take them down to a colored whorehouse, and laugh and yell an get drunk and have a high old time, but they was just as upset as I was, an we all knew it; we was all scared of the Army an life an all that shit; an what we really wanted most of all was to get *comfortable,* you know?

"It wasn't money, I found that out in a hurry. Money, man, I could get money. I *had* money. That's how goddam dumb I was then. I thought me an my brains and my good right arm could get me all the money I wanted. You know? The big problem was I guess I was just *empty* most of the time. When I first got out of the house, run off to Portland, that's when I met you, an had a bed of my own, I thought that was the best goddam thing in the world; a bed you could spread out in, a room that was *quiet*. You know that feeling? But, shit, it got old, not that I ever wanted to go back to the housing project an live like a hog; but I was just plain empty. A long time before I went to college I thought, well, fuck the niggers, I aint gonna worry about that. I don't want no troubles I aint made for myself, I aint gonna join no black club; that's just lookin for protection cause you're scared. I wasn't scared, I told myself, cause I had my brains an my right arm, an that made me different; I was unique, like Willie Mays. Because you know all that keeps the niggers apart an down is the lack of money; and I could get all the money I wanted. And if any white cat wants to call me nigger an spit in my face, I figured I could take that. It happens, you know. Some cat in some backhole poolhall says somethin about the *smell,* or somethin. He says, 'Man, what's that awful *smell?'*—meanin *me,* an I come back at him real quick, 'I guess that must be the smell of *big money;* I guess you aint ever smelled a fifty-dollar bill,' an haul out my wad and ask the man, 'Do you want to take some of this home and get a good sniff at it?'—and some of them dumb fuckin crackers'd get so mad they'd play me, and I'd take *their* money home an smell it, and it smelled *good.*

"Well, an sometimes they'd lose their tempers, too, and take me out an beat me up an take the money back, and mine too, but that's a lot tougher than it looks when my money is on the line. I left a few surprised cats around, man.

"Don't ask me what happened next, man. It was too funny. I was goin with this chick from the college, and one night I get real scared and can't sleep and can't think an lay there in my bed feelin the horrors come down and sit on my chest an I'm thinkin about all that shit, you know, there aint no God and the world is the worse fuckin place there is an we're all out to eat each other up and everything goes, an I'm just a speck in a universe full of specks an one of these days there's gonna be one less speck an nobody will know; all that cryin shit, you know, an somehow it got stuck in my head that love was the answer, an I was goin with this girl, so I must of loved her, so I gets up out of bed and jumps over to her place, she was livin at home, an bangs on her window, an in about twelve seconds I was married, workin at the bowlin alley and had two kids. *Wham!* My old lady wanted to be a social worker, dig, and I was gonna work in the bowlin alley—I didn't give a shit for college—while she finished up her schoolin, groovy, I had the money, but then she got pregnant and all I hear from her is bringin new life into the world an all that crap until the baby comes, an she's gonna go back to school anyway, an here comes the second kid, an that was that. Man, my whole life changed. For a while I dug it, naturally, I had me a good job at the alley, and they put in a bunch of pool tables an I had that all goin for me, I was a pretty big man there for my age; but every once in a while the whole bit got old and I'd hit the road again, leave the shoeshine stand in the hands of my *assistant;* you know, and head for San Francisco, LA, or Chicago. Sometimes I won, sometimes I lost, but I always kept the caseroll tight, and when I'd get lonely, I'd come home. Man, how *dull* it got."

It was at about this time, three weeks after Jack started working in the kitchen, that Claymore disappeared from San Quentin. Everyone was delighted, and began making book on his capture. With not too much else to do that had the spice of life to it, gambling was very important to some of the convicts, and they would bet on almost anything. Of course the biggest bets were on the men in death row, and of them, the most action was on Caryl Chessman, who had been there over four years already and whose arrogant, intelligent face inspired nearly everybody. To them, to some of them, he was one little man, using his larceny and his brains against the entire machinery of the State. If he finally won, there was an unconscious yearning in many of them that the State, the machinery, *all,* would just fizzle away and the gates open and they could go home. The odds on Chessman at this time were three to four against. Jack saw him once, crossing the big yard under escort; he was surprised at how small Chessman was.

The odds on Claymore were a little more sentimental; after all, he was an expert in a sense, and so the betting was a flat even-money proposition.

The night they heard about it Billy was excited and nervous in the cell. "Man," he said to Jack, "me and that Claymore are *connected*. I can feel it."

"What do you mean? Because he's a Negro?"

Billy rubbed his mouth. He did not look either happy or unhappy, but disturbed. "I don't know. When he first come in here and headed up that pipe I could feel it, you know. Connected. That's all."

From Billy's mood, Jack decided not to ask any more questions, and spent the time until lights-out reading in his history book. Afterward, in the semidarkness, he heard Billy say from above, "That man's *got* to stay free."

Now, this was something Jack could not understand. He knew, of course, that *free* meant outside the prison, and that he himself wanted that, especially when he awakened in the mornings to the cell, or stood by the door while the guard at the end of the long walkway pulled down the heavy bar that locked the cells; at such moments there was a heavy tension in him to just run, run down the gallery past a thousand cells or throw himself off the side and into the court; a pain starting at the edges of his eyes as he sat still for the count or put on his shoes—that he could understand, but not Billy's passionate need for Claymore to stay free. Personal freedom, yes, of course; but why freedom for somebody else? It did not make sense.

"If you want to escape," he said to Billy, "why don't you try?"

Billy laughed. He did not even bother to answer. When they heard Claymore was caught and on Alcatraz, Billy brooded for days.

FOURTEEN

Eventually, with so much time ahead of him, Jack got used to San Quentin. The yellow walls, the tall barred windows, the girders in the dining hall, became as familiar as home to him; even the smokestacks, through one of which the cyanide gas and a man's life had too often risen, wrinkling the sky for a few minutes above the north block at around ten in the morning. He even learned how to play dominoes, out at the picnic tables in the big yard. He had to—the enemy here was even more intangible than in reform school or the orphanage, and his fear that he would become accustomed to the life and even learn to *like* it was outweighed by the need to survive each day. For this it was necessary for him to become a *con*, to join the club; at least on the surface. He learned the language and he learned the ropes: that a man who never got into trouble with the *screws* was almost as bad as somebody who was always in trouble; that when you were asked to pass contraband you did it, not as a minor piece of defiance but because without some kind of connecting force of law among the inmates the prison would become an anarchy and the prisoners less than men. It was necessary for their self-esteem that they consider, no matter how comically, that they were in charge of their own destiny, and to break the rules a little demonstrated this. It also got stuff passed, which was probably even more important. The perfect convict, the man who lived entirely by the rules set down for him, was not a man but a vegetable. And the constant troublemaker, no matter how sick he was inside, was actually doing just what the State expected of him, therefore justifying the existence of the prison. So it was a matter of delicate balance between defiance and obedience.

But naturally, he learned, there was no unanimity. Not all the prisoners gambled, not all of them did any particular thing;

they didn't even all agree that prison was wrong—many not only thought it was right but admitted that they belonged in there. On this matter, Jack was not certain himself. Deep inside there was a tickle of guilt, an admission, perhaps, of the justice of prison existence. With Billy Lancing it was just the opposite. Penology was something Billy could get passionate about.

"Prison stinks, man. It really stinks. Think of all them mother-fuckers on the outside who don't know what it's like and think we belong here. Man, think about them cats. Aint a one of them don't break the law every time it gets in their way; man, I read a book once that said most of the money lost in crime in this country was stuff like stolen paper clips, shit like that, bank presidents runnin off to Mexico; and think a minute about the guys in jail because they ran *gambling games!* Can you believe it? Gambling? Every fuckin lawyer and judge in the fuckin country plays poker at his fatass *club,* an then goes down to court and gives some poor asshole two years for playin the same goddam game! What the fuck is this shit? And *cheat* you? What fuckin businessman wouldn't cheat you if he got the chance? *Shit!*"

Jack laughed at him. "You're sure pissed off. Somebody cheat you?"

Billy looked at him incredulously. "Cheat me? What the fuck do you think my fuckin sentence is? Fair play? I bop one check in my entire fuckin life and get one-to-five! What the fuck would you call that? And here some chickenshit accountant draws thirty thousand dollars out of the till an they give him *six months!* Look around you, man, all you'll see in here is the fuggin chicken thieves; all the big boys, the pros, the white-collar cats, are on the outside, or down in Chino out in the sun. Sure, fuck yes, you got to do somethin with the criminals, but you got to do it to *all* the criminals, or the whole thing is *horse-*shit."

Jack said, "Well, what did you expect?"

Billy snorted. "Now I'm locked up, I don't expect nothin. But they better not let me out of here."

"You don't mean that."

"No. Fuck no. Let me out and I'll kiss every ass from here to the Supreme Court to keep from comin back."

"Okay," Jack said. "So there's a lot of injustice. So what? What's that got to do with you?"

"Nothin. Only, I do hate it. Man, justice is based on the idea that we all got a right to live our lives any way we fuckin please, so long as we don't fuck up anybody else. Okay, I did wrong. I'll pay, I'll do my time. But I hope you don't think I'm doin this time cause I bopped that one little check. I hope you know I'd be home free or at worst out on *probation* if I had the money to buy a good lawyer." He had his hands in his pockets and his skinny shoulders hunched up, grinning down at Jack on the bunk. "I hope you dig that lawyer scene. Did you have a lawyer?"

Jack explained to him, for the first time, what had happened in Balboa County. Billy listened, smiling, nodding his head as if the story confirmed his thesis.

"Yeah. They sucked you in royally, tellin you that if you *cooperate,* everthin gets better an better. Man, don't you know the *machine* don't need your help? The only thing you can do to the *machine* is fuck it up. You can't help it. But you can slow it down. Now, like my case, man. I forged a check, dig? I won't give you the whole scam, but like it was a payroll check, some cats got this check protector and print up a bunch, and hand em out to cats like me to cash, for a quarter of the money. So I'm broke an I cash the fucker, an three days later a couple dicks come in to the Palace an haul my ass to jail. On an *information;* like, somebody turned me up, dig?

"So me an this dumb kid lawyer goes to court, see, and this bartender gets up an says he seen me endorse the check an he recognizes it, an then some cop gets up there an says they got about fifty checks just like it an endorsed the same way, an my lawyer just sits there. The gas is, I didn't endorse any of the checks at all! So they got me for a whole goddam crime wave!"

"Well, you got screwed, that's all," Jack said.

"Yeah, but my point is, a good lawyer could of got me off. I studied up on this, man. Like, the bartender says he *saw* me, an he says he saw me *write*. Well, man, a good lawyer's gonna hire a expert to come and *prove* that endorsement aint in my writing, dig, so that makes everything the fuggin bartender says bullshit. An he was their only witness, cause the cat that turned me up sure hell aint gonna show up in court. Hell, whoever it was only turned me up to take the heat off himself."

Jack thought about that for a while. "Well, why don't you make an appeal, or something? Like Chessman?"

Billy sneered at him. "Are you out of your skull? Who's gonna pay for the fuggin *transcript?* The Urban League? Fuck it. I'll do my time. But what grinds my ass is all the goddam people takin away my rights, stealin my money, makin it tough on my kids, an gettin away with it. I'm talkin about *crime,* not law. They don't even *have* laws for some of the shit they pull."

"I don't know what the hell you're talkin about," Jack said.

"You wouldn't. You're white."

"Oh. That. Well, I'm here, too. You ain't in here because you're part Negro; you're in here because you forged a check."

"Sho, man, I aint talkin about that. You're in here because you're too fuckin dumb to keep out. So am I. But I was talkin *in general,* not you and me."

"Why bother?"

"I give up. You are the dumbest cat I ever met."

"I just don't see it," Jack said. "They put us in here because it was easier than leaving us outside on the street. They had the power and they used it. I'm no victim of injustice. I'm not a victim of anything."

"Sho," Billy laughed. "You're in here cause you love me."

Lately it had been coming up like that, accidentally, in joke, or a casual touch, or a reference to somebody else; but it was getting to the point where their evening dialogues were tinged with it and making them both nervous. Once, when they were half-undressed for the night, Billy was trying to get past Jack to go to the toilet and he brushed against him in such a way that

Jack could feel Billy's fingers against his thigh. There was a quick shove, an exchange of profanity, and both went to bed infuriated, their friendship dissolved. Jack lay there angry and offended, tense beyond reason, and Billy lay above him mortified and angry, equally tense.

"I wouldn't touch you with a ten-foot *pole!*" Billy hissed down angrily through the darkness. After a few moments of electric silence, Jack heard him chuckle and add, "Even if I *had* a ten-foot pole." But it was several days before Jack built up his nerve enough to apologize.

Sex in prison is a matter of three choices: abstinence, masturbation, and homosexuality. Jack was familiar with all three, in varying degrees. At the orphanage the boys had been watched very carefully to see that they did not indulge in any "obscene practices," but naturally the boys managed, as they always do, furtively, quickly, and in darkness. The few homosexual episodes Jack remembered from the orphanage were all of the brutal sort, in which a small or weak and generally unpopular boy was forced by a ring of grim youths to submit himself to rape. The emotional climate of the orphanage did not seem to encourage crushes or pairings of any sort; only gang activity. Any boy caught masturbating, Jack remembered, was subjected to incessant and cruel joking from the other boys, and public humiliation from the administration. But it was clearly understood among the boys that all this was merely "something to do" and that Sex meant Women. In a way, Women meant growing-up-and-getting-out-of-here, and one of the first things Jack did after running away was to visit a whorehouse. Although he had taken part, often as a leader, in the rapes and circle-jerks, he dropped all that sort of thing on the outside, and like most boys of high-school age, resorted to masturbation only when he had to, and even then felt angry and shabby about it afterward.

At the reform school there had been precious few effeminate boys, and again sex life in the cottages was a group affair, the strong taking from the weak; but Jack didn't join in much because he spent most of his time in the hole. There, of course, he could masturbate all he wanted, but he didn't. It just made things worse.

Of the three alternatives, abstinence was the one he knew best, and he hoped that in San Quentin he would be able to forget about sex. He did not see how, with two men to a cell, you could get away with masturbating. These were all grown men. Masturbating was a kid trick, he thought, and only a childish man would resort to it. He learned very quickly that men in prison were treated like children and expected to act like children, even in, one might say especially in, the matter of sex. But he still did not see how he could get away with it.

But one ceaseless night he got to thinking about Mona, and from her his thoughts went without volition to vague erotic images of other women he had known, their flesh glowing before his eyes. He tried to think of other things, but it didn't work. A breast, a nipple, a smooth flank would interrupt the flow of thought and he could feel his penis thickening and hardening, beyond his control. It should have been no problem at all, just jack off and forget about it. It had to happen once in a while. Either that or cut it off. It was infuriating to think that one organ could be in charge like that, turn his mind, make his whole body tremble; it was disgusting. But not two feet above his head Billy Lancing was asleep, or perhaps even *not* asleep, and he might hear Jack's movements and lean his head over and ask him what he was doing. Or he might even know, understand, and say nothing. In the morning he would look amused. Jack had never heard Billy making any such noises, and often Jack did not get to sleep until long after midnight. Therefore, Billy did not masturbate. He had conquered his sexual desires. If Jack gave in, he would be the only one in the cell to give in. Furiously he threw himself over on his stomach and waited for the erection to subside. He thought about how funny it all was. He thought bitterly how funny it would seem to somebody not going through it. Like a bad hangover; a subject of much snickering. He wanted to ask Billy about it, but he did not dare. It was too personal.

What made it worse was that most of the men talked about sex incessantly, or so it seemed. To hear them tell it, the most virile men in America were here gathered, temporarily cutting womanhood off from their prowess. Yet you could not be in prison long without hearing about the love affairs that were going on right there, between the men themselves. Now that Jack seemed to have sex on the brain, he seemed to hear about nothing else. It was a commonplace to hear a man bragging about all the women he had slept with, and then without apparent transition begin discussing the cute little Mexican who worked in the bakery. It was all very embarrassing. One day while Jack was walking past the salad table with a stack of hot clipper racks, he happened to glance over in time to see one man slip a plastic ring on the finger of another man. Both were ordinary-looking men, one a burglar and the other a thief, but the expressions on their faces were ones Jack could never remember having seen on a man: one of them shy and coy, an outrageous burlesque of maiden modesty; the other simpering with equally feminine aggressiveness.

Another con, one of the cooks, saw the look of disgust on Jack's face and gave him a steamy wink. Jack was actually embarrassed and could feel his already hot face reddening.

After that the prison seemed alive with affairs. It was unbelievable. These were grown men, and not queers, either. You could expect this from the few homosexuals, but to see a hardened old thief kissing a stubby Negro when he thought nobody was looking was beyond belief.

Finally Jack was approached. He was standing at the salad table, slicing carrots with a butcher knife, and one of the cooks came up behind him, made a remark about something inconsequential, and pushed his body up against Jack, his fingers touching him briefly on the hips. After the momentary shock of the contact passed, Jack said out of the corner of his mouth,

179

"Take it on the heel and toe, or I'll have your balls for a watch fob," and the man backed away, offended, and said, "You don't have to get bitchy about it." Jack turned and gave him an evil grin, holding the butcher knife low and twirling its tip. "Split," he said.

Yet even having refused the man had a *bitchy* quality about it, as if he were queer, and was available, but just not to this particular cook. And besides, there was no denying that the pressure of the man against him had roused him. It had been pleasant, damn it.

Another time, a con said to him, "Oh, we know you're playing hard to get." There did not seem to be any answer. It had been on the tip of Jack's tongue to say, "Oh no I'm not," but that hardly would have cleared the matter up.

But it was not just a question of courtship and seduction, which after all, he reasoned, probably helped a lot of the men forget themselves for a while. There were also the prison wolves, homosexual rapists, who would get it into their heads that they wanted a particular man, and then go after him with single-willed determination until they caught him in a corner somewhere. These wolves sometimes worked in pairs or threes, and it was very difficult to avoid them once they had their eyes on you. Things had been quiet for a while, because just before Jack arrived a man had been killed in the shower by one of these wolves, and there was a big crackdown. All the known wolves had been moved around and were being watched carefully. The one who had done the knifing hadn't been caught, but the population was certain that it was a factory worker named Clifford, a gigantic Negro armed robber who had his fingers into almost every racket in the prison; an organizer, a dominant personality, a natural leader. Even the guards were afraid of him. He was serving life as a habitual criminal, and so had settled down to making the prison his own private territory. Even the tightly knit, secretive Muslim group was afraid of him, though they claimed to admire him.

Jack was not afraid of Clifford or the other wolves, but Billy was. He had been caught twice, he admitted, and both times he thought he was going to be killed. "So I just laid there and *took* it, man," he said. "What the fuck, I ain't going to die for a virgin asshole."

The really bad times for Jack, now, were the hours spent locked up in his cell with *another man*, with live flesh, a warm human body that grew more attractive each night, until Jack's fantasies no longer were about women but about Billy; how they could grapple together in secret as so many dozens of others were doing probably right at that instant, all up and down the tiers of cells, in secret and private, enjoying the flavor of each other's hot thrusts; while he, Jack, lay in murderous frustration and agony. After a while it was even funny. He knew that the only tangible thing that stood in his way was fear of refusal; that, and a strong reluctance to make the overtures. He didn't even know what to say to Billy. He was not going to get up in the middle of some dark night and tap Billy on the shoulder and say, "How about it?" or, "Say, let's you and me screw," or anything of the sort. Nor would he invite Billy into his bunk, winking and grinning and pointing. What if Billy laughed at him? What if Billy groaned with passion and tried to *kiss* him? It was impossible.

So they lay there, both of them, in the smutty darkness, each dreaming and wishing the other would make a move. Billy, of course, was afraid that Jack would break his neck if he got funny.

One morning on the big yard, Jack was watching a game of dominoes between two of the best players in the prison, and a man standing next to him, whom he knew only slightly, said, "That Billy's awfully sweet, isn't he?"

"I guess so," Jack said. He was getting resigned to this kind of talk, even though it sent a pang of guilt through him.

"You *guess* so?" the man grinned. "Who would know better than you?"

"What's that supposed to mean, motherfucker?" Jack snarled.

"Shut up, you guys," said one of the players.

That night Jack said to Billy, "What's all this shit about you and me?"

"You and me what?" Billy asked.

"You know goddam well what. Everybody in the joint thinks you and me're shacked up."

"Well, we ain't," Billy snapped. "So why bug me about it?"

"Because I think you probably started it yourself, that's why, you little shit."

Billy looked disgusted and climbed up on his bunk with a book. Jack was ashamed of himself, but he would not apologize. "Piss on the little bitch," he thought.

A few nights later Jack heard strange noises from the upper bunk. He knew what was going on. Still, out of spite, he whispered, "What's goin on?"

The noises stopped. After a moment, Billy's furious whisper: "I'm jackin off! What the fuck did you think I was doin?"

Jack giggled. "I thought you had somebody up there with you."

There were moments of silence.

Jack whispered, "Well, go ahead. Don't let me stop you."

"She-it," Billy said. "I done lost mah train of thought."

Gutty little bastard, Jack thought. He went into a deep and pleasant sleep.

But if homosexuality was absurd, what about no sex, or masturbation, or normal sex itself? Wasn't it all equally absurd, futile, and comical? Think of the things people do to each other, and for each other, just to get rid of an itch! Think of how it must look to an observer! Think of a creature so constructed that in order to survive, eat, sleep, procreate, get the snot out of its nose, it had to be triggered by pleasure instead of rationality; think of an animal that wouldn't have sense enough to evacuate its bowels if it weren't *fun*, and who, blinded by that very pleasure, actually pursued it as if the pleasure was the goal! Think of the lengths this creature would go, to make sure his itch was stroked by one particular person, of one particular size and shape, when in truth any other person would accomplish the same end! What a joke! Imagine a man horribly afflicted with psoriasis, great itching scabs covering his entire body, who got it into his head that no one but a certain girl's fingers could relieve him; think of this man in all his agony dressing in an itchy woolen suit, his whole body trembling, screaming out, while he stands before a mirror combing his hair, scenting himself, then rushing across the city to the home of this girl, waiting on her, babbling to her about home and future and love and flowers and sweetness, while beneath his suit his body cries out in anguish to be scratched; think of him, seated on the couch beside her (she all modestly pulled away into the corner, and he knowing deep in his heart that she, too, itched and must be scratched or die) and secretly rubbing himself against the couch for some partial relief, until the great moment comes and they strip themselves and expose their scabby reddened bodies and begin, modestly, delicately, to scratch each other while the pleasure of it all swells up into their minds and blots out all thought; until, finally, and naturally, they lie back exhausted, knowing that soon, very soon, they are going to start itching again . . . just think of it!

It struck him with horrible force. His parents, whoever they were, had probably made love out of just such an itch. For fun, for this momentary satisfaction, they had conceived him, and because he was obviously inconvenient, dumped him in the orphanage; because he, the life they had created while they were being careless and thoughtless, was not part of the fun of it all; he was just a harmful side effect of the scratching of the itch; he was the snot in the handkerchief after the nose had been blown, just something disgusting to be gotten rid of in secret and forgotten. Cold rage filled him, rage at his unknown parents, rage at the life he had been given, and for such trivial, stupid reasons! For one wild second of ejaculation! For that, he had been born. This same thing that was keeping him awake nights, and inexorably turning him into a prancing faggot, was the cause of his existence. Fifteen or twenty minutes on a forgotten bed between two probable strangers had given him twenty-four years of misery, pain, and suffering, and promised, unless he were to die soon, to go on giving him misery for another forty or fifty years, locked up in one small room or another without hope of freedom, love, life, truth, or understanding. A penis squirts, and I am doomed to a life of death. It has got to be insanity; there has got to be a God, because only an insane God could have created such a universe.

There was no reason at all why Jack should not do exactly as he pleased. He and Billy became lovers. It was an arrangement, coldly conceived for sexual satisfaction, without even words that first time, but limited by coldly precise and rational language from there on out. The terms were that they would use each other's bodies for that ornate form of masturbation called Making Love, but there was to be no question of emotional involvement, or prying into one another's soul. This, they decided coldly, would keep them from going crazy or queer.

FIFTEEN

Things had been going much too well at the bowling alley, perhaps that was what was the matter. Billy's shoeshine stand was right next to the check-out counter and only a few feet from either the all-night lunch counter or the pool tables, and he had a team of four boys who did the actual shining of shoes (although Billy would take over for special customers, big spenders, etc.) and there didn't seem to be anybody in Seattle who could beat him at his own games of one-pocket, nine-ball, or straight pool. He was making money, very good money, not only from his stand but an actual salary from the management:

Billy was in charge of maintenance, and he had discovered in himself a talent for managing things, for halting arguments, for overseeing the hundred details of a 24-hour establishment without undue strain on himself.

Perhaps Billy's status as resident pool artist was as important to the management as anything else. Billy drew people to the bowling alley, especially from 2 A.M. to dawn, when nothing much else was open, and the poolhall habitués from all over Seattle would gather, sitting in the double row of theater seats overlooking the pool section. These men, especially the better players, respected Billy for his talent, and among them there was an inner circle, including and revolving around Billy, of men who had been out on the road and played in the big poolhalls of San Francisco, Los Angeles, Chicago, Philadelphia, and who could talk about the great players and the great games; who had adventures of their own to tell the younger men, the boys, who had never been on the road. And of course they all played, especially the kids, and the usual winner of the games they played—two-bit nine-ball, dollar snooker, an occasional five-dollar game—was the house, and so the house did not mind if they came around when they were broke, because the house knew that when they did have some money they would bring it and spend it.

Especially the kids, who were getting their taste of night life savored with illegality and the dirty game of pool; it often pleased their sense of daring to mingle with a Negro, even a pale one like Billy, buy him cups of coffee and listen to his advice on how to hold a cue, make a good game, assess a mark, learn the language. And these kids came in handy for Billy, too, as the source of his maintenance manpower. They would show up broke, with not even enough money for coffee or cigarettes, and Billy could hire them for the one night to sweep down alleys, empty ashtrays, sort pins, or even sweep out under the pool tables, the work being no disgrace because Billy was their boss. They worshiped him, these kids, and he knew they did, and basked in it.

It was not just his talent that drew them. Billy was one of the few, one of the very few, poolshooters with money. Another was old Larkin, a short gray man who wore dark blue suits, wine-colored shirts, and a gray hat. He was a snooker expert, retired from the postal service after forty years of traveling around the country on trains, but old Larkin carried only three or four hundred dollars on him and he was getting old and cranky. Billy always had at least a thousand dollars buttoned up in his left shirt pocket. Just knowing it was there made him special in the eyes of the kids; they were just at that point in life when money begins to show its importance, and a thousand dollars was a lot of money.

It was his caseroll, and he had had it for so long now, since the wild days on the road, that he sometimes dreamed about losing it and would wake up chilled with the remembrance of the emptiness of being broke and alone; sometimes it got awful, and cursing himself he would have to get out of bed and go to the chair, feel in his pocket to see that it was still there, and then even carry his shirt into the kitchen, turn on the light, and, still cursing his fears, take the money out and count it. Then he would go back to bed, and his wife might stir and ask him sleepily, "Where have you been?"

"Checkin the kids," he might say. Often he would do just that, go quietly into their room and tuck them in, feeling that incredible tenderness allotted only to parents, and then return to his bed and his bad thoughts. But most of the time he was not at home nights, slept days, and the children were merely loud noises in the other part of the house. But his son and daughter had much to do with his increasing worry over his caseroll; for so long the roll had been his edge, his margin, the means of his escape at any time from whatever world he inhabited, and lately it had become more than this and yet less, as he thought about the children and what they were, and who they were.

Years before he had said and meant, "Fuck the niggers"—

he had seen too many of his friends swallowed up in bitterness, and he wanted to escape, not drown. But now there was no escape and he was in the awful position of seeing his children grow toward that moment when they would know, would be shown, told, that they were niggers and not human beings.

Because no matter how Billy twisted and dodged his way through life he could not get away from the central fact of his existence; whether he liked it or not, he was black, and there was nothing he could do about it, no action he could take without first thinking about it. It was just there. He could not love it or fight it or be proud of it, it was just there. He could not even hate it any more.

His children were beautiful; how could anybody be so cruel? They were so affectionate and full of joy, so eager and innocent; why did somebody have to come along and with one stiff, ugly word, cut the innocence out of them? From the moment they understood *that word* they would proceed through life half-murdered of their ability to love; the moment their eyes became wary they would cease to be children, and Billy was certain that he himself would not love them so much. It might have been better, he thought with bitterness, if they had not been born at all; and then he saw them in his mind and knew that he could not stand their nonexistence; life without them would be life without life. And some day, a white kid, innocent himself, would tell them who they were, and there would be no path for Billy's rage, no one for him to murder, only the emptiness of despair and frustration as he saw the hurt eyes of his children.

Sometimes he saw it that way, but other times he would try to remember his own reaction. It was a hurt, yes, but children get over hurts. It was not as if they were alone with it. And for that matter, they probably would not hear *it* from a white kid at all, but from their own playmates. As he must have. They are alive, he thought; they have to put up with misery, like every living human. That's the only way you ever learn anything.

So it might have just been self-pity, like when you lie there and torment yourself by seeing them killed by a car or turning out idiots. Self-pity and the night-dread of losing his money.

Because the roll was the secret—with it he could cushion his children's pain. Not prevent it; that was impossible; but take away some of the hardest edges. Money could make the difference; he had always believed it. He hadn't really known what money was for until he had children. It is for them. Good skirts and sweaters for the girl, a fine mitt and shoes for the boy. College; it had failed for Billy but it would not fail for them, because he had gone to college to *find* something and they would go to *get* something; the personal right to jobs where you dressed nicely and met nice people who would have you over for cocktails before dinner on the patio. What difference did it make if all your friends were colored, as long as you did not have to live through the black agonies of poverty or the humiliations of government aid? The roll could do that. It was not his to play with. It belonged in the bank. Yet it was only a thousand dollars. It was pitiful. It was nothing. A little frantically, Billy felt the need for hundreds of thousands of dollars; he felt trapped and cornered without thick wads of money to save him, save his children.

And again, he would think about leaving them. Maybe that was the best way, after all. Teach his children the first hard lesson himself. "You can't trust nobody." And flee from all that burden, his children already tempered against injustice. Billy often thought of leaving his wife. He loved her, yes, but that was not enough. Maybe love is enough for a woman, he would think, but it's not enough for a man. A man has got to have his *life*. He and his wife were constantly picking at each other. She knew, and of course he knew, that he did not have to spend all those long hours at the bowling alley. He was a man of some importance (isn't that a joke? he thought) and he had assistants who could run things. She wanted some family life, some evenings out among friends, and Billy did not have a single real friend in the Negro community. She, of course, had dropped all her friends from college when she married Billy. She had to make do with the neighbors, and they were a poor lot. None but she among the women had been to college, and all they ever found to talk about was children, clothes, food, prices, television. When she was not busy with the children she was horribly bored, and she would not watch television, even though they had a set. The neighbors thought she was too sensitive about television, but to her it was just the white man's world shoved rudely into her living room, and she would not have it. She let Billy know several times how dull things were.

That was a woman's place, he would think angrily, to stay home and keep house and mind the children. If that *bored* her, tough shit. Nobody said life had to be one thrill after another. But inside himself he knew what a stupid lie that was; he knew he stayed away from home because he could not stand the boredom either, and secretly he sympathized with her—only he could not see how both of them being bored would help matters. It was a bind. He often dreamed of running away, and several times he did go out on the road, but he always knew he would be back.

So what was his *life?* Look out there at all the ten million things life can be, and tell yourself which are yours, and which you will never do. And there was the agony of it; so much he wanted to do, and so little he could do. Why wasn't he content to be what he was? After all, look at it rationally. He was one in ten thousand already. He was a man of importance. He could earn enough money right where he was to support his family properly, and all that other dream-nonsense was wrong. He did not need hundreds of thousands of dollars for his children, he didn't even need them for himself. He had a good life. He was one of the rare ones who actually loved his family, and one of the pitiful handful of Seattle Negroes who could earn a good living. He knew he had quit the road life for college because he had seen this possibility; he knew he could not have stood the life on the road much longer; the loneliness alone was murdering him; and he knew he quit college and got married not for any abstract reasons but because he had fallen in love and wanted with desperate urgency to begin his family. All this was true. What was the matter? Talent?

So he was a talented poolshooter. There were better in the world. He would never be champion, and so what? What was being champion poolshooter? That was no great thing to be. Certainly he got his few rare moments of joy, his first and his fullest, out of the game; but so what? He was a man now, with the responsibilities he *wanted* and *needed*. He did not feel whole without them. But, of course, he did not feel whole anyway. He felt that he needed to be challenged. It had been a long time since he had felt his heart in his mouth. He knew what he was: out of the running. He missed it terribly. He missed victory, and he even missed defeat. He had everything he had ever dreamed of, and it was not enough.

So he got himself a mistress. What else, he thought ironically. Isn't that what the fellow does? He dreams of greater things, so he gets himself a girl friend and comes on with her about how Tom he is; he takes all that damned anxiety and focuses it in one place; he *bunches* it. Cool; now when I feel shitty, I can blame it on *her*.

Billy's wife, like himself, was pale and semitic, with thin lips, small breasts, and slender limbs. Neither of them had more than an eighth of Negro blood. This was satisfactory, and Billy always thought if he ever fooled around on the side it would be with a woman even paler than his wife, perhaps a white girl. Just a fling, a fillip, getting some strange just for the sake of strange. But that is not how it happened. Actually he fell into a panic of love for the blackest girl he had ever seen in his life.

Early in the affair he felt confident and happy, even though he knew he was completely out of control. The girl, Luanne, worked at the lunch counter in the bowling alley for about three hours one night, and then was fired for being drunk. She was short and slender, with large breasts and buttocks and a thick gravelly voice that reminded Billy of Bessie Smith at her guttiest; she was fired after spilling a cup of coffee down the front of a customer and then laughing about it, and when the manager came out of his office and tried to reason with her she put up a fight and Billy had to come and help them eject her from the place. Two others, white men, had her by the arms and were pulling, and Billy got behind and shoved; close up to her like that he could smell the French whorehouse perfume she was drenched in, and for days the memory of the odor stayed with him, and finally he went into the office and got out her employment card and copied down her telephone number. He had a fine time planning the affair in his imagination, and it was only a week later, when he actually telephoned her, that he felt even the slightest doubt.

She vaguely remembered him, and he came on all niggery and boasted his way into a date with her, and after that one furtive night with her, which ended up on the shabby carpet of her one room (they didn't find the time to pull down the bed), all the real pleasure went out of the affair, and Billy became obsessed. She had been fantastic, beyond anything he had ever known. He could not keep away from her, and he felt terribly guilty. He wondered how long he could stand it. When he would come home early in the morning and climb into bed with his wife, he dreaded her awakening for fear she would want to make love; he did not have an ounce of energy left in his body and he was afraid she would understand, and move away and take the children. The thought of this almost panicked him; it was all right for him to dream of leaving her, but the very hint of a suggestion that she might leave him was terrifying. And what if she, too, had a lover? After Luanne, Billy knew to a certainty that he had been a poor lover with his wife, infrequent, hurried, uninventive—in short, everything he suddenly *was* with Luanne, he had not been with *her*, his wife, the woman he ought to have been loving in increasing depth and passion; the woman he had been neglecting, avoiding, keeping fed and housed and clothed and little else—the woman he had imprisoned to raise his family. Wouldn't she have every right to seek out a lover? And wasn't it possible (and the way he felt about himself, statistically probable) that this lover of hers would give her the passion and depth of intimacy she needed and didn't get from her husband? And wouldn't she be tempted to run away with him?

It did not occur to Billy yet that she, if his nightmares were true, would probably feel as guilty about it as he did; it did not occur to him that she ought to feel guilty. He was the one in the wrong, not she. If she went into an affair, it would be out of need; but in his case it was—well, something else. Pride, randiness; something less honorable than need. He knew that. He did not even like Luanne; every time he left her furnished room he swore to himself that he would never return and that in a couple of days, when he had his strength back, he would come home and make love to his wife as she had never been made love to before. But he never did, and by the time he had his strength back he would again have visions of Luanne, and cursing himself he would telephone her for a date.

Luanne did not care; that was part of her attraction. She was unwomanly in that she did not need affection, lived without it, considered it corny and disgusting. Anyone who would bring her a few dollars, a handful of joints, a bottle, was welcome. She loved to make love and seemed to have an endless supply of wriggles, groans, and passionate profanity; but between bouts she was terribly dull. When she was drunk or naked, Billy decided, she was a ball; but sober and dressed she was nothing at all. Another thing she lacked, from Billy's viewpoint, was time. A girl like that was popular, and Billy had to content himself with being squeezed in between the other men in her life; many of them bigger and blacker and tougher than Billy. At one point there were no fewer than three pimps hanging around dreaming of the fortune to be made of this abundance, but she never did fall for their patter; life was too easy to go professional.

There was no question about it, Billy was beginning to despise himself; with desperation he cast around for something, any part of himself, he could admire. At about this time, when Billy could hardly shave for fear of seeing his own eyes in the mirror, the high-roller hotshot from Phoenix hit town and began knocking off all the poolshooters.

Billy heard about him long before he saw him; how he had come into the Two-Eleven downtown one afternoon, this short, stubby Arizona guy, and had bulled and bragged around about what a great eight-ball player he was, and then had finally been challenged to a game of straight pool by one of the hangers-on and been beaten out of twelve dollars and fled, claiming he had to "get out to the horses"; had come back the next day and gotten into a snooker game with old Larkin on the big English table, telling everyone he had never played snooker "on a football field" before, and betting two dollars a game, and sent old Larkin to the rack in five games. Nobody in Seattle could beat Larkin at snooker. After Larkin went to the rack, the Arizona guy bellowed out that snooker was a kid's game and anybody could win, especially against a man at death's door like old Larkin. He, the Arizona guy, preferred a game with some skill to it, like eight-ball. Naturally, Billy and all the other poolshooters were intrigued. Eight-ball is to snooker what checkers is to chess. Then, before the Arizona guy ever showed up at the bowling alley (everyone just naturally assumed he would come looking for Billy), a rumor was started that he had been on television in Chicago, *demonstrating* snooker, and that he had beaten Willie Mosconi and Joe Bachelor at straight pool, Hollywood Slim and Alabama Shorty at one-pocket, and finally, that Hoppe himself refused to play him. Nobody knew what to think. Billy, personally, discounted all the rumors. He had never heard of this guy. Surely, he reasoned, I ain't been off the road that long.

Billy was behind the check-out counter tipping cues late one night when there was a stir of conversation over at the theater seats by the pool section. He looked up and saw old Larkin, his face twisted in old man's sour distaste, pointing toward the entrance. Billy turned and saw a very short plump man in a blue short-sleeved shirt and white slacks striding in, followed by two large mean-looking LA-type hoods in windbreakers. Billy went back to his work, but kept his ears open. After a bit, this is what he heard, in a vibrating basso, almost a bellow:

"Is *this* the famous all-night bowling alley? I don't see any shooters. I said I'd play eight-ball all night for any price and you all just sit there and look at me. What is this? I heard Seattle was a money town, but I guess it's just another *dollar* town. Who wants to play a thousand points of billiards for ten cents? Split the time. That's the game for this town, billiards. Couple old men fussing around an old table that ain't even got any pockets! Who wants to bet on two whales fightin a sardine? I'll take either side of the bet. Where's the quick money? I'm a sport, where's all the other sports? Eight-ball? I'll play anybody!"

Billy knew this long speech had been directed at him, although he had not looked up once, and he knew the fat man was not looking at him. He came out from behind the counter in a Stepin Fetchit shuffle, his voice high and niggery: "*Eight*-ball? Wha fo youall wont to play that lil ol kid game? Ah'll risk mah ol black hide own one-pocket, *maan!*" Billy hoped the fat man disliked Negroes; it would be to his advantage.

"I didn't come all the way to Seattle to play the shoeshine boy," the fat man declared. So Billy knew the Uncle Tom routine wouldn't work. He said, "Well, then I guess you come all the way to Seattle just to *talk*. All talked out back home, ey?" Billy grinned at one of the LA hoods, and the hood grinned back, and winked.

"Aint I seen you in the movies?" Billy said to the hood.

"Damn right," the hood said proudly. "I been a killer in two pictures. They got me in Central Casting."

"What a fuggin lie," said the other hood. He was younger, not much over twenty-two. He said to old Larkin, "Hey, you want to play some snooker here? Three dollars?"

Larkin muttered to himself and then said, "No, I want to watch the big show."

"You aint scared of me, are you?" persisted the kid. "I don't even know how to play. But I'll play you."

The fat man looked discomfited. "Talk? Money talks. I reckon I'd play eight-ball with the king of Sweden if the money was right."

"Eight-ball?" Billy sneered. The crowd was enjoying this. Nobody was playing pool any more; everyone was gathered around listening and grinning slyly at each other. Among the kids there was the certain belief that nobody could beat Billy Lancing, and they were all looking forward to seeing the fat braggart stranger put in his place.

"You don't want to play." The fat man dismissed Billy. He said to the crowd, "He don't want to play." He looked strangely baffled. "I guess I'll have me a sangwich."

"You do look a little undernourished," Billy said.

"Oh, that's all. That's all. Get your stick, Sambo." He headed for the wall racks where the house cues were kept. Billy shrugged and went back of the counter for his Willie Hoppe Special, returned to the number one table, screwing the shaft of the cue into the butt, running his hand over the high gloss of the wood, checking the firmness of the leather tip with his thumbnail, chalking up, while the fat man rummaged over the cues, testing, weighing, sighting, and finally returned with a 22-ounce club with a billiard tip. "This'll do," he declared. "Warped as an old lady's sexlife. Ha ha."

Billy happened to look over in old Larkin's direction, and for the first time began to feel apprehension; old Larkin's face was screwed up in an insufferable smirk. He must have hated Billy and been looking forward to seeing him beaten. Billy felt a twinge of doubt, and he had to keep his fingers from reaching up and touching his caseroll through his pocket. He grinned tightly at the fat man. "How much we goin to play for, tubby?"

"A friendly game, that's all I ever play," the fat man said. "But I reckon you got a flock of little pickaninnies runnin around dependin on you for food and whatall, so let's just play for a couple dollars. Sound like a friendly game to you? Make it easy on yourself, boy."

"Win, place, or show?" Billy said acidly. Quickly he swallowed his anger. That was the worst thing he could do. He smiled. "Two dollars is fine," he said.

There was a murmur of disappointment from the crowd. Billy tossed a coin, lost, and racked the balls for eight-ball. He backed away from the table to watch the fat man shoot. Everyone was quiet now; all Billy could hear were two hard-core bowlers over on the other side, and the faint, insipid music from the speaker system. He felt the coldness of the air conditioning on his cheek, and he suppressed an urge to rub his hand across his mouth. He wanted a cigarette very badly, but refused to light one.

The Arizona guy looked like a plump child bending seriously over the table, his fat fingers dead white in the glare. He broke with a *thwack*, drawing the cue ball back toward the end rail, and sank the twelve and the four. He walked around the table rapidly, choosing the striped balls, and sank them one after the other, following the fifteen past the side pocket for perfect position on the eight, called it in the corner and sank it. His lips, which had been pursed in concentration, went flaccid again and he straightened up and grunted. "Huh. Lucky. *Rack!*"

Billy dropped the two bills on the table, and began fishing balls out of pockets and rolling them toward the end. "We rack our own balls here," he said.

"Some joint," the fat man reflected. He chalked up and waited for Billy to finish racking. It was winner break, of course. The fat man stepped up, broke, and ran out again. He won six straight games, and Billy did not shoot once.

"That's all," Billy said. He felt remote, almost as if he were dead. He unscrewed his stick, as if he had been driven to the rack.

"You're right," said the fat man. "Two dollars a game. What's the matter with us? The house is winnin all the money. Let's play for something."

"No more eight-ball," Billy said.

The fat man looked surprised. "Name your game," he said.

"One-pocket," Billy said. With something near dread, he added, "For any amount you choose." He glanced at the crowd. You're waiting to see me die, you sons of bitches. It was as if he had never seen them before. They had disgusting, stupid, greedy faces. They were not his friends. He was just entertaining them. He should pack up his cue and quit. He did not want to play the fat man. He did not want to play at all. He was tired. But no, that wasn't true. He *did* want to play, not for the crowd or for the money, but because for the first time in a long time he felt the *challenge*. There was no question about it; this man was *good*. But in his heart, Billy knew he could beat him. When he had this feeling, he never lost. And he had it now. He laughed aloud. "Come on, butterball. Less play one-pocket."

"*One*-pocket?" The fat man was hurt. "One-pocket?"

"For twenty a game," Billy said. Somebody tittered nervously.

"I don't play one-pocket," the fat man said. "It's the dullest goddam game ever invented. How do you stay awake?"

"Well, what's your best game? We done played your *road* game, now, what do you play at home?"

"Eight-ball. That's all I play. I'll play you eight-ball for ten or twenty a game. I'm a sport. I know I got no chance against you."

Billy was flabbergasted. "No chance? Goddam, man, I aint even shot!"

"That's right; I never did see you shoot. How do I know how good you are?"

"You don't want to play," Billy said. "You got my twelve dollars. You go back home and tell everybody you beat Billy Lancing out of twelve dollars."

"Why should I tell em that?" the fat man asked. "Who ever heard of you?"

"I'll tell you what, you chicken-livered tub of guts; I'll play you any game on any kind of table in this joint; but I won't play you eight-ball. I'll play nine-ball, six-ball, bank pool, cribbage, one-pocket, straight pool—either rack or lineup; I'll play you rotation or snooker, balkline or three-rail billiards, pee-pool, golf; I'll play you one-handed or ten or no count; anything you want—*but*, I don't want to waste your time or mine, so the minimum price per contest is twenty dollars, and the maximum price is whatever you think you can handle. Now, do you want to play pool or do you want to go have your dinner?"

The fat man did not say a word for at least a minute. He looked as if he was in shock. Then he bellowed, "Twenty dollars? *Twenty dollars?* I feel like I'm being nibbled to death by a duck! I come in here to play some friendly pool among strangers; but you don't want to play friendly pool, you want to *gamble!* Now, if you want to gamble, I'm willin, but let's *gamble*, not piss and fart away our time at twenty dollars! Let's play for money!"

"There he is, folks," Billy said to the crowd, "the world's champion bullshit artist; he don't have no *foldin* money; all he's got is *talkin* money; cause if he had the *green* kind he'd make a game with me. He *knows* he can beat me; what's he *scared* of?" Grinning happily, he turned to the fat man. "How about fifty a game, sportsy?"

The fat man rolled his eyes. "Fifty? How long has it been since you saw fifty dollars all in one heap? I hear you talk but I don't see your money. Have you got fifty dollars and fifty cents all mixed up in your woolly old head?"

"How about a hundred?" Billy asked happily. He did not reach for his pocket yet, but leaned back against the table and pretended to inspect the tip of his cue.

"We talkin mouth bets, I raise it to a million," said the fat man. "Hell, two million, I aint proud."

"I'll tell you what," Billy said. "I always carry a little *caseroll* on me, just in case, you know. If you can match it, less play for it."

"Match it? Why, son, if I couldn't match anything you carried around in your little old pocket, why I'd just naturally die of humiliation. Haul out your thirty-four dollars and fifty cents and let them bills get a breath of fresh air. I'll not only match it, I'll play you any game you choose for it. I hate to waste time."

Billy removed from his shirt pocket ten one-hundred-dollar bills, unfolded them, and fanned them out on the table. He smiled wolfishly. "You're gonna look awful fuckin stupid if you can't come up," he said.

The fat man stared at the thousand dollars.

"Match it, or just die of shame," Billy said.

After a reflective pause, the fat man drew his two friends aside and they talked quietly, getting their rolls out and putting them together. The fat man came back to Billy and laid a gigantic heap of bills on the table. "There's four hundred and twenty here," he said. He looked sheepish. "That's all we got on us tonight. The fuckin horses, you know."

Old Larkin got up and came over to them. He did not look at Billy. "I'll back you for two hundred," he told the fat man. He got out his roll and peeled off ten twenties, leaving the roll thin as a pencil. Billy did not mind at all, but he grinned at the crowd and said, "I love a *patriot*, don't you?"

"Six-twenty, then," the fat man said. It was actually a question.

"You're sure greedy, aint you," Billy said. "You see my money, and you're just so goddam sure you can beat me, you just *got* to play. Well, okay, we'll play." He got a twenty out of his pocket, from his regular roll, added it to six of the hundreds, and crammed the other hundreds into his pants pocket. "We'll play, baby. One game of one-pocket, for six twenty."

"You want to play for all of it?" the fat man asked.

"Sure," Billy said. "Why fuck around? Lag for break, or flip a coin?" He grinned at old Larkin, whose face had gone gray.

It was really over before the game started. Billy knew it, he knew he had defeated the fat man's spirit, and all that was left was to win the actual game. The fat man won the toss and broke safe, as one always does in one-pocket, and then Billy sized up the lay of the balls very carefully, his whole body burning with a kind of calm ecstasy, shot what would have been a safety even if he had missed, a two-rail bank that dropped into his pocket without even touching the side rails. Then he made two more balls and left the cue ball frozen to the far rail. The fat man shot safe, and Billy made another bank, this time three rails and the cue ball safe anyway, made the shot, and ran out. The game was over. Billy took all the money, counted it, put his thousand dollars back in his shirt pocket and the rest in his pants pocket. Then he went back to the counter and began tipping another cue. He did not even see the fat man and his friends leave.

But it was not over yet, and Billy knew it. He went home at four in the morning and lay in his bed unable to sleep until well after sunup; he listened to the rain and wondered what part of himself he had opened up by defeating the Arizona fat man so thoroughly, so finally, and (what seemed worst of all) so dramatically. He remembered how incredibly sweet it had been, and how terribly he had missed that kind of victory; and he wondered why he now felt so down and empty. His wife knew something was the matter and did not bother him with questions. After she fed the children and ate breakfast, she took the little boy and girl to a neighbor's and left Billy alone in the house. He could hear her bickering with the little boy about putting his rubber boots on. He wondered where they were going until he heard the little girl say something about it, and then he knew his wife was being considerate. This irritated him. Finally he fell asleep, and dreamed of vast clicking pool games.

When he awakened in the late afternoon, none of the tension was gone. He ate, and caught a bus back to the bowling alley. He had never managed to buy a car; no car seemed to fit him. He would not have a cheap car, and the usual Cadillac embarrassed him, yet to choose a different expensive car would have been to play their game, too, not to mention the down payment money that would have had to come out of his caseroll. He tried to make himself busy at work, but it seemed futile and dull, and so he went to see Luanne.

For once she was home alone, but in a sullen mood, and for an hour she and Billy sipped quietly at the whiskey he had brought. The place was so sordid. Instead of a kitchen there was a table against the wall with a hot plate on it and, even though Luanne ate out almost all the time, garbage bulged from wet sacks under the table and spilled onto the linoleum, and she had a tiny back porch also covered with old magazines, sacks of garbage, bottles, newspapers. The wallpaper in the room was puce, with heavy purple grapes and green vines decorating it, and the ceiling looked dirty. The bathroom was unspeakable and smelled of urine and face-powder. The slovenliness of Luanne's place, Billy reflected with irony, had once seemed romantic and sensual to him, but now it was just filthy. He wanted to say to her, "Why don't you clean this goddam place up?" but he knew what she would say: "If it bugs you, baby, clean it yo'*self*." And of course she was right.

He wanted to tell her how frightened he was, but she would have asked him what was frightening him, and he would not have known what to answer. She could be amused at the idea of generalized, even abstract, fear. *Angst*, Billy thought, drawing the word out of his memory, that's what I got; eighteen pounds, four ounces of *Angst*. I'd be better off strung out; at least I'd know how to make me feel better. He knew Luanne was never troubled by such feelings. Or if she was she didn't know it, would get drunk or loaded or find a man, and get rid of the bad feeling. She felt good, bad, or indifferent: it was that simple for her. She could go on a five-day drunk, sleep with eight or ten different men, get into a razor fight, end up in jail, get out and be ready to start all over again; she could talk, argue, listen to music, or dance with a rapt attention that involved her entire being, and five minutes later she could be bored and sulky. In fact, he realized, she seemed simply to absorb the mood of the place she was in, the feelings of the people with her, and she was sulky now because Billy was *down* himself; he had noticed in the past that when he had come over ready and willing to have a good time, *needing* a good time, she was always in the same mood. She was a sponge. There was that whole sponge world; the black world he had fought so bitterly to pull himself out of, a rathole in American society reserved exclusively for Negroes who refused to be like Billy and refused to climb into the middle class, who demanded their pleasures and terrors *now*, could not, would not, wait for the calmer satisfactions Mister Cholly promised but never quite gave. Billy snorted to himself. He envied them their quick pleasure, but he knew he was too white, too far gone, to travel that road; he knew he would be frightened. Yet he knew too much about the other world to try to pretend to join it. So he was not a member of anybody's club, and he was lonely. Just a tourist, he thought; never a resident. Blah.

He was trying to think of a way to say good-bye to Luanne that would be neither ambiguous nor corny, when somebody pressed the buzzer. Billy felt a start of fear and gritted his teeth in self-anger.

Luanne opened the door and a big black man named Uncle Vance came in; Billy knew him, stood up and shook hands with him. He was not afraid of Uncle Vance. In fact, Uncle was kind of funny; blue-black skin, three teeth resembling yellowish fangs, two in his lower jaw and one in the upper; a suit that had once been in fashion and even a little flashy but was now spotted and shabby, the cuffs too thick, the pantlegs too billowy, the coat too long. He was even wearing a necktie with a Windsor knot which Billy could tell was never untied but merely slipped loose and over his head; the knot looked grimy.

But Uncle Vance was a nice man, and immediately, Billy was angry at himself for putting him down. Uncle Vance ran a trucking company, which is to say he and the finance company owned a truck, Vance's eighteen-year-old son drove the truck, Vance went around getting loads to haul, and the finance company took the profits; but then, the very fact that Vance had the truck—the doors of which were lettered: VANCE TRUCKING COMPANY—FAST HAULAGE—ANYWHERE, ANYTIME—made him a member of the middle class in good standing, a voice in the church, a member of the Negro post of the American Legion, all that. He was a respectable man. He was not a man to settle things with a razor, and in fact he belonged to the NAACP, whose members, one wit cracked, spent their Saturday nights hidden in their basements.

He accepted a cheese glass of Billy's whiskey and the three of them sat listening to the radio. It was dark out, overcast, and through the open window Billy could smell the impending rain. It rained a lot in Seattle, winter and summer. It was one of the things people in Seattle talked about. That and Boeing. And how green everything was. Of course, you pay for the green with the rain. But wasn't everything so lovely when it didn't rain! Think of the fools in Harlem. But they didn't talk about this. They sat and listened to the radio and waited for the rain to start.

Finally Uncle Vance broke the ice. "I heard you won a large amount of money from some Cholly down to your bowling alley," he said. "Six hundred dollars, was it?"

Luanne looked at Billy, and he smiled and said, "Yes, I did just that."

"Nice money," Luanne said. "We runnin out of whiskey."

Uncle Vance looked at Billy uncomfortably, and then with an embarrassed air, reached into his coat pocket and brought out an envelope, which he opened with his thick fingers, and removed three small, tightly rolled marijuana cigarettes. "I have these," he said. "Would you care to share a few puffs?" Billy nodded, amused, and the girl said, "Well, you are sweet," and Uncle Vance gave up being embarrassed by Billy's presence, licked down one of the joints, lit it, drew his lungs full of smoke and air, and passed it to the girl, his eyes standing out of his head; she toked, passed it to Billy, and he drew deeply, hoping it was good marijuana and he would feel it hit him right away. They passed the joint around several times before Billy knew it was not going to be any good; it was probably locally grown and for that matter full of twigs. He felt a little high, but the whiskey obscured the feeling, and none of his tension seemed to have gone away. Abruptly, he stood up. "I got to go to work," he said.

Vance tried to look politely upset, but it didn't come off, and Luanne was obviously glad to see him go. She and Vance probably had an appointment anyway; Billy had come over without telephoning. Billy wanted to tell the girl good-bye, but he couldn't with Vance sitting there looking so stiff and respectable.

Vance walked down the hallway with him. "Maybe sometime we could talk a little business," he said.

"Maybe," Billy said. He felt a strong yearning for he did not know what. He looked up at Uncle Vance in the dark hallway. *He* could come here, sneaking back down into the rathole, forbidden cigarettes in his pocket, to snitch a few pleasures he obviously did not get in his own respectable circle, and he could even be proud of himself; he and Billy could meet on this neutral ground and even share the girl and the whiskey and the marijuana, and even talk about discussing business. It seemed stupid.

"You ought to invest some of that money," Uncle Vance said. "While you still got it. You got to think of the future, boy. You know that." He chuckled softly. "Things are gonna open up one day, Billy, and those of us with the cash invested are goin to be on top."

"Oh, yeah?" Billy could not help saying. "When does all this happen?"

"Take it easy, Billy. Maybe not for a while, maybe not in our lives; but we got children, both of us, and we got to think about them. Maybe in their time, you know?"

Billy left the building and caught a bus for the bowling alley. He was angry. Of course Vance was right and his was the right way; and of course Luanne and her *spade* friends were right and it would never happen and it was too much work and they were too angry and too full of passion to wait for anything; and of course the liberals were right and the time was coming, and the niggerlovers were right, too, because the niggers were pretty to look at, and the niggerhaters were right, too, because the niggers were sloppy and lazy and sensual, and so just naturally everybody was right except Billy and he was alone and that was just tough. But I don't *want* to be a Negro; I don't *want* to be a white man; I don't *want* to be a married man; I don't *want* to be a businessman; I don't *want* to be lonely. Life seemed to be a figure eight. It terrified him, sitting on the bus, as if time had opened black jaws and swallowed him.

The fat man burst into the bowling alley a little after midnight, his two friends with him. He walked right up to Billy, who was seated in the customer's chair of his shoeshine stand watching a game of nine-ball on the number one table.

"Come on down out of there, my friend," the fat man said. "We got to talk."

Billy grinned down at him. "I'se comfy," he said.

"What would you like to play tonight?"

"You rob a bank or somethin?"

The fat man smiled coyly. "I got money. What do you want to play?"

"What makes you think I want to play at all? I'm *tired*. I *worked* all day, mon."

"Shee. You'll play. Come on, what's your best game?"

"One-pocket."

"Never. You're the best one-pocket player in the world." The fat man reflected for a moment, and then said, as if it had just occurred to him, "How about some eight-ball?"

"Not in this life; you're the best eight-ball player in the world." Around and around, Billy thought.

"Well, I brought the money, I'd like to gamble."

The crowd was beginning to gather again. It was going to be just like last night, except for one thing; Billy would no longer have the emotional advantage. He did not know just exactly what this advantage was or how you got it, but he knew it was gone. He really did not think the fat man could beat him, though. They argued, showed off for the crowd, joked, insulted each other, and Billy made the fat man show his money, and they ended up at the far end of the pool section playing straight snooker. Billy lost the first three games, each time with the seven ball crucial, paid off $150, and quit. They settled their time and then the fat man said, "I aint sleepy. Hell, let's play some nine-ball just for fun. Five dollars a game."

"Okay," Billy said. They took the number one table and Billy racked it for nine-ball. The fat man won the toss and was standing ready to break. He looked at his two friends, who were leaning against the number three table, and he laughed. They both grinned. The fat man turned to Billy and laughed again. "I got you now, sonny," he said. "And I won't let go."

"We'll see about that," Billy said. "If you're too good, I'll hit the rack; but you ain't that good."

"You won't hit the rack," the fat man said with assurance. "I *know* you. You're *dead*." They eyed each other steadily, and Billy knew the fat man was right; he would not quit, neither of them would, until the other was broke. That was it; that was the center of it all, the nugget of truth he had been searching for all his life: to do something that was endless, to risk it all on himself.

They played until four o'clock the next afternoon; most of the crowd had gone home, slept and come back. For several hours they played for five a game, and then jumped it to ten. Billy could not remember whose idea the raised bet was. It did not matter. At the end he was broke: casemoney, salary, winnings, everything. He had played his best, he hadn't dogged it; it was just that over the long haul the fat man was just a tiny bit better than he was, and so took all the money. It was really very boring. When it was over Billy signed for his share of the tab and went into the bowling alley office and talked to the manager, getting an advance on his wages. Then he came out, still carrying his cue. The fat man and his friends were sitting at the lunch counter, eating cheeseburgers. Billy unscrewed his stick and instead of putting it in its wooden slot back of the checkout counter, reached down and got out his leather carrying case, dusted it off, and slipped the two halves of the cue in. One of the white kids wanted to talk to him, but Billy brushed him off, and started out of the place.

"Where you goin, Billy?" the kid asked him.

He smiled. "Out to win that money back, boy. You think I *like* to lose?" But he knew it was a lie, and he was leaving out of shame. Outside, it was raining hard. Conscious of the deliberate irony, he took a cab to the Greyhound bus depot. He did not telephone his wife. The shame included her. I am a child, he thought. When am I going to grow up?

SIXTEEN

"Night or day it's all one in those damn 24-hour joints," Billy said one slow evening a few days before he was killed. "That's the hell of it, man; they're air-conditioned, open all night, *soft music playin,* an you don't know what day it is after a while, or if it's winter or summer. Time dies in a place like that, you feel pulled loose from it, like dreaming, dig, you don't even know if you're hungry. Like comin out of a movie, dig, and it's bright sunlight out and you're blinkin away and people are walkin around on business and you wonder what the hell world you fell into.

"But how do you stay away from it? It's like so *safe.* Anyway, pool cracks me up. And it aint simple, either. You never were good at it, were you? Maybe you felt it, anyhow. Everything is *connected.* You know, it's your turn to shoot. It starts then. You come up to the table, sightin the shot, lookin over the layout, and you can already feel how all the balls, just sittin there on the table, are *connected,* an you're connected to *them,* an your cue is part of your arm, and you chalk up and feel the connection there, and it gets good, man, and I mean good, cause you're buildin up all that good stuff, you know you can make any shot in the world and the shot is there—it aint somethin you can see but it's *there*—that feels good, like, a lush might walk into a bar someplace an when he walks in he's all pulled apart, but he sees all them rows on rows of bottles and he feels em and they feel him, an he sits down at the bar, all connected to the whole world, an orders his drink, an he throws that shot of liquor back into his throat an it's like comin in your head. The same for me on a pool table. I can feel it. So it's there. I sight the shot, bend down, and there's somethin goin on between me and the cue ball and the object ball and the pocket, and I feel it build up, shoot, an that's *it*. You waited for that all your life. The connection is *made*. The thing is complete. It's inside you now.

"But, if you miss the shot, the ball hangs up in the pocket or you miscue or somethin, that connection is broken and some of you *dies*. I've felt that, too. I *know* it's the truth. Somethin busted and gone, not a run of a hundred balls is gonna bring it back. When you lose you lose forever, an when you win it only lasts a second or two. That's *life*. I aint lyin. I aint comin on. Why should I?

"Everythin in the whole fuckin world is connected, I think; and the connection turns you on, an the broken connections burn you out. Suppose like you see this woman, see? You send out a hot line of connecting stuff to her if she's your action, and if you're hers, *wham*, you connect; you don't have to say a word, it's there and you both know it. But you know what we really do; we think about other things, or come on or get smart or worry about ourselves, and fuck up the connection. Then do we know it's gone? No, man, we keep tryin an it just gets worse and worse. It's like you get this tremendous urge to bust a window with your fist, dig, and if you went ahead and did it right then, *wham*, for about a half a second there you'd feel like the king of the world; but instead, you get to worryin about cuttin your hand and all that shit, so you hesitate and then get pissed off at yourself and bust the window anyway, only you're self-conscious about it and don't get any pleasure out of it at all."

Billy looked tired and gray, and Jack could not understand why he had been talking like that. Afterward, later, he knew that Billy had already decided, and he was taking this last chance to tell Jack who he was.

"Now, man," Billy said, "I know how *silly* a lot of this sounds, dig, a *philosophy* of the *poolhall*; but shit, I looked around myself and I asked myself, what is my life, anyway, and the answer was quick and easy, my life is what I *got*, an if I don't find anythin important in it, I'm dead. But, you know what it's like when you get high sometimes and *everything* seems important? Well, it's like that. If the way I feel about pool aint important, what the hell am I? So I sat down and tried to think up words for it, and the only one I could come up with was *connect*."

He looked down at Jack's hard, battered face. "You and me, now," he said. "We're connected. That's good. And when the connection breaks, it's over, that's too bad, but it's finished and a man would be a fool to try to make it go on when it's all over. You dig? We *got* it, you don't even have to admit it, but when we think of each other, we feel good, and that's *it*. But when it busts, it's busted, and that's the end. Nothin happens twice."

Now Jack understood him perfectly, and he lay silently on his bunk, his arms at his sides. He did not seem to be looking at anything, although his eyes were open. He felt powerless to move or to speak, but he wanted Billy to speak, he wanted Billy to say it all, and it would be said.

Very softly, Billy spoke: "Not the sex. That's not the connection. You and me, we're the connection. You live an I live, and we love each other. Do you know that? The sex, that's—well, *joy*. I got to admit it. How many times we wrecked it because we was afraid to admit it was *joy*? How many times we had to play like we was just jackin off? How many times we have to pretend it wasn't *love*. Now you know it's love and I know it's love, and I'm tellin you I love you. And I want you to tell me. To say it. In words."

Billy waited. Jack could not speak. He did not want to speak. He was embarrassed. He had been afraid this would happen someday, that it would become romantic. It was awful, and because he did love Billy he wanted to tell him so, but he did not mean the word the way Billy obviously meant it, and so he could not speak.

Billy said, "Jack. I want you to kiss me. Once. That's all. You can't talk; at least, at most, kiss me. You got to. If you love me, kiss me."

Jack closed his eyes. "No," he said.

"All right," Billy said. "All right."

Jack got the story in bits and fragments, but what happened was this: Clifford, the wolf-pack leader and hardest nut in the place, made up his mind that he disliked Jack, probably as the result of some chance remark—they had never exchanged more than half a dozen words in a year—and Clifford let it be known that he would have Jack's ass within a week, and was betting five to one Jack would stand still for it. Billy found out about it. He was terrified of Clifford, but the morning after he and Jack had their last long talk, he went up to Clifford's group on the big yard, looking tiny among the huge Negroes, and said to Clifford, "If you don't lay off Levitt, I'll see to it you're sorry." They all laughed, and one of them moved his arm quickly and Billy stepped back, stumbled, and almost fell down. Jack saw this and asked Billy about it later, and all Billy said was that he was getting a bet down. But his face looked strange, grayish, drawn, and that night in the cell he didn't talk at all. Clifford had gotten a message to Billy; he would get Jack the next afternoon.

In the morning break on the big yard, Jack saw most of it. The day was bright and warm and the men loafed and talked in small knots, or strolled by themselves back and forth. Jack was watching the domino games when he saw Billy leave one group of men and head across the yard toward Clifford's group, just in the shade of the shed roof. Jack saw Clifford detach himself from the group with a grin and a wave; saw the two men approach each other. To a guard looking down, to anyone, it looked as if the two men were merely crossing the big yard and would pass within a few feet; a coincidence. The only reason Jack was watching was that Billy looked so stiff; he almost seemed to be marching, and his face was thin and frightened, his shoulders hunched up. He looked strange; usually he was loose and happy-looking. Clifford, as he approached Billy, loomed up over him, gigantic, black, but even his face was a little drawn; and they passed each other, very close, brushing together for a tenth of a second, but passed on, and for a moment Jack thought they were passing contraband. Clifford's face was toward Jack now, and he looked astonished, his mouth loose, his eyes large. Billy, from the back, was ambling along slowly, and he seemed to have his arms folded over his chest. Then Jack saw Clifford fall to his knees. He still looked astonished. Then he fell forward, flat on his face, his legs twisting out and jerking slightly. Everyone, including Jack, turned away. No one saw Billy fall.

Clifford was dead in three hours, a sharpened spoon handle deep into his abdomen. Billy lasted almost five hours before dying. Clifford's knife had a seven-inch blade, and all of it had been buried into Billy. A guard brought the word to Jack, who was celled on the shelf pending an investigation. The guard was a young man. He said, "Your buddy copped it."

"When?" Jack said.

"Oh, about an hour, hour and a half ago. The shit's gonna hit the fan around here again." The guard passed on.

Jack wept that night, bitterly. He could find no thought to comfort himself. He could not even be enraged, only desolated, and more lonely than he had ever been in his life. There was nothing for him to do but weep, and he wept.

PART THREE

Meaningful Lives

1956–1960

SEVENTEEN

Jack Levitt was 26 years old when he got out of San Quentin. He had finished high school and had even taken two courses by extension from the University of California; he had worked in both the kitchen and the bakery, and he had not gotten into one single fistfight. Custody felt he was a good risk, and Rehabilitation considered him to have taken great strides toward the goal of maturity. After the death of Billy Lancing, Jack broke down and cried only once more, when the news arrived that Claymore had escaped from Alcatraz.

According to the newspapers, Claymore had not escaped at all, but had been drowned in attempting escape. He must have drowned, the Federal authorities reasoned, because no one ever escaped. True, his body was never discovered, but, they reasoned, it had probably been washed out to sea. Jack did not believe this, and he didn't think anybody else did, either. Claymore had escaped, and it made Jack cry in his cell, much to the amazement of his cellmate, an old safecracker. Billy had felt "connected" to Claymore, and this is what made Jack cry. He wished Billy were alive, to celebrate Claymore's freedom. He wished there were a heaven, so Billy could look down and see it and rejoice.

Claymore's escape plan had been very simple: He waited for a foggy day and for a moment when no one was looking at him, got outside, jumped into the bay, and started swimming. It is supposed to be beyond human endurance to swim from Alcatraz to shore without extensive training, thick grease on the body, etc., especially because of the strong currents; but if Claymore's desire for freedom was strong enough, he could make it. Then, he would have to be able to wait, hidden, somewhere along the shore of San Francisco, for the early morning hours; and if he survived that, did not die of exposure or become so weak he could not move, he could begin to make his way through the police-watched streets toward the Fillmore District. If he could make it that far, he was probably safe. It would not be hard for him to find Negroes who would not turn him in. So it was not impossible, merely difficult—about as difficult as climbing Mount Everest. A few years later three more men escaped from The Rock, and after that the Federal authorities lost heart. The whole function of Alcatraz was its hopelessness, and if the convicts started leaving any time they felt like it, well. . . . So today it is closed, deserted, and remains a monument to man's incredible stupidity on the one hand, and to his incredible courage and love of freedom on the other.

Jack's escape from that other blot on the pride of the human soul, San Quentin, was much less dramatic. He was paroled at the end of eighteen months, in spite of his bad record and in spite of his even worse appearance before the Parole Board. He felt like punching them all right in the face. For so long now he had not permitted himself to think about getting out, and now, with this invitation to appear before the Board, he could not help himself; he wanted out so badly he became terrified that they, the Board, a handful of men who really knew nothing about him, would refuse to let him out. So he stood there in front of them, his face red and tense, his fists clenched, answering their questions, trying to seem contrite and mature, wanting to smash them, and when he went back to his cell he knew he had botched it completely and he would have to wait at least another year.

But he was wrong; his record at Quentin was good and they considered him a good parole risk. So he left San Quentin absolutely determined not to go back, as much for their sake as his. Because that strange, awful place had actually tried to help him. They, it, had treated him as a man whenever Custody would let them, and tried to find a way to reach him through the layers of hardness, and where they failed they at least tried, and whether it was San Quentin or Billy Lancing that had reformed Jack was a moot point: he was reformed. He came out wanting to make something of his life.

There was a job waiting for him in a bakery on Union Street, near Fillmore. The building was set back from the street, and out in front on its own sidewalk were little marble-topped tables and wire chairs beneath a striped awning. Three trimmed acacia trees completed the decor, and there was a boy in a white jacket to wait on the tables and sell baked goods from the glass counter inside. The proprietor always sat on a high stool behind the cash register; he was a small man, usually dressed in a gray suit and vest, with a plump, pallid face, receding hair, an amused mouth, and blank, colorless eyes. His name was Saul Markowitz, and he opened the bakery each morning at six promptly by wearily pulling back the grating and unrolling the awning, and at that hour his best customers were the servants of the rich of Pacific Heights, who would come in for a quick cup of *caffé Wien* and a hot *croissant*; fresh, hot *croissants* were the specialty of the shop, and the servants would pick up a foil-lined box of them to take back to their people. Also at that hour there might be a few from all-night parties, drunk, sitting at the little tables eating their *croissants* and pouring brandy into their coffee, talking the brittle patter of people who don't have anything to do with themselves. Saul Markowitz knew most of his customers by name, including the servants; he addressed them, joked with them, and kept his eyes remote. Many of his customers thought he was contemptuous of them, but they came back anyway.

Saul Markowitz often recruited his bakery help from San Quentin; they would come, work, be with him for a few weeks or months, and then move on. He would always get another. Jack could not understand at first what it was Mr. Markowitz wanted of him. He knew that Mr. Markowitz had a reputation for a special kind of wit: perhaps hiring ex-convicts was witty. Mr. Markowitz had been asked by Herb Caen why he had named his bakery "Rosenbloom's" and had answered, according to the item in the column, "Who'd come to a place called 'Markowitz's?' "

But Jack was glad for the job and grateful to Saul Markowitz; he worked hard and made no trouble. There were two bakers, and Jack was the helper. He wore a white tee shirt, white duck trousers, and a white apron, and most of the time his face was smeared with a mixture of sweat and fine flour. He hauled sacks of flour around, greased pans and put them in the oven and pulled them out, stocked the display shelves, washed pots and trays, and stuffed himself with baked goods. It was a good job, hard hot work and fair pay, but after a while the smell of the place sickened him, especially when he would have to bend deep into the lard barrel and get the last handfuls of dead white lard from the bottom. The bakers were a pair of noncommittal types whose only conversation, aside from giving orders and cursing, was about union matters. They did not appear to have any life outside the bakery. They left Jack alone and he left them alone.

No one at all, in fact, paid any attention to him. He worked his shift, went home to his furnished room on Pine Street, read, went to movies, visited his parole officer, and that was about it. He did not violate his parole for two weeks—in his case, one of the conditions was no drinking—and when he did he carried it off as if it were a desperate caper, walking several blocks to buy the pint of whiskey, hiding the package under his jacket as he walked back up the hill, locking the door to the room—all with the heavy sense of dread and expectation of a teen-ager visiting his first prostitute. He sat on the edge of the bed and uncapped the bottle and took a quick swig, and almost immediately lost his temper. It was disgusting that he should have to sneak around like that, just to have a little drink.

Well, he would fling it in their teeth. He drank off about half the pint, jammed the bottle into his hip pocket, and took off for Market Street. When he left his room he was angry, and determined to make trouble, but by the time he got down to Market he felt just fine and sauntered along with the early evening crowd, savoring the pure freedom of it, the way people all dressed differently, the way the women looked and smelled, the way the streetcars sounded, the glitter of the lights, the strange, exciting music from the hot-dog joints, the corniness of it all, the cheapness, the vulgarity which is vulgar only if you haven't been away for such a long time and in a place so dull as prison; there was a lot of stuff in the newspapers about "cleaning up" Market Street, and Jack wondered why they wanted to do it. Didn't they know how beautiful it was? Didn't they understand that for some people the opera, the drama, the ballet, were only boring, and yet a peepshow on Market Street was art? They want to make everything gray and tasteful. Don't they understand how awful good taste seems to people who don't have it? Ha, what do they care about people with bad taste! Nothing! But I do. I love them. They wear cheap perfume and carry transistor radios. They buy plastic dog-turds and painted turtles and pennants and signs that say, "I don't swim in your toilet, so please don't pee in my pool!" and they buy smelly popcorn and eat it on the street and go to bad movies and stand here in doorways sneaking nips of whiskey just like I'm doing, and they're all so nice.

At the moment, glowing with whiskey, Jack loved everybody.

He even loved that policeman, damn him, who made Jack hide his bottle for fear of being sent back to San Quentin for three years. But the policeman, damn him, went away and Jack took another nip. I aint going to get drunk and mug my fellowman. And go back to prison. Hell no, I'm gonna get drunk and go to a movie, some cheap Technicolor Western full of noise and easy choices, or maybe even pick up one of these beautiful sleazy-looking broads. . . .

He was suddenly very dizzy. He was not used to liquor any more. But it wasn't that. It was the idea of having a woman that made him dizzy, and he knew it. He leaned up against a building, watching the people surge past him, and took another drink without thinking. The bottle was empty. He made his way across the sidewalk to a trash receptacle and dropped the bottle in. A couple of sailors went past, and one of them looked at Jack, made a face, and stopped.

"Say, buddy," the sailor said, "where can a man get a piece of tail in this town?"

"I look like I ought to know," Jack said.

"Yeah, you look like you ought to know. Do you?"

"Nope. Less ask a cabbie."

"Why didn't you think of that, Normie?" the sailor said to his buddy. "You're supposed to be so goddam hip."

Three hours later they were all filthy drunk, and were asked very politely to leave a bar deep into the Spanish Mission District. The bar was full of Mexicans, and the two sailors and Jack put their heads together and in whispers and giggles admitted that it would be foolish to start a fight. They left and wandered down the street until they found a cab. When they were in back one of the sailors said, "Where to now? Less find that whorehouse."

"Nearest whorehouse is in Stockton," the cabbie said over his shoulder.

"I got to go home," Jack muttered doggedly. He told the driver his address, and they moved off.

"Go home," one of the sailors said. "Why do you have to go home? We got to find a whorehouse an get fucked."

"No fucking," Jack said. "Too drunk to enjoy it. First one has to be good. I got to go to work tomorrow. Thass why."

They couldn't talk him out of it, and had to let him off on Pine Street, in front of his place.

"We goin to Stockton," one of them said. He was sticking his head out the back window, and abruptly he vomited down the side of the cab, just as it moved off. Jack gave them a salute and went up the stairs, drunk and afraid. When he got in bed, the fear subsided a little. He was safe now. Nobody could pick him up and put him in jail. He was safe. But he could not go out and get drunk like that again. He could get in a fight or get braced, and go to jail, and back to San Quentin. They had him. He was free, but he couldn't do anything. Those sailors. Talking about their 72 hours of *freedom*. What did they know? He fell asleep.

In the morning he had a vicious hangover, far out of proportion to the pleasures of the evening, and he went about his work dully. Out in front, while he was putting a tray of cherry tarts (which smelled disgusting) into the display case, a group of late partygoers were seating themselves around a couple of the little tables, and Jack saw beyond them a Rolls Royce parked in the yellow zone. What attracted Jack's attention was a pair of men's shoes sticking up out of the back window. Jack grinned painfully and hoped the man in the car felt worse than he did. He straightened up after placing the tray on the shelf, feeling the needles of pain back of his eyes, and found himself face-to-face with a woman, one of the party outside, pretty, disheveled, her eyes glassy. She looked rich and expensive, and young. Her lipstick was freshly applied and dark against her skin, but her mouth was puffy and reddish around the edges. She was staring at Jack from behind dark glasses. She pointed down into the case.

"Gimme one of those fucking tarts," she said in a bored but expensive voice.

Mr. Markowitz and the counterboy were both out at the

tables, hovering over the drunks, but Jack said, "I don't do that," and went back into the bakery. The woman's vulgarity had irritated him, perhaps because he had always supposed the rich had their own vocabulary to go along with their money. But then maybe the woman wasn't rich at all, but just ran with the rich. Maybe none of them were rich and had just stolen the Rolls. Maybe the guy inside was dead, a couple of bullets in his chest. Ha ha. Maybe the woman will take pity on me and buy my freedom.

Mr. Markowitz came into the bakery, his face composed and intent. He came up to Jack, who was greasing pans.

"Look here, my boy," he said, "one of the customers said you insulted her. What happened?"

"Nothing," Jack said. He kept on greasing the pan. "She asked me to wait on her and I said I didn't wait on people. That's all."

Mr. Markowitz shrugged, his eyes blank. "I'll tell her it's a union regulation or something. You sure you didn't do anything? She's kind of funny."

Jack reported the conversation as accurately as he could, feeling nauseated from the smell of lard and irritated with Markowitz for not just taking his word and getting the hell out of there.

"Well, it sounds like her all right. But we got a business to run. You should have helped her. Suppose you trot on out there and apologize to her. Okay?" He patted Jack on the shoulder, smiling.

"Do I have to?"

Mr. Markowitz looked at him carefully. "No, you don't *have* to. But what the hell . . ."

"Okay," Jack said. He went out to the tables, wiping the lard off on his apron.

There were three women and two men, and one of the men, with curly gray hair and a gray mustache, looked embarrassed. The other man was younger, slouched down in his chair, his face bearing an expression of righteous indignation. All three women were unapproachably beautiful, and drunk. The man with the gray hair did not look drunk.

"I'm sorry if I said anything wrong," Jack said to the woman.

The younger man said, "Is that your idea of an apology, sonny? Just because you're an ex-convict doesn't make you exempt from manners. Let's hear you apologize."

"John," said the man with the gray hair, "for heaven's sake."

Jack looked at Mr. Markowitz and said, "Yeah." Mr. Markowitz was expressionless, not even wearing his usual smile.

"Well, it just infuriates me to see some *thug* insulting a woman like Sally, that's all," the younger man said. He had a nasty voice, irritating and cultured.

Sally herself was grinning up at Jack crookedly, drunkenly. She said, "I don't mind it at all. Maybe that's what bothers you, John. That and the fact that you're chicken-livered."

"Oh, dear," the man with the gray hair said mildly.

Jack felt impotent. He knew he had been called out here as an exhibit, something for these people to amuse themselves with; and he knew he was probably expected to lose his temper. Mr. Markowitz had obviously told them all about him. The younger man was getting up, rockily, as if he were ready to fight Jack. Everything was disconnected; Jack still felt sick and hung over, and he did not want to lose his job. He looked at Saul Markowitz, who simply looked back at him.

"You goddam thug," John said to Jack. He had moved out onto the sidewalk and was standing in a half-crouch.

Jack said to his boss, "Who are you going to back up?"

"What a tragic choice," Sally said.

"Nobody," Saul Markowitz said. He turned to John. "I think you've had too much to drink, John. Maybe you'd better go home. The tab's on me."

"Okay," John said, not moving. "But what about your ugly thug? Is he going to apologize to me, or do I have to take him apart?" He grinned loosely, and suddenly threw a wild, roundhouse punch at Jack.

Jack parried it easily with his left and crossed sharply with his right. John went back, on his feet, for a dozen or more steps, and then collapsed on the sidewalk, his knees drawn up, his arms out.

"Well, that was easy," Sally said into the silence.

"John is eighty-six," Saul Markowitz said, "and you're fired." He got out his fat wallet and peeled off two hundred dollars and handed it to Jack. "I'm sorry. But you could have handled him without that."

Jack took the money, counted it, and stuffed it into his ducks. The gray-haired man came up to Jack. "I'll take you home," he said.

"I have to get my other clothes," Jack said.

"I'm sorry about all this," Mr. Markowitz said.

"Yes, I suppose you are," the gray-haired man said. Jack went inside and got his clothes out of his locker and said good-bye to the bakers and came back out front. They had picked John up and put him in the back seat of the Rolls, along with the passed-out man and two of the women. Jack and Sally sat in front, Jack by the window. He had never been inside a Rolls-Royce before; it wasn't as luxurious as he had supposed, but he liked the smell of the leather.

"What a sullen, rotten, depressing morning," Sally said. "Like every fucking morning of my fucking life."

"Why don't you shut up?" the driver said gently. "You started it, you know."

"I know," she said. She put her hand on Jack's leg and squeezed. "I just wanted to see this piece of meat in action. And John's so easy to get riled. All you have to do is attack his fucking *macho*, and he's off."

"Do you have to use that word so much?" the gray-haired man asked. He wheeled the silent automobile up the hill and into Pacific Heights. "We're going to get the idea that you don't really understand the implications."

The two women in the back seat had been talking to the passed-out man, and one of them leaned forward and said, "We're going to have to have help with Charles."

"I'm going to KILL MYSELF!" a voice bellowed from the back.

"No you're not, Charles," the woman said. "We're going to take you into the house and give you a nice bath."

"I am going to CUT MY THROAT!" Charles yelled.

Sally giggled and leaned close to Jack. He could smell her perfume faintly. Her hand was still on his leg, which he did not mind at all. He minded none of it. First he had been the sideshow, now they were.

They stopped in front of a large white house on Pacific Street, with a red tiled roof and wrought-iron balconies from the third-floor windows, and Jack and the gray-haired man helped Charles into the house. A Negro woman dressed in black opened the heavy paneled door, and said "Oh, dear," and helped them get Charles up the stairs and into the largest bedroom Jack had ever seen in his life. The whole bedroom was done in crimson and soft white, and while they undressed Charles his wife came in and pulled back the drapes, and Jack saw the whole marina below them, the yachts, the brilliant blue bay, and beyond, looking so close, Alcatraz. On their way back to the car, Jack said, "Does he own this place?"

"Yes."

"He must be pretty rich."

The gray-haired man laughed. They made other stops. They unloaded John, who was awake and sullen but not speaking, in front of an apartment house on Washington; and the gray-haired man took his wife, the other woman in back, to their home, another Pacific Heights mansion, but not as large as the first one. Then he drove Sally to her apartment on the east side of Telegraph Hill. Before she got out of the car she kissed Jack on the mouth and said, "I'm really sorry I got you fired. Come and see me if you need a job or anything." She got a card out of her pocketbook and handed it to Jack. Then the two men drove off.

"Where to?"

Jack gave him the address.

"It was really as much your fault as anyone's," the man said.

"We all take the blame and pass it around, but it was your fault. All you had to do was recognize the situation."

"Fuck the situation," Jack said. "I'm sleepy and hung over and pissed off. Did you drive me just so's you could tell me it was all my fault?"

"No, I thought maybe you'd have a drink with me, and we could talk. I imagine jobs aren't very easy for you to find."

"I'm not supposed to drink," Jack said. "But screw it. I'm not supposed to lose my job, either. You know, if your friend decides to push it, he can get me thrown back in. I committed a battery on him."

"He won't. He was humiliated; that's about all he wants."

They drove down Columbus to Broadway and parked the car. After they had gone into a small bar and sat down the man introduced himself as Myron Bronson and they shook hands formally. The waiter came over and Bronson ordered Irish whisky with water back for both of them.

"There was a party last night," he said. "If these things go on too long, they always end badly. You have to understand that these are very nice people most of the time. This morning they were all in a mood to hate each other, and you got fired. By tonight they'll have forgotten all about it, or remember it in context of a hangover, as a way of inducing guilt."

"What about you? You're not drunk. What are you doing with them?"

Bronson smiled. "I learned to drink a long time ago, when there were some rules. But you'd be surprised about John. He's really a very nice fellow. He's the one you hit. He's a lawyer, and a very good one."

"What about you? What do you do?" Jack was thinking about the Rolls parked outside.

Bronson said, "I have some money. I don't really do anything. I have an office with a desk in it that cost more than most people make in a year, but I don't use it very much." He raised two fingers for more whisky.

"You're a rich man," Jack said.

"I suppose you could say that. Yes. Of course."

"Did you earn it, or did somebody give it to you?"

Bronson looked amused. "Why are you asking me all these questions? Are you trying to get even? It doesn't make any real difference where the money comes from, as long as I have it. It's impossible to *earn* the kind of money I have, so you'd have to say it was given to me; but I'm not like Morgan; I don't think God gave it to me. But I'm glad I have it. Let's not talk about money."

"Very boring," Jack said. He finished his second shot. "Now let me buy you a drink." He waved his hand at the waiter.

"Hangover gone?" Bronson asked.

"I do feel better," Jack said. He liked the rich man. He liked the way he dressed, and he liked his somewhat long, curly gray hair, and his mustache, and his fine gray eyes, and his amused smile. The rich man looked like a good rich man, not a bad rich man, although Jack was not sure what the distinction was, and just being with him made Jack forget his new problems, as if all he had to do was ask Bronson and Bronson would give him a whole wad of money and everything would be fine. It was a pleasant feeling. He wondered if Bronson felt this way all the time; never having to worry about money.

"What's it like to be rich?" he asked. "No shit. We're not friends, we'll probably never see each other again. So you can tell me."

"I suppose you're right. When I was a boy," Bronson said, "I was a Mormon. I was sent to Germany by the church to be a missionary. I got there in the middle of the German inflationary period. Nineteen twenty-three. For ten thousand marks you could buy a newspaper. Upper middle-class families were dining on cabbage soup. Nobody had any toothpaste. Some people just laughed at me. That was all right. Others thought I had an answer to their problems, and that was bad. That kept me awake nights, that look of hope in people's eyes, as if all their troubles came from believing in the wrong God. But that didn't happen often. Anyway, the whole thing struck me as a gigantic fraud; the

227

church, the religion, the belief in the myth, everything. But I didn't stop yet, because, you see, the money was coming from the church. And my family. So for weeks after I was absolutely certain there was no God, I kept on with my missionary activities. I felt like a fool. Eventually I gave it up and went to Paris to be a poet." He laughed. "My father and mother absolutely refused to send me any more money. I absolutely refused to come home. All of this absoluteness by mail. Finally my father changed his mind and sent me money. I became an expatriate. I spent most of the money on girls, and the rest of the time, when I wasn't trying to make friends with the older Americans, I would stay in my room, reading *Black Mask* or trying to write poems about what I had seen in Germany. I suppose they were just awful, but some of them got published. The problem was in getting the French prostitutes to see the importance of this. Besides, my artistic conscience was bothering me. You see, I really wanted money, a lot of it. I didn't want to believe that that was what I wanted, because it seemed such a shabby ambition. At any rate, I went to New York eventually, after my parents' money ran out, and 'immersed myself in the roots of my native soil,' which is to say, starved. This went on for six months. It was awful. I suppose I went insane. I started making money; I had a flair for the kind of intricate blackmailing necessary to life insurance sales, and after a while I began investing. Since I thought of myself as a cynic and a thief anyway, I had no trouble doubling, then tripling, my investments." He smiled at Jack. "You have no idea how intense I was in those days. I was a priest. I made a lot of money and I managed to keep it. That's all. I'm still in the life insurance business. I own three companies."

Later, when Bronson let Jack out of the car in front of his building, he said, "Look, don't feel too angry with Saul Markowitz. He spent five years in a Nazi concentration camp. He's a very withdrawn man."

"I haven't got a worry in the world," Jack said. He was drunk from the fine whisky, and he waved good-bye to Myron Bronson and loped up the stairs. When he woke up in the afternoon he was angry at himself for not having conned Bronson out of something, but then he realized it would have been very difficult to do, if Bronson's story of his life was true. Somehow, it did not sound true. It was all too easy. Yet, such things did happen, he supposed.

It would have remained an episode, one of those odd meetings that happen to people who drink a lot, if it hadn't been for Sally's card, which Jack found a few days later on his bureau. He had already been to see his parole officer and the two of them were trying to find him another job. Saul Markowitz had already called the parole officer and had smoothed things over, so there wasn't going to be any trouble. When Jack found the card he remembered that she had said something about getting him a job. He decided he would use it as an excuse to go see her. Maybe there would even be a job in it. But that was not why he was going to see her. He had not slept with a woman in two years, and the thought of her made him weak with desire. It was like getting out of San Quentin; first there was one life and you just got used to it and pretended that there was nothing else, and then suddenly you remembered all the other things that could be done, and the urgency became frantic, everything else blurred away. Jack bathed and dressed in his cheap slacks and sport coat, and then to burn away the excess nervous energy he walked all the way from Pine and Jones to Telegraph Hill. When he got to her apartment, after going up and down the wrong streets twice, he was steamy hot and angry, half-certain that she was not there, or not alone, and that he should have telephoned, or she would not remember him, or would remember him and cut him cold—but none of that was true. She opened the door and laughed in recognition and asked him in, and he walked past her into the apartment, his stomach muscles hard with tension, his face burning. He felt like a child who has come to beg some free candy from the grocer.

EIGHTEEN

She was not beautiful, Jack decided; just very pretty. She had the high cheekbones, well-defined nose, and blue-black hair of an Indian, but her eyes were as blue and intense as his own, and her skin was pale rather than sallow. She wore her hair up to show her slender neck to its best advantage, and as she turned around for him to follow her into the apartment, Jack automatically looked down at her ankles. They, too, were slender. Jack fell in love with her. He was not sure exactly when he fell in love, but he always remembered thinking, as he glanced down at her ankles, "I'm in love. With her." He felt ridiculous.

After three quick drinks and twenty minutes of tense (for Jack) conversation, they went to bed. The telephone interrupted the conversation twice; the first time a woman friend of Sally's, the second time her date for that evening, and she, her eyes on Jack, said into the mouthpiece, "No, I'm sorry as hell. My damn period just started and I feel awful. I'm going to take a couple of Nebs and"—she winked at Jack—"go to bed with a fat novel."

After she hung up, Jack said, "Did it?"

"Did what?"

"Did your period just start?"

"No, but it's a beauty of an excuse, isn't it? Takes the heart right out of them." She stood in the middle of the room, looking down at Jack. He was seated cross-legged on a cushion beside the small fireplace. "You didn't come over here to talk, did you?"

"Well, you said something about a job."

She laughed. "That was just to get you over here. I don't have any jobs. Unless you'd like to be paid for sleeping with me. Have you ever taken money for it?"

"I've never had an offer," Jack said. He stayed on his cushion. "I've never met a chick like you, either."

"I'm debauched," she said. "The coachman got me in the back seat of the family phaeton when I was twelve; and from there on out it's been all downhill."

"Why do you talk such bullshit?" Jack was vaguely irritated. He had come over here to rape, not be seduced by a fast-talking whore. She had him off-balance and he did not like it. He felt inferior and young, and even intimidated by the expensive furnishings of the apartment.

"Why, isn't all talk bullshit?" she asked. She had her hands on her hips, and her face was in shadow. "I've been waiting for you to say something obvious, but you don't seem to know how. Don't you know how to score with *chicks like me?* You're supposed to talk in double entendres, and then come up behind me while I'm mixing the drinks, and put your hand on my fanny. Then I turn around, grunting like a hog, and lay a big fat spitty kiss on you. Then we take off our clothes."

Jack stood up. "I don't know what the hell you're talking about, but if you want to go to bed, let's go."

She grinned. "Just like that?"

"Just like that."

"Aren't you afraid I'm making fun of you?"

"No."

"Well, then; one of us is going to have to *lead,* and the other *follow.* One of us has to make the first move. Are you the type that likes to make the first move, or do you prefer the girls to do all the work? Or, I guess we could sort of stare at each other, and go *'Ooh!'* and fall into each other's arms."

"I want it without all the bullshit. I haven't slept with a woman in a long time."

Something changed in her eyes, but her mouth was still amused. "Oh, really? Neither have I."

"Jesus!"

"Well, why are we standing around talking?"

"How the fuck should I know? Let's go."

He took her hand and led her back into the bedroom. The bed was unmade. He was afraid she was going to ask him to

2 3 1

ignore the mess, but he should have known better. She broke away from him, humming, and started to undress, slipping out of her slacks like a man, pulling her sweater over her head and coming up to Jack for him to unhook her brassiere. That cleared away the fog, and for the first time that night Jack began to feel really passionate and happy. In a very few moments they were on the bed naked together and not talking.

Jack had been afraid that after all that time it would be over too quickly, and he tried to put off the moment of penetration as long as possible, and then even that became dangerous and he entered her quickly; he had been right, and they were finished almost before they started; but before Jack had time to feel sorry about it, Sally went down on him, her appetites increased rather than diminished, and Jack did not have time to consider what to do, it was there in front of him to be done, and he dissolved into the animality of it, and for the next hour vanished into an ecstasy he had forgotten existed. It was too good to think about, too sweet to investigate, and on his third climax he almost fainted, and although his eyes were open he could see nothing but bright colors, as if he had gone blind to form, and then with one final teeth-rattling spasm he did subside into unconsciousness.

They were awakened around midnight by the telephone. It went on for fifteen sputtery rings before quitting, and by then they were smoking cigarettes in the semidarkness. He could feel her smooth skin against him, but he was beyond arousal.

"I suppose," she said, "that I ought to tell you what a wonderful lover you are. For your manhood's sake. But I'm so sick of that *macho* crap. I think you've really got it. But not as a lover. You're okay, but you don't know much. You've got vitality, but any teen-age boy could do better. And of course any woman. But all you really need is practice. You're out of practice."

Jack laughed. "God, you're a nutty broad. You'll talk about anything, won't you."

"Can you think of anything too good or too awful to talk about?"

"I guess not. I want a drink."

"So bring us both one, baby."

When he came back with the bottle and glasses, she was sitting up, with the nightstand light on. She looked very beautiful, and he was certain he was in love with her. He wanted to tell her, but he was afraid of what she might say. She seemed capable of making fun of him about it, or analyzing him. He did not want that.

"How do you guys make it in prison?" she asked. Jack went all tight inside, but he managed to finish his drink without speaking. Then he said, "That's none of your business."

"Oh. Did I step on something sacred? Or vulgar?"

"It's just that—"

"I get it. You're embarrassed. I guess I know what you do. I guess you have to. God, I wish I had a penis!"

Jack had been angry and exasperated, but now he did not know what to think. "*Huh?*"

She laughed. "None of that Freudian crap. I just wish I could be a man for a while, or me with a man's penis. I'd love to do it to a woman or to another man. I love it so much I'd like to fuck the whole world, one, two, three at a time. The whole world! Don't you feel that way sometimes?"

"Hell no. You must be a nympho or something."

"Are you kidding? Do you know what a nympho is? It's a skinny nervous woman who fucks to keep from going crazy. That's not my problem at all. I'm not frigid; I'm just not tender and shy, like a textbook All-American feminine, that's all."

"What *is* your problem, then?"

"I just told you. I want everything sometimes. And I'm not going to get everything. Ever."

There was something terribly wistful about her face, and Jack leaned over and kissed her gently, knowing of no other way of telling her he understood. He was about to whisper that he loved her when she broke away from him, tossing her head impatiently. "Don't. I don't like to kiss while I'm thinking."

"Then stop thinking."

She laughed and then hiccupped. "Oops. Too much drink." She held out her glass and he filled it halfway and took a long gurgling drink from the bottle.

"Do you mind if I spend the rest of the night here?" he asked. "I'm too pooped to go home." She didn't answer right away, so he changed the subject. "Gee, I wish the fellows in Quentin could see me now."

"I know what," she said. "Let's go down to Vegas and fuck around for a few days."

"Tonight?"

"No, silly. In the morning. We'll fly down. Fuck all day and play the slots all night. Sound good?"

To Jack it sounded very good, like an adolescent masturbation fantasy, but good anyway. "You're really something," he said. "You're like a man, you know that?"

She giggled. "In what way?"

"The way you talk. That's all. The way you think."

"Anything wrong with that?"

"Hail, no," he said. "Let's go to sleep."

"If you feel anything funny during the night, don't worry, it'll be me. Playing little games."

Jack went to sleep thinking that he was a long way from San Quentin, a long way from anything he had ever known. It was easy to go to sleep thinking it would go on like this forever.

In the morning he was a little surprised that Sally still wanted to go to Las Vegas. She said, "We'll take a cab over to your place and get your things and then haul ass for the airport. We'll probably get there by the middle of the afternoon."

Jack scratched his head. "How about letting me make breakfast for us? I cooked in the joint."

"Okay. I have to make reservations."

Jack went into the tiny kitchen. From the window over the sink he could see Alcatraz dazzling in the bay under a perfect sky. It was only seven in the morning, but there were already a few sailboats out, their white sails and bright spinnakers canting before the breeze. Jack could guess how the men on The Rock felt about the sailboats. They wished urgently that they could get their hands on one of them and sail off to Mexico or Venezuela. He wondered how the people on the boats felt about Alcatraz. If they didn't suffer from guilt, they probably thought it was interesting—part of the attraction of the Bay area. Jack felt good just from knowing he wasn't on The Rock; he did not feel sorry for the men out there; he didn't feel sorry for anybody. He felt too good. His body could still remember the night, and for the time being he didn't have a worry in the world. It was damned good to be out of prison. He thought about Claymore. Claymore must have known how good it was. Jack had never known before. He had been a punk, with a punk's outlook, a punk's self-pity and conceit, thinking the world was out to get him. That was stupid; he was mature now, time to enjoy life. And how lucky he was to have fallen into *this!*

"You know," he called out to her, "if I hadn't been railroaded into the joint, I wouldn't be here right now."

She came into the kitchen, dressed in a light-blue sweater that almost matched her eyes, those remarkable, penetrating, honest blue eyes, that seemed in the morning light to have a tinge of lavender in them, like the eyes of a Siamese cat. He drew her to him and kissed her, and the kiss seemed to make her girlish and innocent, the way she put her hands up on his chest and looked at him.

"Was it worth it?" she asked him.

"What?"

"The years in prison. To be here."

He laughed happily. "You're goddam right it was."

"Would you do it again?"

"Nope."

She laughed, and watched Jack light the burner, grease the pan, and break the eggs into the already sputtering fat, as if it were a ritual of the utmost importance.

"You know," Jack said, "it seems screwy makin eggs for two people. I'm used to workin in the hundreds."

"Do they have regular eggs up there?"

"Mostly powdered, but once in a while we had fried eggs. A friend of mine, my partner for a long time, used to crack jokes like, 'Hey, sixty-four sunnyside up, three hundert forty-three easy over, two hundert twenty-eight chopped an messed around, an *snap it up!*'" They laughed, and Jack remembered Billy's narrow shoulders hunched up in mock efficiency, his head canted forward in urgency. "And he used to say things like, 'I wonder what the *poor folks* eat!'"

"Speaking of poor folks, I made us reservations at The Sands."

They sat at the little table in the alcove to eat their eggs and drink coffee. "Listen," Jack said, "I'd like to go, really, but I'm not supposed to leave the county without asking my parole officer; and I don't think he'd go for the action. I'm supposed to be looking for a job."

Sally made a face. "Do you do everything he tells you?"

Jack was a little irritated. "Listen, I don't want to go back to the joint just for a little party. And besides, I aint got the money to go to Vegas." He looked down at his plate. "So that's it, baby."

"You big strong men kill me. I suppose you'd flip if I said I meant to pay for the trip. I have all kinds of money." For a moment, Jack wondered if she wanted to be with him as much as he wanted to be with her; but he rejected the thought. She finished eating and lit a cigarette, puffing rapidly, flicking the ashes onto her plate. "Does your parole officer have to know?"

"I goddam sure aint going anywhere without tellin him." As he spoke, Jack wondered if it was true, or if he was just setting up conditions of behavior for *her* benefit.

"Maybe I'd better get myself another man. You just don't seem to have it this morning."

Now Jack was on surer ground. "Not enough *macho*, hey?"
She leveled her eyes on his grinning face, and then had to
laugh. "All right, I'm sorry. I never apologize. I don't know why
I apologized to you."

"Maybe because I'm bigger'n you."

"Partly that. Braggart."

After breakfast Sally cleaned up the kitchen, and Jack watched
with approval. That was good, she was neat. A rich girl, but
she had enough sense to keep her living quarters clean. As if,
Jack thought with dismay, he was measuring her against his
standard of what a "good woman" ought to be. As if he wanted to
marry her. If, that is, she passed all the tests. Rich, neat, a good
lay, attractive. Of course, she talked too much, and too much like
a man, but he could knock that out of her after a while. He was
disgusted with himself. He went and took a shower.

Later they did what she wanted, flying first to Los Angeles,
where Sally got into a telephone booth and made at least ten
calls and talked for over an hour while Jack had a few drinks
in the bar, and then getting on a flight for Las Vegas. There
was a piano on the Vegas plane, and a man who played and sang
requests. It was in the middle of the afternoon, but most of the
people on the plane were half-drunk. They stayed in Las Vegas
five days, and on the third day Jack got on the telephone to
his parole officer and explained what was going on, and got
his permission to marry Sally. The parole officer said he was
as much as washing his hands of Jack, and that any slip at all
would be enough to land him in prison again. Jack explained
very carefully that Sally had lots of money and he could take
his time looking for work, or even go to college for a while,
but the parole officer was still angry, and told Jack he had
committed enough violations already to land him back in San
Quentin, and he, the parole officer, was stretching his own neck
out on the block by not calling Jack on it. Besides, he said,
he had found a job for Jack, which, if it panned out, could
lead to big money. It was working for an outfit that sold carpets,
as a carpetlayer. He told Jack these guys make around ten

thousand a year when they get going. He had obviously done himself proud just to get Jack the chance at the job, and now he was mad because Jack was in Vegas marrying a rich woman. "I'll want that job," Jack told him. "That really sounds great. Goddam, man, you know I want that job." The parole officer was somewhat mollified, and Jack promised he'd be back in a few days at the longest and ready to go to work. When he hung up he was sweating so much, even in the dark air-conditioned room, that he had to take a shower.

NINETEEN

They had argued over whether he should call his parole officer. "You're not doing anything criminal," she said. "They can't do anything to you. It's none of their business."

"They think it is," Jack said.

"Well, I don't like it. I don't like the way they try to lead you around by the nose."

"Well, that's the name of the game. I got to call him." He reached for the telephone, and Sally walked out of the room. He didn't see her again for two days.

After his shower he went down to the casino, wearing the lemon slacks and blue sport shirt Sally had gotten him as a present, feeling the clamminess of the air conditioning through the thin shirt. Sally wasn't at any of the tables or in among the slot machines, but Jack wasn't worried yet. He felt too good about the way things were going. He had to keep reminding himself he was not in prison any more, not even working in a bakery, gagging over the lard barrel or wiping damp flour off his face. He was now a well-set-up gentleman of leisure, making the "Vegas scene," a young man for whom life had done a complete turnabout, the fiancé of a rich and beautiful woman. Jack wondered what it would be like, never having to worry about money again. Of course, he had never worried much about it in the past, but now he could do anything he wanted. He decided he wanted to go to college and study the liberal arts. It would, he felt, give him a greater opportunity to appreciate life. He did not mean to waste his life, the way these people were wasting theirs.

He watched them gamble: the fools at the little roulette setups making their nervous scattered bets, most of them with stacks of four-bit chips, one with a barricade of expensive domino-like plaques that Jack didn't even know the value of; betting numbers or thirds or quarters, red or black or odd or even, betting against one of the most powerfully house-favored odds in the joint (it may have been a luxury hotel to some of the guests, but to Jack it was just a rug joint), bucking a vigorish that did not change no matter how trickily you bet. Jack had not always felt contempt for people who gambled, but now, with the prospect of being rich before him, he suddenly did not see the point of it. When he had gambled in the past it had always been for money, never for pleasure. The pleasure had come from winning money because he needed money. The people he saw around him in the casino did not look as if they needed money, at least not enough to buck the house. It was sensible, of course, to gamble against the house if your income was so small you didn't have a chance anyway. A man making fifty a week and without hope of ever making more could come against the house odds with the genuine hope that he would win a fortune at the risk of almost nothing, because when you start with peanuts all you can lose is peanuts. Negroes shooting craps with relief money were far more sensible than the middle-class gentleman wagering three hundred dollars he can afford to lose, for one reason: the Negro expects to win and the gentleman expects to lose. Gambling, Jack decided, belongs to the poor. The rich or the well-off just make asses of themselves. He liked this new attitude of his; it made him feel superior to everybody in the room.

It bothered Sally that Jack, after the first few halfhearted bets at the dice table, quit gambling. She had the fever. She was a slot-machine player, thumbing the heavy dollars into the machine as fast as the wheels stopped and the machine clicked, while Jack stood by and watched ironically. Sally figured that the slots were the best gamble in the house because they were "fixed to pay." So that people would take their slot-machine winnings and go to the tables, get hooked, and lose everything. But Sally was clever, she would win and quit; nothing could induce her to move on to the big deadly tables. Jack laughed at her.

"Fixed to pay?" he asked. "How do you figure?"

"Oh, everybody knows that. Some of these machines are set to pay off as much as ninety percent," she said glibly.

"Which is eight and a half percent worse than the line at craps," Jack said.

She gave him an odd look. "What are you talking about?"

"Look, if you put a hundred dollars into this machine, it pays you back ninety. If you bet the same hundred, a dollar at a time, on the pass line at craps, you get back ninety-eight fifty. If the odds are working. Either way, you lose money. You can't," he said dogmatically, "change losing odds into winning odds. No matter what you do."

"Oh, nonsense. They must mean that the machines pay off ninety percent *of the time;* that's entirely different."

"Horse-frocky."

"You're infuriating." But in a few minutes she moved over to a craps table and religiously bet the pass line, a dollar at a time. Over a period of seven hours, she lost more than three hundred dollars and went to bed with a splitting headache. She blamed Jack for the whole thing.

"I *always* win at the slots," she said.

She had never been more feminine, and Jack loved her for it. But by the time they woke up again she was the old Sally. "You're right," she told him. "I was wrong. But hell, we're here; let's play the dime slots, just for fun." They did and it was fun, and they actually won a few dollars.

They were a little drunk most of the time, and it cut into their lovemaking just enough to keep them from overdoing it; yet, when they did come together it was good, and afterward, Jack would lie beside her and never want to leave her. Not ever. He wanted her beside him. He was afraid to tell her about it, actually, afraid she would laugh at him, and he would lose her.

On their second night there had been a floor show that Jack wanted to see and Sally didn't. She was still in love with the slots, and Jack went ahead in and watched the show, very conscious of himself, very conscious that these were the big-name entertainers, the most famous people in the world, and he might later on be standing right next to one of them out in the casino or in the men's room or someplace. The fact is, it was thrilling. Later he told Sally how he felt about it, and she scoffed at him and said, "They're assholes, every last one of them. Believe me. But you go ahead and worship them if you want. That's what they live on."

"I don't *worship* them," Jack said furiously.

"Of course not."

"You're laughing at me."

"Why not? Does it offend your manhood?"

"Balls!" He went to the bar. When he came back to the machines, she was gone. He looked around for her, but she wasn't anywhere. He went up to the room, and she wasn't there, either, and he began to get a little nervous. It always made him go a little off-balance when she wasn't around, and that was irritating. Even so, he undressed and went to bed with a bottle of I. W. Harper and a paperback mystery. Finally he was groggy enough, and he threw the book across the room and turned out the light. But sleep would not come. He lay in the dark waiting for her. He knew she knew other people at the hotel; she was always seeing someone and waving, or being talked to by groups of handsome young men and women whom she airily dismissed as "the television crowd" and never once introduced to Jack. She was probably at a party somewhere. He waited three hours or more, and when she came in, turning on the light as if she did not expect him to be there, or asleep, he said, "Where the hell have you been?"

She turned to him. "Ask me that again and see the last of me." Her face was hard. "Who the fuck do you think you are?"

Jack nodded, hating the feeling of relief. "Okay. You're right. Okay. Come to bed. I want you."

She undressed slowly, in the middle of the room, dropping her clothing at her feet. "This is where we agree," she said. "Without this between them, what man and woman can talk to each other?" She laughed, naked, her arms over her head in a deliberately corny pose. "You like me?" she teased.

"Bring that thing over where I can get my hands on it."

"Come and get it."

They made love on the floor, in the middle of the small room, and then, after the period of calm timelessness passed, she said, "We shouldn't let this go. We ought to get married. What do you think?"

"I love you," he said. "I was afraid you'd laugh at me if I told you. But I love you. I want to marry you."

"I love you," she said. "We have to get married. This is too good. I'll never laugh at you."

She crawled over on top of him and they kissed deeply, Jack conscious of the need to make this kiss sincere, and after a few moments she sat up and slid down on him easily, her arms out, her body moving slowly, her black hair down over her shoulders, her eyes on his; it began tenderly but moved quickly into the erotic, and Jack felt demonic, as if he had endless power.

"I'll blow you through the roof," he said between his teeth.

"Blow me through the roof," she answered. Slowly she increased her tempo until they were both bucking and writhing like animals, and when it finally happened he clutched her to him so hard he almost cracked her ribs. "*Oof!*" she said.

■ ■

Now she was gone again. He wandered through the casino, the coffee shop, out by the swimming pool. Everywhere he went it was noisy with people, a continual din that he associated with the lower but similarly constant noise of San Quentin. But these people were not in prison, not even in a metaphorical prison. Jack had known convicts who said that everybody was in prison, that life was a prison, or society a prison, even being stuck with your own identity was a prison; but Jack no longer believed that: prison was prison, nothing else. People might be in *trouble,* or feel stifled or restricted, or even trapped, but they weren't in prison. It just wasn't the same thing at all. The hotel might be a "glittering trap" for the bored and lonely, but that was a hell of a lot different from being sent to prison.

Just to prove it, Jack left the buildings and walked out into the desert. The transition was dramatic; the desert afternoon was blistering hot, and the purple mountains in the distance wavered in the heat, almost invisible through the thermal density. There were sounds, but not human voices. He could hear cars on the highway behind him, and he walked across the hot baked desert ground rapidly, away from the sounds of the cars and toward the mountains. It was a lot like the eastern Oregon country, but much lower in elevation, and somehow dirtier. Nature here was not more beautiful than the works of man, because nature had forgotten to air-condition the place or clean it up, and only the distant view was attractive. After a few minutes, Jack no longer believed in air conditioning—it did not seem possible that any place could be cool when it was so hot.

Even so, he was glad to be alone, and he felt satisfied that he was paying for his aloneness by absorbing the terrible heat. He turned, and he could see cars wavering along the highway like mirages, and he could see the high-voltage electrical towers crossing the sands, wriggling in the heat. He would have to walk miles to get away from it entirely, to be in a place where he wouldn't see the buildings, the cars, the power derricks; and even then he would probably come across tourists on horseback, enduring the heat so they could say they didn't spend all their time in the casinos and had the bad, black, blistering sunburns to prove it. Jack turned back, feeling immediate buoyancy from the air conditioning as he stepped inside. But he had enjoyed being alone; he had even forgotten, for a few minutes, to worry about Sally. He began looking for her again, now that he was used to being cool.

His loneliness was complemented now, he was no longer really alone, he could no longer stand to be alone, which is to say, without *her*. He needed *her*. It made him think of Billy Lancing, and how much he had needed Billy, and how much Billy had needed him. If it had not been for Billy, Jack would not have been able to understand how he really felt, or understood that he was alone without *her*. He could say to himself now, coldly, that Billy had died for the love of him; he could take pride in it. He had been loved *that much!* He did not worry himself with the thought that he never would have died for Billy; he had not loved Billy as much as Billy had loved him, and he knew it, admitted it, and was not ashamed of it. But now he loved Sally that much, and Billy had showed him what it meant.

He looked around the casino. No, not one in sight. No Negroes at The Sands. Only fat white businessmen faking the nigger talk over their cold dice, acting out something they had seen in a movie, or read about in a cheap magazine, but had never seen or felt. Twenty-five-grand-a-year incomes, and blowing a little of the surplus in order to feel like a sport. And gosh, you know who was standing at the table, right next to me? *Frank Sinatra!* And you should have seen the bets he was fading! Made my three hundred look like nothing. I says to him, "Frank, what do you think about . . ." . . . Yeah, like shit you did. You lost your three hundred, or shall we say, hundred and a half, dying over every silver dollar just a little more, sweat running down from your armpits to the place where your belly is cinched in too tight by your belt; your crotch so hot from nervous fear you think you have the crabs; calling out, "Tennessee Toddy, all ass and no body!" to a pair of dice so wet they almost

slip out of your fingers; and then go back to your room black
with despair because you lost instead of won and last night you
put your hand on your boss's wife's knee or fucked your sec-
retary, and now wondered if it had been such a hot idea after
all, the way she thrashed around and said she loved you and
your wife home thinking it was stag only. Or maybe you got
yourself a call girl and now wondered when your pecker would
start to drip greenish pus the way it had in Germany when you
were in the Army. Or maybe you won a lot of money, really
a lot, and your wife was with you and you were coming on
hip with sunglasses and talk about the odds and what games
Scarne recommends, and drinking milk at the tables like a pro,
wondering deep inside how you could keep your wife from
spending this dough (it was dough or bread, but not money)
you had just won and wanted desperately to take out of your
pocket and kiss greedily and scream out that you had *won*, and
never wanted to spend because you had nightmares about
money . . .

Or maybe you were just having a good time. Shit.

Jack felt contempt for his patronizing attitude. He had lost
his temper at the casino. That was stupid. So there were no
Negroes at the hotel. So what? What do I care? It's not my
problem. Why blame it on the customers? They were just assholes, like everybody else.

When Sally finally showed up after having been gone two
days and nights, Jack did not ask her where she had been. He
shaved, showered, and took her downtown and married her. Just
as quickly as he could. She was very quiet, almost wifely, and
suggested they fly back to San Francisco right away. On the
plane she told Jack she was now just about broke. Her money
had been alimony, and now she wouldn't be getting any. For
the last two days and nights she had been in Los Angeles, talking to her lawyer and her ex-husband's lawyer, trying to get a
settlement. But they couldn't do it, and so she was broke. She
looked surprised when Jack laughed.

"What's so funny?"

"I have a job waiting for me. It looks like I'm going to need it." To himself, however, he admitted that he was bitterly disappointed. He wanted to ask her why didn't they just *live* together, and keep the alimony coming in. But he knew the answer: Sally wanted to be *married*. All right, they were married. Jack knew it had all been a false dream, the idea of being rich, and he was not really bothered. Still, she should have asked him, or at least told him.

She snuggled up next to him. "My husband and protector," she said. "My breadwinner."

"My balls," Jack said. They laughed.

TWENTY

Sally's first husband was an actor; they had met while she was a twenty-year-old junior at Mills College—a scholarship student among the sloppily dressed, shaggy-haired rich girls —and he had come out to take a part in one of the school plays. There was something about him that cut deeply into her, a drawn look of constant hunger—for food, for acceptance, for love, for fame, she did not know what. But one thing she was certain of, after she had seen him act: if there was any justice in the universe, this young man was going to become rich and famous. He had talent, the kind that makes you love its possessor, yet at this point it was visible only to Sally. Most of the girls thought he was cute, but funny-looking. They did not know he had talent as an actor, because they did not know what talent was. They only knew that he slopped around at rehearsals, was shy, did not smoke, and secretly picked at his nose. They laughed at him for forgetting his lines and for the way he would frown and place his thumb and index finger on his nose when he was trying to remember something. Most of the girls belonged to the smooth-flowing-grace school of amateur acting, and thought that he moved jerkily. Everyone but Sally thought he was the weak point of the production. They were all afraid that when the play was on he would stop in the middle of the action, hold his nose, and snap his fingers for someone to throw him his line.

But of course he did not. After she had finished her work backstage, Sally went out and around to the back of the hall to watch the performance, and *he* was the only one onstage. The subtleties, the graces of the other performers were washed out by the lights and the presence of the audience, and only *he* seemed natural, real, and yet even more distinct than reality; when he said a line you could hear it sharply, even if it was supposed to be a mumble, and when he began a movement you could predict its course, sense it with him, actually participate in the action. And of course he was the only one whose makeup was not grotesque. Sally could tell at the end, when the cast lined up for their curtain call, that she had been almost the only one in the house to recognize his beauty, and it made her bitterly angry; she rushed out of the building with tears in her eyes and ended up wandering alone through the eucalyptus groves, full of hate for the people who could not, would not, recognize his talent, and full of love for him and for herself.

A month later they were married, and Sally supplied to him the two things he lacked: ambition and direction. She discovered he was really just a bum, whose only true love was sailing on the bay, and whose interest in acting stemmed from the fact that he knew he was good at it, and he knew people paid a lot of money to good actors. He hoped someday he would be discovered, but meanwhile he was content to live a marginal existence on borrowed money, unemployment, the GI Bill, or whatever presented itself. Another reason he liked acting, she discovered, was because actors worked at night, when you couldn't sail anyway.

Sally changed his life. She quit college and got two jobs,

doing high-fashion modeling in a department store days and selling tickets in a Market Street movie theater nights, supporting him while he suffered through books on acting and a few courses at San Francisco State, and took the meager roles offered by the San Francisco amateur theater. She did not make him sell his half-interest in his little El Toro boat, but she kept him so busy he hardly ever had time to go out on the Bay. When television or movie companies came to town to shoot exteriors, she made him go out for the extra parts, and meanwhile they were saving enough money to get to Hollywood. But the miracle happened, and he was "seen" in one of his television bits, recognized for the qualities Sally herself saw, and offered a contract.

For the next two years he was seen getting shot, clubbed, knifed, hanged, or otherwise knocked apart by the various avatars of the fastest gun in the West, and he had parts in two films. One was a science-fiction thriller in which he, an accountant for a firm engaged in top-secret government research, is "absorbed" by a blob of goo. In the other, an adventure story set in the big woods, he played a lumberjack who loses his nerve, and then dies topping a tree (the top of the tree splits, and he is squeezed half to death, and then falls). Then he got a good part on "Playhouse 90" as a farm boy who hungers after the wife of the hired man—a subplot to the main event, a rewrite of *Desire Under the Elms* with a big rock instead of a tree as the God-symbol; and then he was given his own series.

It was a Western, and he played the part of a sheriff in a small Colorado mining town. The device of the show was that he carried no gun, but had a knife up his sleeve. He would not pull the knife unless extremely provoked, but if he *did* pull it, woe unto the provoker, for he always aimed to kill. They filmed twenty-six original episodes, and five years later the series was still being shown as reruns. Meanwhile Walt Disney had given him a contract and he was a made man. He was a rich and famous actor. You see him all the time, these days, having serious conversations with dogs and sadly killing Indians.

Sally left him. She could not stand his success, the fact that without growing at all he had grown beyond her, and she could not stand seeing the talent she had loved being used as a mere device. This, she understood, had been what she herself had done, and it hurt her. Especially because *he* did not see it at all, *he* did not know that his great beauty as an actor was being wasted, used up, for trash. He was perfectly happy. When he was working he got up early in the morning and went to the studio, made up, sat and waited for his part, did exactly what the director asked, and when the shooting was over, went home. When he was not making a picture, he was sailing. He now had a 70-foot schooner with a paid crew of five, and the head of the crew, a salty old Mexican he had met in Santa Monica, was his constant companion and in fact appeared in all his movies in bit parts. When Sally left him he sold his house and moved out to the boat in Santa Monica, and when the divorce proceedings were held he appeared in court, agreed that Sally was to have one-third of his income, and shook hands with her. Everybody was happy but Sally.

When she came back to San Francisco she discovered that among the set whose central ambition seemed to be getting their names into Herb Caen's column she had a certain currency as the ex-wife of one of the ascending giants of Hollywood, and so instead of reverting to her maiden name she kept his, using it as both a shield and an entrée. In Hollywood she had been a nothing, the wife of an actor, someone to whom you made a point of saying hello; in San Francisco, on the other hand, she was a celebrity in her own right, someone who had given up *all that* to return to the only really cultured and exciting city in the Western Hemisphere. Sally knew what a damned lie it was; she knew she had run away from all that excitement, all that bubbling creativity, because down there she had been only a bystander; she knew she had come back to San Francisco to find some thing, some place, where she could again be central. And so she married Jack Levitt. Which fact was duly reported by Herb Caen, and all San Francisco, or at least Sally's set, was agog. Her friends were even more agog when they dropped around to the Telegraph Hill apartment and discovered that Sally didn't live there any more and had left no forwarding address.

She was, in fact, through with café society. She had found something meaningful, and she was through with wasting her life. At last she was in love—this time it was truly love—and she awakened each morning with the brightness of it in her heart, and an eager joy at the prospect of transforming his life and hers into something permanent and meaningful.

But it was not going to be easy. For one thing, Jack did not get the carpet-laying job that promised to go to ten thousand a year. Perhaps the man doing the hiring didn't like his face. So while the money they had lasted, Jack looked around for work. At Sally's suggestion he applied to Federal Civil Service, taking the general entrance examination with hundreds of others, and despite the nervousness epidemic in the cafeteria where the tests were given, Jack thought he did pretty well; he felt almost certain of a rating of at least GS–6, and perhaps even higher. Meanwhile he and his parole officer looked for other kinds of work (Jack hadn't told him about the Civil Service exam), and nights and afternoons he and Sally worked on their new apartment, trying to make it habitable.

When they were settled, there were paintings and drawings on all the walls, drapes on the windows, books and small objects on the shelves, food in the kitchen, and, somehow, perhaps through the expense of work they had put into the place, a sense of belonging, of habitat, that made them both feel comfortable and cozy just being there. The rent was $65.00 per month, and they paid their own gas and electricity, but the heat and garbage were free. They got a telephone at the cheapest rate, unlisted, and they were home.

Jack found a job parking cars for a nightclub on Broadway, and they waited for the answer from the Federal Civil Service.

When it came and Jack read it out in the foyer of the building, he was not really surprised. Sally, however, exploded.

"If the fucking Federal Government won't hire ex-convicts, how in the goddam hell do they expect anybody else to?"

"What did you expect?" Jack asked. He had not really felt irritated until Sally read the letter. She was standing in the kitchen, and he was leaning in the doorway. "They think I'm a rotten vicious criminal; would *you* hire a rotten vicious criminal?"

"What do they mean, 'Untrustworthy'?" she blazed. "How would *they* know? Jesus Christ!"

"No use blowing your stack." He took the envelope and letter from her hand and dropped it into the garbage sack under the sink. "I was a sucker to shoot for it."

"That's the goddamndest criminal piece of horseshit I ever saw in my life!" she yelled. She stooped down and retrieved the letter. "I'm going to take it to the American Civil Liberties Union! We'll see what we'll see!"

Jack was amused, but still angry. "That'll do a lot of good. Listen, forget it."

She stared at him. "Forget it? Why should I? It's a criminal injustice. We have to *do* something about it!"

"Oh, come on. Sure it's an injustice. It's even a crime. So what? Don't you think society ever commits crimes? Hell, they do it all the time. And get away with it. Listen, I committed some crimes, too, you know. And if I can, society can. They aint no better than me, and I aint no better than they are. We're even, dig? Do you think I could look myself in the face if I didn't think society was a crock of shit? God *damn!*"

"What's getting to you?" she wanted to know. Jack's face was red and his eyes burned angrily. He tried to pace up and down in the living room, but there was too much furniture in the way, and after stumbling twice, he threw himself into a chair.

"Whaddya mean, what's gettin to me? Jesus! You act like you got rights or something? Are you out of your mind? Listen, I gave this a lot of thought, baby, and there aint no justice and so you might just as well forget it, and do what you can. Dig?"

"I hate it when you say 'dig.' That's a disgusting word."

"I'll quit sayin it if you'll stop yelling 'fuck' every three minutes. Okay?"

She stamped out into the kitchen, but came back in a few minutes still holding the letter. "The ACLU will tear these bastards apart," she said. "The idea of prison is to reform people, they haven't any right . . ."

"Now, where did you get *that* idea? The idea of prison is punishment, an any reforming done is strictly incidental. Society don't give a fuck what happens to you, and you know it. Society is an animal, just like the rest of us."

"I didn't realize you were such a philosopher," she said.

"I didn't realize you were such an *innocent*," he cracked.

But Sally did send the letter to the ACLU, and the ACLU did nothing, and the rolls of the Federal Civil Service remained pure, and Jack kept working at the North Beach parking lot.

Perhaps what held the marriage together in those early months was Jack's naive sincerity as much as anything else. He really wanted to make a go of it. He had thrown most of his life away by looking out for Number One, he felt, and now it was time to be mature, to find the real meaning of his existence by looking out for other people, in making himself a *family*—he had never had a family of his own, and so, he reasoned, he could start with a clean slate, and do it according to the book.

He had heard enough and read enough about marriage to know that sex was central, the very root of the relationship between man and wife, and so he was very careful to be more than fond to Sally, to be passionate, to give her the kind of manly loving that had first drawn them together, the thing she had missed so much in her life—he would give her this, it would be the perfect ending and delicious beginning to each day, whether he felt like it or not. He decided it was his obligation, and for weeks after they were settled in the new place and he was getting used to the routine of work, he dishonestly pretended that everything was fine. But it was not; he knew it, denied it, felt it get worse, and finally would come home at two or three in the morning after the last drunk customer had been poured into the last expensive automobile, with his mind desperately fending off the hope that for once Sally would be asleep and he could crawl into bed and get some rest. He had read in a paperback mystery the line, "Sex is nice, but there are times when you'd rather cut your throat," and he knew that feeling. He hated having to induce passion in himself, and he hated having to be deceptive in this, the admittedly central thing in their marriage—perhaps, he often thought, the *only* thing in their marriage. Because Sally's desires seemed endless. Of course, he reasoned, this was lots better than the other way around. He had read about such things; the couple get married and from that day forward the old man has to play rapist to his neovirgin wife. He was glad Sally was not like that, but he wondered about himself.

Increasingly, the core of his anxiety was the fear that he was homosexual at heart. He could not ignore the facts of his life: until Sally, the highest point of his emotional *development*, as he was beginning to think of it, had been with Billy Lancing; and even though there was plenty of evidence to prove that he loved Sally more and in a very different way, he *had* been deeply involved with Billy, they *had* made love to each other, and now he *was* getting awfully tired of making love to his wife. He tried to picture how it would be with a man again and searched himself for a thrill of guilty pleasure, but always it seemed so stupid and ugly, seen, as it were, from the viewpoint of a third party. Again, he would wonder if it just wasn't the basic difference, biologically, between men and women—that women could reach orgasm after orgasm, while a man just naturally went limp after a while. He wanted to ask somebody, stop a stranger on the street and say to him, "Listen, Mac, do you lay your wife twice a day? Or am I overdoing it?"

He could see what they meant when they said sex was important; he was hardly able to think of anything else. But he was also firmly resolved not to be the first to pull the "headache" bit or say, "Not tonight, honey, I'm beat." That was a woman's trick. And after all, Sally was the woman in the marriage, not him. He thanked the gods of biology that there were at least three or four days a month when even Sally would hold back, but he discovered that even then she was willing, if not eager, to please him in other ways, and not averse to being handled herself. So there was no respite. Often he wondered if everyone's private life was as strange as his, so at variance with the public image of marriage. One thing was certain; it wasn't anything like anything he had ever dreamed of. He was glad he had not stopped a stranger on the street, because he knew now the stranger would have lied, just as Jack would lie if somebody asked him about his private life. Maybe that was what they meant by "private."

But of course there were other things to occupy him; the Sex Problem was enormous, but not all that enormous. There was also culture, the matter of what did he want to do with his life, how was he to improve himself in order to enjoy life to the fullest, to be able to draw pleasure from as many possible sources and to understand the natural pains of existence so they wouldn't trouble him too much. He wanted a full life, which would have in it love, a kind of work he could love, sports, art, books, the theater, hobbies, friends, and most of all—most important, the pinnacle—children. This was very important to Jack. It was the reason people got married in the first place. It was the sole rational reason for monogamy—people got married so children could have parents and a home, and be brought up properly, with love, to understand the world and so not fight it, not be blinded as Jack had been for so many years by his own selfish egotism. Naturally, he wanted a son. He figured that having a son, and then perhaps another, and then a daughter or two, was the essential part of the fullness of life. He had seen enough of the emptiness of life to last him forever. He did not fool himself into thinking his life had been *wasted;* no, that was not it, just that he was through with emptiness, it was time now for the rich part. He felt, naively, that he was entitled to it. He had worked for it. He had thrown more than a quarter of a century into the earning of it.

He even reasoned, a little smugly perhaps, that people who hadn't been through the mud as he had, and by that he meant people who hadn't dragged *themselves* through the mud, hadn't seen society and man at its and his worst as he surely had, were missing the really rich pleasures of life because they had nothing to compare them to. Having your own apartment, for example, might be pretty interesting to the ordinary citizen but it could never be as vital as it was to Jack, who felt an actual pleasure at the sense of paying for his own walls, walls that he could get out from behind any time he wanted. He also felt, again a little smugly, that his life had given him a better understanding of some of the works of literature that he was now conscientiously plowing his way through, because he had seen, felt some of the things they described, and he had not yet worn out the pleasures or forgotten the pains of "life," which was supposed to be what literature was about.

At first Sally helped him. She took him to operas, where they sat in cheap seats, and explained to him as best she could what was happening and why it was supposed to be great; and she would accompany him to football and baseball games and listen when he explained to her what was going on and why it was supposed to be exciting. She took him to art movies, galleries, poetry readings, and it made her laugh and feel tender to see the way he seemed to be discovering everything for the first time. One day they packed a lunch and drove down the coast highway, and when they crested the hill overlooking Pacific Manor and saw the ocean and the long curved white beach, the land rising past the few houses to the soft brown mountains, Jack was entranced; it was such a sudden transition: from the mile after mile of Henry Doelger Homes, an endless series of repetitions of pink, blue, green, brown, and white houses; and then bursting over the hill to see all that wide blue ocean. He stopped the car on the shoulder of the highway and got out, just to have a good look. When he got back in, he said, "You know, I'd like to live out here some time."

"It would be nice," she admitted, "except for the way the salt air gets to everything and ruins it. And it's so foggy most of the time."

"I wouldn't mind that. It's so wide open."

They drove through the scattered beach towns and up into the Devil's Slide area past Pedro Point, and Jack could see the waves crashing into the ocher cliffs four hundred feet below the narrow rim of highway; the water looked impossibly deep and blue, and out a way from the cliffs there was a slow-moving ribbon of dirty-looking foam, and he wondered if that meant the tide was going out, or if it had anything to do with the tide at all. He realized that he really didn't know anything about tides. There was so much for him to learn about things, even unimportant little things like tides, which everybody ought to know. It made him wonder where he had been all his life.

Eventually the road straightened out and they came to and passed the tiny ramshackle community of Montara, and then came to Moss Beach, and Sally showed him where to turn off onto the dirt road that led to the reef.

The tide was going out, and as they sat on the sand and ate their lunch, they could see the waves beginning to break dramatically over the long brown fingers of reef, and watched a calm lagoon form right in front of them. There was a kelpy iodine smell to the air, and Jack was overwhelmed by a desire to go out and wade in the lagoon, to get into the water. He took Sally by the hand and led her down to the edge of the sand and they waded out into the weed-filled, gently undulating water. She seemed to understand his mood and said nothing; she understood that he was discovering this immensity for the first time, and she did not want to spoil it for him by admitting that it no longer had the same attraction for her, that she had made the discovery when she was twelve and become bored with it by the time she was eighteen. But she followed Jack through the water, and climbed up onto the slippery reef with him, and watched him discovering the tide pools, squatting in fascination at the perfection of calm and beauty, the scuttling hermit crabs, the tiny green shrimp, the rock fish and snails and flowery anemones, such a peaceful community *right there at your feet;* listened to his exclamations of discovery and answered his questions about which animals were which, until needles of pain shot through the backs of her knees and her eyes smarted from the glitter of the sun on the water; but when she stood up and suggested that they get some coffee and have a cigarette he just gave her a dirty look and then went on staring down into the water, and she had to go back alone.

She watched him from the beach as he went farther and farther out on the reef, and saw him at last on the final edge, staring toward the open sea, breakers crashing beside his tiny figure, and she knew there were all sorts of romantic ideas pouring through his mind about life, the sea, nature, the size of the universe, man is a tiny creature, etc. etc. But she did not feel like sneering at him for it; she began to have images of this man, locked somewhere in a prison cell away from all possible thoughts of immensity, and she felt a great wave of pity for him, for the loss of his youth, for his naive, childlike expectation that the past was all over and he could just start from where he was and bury it all behind him and become a cultured person. It made her feel so bitter she wanted to cry.

Jack was having a hell of a fine time. He was playing a game with the ocean. He was standing at the very edge of the reef, watching the rollers swell in front of him, rising high above his head, and then break and crash at his feet. The game was a modified form of "chicken"—he had already seen that the reef undercut the waves so that they could not hit him full force, and he was watching the waves come in, testing himself for the fear-reaction, the urge to flinch and jump back when a big one rose over him: if he felt scared, the ocean won; if he didn't, he won. It was really such a good game—because the waves were so beautiful and green when they rose before him, and he was watching their beauty and wondering why blue water turned green when it was really *clear*—that he forgot to feel the fear and won each round handily after the first few. He was not thinking of Sally at all, and hadn't really thought of her since she had stood up to go and he had squinted up at her directly into the glare from the beach and seen her almost angry expression as she turned to go. Now he wasn't thinking about much of anything, just watching the beautiful water. He had even forgotten about the tides, and so it was with a sense of genuine surprise that he watched one wave rise much higher than the others and race toward him, hitting him across the chest; he felt himself picked up like a leaf, felt a gentle force with greater strength than he had ever experienced carry him back across the reef, rolling him now over the rock and then landing him in the lagoon, his arms and legs flying. He had a mouthful of salt water, and it tasted bitter. He flailed around trying to get his balance, and accidently his feet touched bottom, and abruptly he stood up. He was about twenty feet from where he started, in calm water up to his waist. The breakers seemed a long way off; as he watched, another one climbed the reef and sent a line of dirty suds toward him. He rubbed his mouth and laughed. He turned, thinking of Sally, and saw her standing, far away, beneath the bluff, her hands at her sides. He could not tell at that distance if she looked frightened or not, but he waved his arm to show he was all right and began wading toward her.

"You crazy jackass," she said angrily. He felt suddenly like a little boy.

"I won't do it again, Mommy," he said.

Three skin divers in black wet-suits came down the bluff from the parking area, big, bulky men with gunnysacks and snorkel breathers and face masks in their hands; one of them saw Jack's wet clothes, already beginning to steam in the sunshine, and laughed and said, "Fall in the water, buddy?"

"Fuck you, Mac," Jack snarled at him. The man looked horrified, and moved away with his friends.

"For heaven's sake," one of them said.

Both Jack and Sally were happy and tired as they drove back to the city, even though they had headaches from the glare. They resolved that next time they came to the beach they would wear sunglasses.

When they got home they wanted to make love, but they were too tired. So they just took hot baths, and Sally went to bed with a book and Jack went to work. When he returned at two thirty she was sound asleep. With real relief he crawled in beside her, feeling the warmth of her body, and sank into a delicious, life-giving sleep.

TWENTY-ONE

Sally's boredom with Jack's program of discovery soon turned into criticism. He did see things from a rather special point of view, and after a while he was no longer listening to her recommendations as carefully, nor was he accepting her judgments of what was good and what was bad. Sometimes it got pretty irritating. Once, for example, he spent a month wading through *Ulysses*, which Sally told him was the greatest novel ever written. He threw it aside late one night and said to her, "Baby, I just can't cut it. That book's as full of shit as a Christmas goose. It's too much for me. I like Bloom a lot, but I can't stand his goddam crazy wife or that asshole Stephen. He's just a turd. I don't want to read about turds."

"Maybe it is a little too advanced for you," she said. She was, Jack realized, just sitting there doing nothing, and probably had been ever since he got home, and God knows how long before that.

"Maybe it is," he said. "Maybe I should go back to comic books. How the hell can you sit there doin nothin? Don't you go nuts?"

"I'm thinking," she said. "But maybe you don't know anything about that."

"Oh, boy," was all he could think of to say.

She giggled. " 'Stephen Dedalus is a turd.' That's something you might see on the wall of a public toilet. Like, 'Donald Duck is a Jew,' or 'Plato eats it.' "

"Do they write stuff like that in women's rest rooms?"

"No," she said. "I always use the men's room."

"We're lucky," he said abruptly. "We have a sense of humor. That saves us. A lot of times."

"Saves us from what?"

"Oh, you know. Arguing."

"I think argument is good for a marriage," she said. "It cleans out the dirty little places; the stuff you might bury away."

Jack agreed, and they had a long talk about marriage, and how difficult it was, and how lucky they were that each of them was such a fine example of a generous, warm, and loving human being. They went to bed feeling smug, satisfied that theirs was a perfect marriage. It was a feeling they often had, and sometimes it lasted for days. But more and more they found themselves arguing about things outside the marriage, things that did not really matter at all, like art, literature, music, or politics. While both of them admitted that taste was a very personal matter, they argued as if each had the proper taste and the other had to be kidding or was being *defensive*. Jack could not finish *Ulysses*, but read *From Here to Eternity* with rapt attention, and at the end hugged the book to his chest and said, "This son of a bitch has *really* been around! Man, what a book!" But Sally merely sneered and said, "Illiterate," leaving Jack in the dark as to whether she meant him or James Jones.

"At least when he wants to say something, he says it," Jack insisted. He began to illustrate from the text, and realized from the way Sally looked evasive that she had not actually read *From Here to Eternity* but knew what it was about from the movie and from book reviews. She admitted this, and did not see why it mattered.

She took him to a production of *Waiting for Godot*, perhaps rather cattishly hoping it would snow him and make him feel inadequate; but when they left the theater and she began talking

260

about Beckett's use of language, Jack interrupted her and said, "Hell, it seems simple enough to me. They're waiting, that's all. It don't matter what for."

"Doesn't," she said automatically.

"Doesn't. They're just waiting. What did you want?"

"It's not that simple," she said, but she was not sure why it was not that simple.

"I've done a lot of that waiting jazz," Jack said. "I know what it's like."

"So have I," Sally said. "What do you think I do all day?"

And it was true. Sally was waiting for—she did not know what. Waiting day after day, perhaps for the nerve to walk out. It was not really the marriage she had hoped for, and she often wondered sickly if any marriage could be. She felt chained by the marriage, trapped, her freedom gone. It was so maddening. She would sometimes just sit around the house all day, anticipating Jack's return, allowing most of the housework to go undone, and when Jack did arrive, she would experience a sharp sense of disappointment. She did not know why. Often she would awaken with a feeling of resolve—to give the apartment a thorough cleaning, or to get a job so that they would have enough money to do more things; but the dullness of the morning routine of breakfast, toilet, dishes, and daily newspaper would take the edge from her resolve, and she would just sit. Looking through the classified ads for work was depressing, too. Women were always wanted for jobs, but no one seemed willing to pay a decent salary. With a twinge of guilt Sally realized that if she got a job, she would want to surprise Jack with it, not mentioning until he asked that she would be making more money than he was. And the plain fact was that such jobs required training, and she had none. She was getting older, and they were not having any fun, and she was becoming a housewife.

The afternoons were the worst times. Even if she had been busy, even if she had been a *good* housewife, there was nothing to do in the afternoon. She almost always wanted to take a nap by then, and Jack was up and around the apartment. If he left early, she was angry with him for deserting her in the apartment, and if he hung around, reading or sitting in the kitchen drinking coffee, she was resentful because he was in her way. By the time he did leave, she would be too full of coffee to nap, and too nervous to do anything but sit. It was driving her crazy. She felt that she actually might have gone out of her mind, if an incident hadn't occurred to break the monotony.

Jack, in the course of his work, had to deal with a lot of drunks, and he knew that the only way to handle them was to get them somehow into their cars, or if they were too drunk, into a cab, and get rid of them; he knew he could not rise to any challenge, he had to withstand any insult without losing his temper, and it really wasn't too hard to do. After all, it was part of his job. But one night, after a series of particularly haughty, drunk suburbanites, he was walking up Broadway alone, on his way home, and there were four teen-agers blocking the sidewalk, arguing with each other. He tried to get past them, but one turned on him and shoved him against the building and swore at him. Jack wanted to get home, so he tried to leave, but the boys surrounded him. He was still a very hard-looking man (he had not yet begun to wear glasses) and perhaps the boys, in their desperate boredom, felt challenged by his obvious toughness. They ganged up on him, and something drawn very tight inside him snapped, and with real joy he took them on, grabbing two by the neck and smashing their heads together, kicking another in the stomach and hearing with great pleasure his grunt of surprise, and then watching the last of the boys, his arms akimbo, his mouth open in stupid fear, backing away from Jack. With a giggle, Jack followed him and hit him in the chest, as hard as he could, and the boy folded up. Two policemen in a patrol car had seen the whole thing and were crossing the street when the last of the boys folded up. They put the arm on Jack, and after calling for another patrol car and an ambulance they took him downtown. Both of the policemen had been delighted by what Jack had done, but they braced him and took him downtown anyway. When they found out he was

262

on parole they were genuinely sorry they had picked him up.

Jack was certain he was going back to San Quentin, and he retreated bitterly into his hard shell, hating himself for his pretended hardness. They offered him his one telephone call and he shook his head angrily; then, rising out of the stupid hardness, accepted, and called Sally.

"I'm in jail," he told her.

"Oh my God, I'll get you a lawyer," she answered.

The next morning, after a great deal of fussing, Jack was released. He had never seen and heard so much bathos in his life. They were all there—his parole officer, his lawyer (Jack had expected to see John, the man he had hit out in front of Rosenbloom's, and was surprised to find that he was being represented by Cyril Whitehead, one of the most famous criminal lawyers in the country), Sally, the four punks, their parents, a representative of the District Attorney's office, two or three other lawyers with the fat, well-bred look that comes from a corporation practice—all these people milling around, talking, touching each other, alternately smiling and looking serious; and the upshot was that while *fighting* was forbidden to parolees, they did have the right to *protect themselves,* and as to the four boys, well, they were all from good, local, prominent families, and were really good boys at heart, and they were awfully sorry (sorry they had been knocked around, Jack thought) and promised not to do anything of the kind again, etc. etc., and Jack and Sally went home, and for weeks she was very loving and devoted to him. She had almost lost him; it could happen just like that.

For his part, Jack understood what Sally must be going through, stuck at home all the time, and a most wonderful solution came to him: it was time to start having children. Even though he only made $72.50 a week, which was really not enough to have children on, it was better just to dive right in now and save Sally from her perpetual boredom that to wait around and perhaps lose her. It was a very rational solution, particularly because Jack felt that Sally pregnant would inspire him to do something really serious about bettering himself, getting a job he could love and making the kind of money they needed. Everything seemed to click into place: that was why the woman stayed home, and that was why men tried to better themselves—children. Just thinking about it gave him a rich, meaningful sense of reality.

He was astonished to learn, when he got home that night, that Sally did not want to have children. Not just yet. It was something he had always *assumed,* and suddenly he remembered that they had never actually talked about it at all, not seriously, not *talked* about it. He lost his temper.

"Look, I'm for it," he said. "We aint getting any younger, and I read that it's best to have the kids when you're pretty young, so's you don't get tired of them too quick. And anyway, it'd give you something to do, something to make plans for. So how about it? Are you just scared?"

"Maybe I'm too old already," she said. They were both in bed now, the night-light on overhead. She looked a little frightened. Her hair was up in pins, and her nose stuck out shrewishly. The light from above gave her skin a sallow, unattractive look, and made her eyes smaller and not blue at all.

"Well," he said, "we're gonna do it. And we might just as well start trying right tonight. You don't have your diaphragm on, do you?"

She eyed him suspiciously. "You know when I put my hair up I don't. You're going to rape me, is that it?"

He gritted his teeth. She was about as lovely as a corpse. "If I have to, I will," he said.

"You mean it, don't you," she said. "You'd just make up your mind like that, and do it." She laughed sourly. "I should have known. It always comes down to that. This is the way you do everything. You sit down and think it out, and then when you've got it thought out, you do it. Nobody else matters. Just you. No wonder they threw you in prison."

"We have to have kids," he said stubbornly. "Or it's all bullshit."

264

"Maybe it's all bullshit anyway," she said. As if saying good-bye to something ineffable, something long gone anyway, she held her arms out to him, and they made what passed for love. Just to be sure, they made love fifteen nights in a row, and the irony was that these hurried matings were the least loving in their marriage. When Sally's period was eight days late (and she was very regular), she disappeared and was gone for a week.

Jack went nearly crazy. He thought she might have jumped off the Golden Gate Bridge, or done something equally dramatic and final. But he was stubborn, too, and he would not look for her. He did not have that right. They were only married, as she had once said, not sewn together.

At the end of the week he was standing out in front of the parking lot on Broadway, in his white knee-length coat, his hands in his pockets, waiting for the crowds to start coming out of the club, when a Rolls-Royce sedan pulled in next to him and Myron Bronson stuck his hand out and smiled at Jack. "When do you get off?"

"Couple hours. How are you?"

"I have a message from your wife."

Jack was not surprised, and he kept his face blank. "Meet me at Vesuvio's about one, then. Okay?"

"Where is it?"

Jack told him, and the huge rich car backed out and tooled off.

Vesuvio's was crowded, as usual, but Jack had no trouble spotting Bronson, with his beautiful wavy gray hair. They took a table by the window, and Bronson ordered Bushmills for them, and they talked.

Sally had been staying in Bronson's elegant Pacific Heights mansion, alternately getting drunk on Bronson's excellent brandy or bitchily begging him to get her an abortionist, on the cuff. One of the sins of poverty, Bronson told him with a shy smile, was the lack of funds needed for a good abortionist. He would have given her the money, he told Jack, if she'd only been a little dishonest and not told him why she wanted it; because she knew that he, Bronson, did not believe in either contraception or abortion.

"Are you Catholic or something?"

"No, I just don't believe in them. When I was very young, not much older than you, I had a vasectomy performed on myself; I had myself neutered, so that, I suppose, I could enjoy what pleasures there were without having to be anxious about getting tied up in a lawsuit, or worse, getting married." He smiled. "I've been married three times since then, and possibly, just possibly, the cause produced the effect. Anyway, I don't like the idea of murdering the possible. Of course, I can afford such ethics, now."

But Jack was not particularly interested in Bronson's problems. "Tell her to come home to me," he said. He wanted to say, "I need her," but didn't.

"Well, she's asked me to give you a message. Please understand the wording is hers, not mine, and that I won't kick her out. I don't think you'd want me to. She's going through something awful; I think she's afraid she's going to lose the only thing that keeps her free, or at least makes her think she's free; I think she's afraid that having a child will make her old. I know it won't, I know what it will do for her, it will complete her; but she can't see that at all . . ."

He trailed off, and sat looking out the window.

"Well? What's the message?"

Bronson sighed. Without turning his head, he said, "She asked me to tell you, 'Inform that son of a bitch I'll have the kid where he can't find me, and then stick it in an orphanage.'"

Bronson knew the message was vicious, but nonetheless he was still shaken by what happened to Jack's face. Bronson had been around a lot, but he had never seen anything like this, not even in 1929. Jack's face turned the color of pale mud. His mouth froze, and his eyes seemed to have turned to lead; cold, dead, lifeless metal. He looked to Bronson as if he had actually died, right at that moment, at the very sound of the words.

Bronson felt something like terror constricting his bowels, and he took a quick drink to cover his fear.

Jack did not see Bronson's reaction; he saw nothing. Twenty years of his life had just vanished and he was standing naked on a cold wooden floor in an endless corridor of shabby beds with cheap metal frames and he was alone and there was no one there to make him unafraid of what had wakened him in terror. He could not call out because if he had called out someone would have come and slapped him for making a fuss, and the other boys would have laughed at him for his fright, for his nightmare, and for not being able to hold it in. And yet deep inside him was the terror, the old terror, the dead, nameless, empty, silent screaming terror that had wakened him with dead horror of emptiness and he died right at that moment, and twenty years later he died of it again and sat there like a stone for minutes; minutes, not hearing the noise of the crowd in Vesuvio's, not seeing the concerned, afraid, gentle face of Myron Bronson peering at him; until, by tremendous effort, he made himself come out of it, buried the memory, and said:

"Tell her if she does that I'll kill her." He got up and left the bar.

She came back to him late that night and found him lying like a stone in their bed, and she kissed his body and whispered her love in his ear and made him come back to life, telling him that she had not meant it, could not have meant it, wanted to hurt him the worst way she could and had known that would do it, and how she hated herself for having done it, and how she wanted the child now, loved it already and wanted it badly, his child, her child, and would love the child forever as she would love Jack forever; and at last he came to life, the first sign of it tears flowing down his cheeks, and then heavy racking sobs out of his chest as they clung to each other, both sobbing now, wordlessly, until it passed and they slept.

TWENTY-TWO

They had an argument about where the baby was to be born. Sally had been reading some books on the subject of natural childbirth and related matters, had been calling and visiting friends who had had babies, and decided that one thing most of the women really wanted but didn't have the courage to face was to have the baby at home, *naturally*, without any pain-killers, attendants, or anything else that would tend to get in the way of the true, age-old experience of women. She had even given thought to having in a midwife instead of a doctor for that final, almost casual moment, when a woman seemed to need a little help. Naturally, she wanted Jack at her side.

"Horseshit," he said. "You'll go to a hospital."

"But that's so *pasteurized*. And anyway, it costs too much."

But he was adamant. "Crap. That's not your reasons. You want to have the *experience*. I've read some of that crap, too. You want to have the kid naturally, nature's way, like a goddamn Indian squaw, so's the kid will *really* be yours, so's you'll *really* understand the magical process of birth. Bullshit on that. Do you think that's the only way to learn how to love the kid? Do you think it'll be any more your kid if you go through agony for it? If you love it, you love it. That's all. Don't think of yourself and your experience, and how good it'll be for *you* to feel it; think about the *kid*. He's the one gettin born, not you. He's the one the safety, the sterilization, and all that stuff's for, not you. Well, it's for you, too. Do you want to risk your life and his for the sake of a goddam *experience?*"

"You just don't understand! It's how a woman feels, if she's a real woman!"

"Are you in doubt? If so, tough shit. My kid's gonna be born in a hospital. Period."

"You're just frightened. You can't face the responsibility.

Maybe subconsciously, you can't face the responsibility of having children at all. Maybe you're not *ready*."

"I'll face anything I have to face; but I'm goddamned if I'll go out looking for it. Shit, yes, I'm frightened. So what?"

"I'm the one that has to have the baby! I'll have it where I please!"

And so she did. Nothing he said, from ridicule to outright rage, could change her mind, and at last he gave in, half-expecting her to get apprehensive and decide on the hospital after all. But she didn't. She had the baby in their bed, attended by a doctor, a nurse, and Jack. The nurse made Jack leave the bedroom while she prepped Sally—which he couldn't understand, since he was to be there for the "grand opening," as Sally called it. The doctor arrived about an hour later, a small reflective man who did not seem to think that anything was out of the ordinary. During the waiting period he and Jack sat in the living room and drank coffee and talked about Russian literature. Jack had been reading the Russians, on Sally's sly recommendation, and a few library volumes were scattered around the room. It turned out that the doctor liked Chekhov best, perhaps because he had been a doctor, and Jack preferred Dostoyevski, perhaps because he had done time. Jack and the doctor agreed that Russian literature was "full of life."

The actual birth of the child was slow and easy, but very painful to Sally. Her face was pale and wrinkled with pain. Jack, standing there holding her hand, did not know what to do with his eyes. He did not want to watch the baby coming out, and yet he could not bear to look at her face. He compromised on the doctor's face until the baby actually began to emerge, and then there was no question of looking away. Jack felt anguish, but he felt much more than that, as if the dream were over and life was suddenly real; an experience of such immensity that he could only stand transfixed and watch his child being shoved out into life. Sally did not cry after the child started coming; her only sounds were determined grunts; and when the baby was free and the mess started coming out, she gave a sigh, not of relief but of accomplishment, and Jack looked at her face. She looked sleepy. He heard the vigorous slap, and turned to see an unlovely mess, all balls and slime, hanging down from the doctor's hand, and braying faintly with life. As Jack watched, a tiny stream of urine sprang from the child and wet the front of the doctor's gown.

"He's a beauty," the doctor said. "The good ones always pee on me." He looked at Sally, admiration in his eyes. "You can be proud of this one. A fine boy."

"I'll bet you say that to all the mothers," she said in a faint voice.

"Of course I do," the doctor said.

Myron Bronson telephoned to find out what had happened, and after Jack told him, he said, "Look, I'd like to be the boy's godfather. Would that be all right with you?"

"Sure," Jack said.

"That would mean he would have my name. Is that all right? Would you name him after me?"

"No," Jack said. "I already have the name. I'm sorry. Can't you be godfather anyway?"

"I suppose so. What's his name?"

"Billy."

He had known he was going to name the baby after Billy Lancing all the time, but he hadn't mentioned it to Sally, and at first she objected, wanting him to be named John (for Jack) Myron; but there was something about Jack's expression that kept her from insisting, and so the child was christened at Grace Cathedral as Billy Lancing Levitt. The function of the religious ceremony and paper work was to provide the child with a church background just in case he needed one; not because either of his parents was Episcopal. They decided rationally that they had no right to deny him the security of a faith, and they decided rationally that of all the faiths around, Episcopalianism was the most secure. Myron Bronson came through with the traditional silver mug, but containing a rolled-up thousand-dollar bill, and the child was driven to his christening in a

Rolls-Royce. The whole business had an air of unreality about it for Jack, and throughout he tried to concentrate on the image of his dead friend. There was nothing to remind him though; even the name seemed not to belong to the old Billy but just to the new one, the small red face in the huge white bundle. At first it had seemed like a good idea but among these rich trappings it became just silly and sentimental. It wasn't going to bring Billy back; it wasn't going to commemorate his good qualities; Jack was not even sure the old Billy really *had* any good qualities except the strength to die. Anyway, it was all very stupid, and Jack did not care anything about the kid; he was just an added irritant. Except for the thousand dollars.

They spent a lot of the money on the child, and then Sally took the rest and got herself some new clothes. After the usual postpartum depression, in which she talked about things like being the wife of a parking-lot attendant and losing her looks, she became engrossed in motherhood, nursing the child herself, reading Dr. Spock when she could get the tattered paperback away from Jack, and taking Billy for long rides in his green-and-white stroller; and when the baby was asleep in its crib, which was most of the time, she would just sit in the living room and look contented. For the first time since they had been married she had enough housework to keep her busy, and it was a real pleasure to take a break and do nothing; not even daydream, just sit there and feel good. It was almost six weeks before they made love again, and by that time Jack was ready to lose his mind from desire, and they had a fine time of it.

Everything seemed marvelous; Jack was gradually learning to love his child, and he was not in any sense discontented with his life. When he would come home from work late at night he would peek in at the baby and even bend down and kiss him and think that this was amazingly good—to be able to love something that hardly knew he existed. But he did not want to analyze the emotion—it was too good to speculate about or attempt to define; it ought to be left alone and just *felt*.

271

He noticed other children in the street and felt a great connecting sympathy with them; he even began to wonder if, when the time came, little Billy would be able to hold his own among other children, and what he would be like when he got older. And then Jack seared himself with the masochistic pleasures of speculating on all the possible disasters that could overtake a helpless child, things Jack could do nothing about, like deformation or idiocy or smothering in the bed, or running out into the street and being killed by a crazy teen-ager on a motorcycle, or catching polio and spending the rest of his life in braces, or going blind or deaf, or not learning how to read; and then he realized he was torturing himself for his own grim pleasure and he stopped it. The hell with the future, he thought. And then admitted he was afraid to think of the future. What if he made extensive plans for the boy and the boy died or was crippled? All the plans would crumble and Jack would go mad from grief. Better, he thought, not to plan at all; let things happen as they will. Perhaps plan a *little*, but not too much. There were things he owed the child, and he had to plan for them.

He remembered that as a child he had never gotten anything from anybody except regimentation; and the toys they were given at Christmas were all used, repaired toys that you could tell other kids on the Outside had gotten tired of and discarded, just like the clothes they wore; and there were certain toys that kids never wore out and that never showed up at the orphanage, such as baseball mitts and electric trains that actually worked; and he remembered that everything they had in the home was the gift of the faceless authority that ran the place, and none of the children ever got anything he didn't deserve.

He thought about the orphanage carefully now, not with any particular self-pity, but abstractly going over the things that had happened to him, sorting out the good and rejecting the bad. He wanted Billy to be properly trained and brought up, but he didn't want to hurt him needlessly; certainly he should not be undertrained as Jack's revenge on the orphanage, or overtrained and deprived as a reaction to this. The trick was to strike the proper balance. There would be no cast-off, shitty toys for Billy, no empty nights with no one to be comforted by; on the other hand there would be tears, injustice, cuffings, yellings-at, and discipline. But the boy would know deep inside that it was done with love by a human being, not abstractly by a machine. Of course, that was what it amounted to; the boy would be loved. It was that simple. He would be loved, and he would know it, and that would give him the strength to face any kind of injustice. Jack had not been loved as a child; he had not even been liked. And it had almost destroyed him. He had been nothing until he had been loved. From that moment (the moment, he thought with a pang, of Billy's death) his life had begun to improve, and with only a few setbacks, it had kept improving. The more he loved and was loved, the better his life got. At once it seemed to Jack like a magical solution to everything. If only everyone loved everyone else! Then there would be no trouble in the world. It seemed so easy. If we all just reached our hands out to each other, what peaks of human joy could we not achieve!

For hours one night he kept this simple idea in his head, wondering alternately why it *would not* work, and why it *did not* work. He tried to think whom he hated most in the world, and ended up realizing that he did not hate anybody. What he hated was ungraspable. It was not a person or persons, it was a thing. He wondered if he could stop hating the *thing*, and decided he could not. It had done too much to him. And he thought about hate; it was a kind of passion, not altogether dishonorable in itself but, like love, capable of the most awful sorts of injustice. Like the way so many people felt about Negroes, a hate not for anybody in particular, but for an idea, an abstraction of a kind of people who were hateful. Because they were to be *feared*.

So it was not hate, but fear. And love does not conquer fear. Or does it? How can you love when you're frightened? Jack knew what he did when he was frightened: he struck. But the joke was, he had never in his life struck the machine itself, only people. In his twenty-five-year battle against authority, he had not landed one single punch. It was a great fight, Ma; I didn't lay a glove on him. *It.* "My boy don't fight till we hear it talk." And that Algren short story, what was the title? "He Swung and He Missed." Beautiful.

Jack was rather pleased with himself for having come to so many interesting philosophical insights, until a few days later he realized that all he had thought of was crystalized in a single terse folk saying: "So go fight City Hall." He had to laugh.

But something still troubled him. It could not be true that he had wasted his life up to now; it was not possible that fighting City Hall was wrong or futile. The folk saying had to be wrong. It was not like Don Quixote fighting a windmill, because a windmill wasn't a criminal, and society was. Society was a criminal because it committed crimes. To fight society *because it was a criminal* had to be good. But was that what Jack had done most of his life? Had he fought to make society quit cheating, lying, robbing, and murdering? Or had he fought because he was scared? Search as he would, he could find nothing in his past to justify his fight. He had not fought the evil side of society; he was not even sure what it was. He had merely *fought.* It left him with an awful sense of frustration, because in his case society, too, had been fighting blindly and helplessly. There had been nothing else to do with him but what it had done. It was not society who had abandoned him, but his name-less and unknown parents; and they must have had their reasons for abandoning him. For all he knew, they were both dead and therefore blameless. Or they did not love one another, or did not have any money, or any of a dozen reasons for not keeping him. What if they had kept him anyway, and did not have any love to give him? What then? Mightn't he have grown into a monster even worse than he was? Jack had known plenty of people whose home lives as children had been, at least on the surface, perfectly reasonable, and they were depraved maniacs compared to him. What about Dale Phipps, born into and raised by a solidly protective Catholic family, who liked nothing so much as murdering people? Jack could not even say with any certainty that Phipps had not been loved as a child. Maybe society didn't have anything to do with it. Maybe where you were born and who you were raised by didn't affect things at all. Maybe some people were just naturally rotten and others just naturally good. But if that was the case, then what could he do to make sure Billy, his son, would turn out good?

Nothing.

It was an awful word. Nothing. It made him sick at heart. He refused to believe in it. He demanded that there be something he could do. He demanded that his love be worth something to his child. If it wasn't, life was garbage. He had to rule out the idea that life was just a matter of accident, of percentages, because it was just too goddam much to stand for. Even if it was true, he was determined to live as if it were false. There had to be some way you could make yourself be *felt*.

One afternoon while Sally was ironing some of the things he had just brought back from the Laundromat, he said to her, "Don't you think this is the answer to the whole goddam thing? I mean, society is just made up of people, and lots of them are rotten, so society's partly rotten. So what we do is raise our kid to be good; and the more people who do that, the better the world gets. And, like, the more we do that, turn out good kids, the more of them there are to turn out more good kids. And the whole thing can snowball, dig, until finally all the rotten people are dead and forgotten." He scratched his head. "Sort of. You know?"

She laughed at him. "What have *you* been smoking?"

"Listen, I'm serious. What can we do better than raise Billy so he doesn't have any of the hang-ups we have?"

"You mean spend the rest of our lives on *him?* I'd like a little more than that."

"Hell no, that'd wreck him. I mean, you know, making him a better person than we are."

"How?"

That was the question, of course. "How the hell should I

know?" he retorted. "Just do it as it comes up. Billy had this theory about life, you know. I told you about it. How we're all *connected*. I mean, like the bad connections—do you remember?—well, the less of them there are, the better your life is. So the thing is to teach Billy to understand his *feelings*. . . ."

"That theory," she interrupted. "Have you any idea how childish it is? '. . . never send to know for whom the bell tolls; it tolls for thee.' Sure it does."

"Well, is that childish?"

She laughed again, and the steam iron hissed under her hands. "You know what I mean. Old-fashioned. It's not a new theory, as you seem to think. It hasn't done us much good, has it? That's one of those ideas that float around."

"I don't think it's the same thing," Jack said lamely. "Anyway, just because it's been around doesn't mean it's no good."

"You're certainly a philosopher these days. My, yes, having a baby makes a person *think*." She held up one of his sweat shirts. "Do you think this needs to be ironed? It's only wrinkled under the arms."

"No, forget it."

"Have you done anything about getting a better job?"

"Not today. I want to figure out what I want to do, you know, permanently."

"All philosophy today. No time to think about making a little more money."

"Oh, get off my back."

But she was right; he had been avoiding the idea of change, putting off the necessary hard thought he would have to work his way through to discover what his life's occupation was going to be. As a matter of fact, he did not mind parking cars. He was reasonably happy; he did not seem to have any ambitions at all.

"We have to get a bigger apartment, you know," she said. "We could borrow down-payment money from Myron, and buy a house. Except that I really don't want to live in one of those damn cracker boxes. But there are some awfully nice places in Sausalito . . ."

"No," Jack said. She had hinted at this before. "We don't live off him or anybody else."

"You didn't mind the thousand dollars."

"That was different."

"Yes, we don't have to pay it back."

Jack was silent. There was really no arguing with her. She just did not understand. "Listen," he said at last. "I think I really will try to decide what to do with myself. Maybe I'll take one of those aptitude tests or something."

"That would be nice," she said dryly. " 'We find, Mister Levitt, that your aptitudes indicate a strong tendency in the direction of either philosophy or running a gas station.' " She looked at him. "Oh, I'm sorry. I was just kidding. But I really think you ought to go to college. I could work, after Billy gets a little older. You need an education."

"Fuck it," Jack said. But he did not really mean it; he was just mad at her. The idea of having her put him through college was very inviting. But there was another way. "Listen," he said. "I work nights; I could go to college anyway. Why not?" He began to get enthusiastic. "Hell, why not? Go to classes in the morning, study in the afternoon and at work. I can sit in a car and study. I could get a lot done."

"It wouldn't work."

"Why not? Hell, yes, it would work!"

"No. Because we don't have enough money to pay for any extras, like books or tuition; and in the second place, I don't think you could handle eight hours of work and college at the same time. It's damn hard, you know."

"Well, shit. It was an idea."

"Yes, you're good at that."

"Oh, balls."

Lately Sally had been like this; she wanted things to change, she wanted a new apartment or even a home of their own, she wanted Jack to begin to find a career for himself, or at least a better-paying job; yet she didn't like any of the ideas he came up with, and seemed always to be making fun of him. It was irritating. Most of the time they were getting along better than they ever had, but there was this one argument about changing their circumstances that always left Jack with a bad taste in his mouth; and also there would be times when Sally would hardly speak to him, and he would be made to feel guilty and would not know why, and would get angry about it and ask her what was bothering her, and if she said anything at all it would be, "Nothing. Does something have to be wrong?" And he would still feel guilty. But otherwise, things were fine. The baby had really helped. Jack had been right about that. But he was careful never to say this to Sally.

TWENTY-THREE

When Billy was around seven months old, he caught something, and was terribly sick for three days. It was the first time he had been really sick, and Jack felt a combination of terror and sheepishness; but sheepish or not, he stayed home from work. Sally was worried, too, but contemptuous of Jack.

"He's got the flu, for Christ's sake. He's not going to die or anything. I can take care of him. Don't you trust me?"

"I'd just as soon stick around," Jack said. "Tell me what the doctor said."

"I already told you. What's the matter, don't you trust me?"

"It's that goddam doctor I don't trust. What does he care?"

On the second night, Billy's fever went to 105°, and he just lay there hot and flushed, not even crying or fussing. Jack and Sally stood over the crib, afraid to touch each other, or even speak, for fear of making a corny gesture. Jack wanted to call the doctor again and inform "the son of a bitch" that if he did not get over there in five minutes flat, Jack would personally guarantee that the doctor would never have another child of his own. But he did not call the doctor. The doctor would be very patient, but Jack would know that secretly the doctor would be laughing at him. The high fever was expected. It was supposed to get very high and then break. It was called "The Crisis."

Jack and Sally went into the living room and sat waiting for it, with the FM radio on. They listened to a panel discussion on the plight of California agricultural workers, and then a series of Beethoven sonatas, with comment. Then the radio station went off the air, and neither of them got up to tune in another. After a minute Sally went into the back, and then returned, her face drawn.

"He's not so hot, now," she said. She sat down and picked up a copy of *Ring Magazine,* thumbing through it idly.

Jack got up and went into the back to check, and she gave him an irritated glance, but did not speak. He looked down at the baby through the gloom. The baby just lay there, eyes open, not moving. Jack put his hand on the baby's forehead. It seemed cool, almost cold. It occurred to Jack that his baby was dead. His legs felt weak. He went into the kitchen and sat down. It was impossible that Billy could be dead. The doctor said it was just the flu. Babies don't die of the flu. Or do they? With proper care? *Could you do everything and still lose your baby?* Jack knew the answer, but he would not let the words form in his mind. He knew what he had to do. He had to get up on his legs and go in there and see if the baby was dead or not. A strange thought occurred to him and helped him stay in the chair. What did you do with a dead baby? Did you have to call the police, or just a mortician? Jack remembered what had happened to a man he had known in the old Portland poolhall days. The man's wife had her baby, and then on the third day it died, and the hospital told the man how much the little coffin, the hearse, and the ceremony would cost, and the man had to tell the people at the hospital that he didn't have any money at all, and no job, that he had used up his last cent paying for the birth; and so the hospital put the dead baby in a plastic bag and handed it to the man to dispose of himself. They also gave him a mimeographed sheet of city and county regulations concerning the disposition of bodies. Jack would not have believed the story, except the man came into Ben Fenne's with the dead baby and the sheet of regulations and wanted somebody to help him. The two men at the front billiard table looked at the man, and then at each other, laid down their cues, put on their coats, and led the man out. Jack never did find out what happened after that. Nobody seemed to want to ask.

But he had tortured himself enough. He had to get up and go in there. He did, knowing that very near the surface of his mind was the hope, the wish, that the baby was dead. It was only curiosity, the need to see if he would feel glad, that conquered his cowardice.

The baby's eyes were shut, and its mouth open slightly, bubbling. Jack felt its forehead. Cool, but not cold. He picked Billy up and held him for a long time. By the way he felt now, he knew his previous wish for the baby's death had been a lie, and he absolved himself easily.

Jack went back into the front room. Sally looked up from nothing and said, "What took you so long?" There was a terrible anxiety in her voice which she did not bother to conceal.

"He's fine," Jack said quickly, passing up the temptation to be dramatic and torture Sally. "He's cooled down and breathing easily. Jesus Christ Almighty, no wonder they call it 'The Crisis'! Whew!"

But Sally got up and went in there and took the baby's temperature with a rectal thermometer anyway, and came back with the exact figures. "Ninety-nine," she said proudly. "That's nothing."

"Nothing at all," Jack said happily.

■ ■

Every once in a while, Jack wondered how long Sally could take it. The incident with the flu was just one—admittedly dramatic—example of the things a mother, a parent, had to put up with. Jack could take it because he was away more than a third of the time, but Sally—she was there day and night, and being responsible for the care of a child, especially one you were learning to love more and more each day, was a dangerous, complicated, and boring job. Day after day it could sap your inner energy until there was nothing left; it could nibble at your courage until one day you awakened in terror and hatred. Jack felt all this in himself sometimes, and he knew it must be even worse in Sally. Of course she was a woman, and women were supposed to be better equipped to handle this kind of thing, but still . . . And anyway, this housewifely business was not Sally's world at all. She had been used to a more exciting life, running around with famous and wealthy people, drinking a lot, being admired and chased and desired—and now she stayed home most of the time, did dishes, washed diapers, cleaned house, played with Billy, read magazines, watched television on their tiny set, and that was about all. They didn't go out much. Jack worked afternoons and nights, and on his one night off a week he liked to sit home and watch the fights on television. When they did go out, it would be around the corner to the Royal Theater to a movie. Once they saw Sally's ex-husband playing a dogcatcher with a conscience who ends up letting all the dogs loose, and somehow gets himself a big country estate and a rich, lovely wife, and they all live happily ever after, 87 dogs and all. It was a terrible movie, but her ex-husband was good—he was really a very good actor—and it was fun watching all those mutts running through the town.

Afterward Jack and Sally walked home, and Jack paid off the Chinese baby-sitter while Sally got undressed right away and went to bed without saying anything to Jack. He followed her, thinking she wanted to make love, but when he put his hand on her shoulder she shrugged it off. He wanted to be angry at her, but he couldn't. He understood. She was thinking about the fact that she was now a lumpen-proletariat housewife, scrimping pennies and washing the shit out of endless diapers (you had to do that before you took them to the Laundromat), and was losing her looks; while her ex-husband was rich and famous, and getting handsomer every year as his face grew older and more manly. All because she had married Jack. He wondered if all the housewives in the world felt this way sometimes, even without the rich and famous ex-husband. He wondered why they didn't all flip their lids and go on periodic rampages. Especially the beautiful or formerly beautiful ones. Life promises them so much, and then it all comes to nothing. It has to, because the promises are false; they have to be false, because they are too promising.

It was all right for him, he got out of the house every day, he was in the midst of the Broadway crowds and could see how stupid it all was, this frantic search to be entertained and enraptured which ends up with your being stalled in traffic on Broadway, red-faced and furious, blowing your horn at the drunken idiot in front of you. He got to see that almost every night, and so he *knew;* and anyway, after work he always stopped in Vesuvio's and had a pitcher of beer and kidded the pretty waitresses and talked to the Vesuvio crowd, before he had to walk up Broadway and home through the tunnel. But Sally— she was always there. It was not like her at all.

So when she blew up at last he was not surprised, just hurt and guilty.

He had come home from work and Sally happened to be up. She was learning how to knit and it had turned out to be more challenging than she had suspected, and she was on the couch knitting something bright green. She would never tell Jack what she was working on, but it looked like a sweater or something for Billy.

He plopped himself down in his easy chair and picked up the book he had been working his way through: *The Hamlet* by Faulkner. After a while he got up and went into the kitchen for a can of beer, and then came back. In a few minutes, he snickered. He had a habit of snickering when he read something he liked, and snorting when he read something complicated or stupid. This time he was snickering at some woolly deal of Flem Snopes's, when Sally cried, "What the fuck is this!"

"Huh?" He looked up at her, wide-eyed. It was hard to pull himself up out of Yoknapatawpha County.

Her eyes were blazing at him. "You've got some whore's lipstick all over your mouth!"

Jack rubbed his mouth guiltily, trying to remember. Oh, yes. The barmaid had kissed him when he gave her a fifty-cent tip. "It was nothing," he said. "Some barmaid."

"No wonder you don't go to bed with me any more," she shouted. "You've got some whore barmaid fucking you!"

"Do you really believe that?" he asked angrily.

"I'll bet you sat yourself down and decided it was time you had yourself a mistress. You cheap hood. I'm leaving in the morning. Nobody does that to me."

"And nobody has. Goddam it. She kissed me, I didn't kiss her. I gave her a tip, that's all. Christ!"

It was one of those arguments that nobody ever wins. She accused him of throwing their money away. He denied it. She accused him of slopping up beer after work every night. He refused to answer her. She called him every dirty name she could think of, and he replied that she ought to know. Eventually, she got up and went to the telephone and called Myron Bronson. Jack went in and took the instrument out of her hand and hung it up. She slapped him. He walked away from her, plopped back down in his chair, picked up his book and beer can, and pretended to go back to his reading. She went into the bedroom and packed. Then she unpacked. She came back and asked him, "Was it really a barmaid?"

He bit off the sharp answer and said, "Yes. It was nothing. Really."

"I'm sorry," she said.

"It was my fault," he said.

"I just imagined a lot of things."

"I don't blame you."

But they did not make love that night, or the next night, or the next, because unfortunately it was her period, and by the time her period stopped she was gone. She took the baby with her.

TWENTY-FOUR

Not long after Sally left him Jack was released from parole, and with a shock he realized he had been out of San Quentin three full years. He had been out for longer than he had been in. He wanted to celebrate, but there was no one to celebrate with. He did not want to go down to Vesuvio's and entertain the lushes with his release from parole. They were fun to talk to, but they would not understand this. He had called Myron Bronson, of course, right after Sally left, really hoping she had gone to him, because at Bronson's Jack was certain the baby would get good treatment. But Bronson did not know where she was. Jack knew Bronson wouldn't lie to him. He even volunteered to help Jack look for her, but Jack said he would not do that; when she was ready, she would come home. He was not sure he believed it; he was not even certain he knew why she left.

He decided he would have to celebrate his release alone, and so he took the night off and went down to the Tenderloin to do his drinking. There was an urge in him to be among thieves and losers; it would be relaxing to be with thieves; he might even meet somebody from San Quentin and they could talk about old times and how good it was to be on the street.

It was no fun at all. He began drinking at a place on Mason, a block off Market, and after eight straight shots his gut felt tight but the rest of him was still empty. The customers were all strangers and the whole place seemed cheap and dull. He left, and on impulse went around the corner to the poolhall, up the dark double flight of stairs, past the empty wine bottles, the urine- and vomit-stained walls, through the glass doors, and into the huge mellow old room. Right at the door was the long row of billiard tables, all but one in use, old men in dark pants and white shirts leaning into the flood of light over the emerald green baize. He walked past them and the big English snooker tables to the long counter, ordered a bottle of beer, and sat watching a pair of young punks playing six-ball. Other punks lolled in the theater seats behind the tables, and Jack saw among them one or two old men, asleep in out of the cold. Poolhalls never changed. The punks never changed, either. The same knowing, wolfish smiles, the same sharp haircuts, the same wise talk.

In fact, the only difference Jack could see between this place and the Rialto in Portland was that this place stayed open 24 hours a day, and along the dim walls large old paintings hung, illuminated by special lights. The paintings seemed strange but not out of place. There was one, very badly done, of some old men playing billiards, but none of the others was appropriate to a poolhall except perhaps the reclining nude, in the pose of Goya's naked Alba. The two on the other side of the room fitted the place only in the sense that they were of an era past; one of a group of harem women, the other of a pride of lions on a sandy rise in the greenish North African twilight—a strange picture anywhere, but here a kind of silent, moody comment on the roomful of small-timers. Jack sat and stared at the lions for a long time.

"Levitt? Jack Levitt?"

He turned around. The man speaking to him had thin blond hair, and cold gray eyes, and appeared to be in his middle thirties. Jack did not recognize him. "No," he said.

The man smiled. "Sure you are. You haven't changed much. Kol Mano. Portland. About a hundred years ago."

Mano, the gambler. Jack recognized him now. They shook hands and Mano sat down next to him. "What's been happening?" Jack said.

Mano shrugged. "I hear you were in Q. How long you been on the street?"

"Three years. Where'd you hear about me?"

"Around. You remember Denny Mellon? You used to run with him in Portland. He's around, too. I saw him a month ago in Emeryville."

"You sure got a good memory."

"I got to. That's my business." He explained to Jack that he was still a gambler, and they ordered bottles of beer. Jack was not particularly glad to see Mano, but it was better than nothing.

"I got off parole today," Jack said.

"Hey, we got to celebrate."

"Yeah. Well. How's old Portland?"

"Terrible. I haven't been back in a long time. They closed the Rialto, tore down Ben Fenne's building, shut up the card-rooms for poker action, everything. They got a lady mayor up there a few years ago came in and really cleaned house. Man, what a gas. She calls in all the cops and tells them, 'Boys, I know what's shaking; I know the location of every gambling club, brothel, after-hours joint in town. Tomorrow I want them closed and the operators on their way out of town. *Get it?'*." Mano laughed. "So the cops, they go to the Scotchman—you remember him?—and tell him, 'Jesus, this broad is serious!' and he thinks about it for a minute and then says, 'Okay, that's all she wrote.' Closed up shop and moved back to Aberdeen. So the whole town is tighter than a tick. The only action is a couple of poker and pan games in Vancouver, and they cut the pots so bad there's no point. And, of course, the country clubs, University Club, and that kind of shit. But that never gets closed down."

He squinted at Jack. "Say, it's been a good ten years since I saw you, no? Lots has happened, man. Remember how I used to have to hold my finger over that hole in my throat? All fixed up."

"Great. You feel better?"

"Well, I lost a great psychological advantage. You remember Mike? The big one, his mother was the abortionist? Well, he opened his own joint up on 14th, near the ball park, half the thieves in town started hanging in there, guys like Clancy Phipps, Jack Morgan, all those heavies. Anyway, he had a little combo playing there, and one night he gets in an argument with the bass player, I guess this was last year some time, and the bass player gets real pissed off, goes home, gets his old man's shotgun, comes back and blows Mike's head off. So he's dead. So's Dale Phipps."

"Huh? I thought he was in the Marines. How'd he get killed? I heard from Denny he killed a bunch of people over in Korea."

"Yeah. Well, he came back to Portland and was stationed out on Swan Island, got married, had a couple of kids, everything. And one night he comes back from duty and there's his house on fire and fire trucks there, and a bunch of people standing around, dig? And he rushes into the house to save his wife and kids, and the whole place collapses on him. So he died. But his wife and kids were out of the place. They saw him run in." Mano shook his head. "Man, what a hero."

Jack looked at him. He tried to remember the mean, sullen, cruel Dale Phipps, tried to see him as a hero, and just couldn't do it. They drank their beer quietly for a few minutes, watching a six-ball game.

"You know," Mano said, "a lot of people got washed down the drain in the last ten years. It kind of makes you wonder."

"Yeah? Who else?" Now Jack was interested; he wanted to hear about other people's failures. Now he was glad he had run into Mano.

"Remember my buddy Case? Little Bobby Case? He's in Alcatraz. Got strung out when he was about seventeen, hit the junk like it was going out of style, and they nailed him in Arizona, he did five there, and they nailed him again, running shit across the border, and he got another two, and then a bit at Lexington, and then finally Alcatraz, on a life term or somethin. I'm not sure what they got him for. We split a long time ago."

"Who else?" Jack wanted to know. "Who else went down the tubes?"

"Well," Mano grinned. "You."

"You remember that colored kid, Billy Lancing? Went to that party up in the West Hills where I got busted?"

"Sure, I know Billy. I see him around once in a while, around the country. He's a crossroader. I ain't seen him in a few years, but he's around. I think he lives up in Seattle now."

"No. He's dead. He died in Q."

"No shit. You want another beer?"

"No."

One of the punks came up to them, and said to Mano in a low voice, "Hey, man, can you lay fi bucks on me? I got a fish wants to spot me the five. What say?"

"Fuck you, honey," Mano said cheerfully. "You couldn't find your ass with both hands. Make it."

"Cocksucker," the punk muttered. He went back to the row of seats, but the one he had been occupying now had an old man in it. He snarled at the old man and went away. Mano laughed. "These fucking kids don't know dick. Not a one of them has the talent Bobby Case had."

Jack felt hot and flushed. He was angry that Mano hadn't understood about Billy, although there was no reason he should have. But Jack was tired of him, depressed, unable to get drunk. He felt his already tight gut tighten even more at the thought that Sally had left him and taken little Billy.

"Well," he said to Mano.

"Listen, I'm going to Hot Springs in a couple days. You want to make the trip?"

"Me? What for?" There was something in Mano's eyes that Jack didn't like, a kind of vagueness.

"I can always use some help. You look like you're still as tough as ever. You know."

"Bodyguard?"

"Sort of."

"What else?"

"Nothing. What did you think?"

"What do you think?"

Mano's mouth tightened in a smile with no humor in it. "When I want a punk, I'll get somebody prettier than you, baby."

"Okay. No, I don't want to go to Hot Springs."

Mano shrugged. "I just asked."

"Nice seeing you again."

In the end, Mano wandered off with his beer bottle, went up to the row of punks, and whispered to one of them. The punk got up and Mano sat down. Jack turned away. He felt terribly uncomfortable. He guzzled the last of his beer, hoping it would cool him off. He did not want to see Mano again. He did not want to see any of these people. He did not like the place at all. He did not know what the hell he had come in here looking for, anyway. Unless it was the ghost of Billy. And that was stupid. The ghost of Billy—even the ghost—would have better things to do than hang around a poolhall, even the poolhall he had been arrested in. This was Billy's headquarters on that last desperate trip to California when his stake was gone and there didn't happen to be any squares around who would play him and he had to go out writing bad checks to get eating money, and this was the place where the two big plainclothesmen came in and picked him up with everybody in the joint looking the other way and some of them sidling out the back door, while Billy looked up at the two hard bored faces and grinned and cracked a joke that nobody laughed at, and went out between the cops, telling the houseman to keep his stick for him, walking jauntily, with that nigger-strut cakewalk shuffle he affected to show he wasn't pretending to be anything he wasn't, down the stairs to his own death. Only he didn't know he was going to die in San Quentin. And he probably wouldn't have if Jack hadn't come along. But I didn't kill him, Jack thought furiously, he killed himself. But over me. He really did that.

Jack got up and went down the counter to the check-out stand.

289

The small, balding man behind the counter eyed him blankly.

"Do you still have Billy Lancing's cue?" The words came thickly up out of his throat.

"Private stick?" the man asked in a bored voice.

"He left it here four or five years ago. He ain't been back."

The man bent down and came up with a thick dusty ledger book, flipped it open, and began going down a list of names and numbers. Then, with his finger on a line in the book, he looked up and said, "Four eight five."

"Is it here?"

"Beats the shit out of me," the man said. "You could look in the tray." He pointed to a high dark wood cabinet of trays. Jack went over, found the drawer, opened it, found the numbered slot. The cue was there, a Willie Hoppe Special. Jack lifted it out. It had a fine layer of dust on the exposed side. It was still a good cue.

"Is it yours?" came a voice from behind Jack. The man from the counter was there, to see that Jack didn't steal anything.

"No. The guy it belongs to is dead. He died over two years ago."

"Oh? Yeah?" The man did not seem to care. "But it's not your stick."

"No. I guess you ought to sell it."

"How do we know the guy's dead? People leave their sticks here a long time."

"He's dead. Take my word. I saw him die." Jack stared hard at the man. "At least, I saw him knifed. He died in the hospital, later."

"Put the stick back. I'll have to ast Earl. Thanks."

"I loved him," Jack said to this complete stranger. "But, see, I never told him about it."

The man made a face. "Oh, yeah. Well, well." He waited for Jack to replace the cue in its slot, and then went back to his counter. Jack went down the front stairs to Market Street, the heaviness still in his chest.

So he had finally admitted it, in the only possible set of words he could use. Still, he did not feel any better. He had loved Billy and it hadn't done any good. He loved Sally, he told her about it many times, but it didn't do any good. He loved little Billy but it didn't do any good. They were gone, and out of his stupid pride and cowardice he would not go looking for them. Suddenly he wanted to get into a fight. He was off parole, he could get into a fight if he wanted to. It would only mean a few days in jail at worst. It would feel good to bash somebody in the mouth. He made his way through the Market Street crowds, hoping somebody would look at him cross-eyed, or would push him. Any excuse. He walked past one of those hot dog and magazine stands, full of tough-looking punks and half-Mexicans, with greased hair and hip clothes. He caught the eye of one of them, a big one with thick stupid lips and acne scars on his cheeks. Jack grinned at the punk hopefully.

Very casually, the punk dropped his eyes; Jack waited, but when the punk looked up it was in another direction. It was useless. He did not even want to get into a fight. All he wanted now was another drink. He went on down the street and into a liquor store and bought three fifths of Jack Daniel's. Very expensive, but only the best. He took a cab home.

He opened one of the bottles in the cab and took a long swallow.

"Don't do that, buddy," the driver said without turning around.

"I'm celebrating," Jack said.

"Yeah? Well, not in my cab. What's the big occasion?"

They can't help talking, can they, Jack thought. They must get very lonely. He told the driver about the end of his parole. "My third anniversary on the street," he added.

"Oh, yeah? What'd they get you for?"

"I cornholed a cabdriver and took his money."

The driver pulled over to the curb fast and got out and pulled the back door open. "Out," he said.

"Have a drink, honey," Jack grinned.

"Aw, shit."

"Come on, have a drink an take me home. I dint cornhole *you*, did I?"

The driver took a quick short drink and got back in. "You're puttin me on," he said.

"Fuck yes, I'm puttin you on. You dumb son of a bitch."

"Leave me alone, will you? I'm takin you home. I know how you feel. Don't take it out on me."

"Who'll I take it out on? How about the niggers? Can I take it out on them?"

The cabbie laughed bitterly. "Sure. They takin over. You know what we call Yellow Cab now? The Mau-Mau Taxi Compny. They hire all the niggers, you know."

"Goddam niggers takin all the good jobs," Jack said bitterly. "Runnin all the banks. Fuckum. Fuck you, too."

The driver sighed.

When they got to his place, Jack got out and paid off the driver. "Hey, pal," he said, "how's about comin in and blowin me?"

The driver stared at him with hatred, and put the cab in gear.

"No," Jack said. "I'll give you fifty bucks."

The driver averted his eyes; Jack could tell he was thinking it over; coming in, seeing the money, trying to get it, knowing Jack was putting him on, yet tempted anyway. Jack laughed at him. "You got your price, don't you?" he said. The driver gritted his teeth and drove off. Jack giggled. He felt mysterious and disembodied. He knew he hadn't really wanted a fight. The cabbie was just working. No reason to hit a working man. Just get inside, go to bed and have a nice long drink.

He woke up in the morning sick with a cold, hung over, and feverish. He threw up several times, and tried to drink some whiskey, threw up again, and went back to bed. He was sick for three days, his head swollen and soggy, his hands trembling. He stayed about half drunk most of the time, and if it did not help him get rid of the cold, it did make him more comfortable. He didn't shave and didn't eat, and the cold just went away of its own accord, leaving him empty, sober, and shaky. He went down to the store and got some food, and when he came back there was a postcard for him in the mailbox. It was a picture postcard of the Mormon Tabernacle, and on the other side was a note from Sally. She was visiting her mother and stepfather with the baby, and would be home on Friday, love. Jack hadn't even known she had a mother and stepfather; if she had ever mentioned them, he had forgotten. He went to bed again after eating, and that night he was back at work.

TWENTY-FIVE

But he could not go on allowing his emotions to rise and fall at Sally's whim. Try as he would, he could not understand her, unless the obvious was true and she had simply grown tired of being married to him. Perhaps to her the marriage had been an experiment, and the experiment had failed. Perhaps all marriages had some of this quality, and if there wasn't a binding force stronger than love—or was it only passion?—something like a religion, a code, a blind facing-away from the messy inconclusiveness of life, a marriage was doomed from the moment the man and woman regained their sight. He did not know. He wondered how many people stayed married out of spite or from fear of being alone. He wondered how many children were raised in homes without love, where the counterfeit was accepted as the coin, where the words were warm and the eyes and heart cold. He wondered why he and Sally had never become friends. That could have made all the difference.

293

■ ■

Later, after it was all over and he had stopped struggling against the loss of his wife and son, and time had washed the bitterness from his blood, he would marvel at how long he had managed to stay innocent, dramatizing his adversity the way a kid does, as if to prove that it exists. By then the past would lie half-buried in his imagination and the future would stand before him as implacable, faceless, and beyond his power to control as it always had—but with the calming difference that now he knew it and accepted it. By then he would realize that the freedom he had always yearned for and never understood was beyond his or any man's reach, and that all men must yearn for it equally; a freedom from the society of mankind without its absence; a freedom from connection, from fear, from trouble, and above all from the loneliness of being alive. By then he would understand that fulfillment was only temporary, and desire the enemy of death.

By then he would realize that all the dramatic alternatives his pain brought to mind could not possibly satisfy him forever, but that they, too, were forms of his lifelong fistfight with an invisible enemy: to have killed her—he dreamed sweetly of this— would have satisfied his childhood urge to murder long after he stopped needing the urge as protection; to have walked, as he saw himself in horrible self-pity, out to the Golden Gate Bridge for the last long drop to eternity would have been only an act of revenge, hurting no one but himself. There were other alternatives, too, born out of a need to act, a need for drama. He could have become a professional thief, revenging himself on a society he no longer loved or hated. He could have gone for junk or alcohol as weapons against his pain; they worked for some men, but he knew they would not work for him. He could have left the city and chosen a square of dirt far away in the mountains of the West and become one of those sour, lonely farmers whose only friends are distant clouds and mountain rims—indeed, it was still an attractive dream, one he could not quite abandon. He could have gone to college and become sharp and gone into business and made ten million dollars and shown them all. He could have turned poet, living the quiet life, accepting in spiritual gain what he had lost in material failure.

Only once, in those months of self-sorrow and anguish, did he actually do anything. Caryl Chessman, twelve years a symbol of one man against the machine, lost his final appeal, and Jack joined, stiffly, self-consciously, a group of young men and women who marched across the Golden Gate Bridge, up the long freeway to San Quentin, and stood in all night vigil to protest the murder. In the long night he came to sense something of these young people: they were different from him; not just a younger generation, but different, harder, more sure of their rights and the rights of man. They were even a little frightening. In the morning, after Chessman was dead and they were walking back to the city, some teen-agers came along and jeered at them, called them filthy names and laughed at their passive expressionless refusal to be angered. Jack wanted to be like the others, untouched by the jeers, but he could not. One young punk stuck his acned face next to Jack's and spit; without thinking, Jack hit him twice in a surge of delicious wrath, leaving him bleeding and unconscious for his friends to carry away. The other demonstrators looked at Jack without admiration and without sympathy, and for the rest of the march home no one spoke to him. He could not help agreeing with them. The only hope for the world, for Billy, was to rid the earth of fighters.

There were other, perhaps more rational, alternatives. He could have remarried. He came to see that marrriage was not an institution, not even an idea, but a rational social process whose function was to raise children properly. He could have more children, and raise them into rational adults. It would be a risk, but it would be worth it. There could be love and dignity in that kind of life. But it was not so easy. He had no work, no profession, no obsession, and it would occur to Jack that a man without a craft might turn too much of his energies onto his family, and burden his children with too much love and too much care. It would be a crippling thing to do, as crippling as the orphanage had been. So marriage would remain an alternative, rather than becoming an ambition.

Gradually, through his books, his records, his long walks alone, the mere passage of time, he would begin to come to terms with his life as it was. He became an observer. He began to taste his food and to smell the air. He saw things and felt them. The earth became real, and at times he was capable of sensing the pleasure of existence. Other times were not so good. There were evenings when he would drink too much and get to feeling sorry for himself, and at such times he was easy to provoke. Among the regulars of North Beach he became known as a likable but unpredictable character, and it amused him to see the wariness in their eyes.

His life was temporary. He continued to park cars for a living, and he stayed in hotels and ate in restaurants, but for the time being, that was enough. Not that he planned to spend the rest of his life this way. He did not plan anything.

When Sally got back from visiting her parents things were different. Often Jack came home from work to find the old Chinese baby-sitter there and Sally gone. She would come in late, often in the morning, and Jack would refuse to ask her where she had been. Often he heard the roar of a sports car outside just before he heard her key in the lock. When she came in she would be drunk as often as not, and sometimes very affectionate. But Jack would pretend to be asleep.

It could not go on like that. One morning when she came in particularly drunk, Jack heard her singing, and heard Billy cry out. He opened his eyes and turned on the overhead light. Sally had the baby in her arms and was dancing at the foot of the bed. The baby was crying angrily. Jack got up and took Billy away from her and put him back in his crib. Sally stood in the middle of the small room, rocking slightly, her face blank. Her lipstick was smeared and she looked just as she had the first time he had seen her. He wondered if his millionaire friend Myron Bronson had brought her home.

"Come out in the kitchen," he told her. She followed him, humming to herself.

He made a pot of coffee, and when they had both drunk a cup, he said to her, "This has got to stop. I won't ask you where you been or what you been doing, but this has got to stop. You can't take care of Billy and stay out all night, too. Forget about me. Think about him."

"You think I don't?" She grinned bleakly. "I think about him all the time."

"Then stay the hell home and take care of him."

"Just like that. Why should I?"

Jack gritted his teeth. *"Because you're his mother!"*

"You think I don't know it? What the fuck do you know about it? Have you ever had to sit in a place like this and know you couldn't do a goddam thing cause you had this *infant* around your neck? That's what it's like, you know. The baby is hanging around your neck and you can't kill it and you can't leave it, and it gets so goddam boring sometimes I want to die and you don't know fuck-all about it. There. It's got nothing to do with you at all, you just don't know."

"Self-pity," Jack said to her. "I thought you were bigger than that. But all lushes are alike, aren't they."

"You're right. Oh, God, how sorry I feel for myself! I can't help it. I'm better than this; I'm better than you."

This admission made Jack feel superior, and he said, "Okay, have some more coffee. Listen, we have to hold this thing together, whether we like it or not." But even as he said it, he knew it wasn't true. He was being stubborn now, not rational. It was, he knew later, the greatest punishment he could torture her with: *holding on.*

It was amazing how long it lasted, even after that. There would be long periods when Sally would stay home and "take care of the baby" (now walking all over the house, a tiny, sturdy, blue-eyed blond replica of Jack), stay home and knit, make good dinners, and seem to be perfectly contented. Jack cooperated; he asked for and got an extra night off a week, thinking that the sacrifice in money was worth the gain in time; and they went out to bars, to parties among Sally's old friends, some of whom were glad to meet Jack and liked to talk to him about prison life; and days they went for drives more often, to the beach or the mountains, Sally and Jack in the front and little Billy in the back in his little car-seat. It was an excellent abstract of a rich, full life.

But then there were times when Jack would come home and there would be the Chinese baby-sitter, and, secretly pleased but refusing to admit it, he would heave a sigh, pay off the sitter, and wait for Sally. He no longer pretended to be asleep, because when she got home they would want to have their argument. Jack looked forward to the arguments because he always won. After all, he had the baby on his side, and all Sally had was the advantage of ending up the contrite sinner.

The arguments would take different turns. Sometimes Sally would say that it was Jack's fault because he didn't have a better job. But he could top that. Smugly he would tell her that rotten vicious ex-convicts like himself were not in demand as bank presidents. Once she retorted that he did not even try to find a job where he would work days, and he countered that by finding one, working in a downtown parking lot. It was a real triumph for him (a triumph of spite, but still a triumph); he worked all day and Sally stayed home with Billy all day. At night Jack insisted that they go out together. If he did not insist, she would. At the end of the month Jack discovered what he had really known all the time—they had no money to pay the bills.

He got scared. "We can't go out for a month!" he told her. "We don't even have enough money to buy food!"

"You're going to keep me locked in here for a *month?*" was her shocked, victorious reply.

"Well, goddam it, we just don't have any money!" There was no answer to that!

"Borrow some from Myron," she said, and before he could

counter with his "ethics" she added, "This time we really need the money. It's not as if we wouldn't pay it back."

Jack accepted defeat and finally called Myron Bronson. Both Jack and Sally were horrified to discover that Bronson was in Las Vegas and wouldn't be back for a week.

In the end, Jack got an advance of his wages, and they ate, but that was about all. They didn't go out.

That lasted two weeks. On the night Jack came home with his paycheck, Sally was not there. The baby was asleep in his crib, but there was no Chinese baby-sitter. When he realized that Sally had actually abandoned the child, the last bit of love in him died; and so what followed did not have any real effect at all. His anger was real, but there was no passion behind it.

It was two in the morning when she called. Her voice sounded strange and distant, as if she were turned away from the mouthpiece.

"What's the matter?" he said angrily. "Where are you? Why did you leave the baby alone?"

"I'm . . . in a phone booth," she said. She giggled.

"Why did you leave Billy alone?"

"I'm not . . . alone," Sally giggled. "We're in here together."

"Who? Who?"

"Me . . . and this big, black *nigger*." Jack heard a distant muttering, and Sally's voice saying, "Why not call you that? That's what you are. That's what I wanted. A big . . . black . . . *nigger*."

"What the hell's going on!" Jack yelled.

"We're in this phone booth," Sally giggled, her voice suddenly loud, intimate, her mouth pressed up against the instrument. "We're sort of, well, fucking in here."

Jack hung up the telephone very quietly. He thought about the man with Sally, who probably did not care whether Sally was "using" him or not as long as he got what he wanted. Try as he might, Jack could not hate or even dislike the man. But when Sally showed up several hours later, alone, he was waiting for her. He had most of her clothes packed into her set of matched luggage.

"You're leaving," he said. "You're not staying here any more. I'll take care of Billy. You get out. Get a divorce. Stay away. I don't want to see you."

She looked at him strangely. She seemed all right, just a little tipsy. "What's the matter?" she asked in a husky voice.

"You called me, remember?"

She looked puzzled. "I called you?"

"Yes. Now, here's your stuff. All packed. I'll call a cab for you. Here's some money. I got paid today."

"Yes, well, but—" she began, but he cut her off.

"So get out of here. You can't have your furniture until I get some. Go on, get out."

That was the end of the marriage. Even as he threw her out he knew that she had been going through things probably worse than anything he had faced, but he could not let that stop him. Billy could have died while she was going through it; he could have begun to feel the emptiness Jack remembered so well, and Jack would not have that. He felt pity for Sally, but pity was not enough.

Jack arranged for a young girl to take care of Billy days, and he took care of him nights. He did not go out at all for several months. He knew what he was doing was not the best thing for Billy, but he could think of no alternatives. When the divorce, from Reno, came through, he did not contest it, and there was no question of alimony or mention of the child. He didn't learn about that part of it until the very end, when they came to get Billy. It was very simple, Sally explained to him coldly, dressed in an expensive suit Jack could never have afforded to buy; all she would have to do was go to court and they would award her the child. She was going to marry again, and her new husband would be—of all people—Myron Bronson. Bronson stood slightly back of Sally, not speaking, while she explained everything to Jack. Bronson had gotten his divorce at the same time she had gotten hers. The courts, faced with deciding between an ex-convict without a wife making only a few dollars a week, and the wife of a millionaire, well, you can see who would get the child. So why not, coldly, just hand him over.

Jack was stupefied. "But I want him," he said to her.

Her expression did not change. "So do we."

And that was that. Except for Myron Bronson's visit. By this time, because he was alone, Jack had moved into the Swiss Hotel on Broadway and was back working nights a block away. They met in the bar downstairs from the hotel. Bronson looked the same: gray hair, gray mustache, beautiful tasteful clothes, gentle eyes. He tried to explain to Jack.

"I didn't want to do this. Really. She came to me when you . . . threw her out. I've been in love with her for years. I'm surprised you didn't know."

Jack tried to muster up some hatred for Bronson, but he could not. "Look," he said. "Is Billy okay?"

Bronson smiled softly. "Yes, he's fine. I love him, too. I always have. I want you to come and see him. But when she's not there, please."

"I will," Jack said. "I'll come soon. I want to see him."

"You have to understand," Bronson said, "she's not really to blame. She couldn't live like that. It's not your fault, either. You two just shouldn't have ever known each other." There was a glass of whisky in front of him, but he left it untouched. "You know, now that she can do anything she wants, and the baby will be cared for, she stays home. With the pressure gone, it's all different."

"Nobody's fault again," Jack said. "Nobody's ever at fault. Not the way you see things."

"No," Bronson said, a little surprised. "I suppose not. Not really." He averted his eyes. "I want to adopt Billy."

"All right," Jack said. "Go ahead."

"I won't offer you any money."

"No. Don't. I'd take it if you did. Look, all I'm good for is fighting. You know? Do you want to fight me? Would that be okay?"

"No. I won't fight you."

"Is there anything I could say that would *make* you fight me? Anything I could call you that you couldn't take?"

"No. Nothing. I'm sorry."

"Then that's it."

"I guess so."

After Bronson left, Jack reached over and picked up his glass of whisky. He did not feel as bad as he should have. He sat there for a long time, watching the cars go by outside, sipping at Bronson's good Irish whisky.

On the Beach
at St. Tropez

Myron Bronson sat under the beach umbrella waiting for his bridge partners to come in from their boats. It was very hot and sticky, and even with his sunglasses on, he had a slight sinus headache. The heat and the late afternoon sun gave the water a bronze look, and the clusters of white boats sat without reflection on the tame water. Billy was playing with some other children down the beach, and Bronson watched with pleasure. Billy's curly hair was almost white from constant exposure to the sun, and his body was tanned almost black. He looked like a little Dane. Bronson thought about his own outdoor childhood in the Rockies and on the Utah desert, and again he wondered if it was not time to go back to America. If they went back now, Billy could start in the fall, at a public school. It would be difficult for him at first—already he spoke more French than English—but Bronson was confident that Billy's good nature and his beauty would see him through the first hard weeks of re-Americanization. Bronson wanted Billy to grow up in America, in the West. Some day, when Billy was old enough, he was going to learn who his real father was, and Bronson wanted him to be able to understand. He did not want Billy to despise, or, even worse, feel sorry for his real father.

Bronson was sixty years old, and he was beginning to expect that he would die before Billy grew to manhood. He would sometimes wake up at night and feel it all slipping through his fingers. In all his life, he was beginning to understand, he had learned only two things: how to earn money, and how to enjoy himself. There had always been a cheap streak in him, a yearning for the fashionable, the flashy, the hip; and he had learned how to turn this to his advantage, to use it for his pleasure instead of as a source of guilt. Well, that was something. But it was not enough. What he really wanted was to endure, to live forever. It was the penalty you paid for living for pleasure, for yourself. You lived so beautifully that when you came to die . . .

But Billy. He hoped Billy would grow beyond him. Of course, right now he was just a sweet little boy, and it was silly to worry about his future so much.

Still, it sometimes made him bitter to think that his Billy would grow up in a world where one man's chances of survival were no better than the next man's; where for the first time in history the rich were not protected. Bronson knew he had "no right" to hate this, but he hated it anyway. Yet he could not help admitting to himself that he got a spiteful sense of pleasure out of it, too. Mankind, after millennia of struggle, finally perfects a weapon long enough, sharp enough, to stab through all the massed ranks of infantry privates and slice its way into the fat bellies of the generals. But perhaps Billy would be one of the generals or the politicians, or just another of the flabby rich, the cigar dropping from his mouth as he first comprehends that the shelter isn't deep enough, the air not pure enough, the food supply not big enough, to outlast this final poisoned, burnt-out, earthly suicide. And then again, perhaps Billy will be still a child, and Myron Bronson will have to hold him while he dies. . . .

A huge man wearing a tiny bathing suit emerged from the water, dripping and shaking himself. He walked up the beach toward Bronson's table. He was one of the bridge players, a man whose family fortune was in graniteware, and there was talk that he might be a candidate for the Senate from his home state of Illinois. Bronson looked at the barrel chest covered with hair, the ballooning belly overhanging the narrow black strip of bathing suit, the hairy muscled legs. He looked up at the man's shiny face, his rubbery lips, his tiny brown eyes. He was an incredible fool, impervious to doubt, a terrible bridge partner who always overplayed his hand and then looked like a hurt puppy when he got beaten, as he almost always did. He sat down next to Bronson and ordered a drink from the waiter.

"Lemme catch my breath," he said. "God, I got to quit smoking."

"Everybody's quitting," Bronson said. He watched Billy run down toward the water, and saw his governess get up from her table, hesitate, and then sit down again, as Billy swerved and ran back up to the other children. Billy would not drown here, not at St.-Tropez. The children here were so well cared for that nothing could possibly happen to them. No one had to worry about his children. That was all paid for.

"Where's Sally today?" the man wanted to know. He was wiping his face with a towel and not looking at Bronson. Bronson had seen him the other night, leaning against Sally in a corner of the garden, pressing her up against a wall, but it had not bothered him. He knew the man wanted to sleep with Sally, but he had also heard Sally, that night in their bedroom, snort and say, "I wouldn't want that fat hog on top of me." Anyway, Sally was sleeping with her first husband these days, and had no time for anyone else.

"Oh, she's off on a yachting party," he said. "She'll be back by dinner."

The man made a face. "That actor feller?"

Bronson nodded. He began to shuffle the cards; the other two players were coming up out of the surf now, and as soon as they were dry, the game would begin. They all played together every afternoon. Almost everybody else played poker, but these four preferred bridge.

Of course, the trick was to get rid of Sally and still keep the boy. She did not want to go back; she had had enough of America. She had finally come into her own, living in Paris, surrounding herself with a circle of writers and artists and a few of the more intelligent young French movie people. She was happy in Paris, and she did not want Billy to go to American schools. She wanted him to go to Switzerland, to boarding school. She did not even call him Billy; she called him Myron. She wanted to change his name legally, but Bronson managed to keep putting it off.

It was really too bad about Sally. She was only thirty-two, but already she was getting brassy and overdone; what had once been charming in her was now grating, at least to Bronson. Billy did not like her any more, either. She would pick the strangest times to be motherly. The only person Billy really loved, in fact, was his French governess. He would feel very bad about leaving her. But it was necessary. The question was, how to get rid of Sally? It was a definite problem. He would have to give it a great deal of thought. He would have to make sure he was doing it for the boy's sake, and not just to satisfy some urge in himself to hurt her. He hoped that wasn't it.

"Okay, let's cut for partners."

Myron cut, and drew the potential senator. It managed to spoil his entire afternoon. He really enjoyed bridge, and he hated to see his partner make such a botch of it.

TITLES IN SERIES

J.R. ACKERLEY Hindoo Holiday
J.R. ACKERLEY My Dog Tulip
J.R. ACKERLEY My Father and Myself
J.R. ACKERLEY We Think the World of You
HENRY ADAMS The Jeffersonian Transformation
CÉLESTE ALBARET Monsieur Proust
DANTE ALIGHIERI The Inferno
DANTE ALIGHIERI The New Life
WILLIAM ATTAWAY Blood on the Forge
W.H. AUDEN (EDITOR) The Living Thoughts of Kierkegaard
W.H. AUDEN W.H. Auden's Book of Light Verse
ERICH AUERBACH Dante: Poet of the Secular World
DOROTHY BAKER Cassandra at the Wedding
J.A. BAKER The Peregrine
HONORÉ DE BALZAC The Unknown Masterpiece *and* Gambara
MAX BEERBOHM Seven Men
ALEXANDER BERKMAN Prison Memoirs of an Anarchist
GEORGES BERNANOS Mouchette
ADOLFO BIOY CASARES Asleep in the Sun
ADOLFO BIOY CASARES The Invention of Morel
CAROLINE BLACKWOOD Corrigan
CAROLINE BLACKWOOD Great Granny Webster
MALCOLM BRALY On the Yard
JOHN HORNE BURNS The Gallery
ROBERT BURTON The Anatomy of Melancholy
CAMARA LAYE The Radiance of the King
GIROLAMO CARDANO The Book of My Life
DON CARPENTER Hard Rain Falling
J.L. CARR A Month in the Country
BLAISE CENDRARS Moravagine
EILEEN CHANG Love in a Fallen City
UPAMANYU CHATTERJEE English, August: An Indian Story
NIRAD C. CHAUDHURI The Autobiography of an Unknown Indian
ANTON CHEKHOV Peasants and Other Stories
RICHARD COBB Paris and Elsewhere
COLETTE The Pure and the Impure
JOHN COLLIER Fancies and Goodnights
CARLO COLLODI The Adventures of Pinocchio
IVY COMPTON-BURNETT A House and Its Head
IVY COMPTON-BURNETT Manservant and Maidservant
BARBARA COMYNS The Vet's Daughter
EVAN S. CONNELL The Diary of a Rapist
HAROLD CRUSE The Crisis of the Negro Intellectual
ASTOLPHE DE CUSTINE Letters from Russia
LORENZO DA PONTE Memoirs
ELIZABETH DAVID A Book of Mediterranean Food
ELIZABETH DAVID Summer Cooking
L.J. DAVIS A Meaningful Life
MARIA DERMOÛT The Ten Thousand Things

*For a complete list of titles, visit www.nyrb.com or write to:
Catalog Requests, NYRB, 435 Hudson Street, New York, NY 10014*

HENRY JAMES The Ivory Tower
HENRY JAMES The New York Stories of Henry James
HENRY JAMES The Other House
HENRY JAMES The Outcry
TOVE JANSSON The Summer Book
RANDALL JARRELL (EDITOR) Randall Jarrell's Book of Stories
DAVID JONES In Parenthesis
ERNST JÜNGER The Glass Bees
HELEN KELLER The World I Live In
FRIGYES KARINTHY A Journey Round My Skull
YASHAR KEMAL Memed, My Hawk
YASHAR KEMAL They Burn the Thistles
MURRAY KEMPTON Part of Our Time: Some Ruins and Monuments of the Thirties
DAVID KIDD Peking Story
ROBERT KIRK The Secret Commonwealth of Elves, Fauns, and Fairies
ARUN KOLATKAR Jejuri
TÉTÉ-MICHEL KPOMASSIE An African in Greenland
GYULA KRÚDY Sunflower
PATRICK LEIGH FERMOR Between the Woods and the Water
PATRICK LEIGH FERMOR Mani: Travels in the Southern Peloponnese
PATRICK LEIGH FERMOR Roumeli: Travels in Northern Greece
PATRICK LEIGH FERMOR A Time of Gifts
PATRICK LEIGH FERMOR A Time to Keep Silence
D.B. WYNDHAM LEWIS AND CHARLES LEE (EDITORS) The Stuffed Owl
GEORG CHRISTOPH LICHTENBERG The Waste Books
H.P. LOVECRAFT AND OTHERS The Colour Out of Space
ROSE MACAULAY The Towers of Trebizond
NORMAN MAILER Miami and the Siege of Chicago
JANET MALCOLM In the Freud Archives
OSIP MANDELSTAM The Selected Poems of Osip Mandelstam
OLIVIA MANNING School for Love
GUY DE MAUPASSANT Afloat
JAMES MCCOURT Mawrdew Czgowchwz
HENRI MICHAUX Miserable Miracle
JESSICA MITFORD Hons and Rebels
NANCY MITFORD Madame de Pompadour
HENRY DE MONTHERLANT Chaos and Night
ALBERTO MORAVIA Boredom
ALBERTO MORAVIA Contempt
JAN MORRIS Conundrum
ÁLVARO MUTIS The Adventures and Misadventures of Maqroll
L.H. MYERS The Root and the Flower
DARCY O'BRIEN A Way of Life, Like Any Other
YURI OLESHA Envy
IONA AND PETER OPIE The Lore and Language of Schoolchildren
RUSSELL PAGE The Education of a Gardener
BORIS PASTERNAK, MARINA TSVETAYEVA, AND RAINER MARIA RILKE Letters, Summer 1926
CESARE PAVESE The Moon and the Bonfires
CESARE PAVESE The Selected Works of Cesare Pavese
LUIGI PIRANDELLO The Late Mattia Pascal
ANDREY PLATONOV The Foundation Pit
ANDREY PLATONOV Soul and Other Stories